THE TRINITY

Printed in the United States of America.

Published by Offense Mechanisms
www.offensemechanisms.com

ISBN-10: 0-9774110-7-9
ISBN-13: 978-0-9774110-7-8

Cover design by Paul Hughes.

THE TRINITY
by David LaBounty

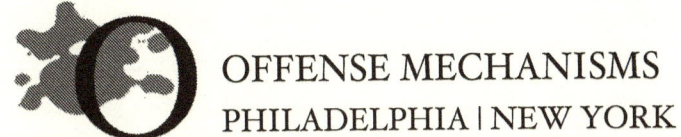

OFFENSE MECHANISMS
PHILADELPHIA | NEW YORK

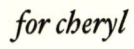
for cheryl

Remember the young man standing in the large picture window. Remember the young man staring out at the damp early dawn suburban street, studying the uniform box-like houses he has known all his life that vary only in aluminum siding and landscaping.

He is waiting for a plain white sedan with U.S. government plates. He is waiting for a sedan driven by his recruiter, who will take him to the processing center twenty miles away in downtown Detroit.

His house is nearly silent. His mother is sleeping in the main bedroom after coming home late from a date the night before. His father is in the basement, the flat sound of the television traveling up the staircase. His father moved to the basement years ago, when he and Chris's mother stopped liking each other, and the television is left on continuously to kill the sounds of loneliness. Chris never was quite sure why his father never left or why his parents never divorced. Perhaps economics, perhaps laziness.

His father turned into a hermit—home from work and straight to the basement—every day, without a deviation.

His mother: reliving her youth, hardly home, never eating with Chris nor studying a report card in two or three years. She dates, often and with great variety, and the men sometimes leave the house as Chris leaves for school.

Chris isn't sure if anyone will bother to see him off. He sighs with indifference. He lights a cigarette and waits, thinking about himself.

Eighteen and blond, pink-skinned, bespectacled, vaguely overweight and definitely out of shape (the result of beer and a steady stream of fast food) and a virgin, an aspect of his life that grieves him to no end. He has never had a girlfriend, nor has he even kissed a girl, an aspect of his life that grieves him even more.

No one among his few friends claims virginity.

Chris strays from the subject of girls altogether.

He has faith that the Navy will change things. He has faith that the Navy will change him, and reconstruct the details of his life.

A car arrives in the driveway, an older, rusty two-door Chevrolet driven by his brother, four years his senior.

As his brother leaves his car, beer cans roll into the driveway and into the street. His brother walks clumsily into the house. Once inside, Chris detects his brother's residential odors—beer and marijuana. Chris looks at his watch and notes that his brother has come home one hour before his job as a warehouseman starts.

His brother is startled by Chris's presence in the living room at such an early hour.

"What the fuck you doin' up?"

"I leave today."

"For the Navy?"

"Yep."

"Do Mom and Dad know?"

Chris shrugs his shoulders.

"No shit, the fuckin' Navy." And his brother ambles out of the small living room and into the hallway. It will be an eternity before Chris sees him again.

The twilight gives way to daylight and another cigarette disappears before the recruiter pulls up in front of Chris's house. Chris walks out without taking a last look inside. He closes the door to his house and a lot of other things.

The recruiter, a Petty Officer Arnold, was a factor in Chris's decision to join the Navy. Arnold is a young man, thirty still several birthdays away, but he appears worldly and wise to someone as sheltered as Chris.

For Chris, there were few choices upon graduation from high school. College? No. His sub-par grade-point average saw to the fact that a four-year university wouldn't be interested. Community college? No. That meant living at home, and Chris wanted anything but that. A job? No. No job he could get at his age would pay enough for him to get his own place, own a car, et cetera, and that too meant living at home, and he didn't want to wind up like his brother.

That left Chris with four choices: Army, Navy, Air Force, Marines.

The Army? No. He didn't want to fight in a trench if World War III started. The Air Force? No. It seemed too technical and just not fun. The Marines? No way. Chris lacked the certain masochistic machismo the Marines seemed to attract and require.

The Navy held the greatest lure for Chris: the travel. He had never left Michigan in his life, save a short trip to Chicago when he was small and his parents still operated the household as a family. The recruiter enchanted him with tales of stops in Australia, Japan, Italy and Hong Kong. Additionally, Petty Officer Arnold seemed the most relaxed, his shirt somewhat untucked and his face round and soft, in contrast to the Marine recruiters, sitting at attention in their desks, belt buckles glaring, faces stern and serious.

Petty Officer Arnold maybe spent a little more time with Chris than was necessary, realizing how impressionable and inexperienced Chris was.

Arnold had many, many tattoos. He tried to collect one from each port of call.

His favorite, a red and green dragon, impressed Chris the most.

"I got this one here in Singapore; I was drunk as a skunk. This Chinaman give it to me. The man was damn near blind, but it came out pretty good, though."

Arnold told Chris about the women he had met during his travels.

"Do you like blondes with big tits?"

Chris said sure, of course.

"Then, my friend, make sure you get to Australia. Them women down there just love American sailors. Their men don't treat women right. Hell, they got eight women to every man down there. I guess they can do what they want. Anyway, an Australian gal will screw you all night and make breakfast for you in the morning. Good luck finding that anywhere in this country. Hell, these days, women want you to make *them* breakfast."

3

"Do sailors ever marry Australian women?" Chris asked, his mind in the middle of a fantasy with a beautiful Australian woman attached to his arm.

"I don't know. Why the hell would you care about that?"

Chris shrugged his shoulders and remained silent.

"Sailors do marry a lot of Orientals, though."

And Arnold told him of the debauchery in Asia, especially in the Philippines, with its inexpensive call girls and even less expensive beer.

"I had me two girls, a real good buzz, a little Flip to drive me around and a hotel for the night, and I didn't even spend twenty bucks."

Chris has never felt especially patriotic, having only a thumbnail knowledge of current events. He likes President Reagan for no real reason, knows that the Russians are evil, and the world he lives in is under the constant threat of communists and nuclear war.

"My friend, our job is the most important in the world," Arnold told him during one of his frequent visits before signing up. "If it wasn't for our military, them commie-pinko-faggot-hippies would rule the world. And they're trying. Look at Nicaragua; we shouldn't have let that happen. If it weren't for those damn democrats in Congress, Reagan would have sent us in there, cleaned that place up. Anyway, we keep the world at peace and keep America free. Be proud of that uniform when you finally put it on."

On the way to the processing station, Arnold gives Chris some final advice.

"Do exactly as you're told, keep to yourself, and you'll be fine. Basic is easy. There'll be every type of fellow you can imagine—old and young, rich and poor, black and white, some real smart and some really dumb, and hell, anymore, gay and straight."

Chris hasn't given much thought to boot camp, just life afterwards, the places he'll see, and the life he'll lead.

In Eastern Scotland, somewhere between Aberdeen and Dundee and just a few miles from the North Sea, lies a small U.S. naval base, a listening post, hidden in a valley surrounded by low and smooth green hills and pastures full of many sheep and tidy farmhouses made of stone.

The base contains just over five hundred Americans, mostly sailors and their families. If one were to travel more than thirty miles from the base, a Scottish person would not know there was an American base just outside the village of Lutherkirk.

The base is an old Royal Air Force installation, built just after the British were brought into World War II. Some of the original hangars remain, and they have been converted into tennis courts, a gymnasium, a galley and the base commissary. The base is still officially referred to as RAF Lutherkirk, and a token RAF Major is the lone British serviceman assigned to the base. He is given the title of Base Commander, but he is only a liaison with the British government, the local community and local law enforcement.

Father Alexander Crowley arrives at the base late in the summer. He is the new Catholic chaplain, and it is his first duty station. He was given the rank of lieutenant after a brief period of Naval Chaplain Corps training in Newport, Rhode Island. Already past forty, he is rather old for the rank; his dark red hair is graying throughout, and the pale skin around his bluish eyes is starting to wrinkle. He is thin in the arms, legs and shoulders, but, due to his recent development of a love of wine, his khaki uniform is taut across his stomach and snug around his waist.

He had been removed from his duties after many years as a parish priest in Houston's Fifth Ward for homilies that had nothing to with religion. He had taken to telling his parishioners about the evil of the Jewish-controlled banking system and the erosion of American culture by too many immigrants and minorities. His parish was mostly African-American, and they became irritated. After many complaints and warnings over several years, the diocese recommended a transfer to another parish, even another diocese, or even resignation. The hierarchy of the Houston diocese sensed Crowley had become bored and frustrated with parish life in the inner city.

But he wasn't bored, he was angry. Faithlessness, bitterness, indifference and a smug and perverted intellectualism had eroded his once youthful and fervent love of Jesus and the Church.

He was born the youngest of seven kids, five girls and two boys all about two years apart, and raised in a small town in Northern Minnesota. His sole brother was the oldest sibling and he had left for work in Minneapolis by the time Alexander was four, leaving Alexander essentially the only boy in a house full of women.

His father was the town's high school history teacher and football coach. His father was a large and outspoken man with broad shoulders, large hands, and an even larger head with a Marine Corps style haircut. He was very masculine and a contrast to his devoutly Catholic and thin and timid wife. He was privately atheist, despite going with the family to Mass every Sunday.

Alex's mother was a homemaker of the most obedient kind, surreptitiously devoted to her husband but more devoted to her church. Rosary beads, crucifixes, and images of Mary and Jesus could be found throughout the house, and she was constantly seen kneeling, especially after a confrontation with her husband, who had despised her by the time Alex was born. But he would never leave her, despite the malaise that crept into their marriage; he had too much comfort in his lifestyle, being a big man in a small town. His peers assumed his family life was perfect.

Alex took after his mother much more than he did his father throughout his childhood.

He was born prematurely, was tiny as an infant and child and had many grave childhood illnesses: mumps at three, measles at five, a near-fatal flu at seven, and chicken pox at eight. With each illness, his mother would pray constantly and convince the local priest to come and pray over him. After each recovery, his mother would tell Alex that God had saved him, and that He had set a special purpose for his life. Because of all the religious imagery his mother surrounded him with, young Alexander Crowley saw his childhood as some sort of an amazing divine drama. He thought of himself as a knight of God, battling disease and pestilence and evil in the world. He developed an early love for Mass and Sunday school, and would join his mother in prayer at home whenever the mood struck her. He read scripture often, especially the canonical Gospels. He was fascinated by the miracle of the loaves and fishes, the walking on the water, the temptation in the wilderness, the cross being carried to Calvary, the brutal crucifixion and the miraculous resurrection. But he was more interested in the Catholic rites than he was scripture; he had a fascination with the sacraments and the lifestyle of their parish priest.

Because of his frailty and his interest in religion, Alex had his mother's undivided attention. She all but ignored her daughters and husband.

His father, sensing and fearing an effeminate nature in the boy, tried pushing sports and hunting and fishing and martial arts training on Alex. He wasn't interested. He would remain small until he reached college, and he possessed no athletic ability whatsoever. In fact, his father was embarrassed when he watched Alex try to play with other boys. Alex felt hunting was barbaric and fishing very boring. Martial arts was tolerable, as it gave him time alone with his father, time his father never normally provided. But he much preferred spending time indoors with his mother, reading the Bible or almost anything non-fiction or church related, and going to Mass and different church functions. His childhood ran the full gamut of Catholicism; he took all the catechism classes he could and was an altar boy throughout junior and senior high school. The Roman Catholic population in his town was small, and no parochial school existed. Alex would have preferred a parochial school to the public high school where he was taunted and left friendless, despite his father's imposing and respected presence.

Early in Alex's senior year of high school, his father died of a heart attack while coaching a football game. As his father fell on the field, Alex and his mother, who were sitting in the stands, didn't bother to run to him. They sat peacefully and watched as paramedics ran to his side. They didn't bother to rise until the ambulance drove him away. This cinched Alex's future (and his desire since childhood): he would become a priest with his mother's strong approval. The vows of celibacy would be no problem, as he had no interest in girls or sex, and felt guilty when any sinful thought crossed his mind. His heart was a bit lighter when his father passed away; he had been wishing for years to be rid of him. He felt a small amount of shame at the glee he experienced upon his father's demise, and prayed at length to absolve himself. It was to no avail. The selfish joy he felt upon his father's death would be his first insight into his innately cruel and selfish nature.

He completed his undergraduate degree in theology at Bemidji State and attended seminary at a small Catholic university in southern Minnesota. He was ordained in the tearful presence of his mother and in the indifferent presence of his siblings.

His first work as a clergyman was as a roving assistant priest for rural parishes in North Dakota, saying several Masses from town to town on Saturdays and Sundays, as none of the parishes had enough people to support a fulltime priest.

After three years in North Dakota, Houston became available. He welcomed the opportunity to leave the Midwest and he welcomed the challenge of serving in the inner city. He rekindled his childhood fantasy life. He pictured himself as a knight of God, as a sort of divine superhero to rid Houston's Fifth Ward of poverty, drug abuse, rampant crime and faithlessness. He failed miserably.

Shortly after his arrival in Houston, Father Crowley's mother developed breast cancer. It spread quickly to her lymphatic system and into her lungs. She passed away within six months, without giving Alex a chance to come home and say goodbye.

Alex was devastated. He was angry with God and angrier still with his remaining family.

He blamed his sisters and brother for their mother's quick demise. He felt that if they had been more attentive in his absence and had taken better care of her, she would have lived, or at the very least, the cancer would have been spotted sooner. Only two sisters actually remained in their hometown, and they had husbands and children of their own. They weren't particularly close to their mother, especially after being reared in the shadow of her beloved Alex.

Father Crowley returned for the last time to Minnesota to deal with his mother's funeral and all the other family business that comes with the death of a last remaining parent. Things were tense between him and his siblings, especially since Alex was named executor of the will, even though he was the youngest child. There wasn't much in the way of finances to settle. The house was sold at a bargain just to unload it, and the monies were equally divided between Alex and his brother and sisters.

After the family business had been settled, Alex returned to Houston and remained solely in Texas for the next several years, communicating with his family only cordially on holidays and after a few years not at all. They never shared his religious zeal, and they felt he looked down upon them. He was fairly self-absorbed as a young priest, and despite the implied forgiving nature of a clergyman, he held a grudge against his family and vowed he would never return to Minnesota, not even in the event of another family member's death.

Despite his pride, Father Crowley felt adrift and empty without a family to come home to.

His faith began to ebb as he neared the age of forty when he realized that after years of frustration, he was a lousy priest.

From his days of assistant priest to head of his own church, he had inspired no one. His Masses were listless and eventually sparse; only the devout would remain, staring hopefully from the pews.

He couldn't speak well; he stuttered and rambled and the eyes in the pews stared everywhere but at him. He prayed and prayed in the early going, praying for the gift of an able tongue, but God didn't intervene. Crowley blamed his parishioners for his poor preaching skills. He felt they were too dimwitted to understand him, and after a time, he blamed their ignorance on their race. If they weren't black, he thought, then maybe his preaching would be more effective and their attention would be more rapt.

He had very little patience for confessions; the paltry sins of the pious irritated him, and the confessed debauchery of the casual believers sickened and sometimes excited him. Weddings and the required pre-counseling he considered a waste of time; he had seen more divorces than marriages, and after a time, he didn't wish to see his parishioners procreate.

And then came the visions.

At first, he saw them as white specks of twinkling light that came only at night as he tried to pray for an able tongue and to be removed from the parish that had become so loathsome. The specks of twinkling white light appeared behind his eyelids and on the ceiling. He thought the lights shrouded small faces, but he couldn't be sure.

He was afraid the lights were demonic, but he was sure they were angels, angels sent to guide him through this difficult period of his life. They began to appear more frequently as he became more disgruntled with his parish, and eventually he could see them throughout the ceiling of his chapel, as though they were sneering at the congregation. He took it as a sign from a god, but from which god, he couldn't be sure. He took the visions as a signal that it was time to turn his attention somewhere else. The zeal he had once had for the Church was gone forever. He became interested in the origin of his visions, and visited New Age bookshops after exhausting his own library on the subject of angels and apparitions. He decided he was again special, just as he felt special as a child when the angels and God had saved him from all those awful illnesses.

He had been a fan of history since his boyhood days in Minnesota, partially due to his father's role as the high school history teacher. He developed a fascination with World War II after it became apparent to him in Houston that he had missed his true calling and that he wasn't cut from a priestly cloth. He had a special interest in the spectacular rise of Hitler and the Third Reich. Something, somehow, made sense to him. He read *Mein Kampf* in a relatively brief period, hiding the book in the rectory in case someone should stumble upon it. He began to understand Hitler's notion of the superiority of the white race—his frustrations in his own church made that apparent. And the struggle Hitler described stirred something in his soul; he could identify with the isolation Hitler felt as a young man as a struggling artist in a hostile Vienna. Crowley felt he was a struggling priest in a hostile church, hostile because of the ethnicity of the congregation.

He felt the world would be a better place if Hitler had been successful, and as he became more infatuated with Hitler, he thought of Jesus less and less and eventually stopped personal prayer—a very large part of a clergyman's life—altogether.

He began performing his Masses by rote, mumbling the prayers and offering communion robotically, without passion. After a time, his homilies rarely mentioned the Father, the Son, or the Holy Ghost, and they rarely referred to scripture. He had also stopped reading the Bible altogether, devoting his readings to anything germane to the separation of the races.

He even tried to find a local white supremacist group in the Houston area. He found a few, but their simplistic, amateurish meetings in far-western suburban Houston basements bored him; he wanted something more spiritual, more fulfilling. He began exploring Hitler's interest in Norse mythology and the occult, and slowly, after the passage of years, he discovered a whole new set of gods to replace the one he had discarded. He was sure the twinkling lights were angels sent from the gods of the north, the same gods revered by Hitler and the Nazis.

With all the social ills in America, the crime and poverty in his part of Houston, problems he blamed on the inferiority of the blacks in his neighborhood, he assumed Christianity and its apparent ineffectiveness and pacifist nature had failed America. He decided covertly and solitarily to join the ranks of another side. He read the ancient *Poetic Edda,* the definitive book of Norse mythology, and he tried to become intimate with all of its deities, male and female: Thor, Njord, Frigg, Freya, Freyr, Tyr, Heimdall, Bakur, Loki, and especially Odin, the supreme Norse god and the focus of all of Crowley's new devotion. He made the leap from Christianity, and Crowley adopted his own brand of religion and supremacist beliefs, molded to contour his feelings.

After many complaints stretching the span of two years, the Houston diocese censured Crowley. He was given two options: resign or accept service in the military, which was in dire need of priests. More than a decade of priesthood and an advanced degree in theology left him unsuitable for other employment. The world offered him no other options; he couldn't go home again. The thought of the military excited him; he craved structure, and if he had to perform Mass, he might as well do it where he would find fewer of those minorities that irritated him so much. He chose the Navy, hoping to influence a young Caucasian sailor or two with his new theology, and the travel opportunities seemed better. He was thrilled when he was ultimately assigned to a small base in Scotland, with Europe lying at his doorstep, the ancient home of his newly beloved Norse gods a short flight away.

July 20, 1986

Dear Wife,

This is strange I know, but today I start to find you. Right now I'm on a plane to Orlando from Detroit, I'm on my way to boot camp for the Navy and then communications school in Pensacola. After that I hope to get a ship out of San Diego maybe, tour the Pacific. I may find you there. I don't care what you look like, as long as you're not my mother. I'll explain when I can, maybe you will meet her, maybe you won't. I'm eighteen now, I like music, rock mainly, some new wave but I don't know how to dance, in fact I've never danced. I didn't go to prom or anything like that. I don't think I'm ugly, but I can never talk to girls and I don't want a lot of girlfriends. I did at one time, but now I want someone I can feel loved by (corny I know, but I want you to know how I feel about everything). Anyway I am very nervous, I'm not in shape at all and I know I'll have to run and do push-ups and all that. I want to be in shape, I want to look good for you. I smoke, I think because my father does. I don't have a lot of friends, just two really, we didn't really do much. We drank, getting my older brother to buy beer for us so we could drink in parks on weekends, or our houses when our parents were away. I'll miss them, one is going to college, and the other one is working the same after- school job he had in high school. I had to get away somehow, and the Navy is my way. I could never meet you at home. More later.

Love,
Christopher Fairbanks

Chris arrives in Orlando for basic training bearing nothing save the clothes he left his house in (black t-shirt, white jeans, unlaced high top sneakers), a pack of cigarettes held dearly in his hand, and his nylon Velcro wallet, containing only his driver's license and his life savings of forty-three dollars.

He arrives at the Orlando airport late in the evening, and is directed to a white government van that carries him and a few other arrivals from around the country fifteen miles to Recruit Training Command Orlando. Boot camp.

Outside the airport, the thrill of seeing palm trees for the first time excites him, and already he is starting to feel like a man of the world.

The first night is rough, as he is shoved into a chair behind a long table with several other tired and out of place young men. They receive a few items such as toothpaste, a toothbrush, razors, soap, and a pocket-sized New Testament edition of the Gideon Bible, a book that Chris is very unfamiliar with. He can't ever recall seeing a Bible at home.

Chris is formed into a company of eighty or so recruits. For the first short night, they are handed sheets and a blanket and shown their barracks, a long narrow room with rows of twenty bunk beds on either side. The first night is basically sleepless, Chris and the others sleeping in the clothes they arrived in.

They are awoken well before dawn that first morning by their company commander, a tan, thin and dark-haired man in a khaki uniform just past thirty, but he seems so very old to Chris. He throws an empty aluminum trashcan down the middle of the barracks.

He yells, "Get the fuck up, recruits! On your feet now!" Chris is nervous. They are sent outside and clumsily marched to the galley for breakfast. They are given five minutes to eat mass-produced scrambled eggs and potatoes. After breakfast, they are sent to the barbershop. Chris's semi-long, feathered blond hair is completely shorn. It will be several days before he has the courage to look in a mirror or even directly at his reflection.

The eight weeks of basic training proves as Chris imagined, push-ups and running, marching and yelling. Most of the recruits are his age, but some are in their twenties and a few are even in their thirties. They come from every region of the country and from every race. Chris finds the variety fascinating and disturbing. There were no minorities in his school, and he feels nervous around the black recruits, who seem to form a loose clique.

Chris struggles with the training at times. In the first week, running proves to be nauseating. The standard number of push-ups for punishment (everyone gets punishment) is twenty-five, and Chris's arms initially shake at a count of ten. Making the bed (or rack, as it is called) and folding and stowing his gear also prove troublesome; Chris has never been particularly meticulous. Not to mention shaving. All recruits are given ten minutes to shit, shower and shave every morning upon reveille, even if they have no facial hair. Chris is still hairless, with only sporadic acne decorating his face. Because of his complexion, he cuts himself badly while shaving. The multiple scars make his face look like a roadmap. Out of discipline, the company commander periodically yells at Chris during inspection, making him shave again, telling him his shave isn't close enough and that he had better shave again. Chris returns to the bathroom (the head, it is called) and shaves and bleeds some more.

Despite the large number of people living in such a small area, Chris remains friendless, talking with others only a little in the evenings when the atmosphere is more relaxed. He has not settled into any sort of friendship or circle of friends, as the rest of his company has. Bonds are made based upon many things, Chris notices. The boys from the South tend to cluster together, as do the few fundamentalist Christians who pray and read the Bible in a quiet corner of the barracks. Friendships are also based on age, tastes in music, and again, race.

In the evening, they are allowed time to polish boots and belt buckles, iron shirts, smoke cigarettes and write and read letters. Incoming mail is passed out nightly, when one recruit is designated to pass out letters from friends and family. Chris is tense during this time; everyone receives mail except for him. The fact that no one seems to love or care enough to write to him makes him feel hollow and melancholy. He is extremely envious of the joy he witnesses on the faces of the other recruits as they read and discuss their letters, especially letters from girlfriends.

Chris creates a fictitious girlfriend for discussions, as girls appear to be the most prevalent and common topic throughout the barracks. Everyone seems to have a girl back home, waiting and writing and sending pictures.

Except for Chris.

He even writes separate letters on a few occasions to his mother and father, but there is no reply throughout his entire basic training. He writes letters anyway, but spends more time than most smoking cigarettes, sitting on the balcony outside the barracks, staring at the palm trees swaying in the gentle and humid Florida breeze.

Chris finishes boot camp ten pounds lighter, his face and neck stained red from the Florida sun. There is a graduation ceremony of sorts, and some parents make the trip, surprising a few of the recruits by arriving unexpectedly. Chris doesn't bother to scan the crowd; only his mother came to his high school graduation, and she was jittery then, as if she was in a hurry for the ceremony to be over. He shares his proud moment with no one. He dons for the first time the dress white polyester uniform with the wide-bottom pants and the black kerchief around his neck.

Still, he is proud of his accomplishment. His company did not remain intact throughout basic training; some recruits got sent back a few weeks, some quit, and some the Navy wisely decided to part ways with. Not everyone can finish boot camp. Chris does.

September 18, 1985

Dear Wife,

If we're married than I am going to assume you want children. I want kids. I want them to be happy, and I want them to feel like they're not alone. If you meet my parents you will understand why this is important to me. My parents have a weird set-up I guess, they really should be divorced, but my Mom won't. My Dad doesn't care, he is kind of lazy and doesn't like things to change, and he wants to keep living in our house in Michigan. I live just outside of Detroit. My mom used to say she didn't want to be divorced because it was against God's word, but she hasn't gone to church since I was a little kid, so I don't know, maybe she is lazy too. Maybe now that I'm gone she may change. I'm the youngest kid, I have an older brother, he's twenty-two and a partier and a stoner and he still lives at home. I had to get away. Boot camp was okay, I'm done. I leave tomorrow for Pensacola where I will go to communications school. Maybe I will meet you there. I don't know if I'm ready, but I feel life will be better if there is someone else out there that can love me. I will be very embarrassed if anyone sees this.

Love,
Chris

Father Crowley chooses to live off base as opposed to the Bachelor Officer Quarters the base provides. He is given a fairly generous housing allowance to offset the cost, and after a few days of being in Scotland, he finds a large, furnished and airy stone farmhouse a few miles outside the base. The house has all the privacy he craves, a long driveway off a main road, the house hidden by ancient wide and leafy oak trees and an old stone moss covered fence.

In the back is a short, unattended garden, and beyond that, smooth rolling green hills that seem to carry on infinitely like a photograph one might expect to see on a postcard.

He decides this is better than a ship.

He purchases a 1975 Austin Allegro, a small, blue two-door car, and he quickly learns to drive on the opposite side of the road, shifting with his left hand.

His troubles in Houston and Minnesota seem very far removed from this tranquil and fresh setting.

However, he is still a priest, and that is his job for the Navy. His office is in the base chapel. Both the Protestant service and the Roman Catholic Mass are performed in this bland, American looking, one-story brown brick building with a large glass door and no windows.

His office is next to the Protestant chaplain's, a man full of contempt for the Roman Catholic Church and for Crowley by association. He is older, gray wavy hair parted to the side, red faced and overweight. He has served in the Navy for twenty years and possesses the rank of Commander. As the senior chaplain, he is also Crowley's supervisor. Crowley will learn to avoid him.

He is only required to perform two Masses per weekend, due to the small number of church attendees on the base, in contrast to the four Masses he had to perform in Houston for the much larger parish. The rest of the time is set aside for counseling and standing in various base ceremonies.

He will have ample free time, more than a normal sailor.

He establishes a routine after a few weeks: Monday through Friday, he sits in his office from eight until two as the odd sailor or spouse may wander in, seeking advice on some subject or another that a priest should have some expertise in. Crowley always feigns interest in the problems of others, but he always thinks their situations silly and their lives pathetic. He feels nauseated but superior when a black or Hispanic sailor or family member wanders in. For them, he shows even more interest, subconsciously not trying to betray his true emotions.

Mass is at five in the afternoon on Saturday and again on Sunday at nine in the morning. That's it.

He goes for drives in the late afternoons and Saturday mornings, strictly in civilian clothes, driving far and often, exploring that part of Scotland—the cities of Aberdeen and Dundee and the villages in between—dotting the North Sea coastline. He is searching for bookstores that may have supremacist literature, stopping in pubs, drinking beer for basically the first time in his life, trying to get a feel for the locals, their political opinions, and their thoughts on race. He finds them provincial, mostly farmers or shop workers or pensioners of one sort or another, fanatical about soccer and hating the English (especially Margaret Thatcher) and when he is close enough to the base, hating the arrogant young Americans and their hi-fi stereos and their cars. He finds the people in that part of the country are basically poor, and the young sailors have more money than their Scottish counterparts.

He is unable to root out any white supremacist sentiment anywhere. There are few minorities in the country, maybe a few Pakistanis in Dundee, a small Jewish population in the larger cities, but none elsewhere.

He is frustrated at first, frustrated with his inability to find compatriots, and he is almost willing to resign himself to spending his three-year tour of duty in self-study and contemplation. He does find books on Norse mythology and books about the Nazis. He wants to read all he can about his true gods and the figures from history that he admires most.

And this is how his first months pass, a cacophony of drink and loneliness and private worship of the gods of the north. He stands outside often, when he can, while at the chapel and elsewhere, and looks straight up into the sky. He is looking for Valhalla and signs from Odin, his favorite and dearest of the ancient gods, the god of all things he admires most: god of poetry, god of love and god of war.

He is ready for war, and he badly wants fellow soldiers in this holy war of races he intends to wage, even if it is only a few.

The village of Lutherkirk is small, one main street with a small store, a chemist shop, a post office, a bank, a garage, a bakery and four pubs. High Street is flanked by three roads that contain mostly simple homes, many multiple-unit dwellings with small gardens and no front yards, with the front doors opening right onto the sidewalk.

Crowley enters the main pub in Lutherkirk early on a Friday evening just as the darkness becomes complete. The pub occupies the first floor of a simple hotel. It is dark, the air is stale, and cigarette smoke shrouds everything. When he enters a pub he typically sits at the bar, but this time, noticing two young men from the base at a table, he decides to join them.

The fact that they are American is obvious. One is wearing a flannel shirt and cowboy boots; the other is wearing a college sweatshirt. The Scottish dress is quite different from that, slightly more formal. Both young men are fair-haired, and the one in the sweatshirt is quite overweight, probably borderline on the Navy's acceptable standards of personal weight. His chest is loose and flabby; he has a double chin and still a few freckles on his cheeks. The one in the flannel shirt is so thin that he appears almost feminine. His shoulders slouch forward and he is wearing tight blue jeans in the fashion of a country music star, with a belt and large belt buckle and a pack of cigarettes in his front pocket.

Again, Crowley sees the white twinkling lights hovering below the ceiling, and he feels the gods are leading him to the two young men. He hasn't seen the lights since he was in Houston, and the initial sight of them makes him nervous and excited. Despite his priesthood training, despite his wayward beliefs, the sight of the apparently supernatural is still disconcerting and intense.

The two sailors, both lowly seamen, recognize Crowley; they know him to be a chaplain—and more notably, an officer. Officers and enlisted don't typically interact. In fact, fraternization between the two military castes is forbidden.

"Good evening, gentlemen," Crowley says with an enthusiasm unusual to him as he takes a seat at the table with the two young sailors, both with nearly empty pint glasses in front of them.

They nod. "Hello, sir." They sit more erectly.

Crowley notices their tenseness. Their discomfort makes him feel smug, secure, powerful.

"Relax, fellows," says Crowley, scanning the pub, making sure there are no other Americans. There aren't. "I'm not here to lecture you about drinking or try to get you to come to church. I'm out for a pint, myself. Even priests need to have a drink now and then."

And Crowley looks more relaxed, like a person who belongs in a pub. Wearing a tartan tam that he purchased in a shop in Dundee, a dark blue wool sweater on top of a white collared shirt and khaki trousers, he looks almost Scottish.

"What are you boys drinking? Lager?"

They nod in affirmation, glad someone is buying them beer, as their funds are running low and payday is a good week away.

Crowley walks to the bar and comes back clutching three pint glasses, dripping beer as he deposits the glasses on the table.

The priest produces a pack of cigarettes and offers one to each of the young sailors. The heavier one, Brad Hinckley, is shocked. He was raised around a Catholic grandmother, and the sight of a priest smoking and drinking surprises him. He also thinks it's cool. All three light their cigarettes and exhale simultaneously.

"So, how long you boys been here, been in this country?" Crowley asks.

Hinckley has been in Scotland six months. The other sailor, Lee Rodgers, just a bit longer. Crowley asks them if they like being there. They both hate it. They hate the weather, which is continually cold and damp, and they hate the people with the stupid accents. The Scottish people are referred to as "blokes" by the Americans, a term that the

Scots find offensive. The two refer to everything Scottish as "bloke."

"This bloke money is too big for your wallet."

"The bloke beer is horrible," they both claim while quickly drinking their pints.

"The bloke music is weird. No good country stations on the radio," says Rodgers. He hails from southern Missouri, just outside of Cape Girardeau.

"The bloke T.V. only has four channels, with weird shows and sheep herding contests, and cricket is the most boring sport I ever saw and soccer is stupid and I can't see any football," says Hinckley, who constantly recalls the glory of watching college football in his native Nebraska. Nothing else in his life matters as much.

Crowley sees potential in these two young men. They are slightly bitter for no good reason.

"Will I ever see either of you in church?" Crowley asks.

They both lie and say yes.

"Better yet, screw church—come to my house, I insist. A sort of Bible study, free food and beer. How's that?"

It is the week preceding Christmas and a priest is usually absorbed in church related duties, but not Crowley. There are things he can do, Masses to prepare, homilies to write, but he is not interested. He will wing it for his Christmas Eve Mass, as he does all Masses. Maybe he'll put up a box for canned goods for the poor. Which poor? The poor on base or the poor Scots? He does not know. Maybe (and most probably) he will throw the cans away.

Yet he may keep them for himself, he decides, as the three unusual friends leave the pub and pile into Crowley's Austin and drive the few miles to the priest's farmhouse.

The priest's cupboards, small refrigerator, and liquor cabinet are stocked for an occasion such as this. He knew it would only be a matter of time before he found some potential recruits; he just didn't expect them to be American. He felt the choice was made by the gods, and he wasn't going to tempt fate and contradict them. He feels their presence in his cold sitting room and looks for the white lights as he shovels coal into his fireplace and strikes a match.

Hinckley and Rodgers stand around awkwardly, staring at the walls in the dimly lit room. Father Crowley has decorated it with abstract paintings and tapestries, and on the mantel stands a small and simple swastika made out of black iron on an iron pedestal.

Hinckley and Rodgers nudge each other as they both see it at the same time. Both are shocked, and despite the history lessons to which neither paid much attention, neither of them is offended.

Crowley feels trepidation as their gazes linger above the mantel. He studies their faces in that priestly way, looking for signs of emotion, but each face remains blank. They continue to look about the room.

"Sit down, sit down." Crowley points to a dusty couch with greasy upholstery that came as part of the furnishings. He wanders off to the kitchen and retrieves three cans of beer, British cans, tall, taller than an American can of beer.

"So, tell me," Crowley says, "where are you two from?"

Nebraska, Missouri.

"Really? What part?"

"Jus' outside of Cape Girardeau."

"All over, but I guess you could say Grand Island because I was born there."

And it is true; Hinckley had a vagabond childhood spread across the eastern part of Nebraska. He had been born out of wedlock. His mother went from town to town, relative to relative, boyfriend to boyfriend, working mainly as a waitress, sometimes as a bartender. Grand Island to Lincoln to Omaha to West Point, back to Omaha to Norfolk, back to Grand Island and Omaha again.

Depending on the nature of her current relationship, Hinckley's mother would drop him off at her parents' house to live, a house in a less desirable part of Omaha that used to be more desirable. He would live with them for months at a time and would attend school there, and in the school, he would be a definite minority, a fact that disturbed his bigoted grandfather to no end.

"Niggers," his grandfather would say, "have ruined this town, have ruined this neighborhood. They all sit around and do nothing except kill each other over drugs and wait for welfare checks. They don't work, and when they do, they're lazy. I ain't never met a good one yet. Shit, when I was growing up before that god-damned Martin Luther King showed up, they all worked, did as they was told. But now, hell... I ain't met a decent one yet."

His grandparents had long paid for the house they lived in and couldn't afford to move. Due to emphysema, his grandfather couldn't work. He had been drawing disability and later on Social Security, and those monthly checks could only go so far. He sat in the living room of their old bungalow watching the sidewalk decay and the parade of longtime neighbors move and pass away. He didn't venture out much. He had to keep an oxygen tank by his side, so he watched a lot of television, the back of the set against the picture window in the living room, so he could look outside and watch television at the same time. He felt he had to keep an eye on his property.

Brad dreaded and feared school. He felt isolated because of his color, felt the fear of the blacks because of his grandfather. Brad would rush home and watch television with his grandfather and only do a cursory amount of homework. On Saturdays in the autumn, their attention turned to college football. They would watch the Nebraska games with a rabid passion; nothing else in the world mattered, and they would spend the preceding week in anticipation of the upcoming game.

Sundays, his grandmother would drag the adolescent Hinckley to Mass, to a church over the Missouri River in Council Bluffs. He would sit stone-faced and inattentive, his thoughts anywhere but on the Mass in front of him. The words of the homily would not reach beyond his ears, and the concepts of Jesus and God and love never meant anything to him.

Ultimately, his mother would leave her boyfriend or get left by a boyfriend and she would come back to Omaha and stay with her parents for a while, until school let out, and then it was off to Wahoo or Norfolk or wherever there was a place to stay and a job to be had.

Hinckley's father was nonexistent; his mother was just eighteen when he was born. His father had been in the Navy and had gone off to Vietnam and died in a gunboat on a river in the Mekong Delta. He left Nebraska not knowing his young girlfriend was pregnant, and no one knew for sure if he ever knew. His parents ignored Brad's mother. Pentecostals of the severest kind, they secretly felt their son died because of his sin, for lying with Brad's mother out of wedlock, and they thought of her as a harlot, as that whore of Babylon responsible for the fall of their son.

After struggling to finish high school in Omaha, Brad had thought of nothing except joining the Navy, a conscious decision to identify with his father. He flew with glee on a plane to Chicago for boot camp at Great Lakes. He was disappointed upon his arrival. He expected to be entering an all-Caucasian world but was almost frightened by the number of minorities: blacks, Mexicans from Texas and California, Puerto Ricans from New York and New Jersey, and even three Asians who really didn't bother him, but he thought of the gooks in Vietnam that had killed his father. He recalled pictures of his father, thin, athletic and handsome, bearing little resemblance to himself.

He didn't excel the way he expected to; the sedentary life in front of the television and a propensity for constantly snacking made him overweight despite his tender years, and he couldn't keep up with the demands of the physical training. He threw up during the first morning run. He struggled to complete twenty-five push-ups, and this weakness made him a target of the company commanders and the butt of jokes amongst his fellow recruits. He hated to be laughed at by anybody, especially by the blacks. So he sucked it up and ran through the pain and nausea, completed the required push-ups and sit-ups by sheer will, and by the end of boot camp he was a model recruit. No one would laugh at him again. He was still pudgy, and this disappointed him. After boot camp, he was sent to storekeeper school on the other side of Great Lakes. It was a short six-week course on how to be a naval supply clerk. He made sure to finish at the top of his class, and then it was on to RAF Lutherkirk, Scotland. *There won't be many niggers there*, he thought.

He made one friend shortly after his arrival in Scotland, Seaman Rodgers. Neither one worked in the communications buildings on the base, so they were sort of outcasts. Rodgers was a disbursing clerk and worked in the base personnel office, passing out and preparing paychecks. Rodgers had joined the Navy out of anger; his longtime girlfriend all the way from junior high school broke up with him at the senior prom, where it was revealed she was pregnant. He knew it wasn't his because she told him she was saving herself for marriage. His outlook on life changed instantly. He stopped being the happy-go-lucky guy his friends and family had come to know. Rodgers had no specific plans upon leaving high school, just to work on his father's farm and get married to his sweetheart Jane, but Jane broke his heart and he had to get away. So on the Monday after graduation, he drove the thirty miles into Cape Girardeau to find the Navy recruiter. "Sign me up," he proclaimed upon walking into the recruiter's office. No one tried to talk him out of anything. They quickly processed him and sent him the next day to St. Louis for a physical, and he was immediately put on a bus for Great Lakes. His parents didn't know until he telephoned them from the bus station, telling him that his truck was in front of a parking meter in downtown Cape Girardeau and that he had left it unlocked with the keys in the ignition. His mother cried and his father called him a damn fool and asked who was going to work the farm with him this summer and said when he saw him again, he wouldn't be too big for a belt. Rodgers apologized, but he couldn't risk the chance of seeing Jane around with anybody else. His mother understood but wished he hadn't done something so extreme. His father called him a sissy.

Rodgers knew he made a tragic mistake when he arrived at Great Lakes and he was formed into a company and yelled at. He felt like a pig being shoved into a crowded, dirty pen. After the first night, he became very homesick. By the end of the first week, he was miserable. He was less than a marginal recruit and was forced to repeat two weeks. He longed to be outside, listening to his music, working the farm from sunrise to way past dark, watching the dust fly behind the trucks driving along the dirt road in front of his house.

He had never been around minorities before, but he didn't like them. No one offended him or bothered him, but he and his friends in school identified with the Confederates. He even flew a Confederate flag from the back window of his truck. It fit with his image of tobacco chewing and country music listening. He felt he should hate blacks; he was a reb'.

Disbursing school was in Biloxi. Rodgers was glad to be in the South, though it still wasn't enjoyable. His rate was mostly female, and none were attractive. Many were minorities, and he felt very out of place. He couldn't wait to get out of the Navy and be back home. When duty stations were assigned, he hoped for and expected a ship; there would be no women, and he would at least get to travel. But his number came up for shore duty, RAF Lutherkirk. He looked on the globe and saw how far north Scotland lay and he started to shiver and curse.

Rodgers and Hinckley arrived in Scotland within a few weeks of one another. They quickly became friends, drinking buddies mainly. Neither worked in the communications department, the mission of the base. Both worked in the support side and therefore had few coworkers and were sort of looked down upon by the other sailors who worked with security clearances inside windowless buildings. They mainly worked Monday through Friday, while the rest of the base worked rotating around-the-clock shifts. They found themselves in the base club every night, drinking, Rodgers talking to Hinckley about country music, and Hinckley trying to relate every conversation to Nebraska football.

Becoming bored with the club, they had taken to wandering outside the base to drink in the pubs. At least there, they were isolated because of their nationality, not because of their job.

So this is how they came to arrive at the pub on the first floor of the Lutherkirk Hotel and to be met by Father Crowley and to find themselves drinking with a priest late on a Friday evening and early into Saturday morning.

Their gazes return to the swastika, and Hinckley has an understanding of what it represents. He's seen many late night war movies with his grandfather and listened to him speak reverently of German order and ingenuity.

"They make the best damn cars and the best damn beer," he would say while draining a can of beer inexpensive and domestic.

Rodgers, despite high school history and being alive in the twentieth century, really doesn't have a clue. The swastika is recognizable, but it is just a symbol in a world full of symbols, like the blue oval on the grill of his Ford truck, the Dingo branded into the heels of his boots, or the Columbia on the boxes of his country cassettes.

Crowley smiles that nervous and disarming smile he learned in seminary for dealing with confrontation, even though he is not about to be confronted.

"Hitler wasn't all bad," he says abruptly. "He just tried too hard."

Rodgers nods and sips his beer. Hinckley looks puzzled.

"I know he is thought of as a monster, but that's not true. His was a beautiful soul, and if you know the right history, you will understand. He strived for beauty. He strived to bring calm to a chaotic world."

"What about the Holocaust?" Hinckley asks. "All them Jews getting exterminated?"

"Lies, mostly lies. They were put into colonies to take care of themselves, and they couldn't take care of themselves without preying upon the good German people. They destroyed themselves. You and me, and people like us, we are the foundation and keepers of this world. We make it go round."

Rodgers nods and sips his beer, humming a tune and recalling the leanings of some of his father's friends, talking bad about the niggers in the north, being on welfare and hard working men like them having to pay for them.

"You both appear to be intelligent men," Crowley says to be flattering but not truthful. "Name me a country in this world that is civil and prosperous that isn't ruled by white people."

Hinckley searches his brain and finds nothing. Rodgers nods and sips his beer. He doesn't know too many countries.

"Exactly!" Crowley exclaims triumphantly. "You can't and you never will because they are inferior, the blacks, the Jews, the Asians.

"You see, people like us, Caucasians, we are chosen. We are special. I don't want to confuse you, but we are descendants of supermen, probably from Atlantis. We need to take back what is ours and restore peace and harmony to this wretched world."

"Aren't you, you know, a priest? Don't you believe in God and stuff?" Hinckley asks.

"Not the God you're thinking of, not anymore. You and me, we were deceived. The whole of Christianity was a plot conceived by the Jews. Notice how they are the 'chosen ones' in the Bible? That was their way of holding sway over those vagabond tribes, and even they were surprised at how quickly it spread. Notice how all religions are scrutinized by Christianity except Judaism? Christianity was started by

Jews. As for me being a priest, well, it's a job. I don't know how to do anything else. Except change the world. Another beer?"

Crowley quickly drains his and Hinckley does the same. Rodgers has long since finished his. In his alcoholic stupor, Crowley's words are sinking into his brain.

Crowley returns with three more tins. "I hope I can trust you guys, you know, to keep this conversation amongst us. By the way, did either of you grow up around black people?"

Rodgers shakes his head. Hinckley nods.

"Did you like them?"

They both shake their head.

"Did they make you feel uncomfortable?"

They both nod.

Crowley beams. He silently thanks the spirits that led him to these two young men. "They shouldn't live among you and you shouldn't live among them."

"So what can a fella do?" Rodgers asks, breaking his silence.

"Change the world."

"How?"

"Separate the races. White among white and black among black and yellow among yellow. Never shall they coexist... nor want to coexist."

"It'll never happen. Not in your lifetime, not in mine. The niggers are everywhere, and there are even Mexicans moving into Nebraska," Hinckley says.

"It will happen, but it will take effort," says Crowley. "A war effort."

"Well, shit," says Rodgers. "I ain't fighting no war passing out paychecks. Sign me up."

"It's not that easy," says Crowley gravely. "You first need to earn my trust. If I take you in, and you join me and the armies back in the States and around the world, how do I know you won't betray me, you know, to the Navy?"

"We'll swear," says Hinckley, "on a Bible or something."

"That won't do." Crowley desperately wants compatriots but is rightfully cautious of two so immature and obtuse. He had hoped to find more cerebral partners, but the gods apparently don't have that in their plans.

"Come back tomorrow, and I will find a way to test your word. If successful, we will start straight away."

Crowley calls a cab for the two young men, to take them the five miles back to base. They finish another beer and smoke another cigarette while they wait for the taxi.

After they leave, Crowley is so excited that he nearly has an erection, a sensation he hasn't felt since Houston. Even then, it was seldom, only occurring when he heard debauched confessions or during that awkward moment when a child would sit on his lap and squirm, shame reddening his face to a crimson hue.

He has a plan of attack. He has formulated this plan since Houston, but the opportunity to carry it out never arose there. The opportunity has now presented itself to him in Scotland, in the Navy, as he had hoped it would.

The previous week, just before the Saturday Mass, a young black couple, a sailor and his wife, had entered his office.

The sailor himself was slight and very dark, dark skinned of a hue Crowley would expect to find only in Africa. The girl was very pregnant and very light-skinned; so light-skinned that Crowley decided she was of a mixed race origin.

Crowley was disgusted at the thought of her mixed ancestry, just another example of the races intermingling. Just another example of the dilution of the white race.

He was polite to the couple. They asked him to baptize their child when it was born.

"I'd be delighted," he said. "Please, tell me, where do you live? I would like to check up on you from time to time, and see how you're doing, with the child and with each other. I long for the time when priests made house calls. I think the world, the parishes, were better places."

"We live in Lutherkirk, right in the village," the young sailor replied. "I guess you could come and visit, though the place may be messy."

"You should see mine," said Father Crowley, knowing that would never happen.

As the young couple left his office to take their place in the pews, Crowley called them back.

He placed his hand on the lower abdomen of the mother-to-be and blessed the unborn child.

In his mind, he said a curse.

A chartered bus takes Chris and a small number of recent graduates to Pensacola and the various "A" schools on three different bases in that city.

He was paid just before leaving boot camp and allowed to cash his first check, about eight hundred dollars, more money than he has ever seen. He has no idea how to save it or spend it.

It is his first trip in public with his uniform on. He is wearing the white uniform with a short-sleeve shirt, white pants, patent leather shoes and the typical sailor's hat, known as a Dixie cup. As he is an E-1, the lowest possible rank, he has no stripes on his sleeves and no service ribbons on his chest. He is a swath of solid white, not unlike an ice cream man. His shaved blond hair is just starting to grow back; too short to lie down, it stands straight up out of his pink scalp.

Still, despite the blandness of his uniform, he feels special. He feels official. He wears the uniform of an organization, and he feels like a part of something solid, like a family or a fraternity. He doesn't feel quite as alone.

Even though his destination is not glamorous, Chris is traveling, going somewhere, to yet another place he has never been.

The trip is about seven hours, a large chunk of it on I-75, the same interstate that runs through his part of metropolitan Detroit. The scenery is uninspiring, flat and lush and green, but Chris spends every moment staring out the window, trying to take in all he can, noting the names of different cities he passes through, exit signs pointing the way to Ocala, Gainesville, Tallahassee.

Just outside of Orlando, the bus driver stops to let them buy beer and cigarettes to take on the bus. Florida's drinking age is eighteen, and Chris is quite content staring out the window, sipping beer and nearly chain smoking. He is starting to feel more like a man as he becomes giddily intoxicated.

It is eight in the evening when he arrives in Pensacola, at the smallest of the three bases there that hosts an "A" school. The alcohol has worn off, and he is feeling the ill effects: tiredness, headache and thirst. He is sent to one of the barracks, a three-story brick structure with two wings that looks more like an apartment building or dormitory than what he expected; there is even a small courtyard with benches and planted flowers. There are young men and a few young women wandering around. The evening is warm, and the relaxed atmosphere is in direct contrast to the more intense one Chris left in boot camp.

He is checked into the barracks, thrust keys and linen and is given directions to his room and told to be at morning muster downstairs at 0700.

His room is on the top floor of the building, down a long, dark hallway.

He nervously opens the door, not sure who or what he will find inside.

The room is small, not much larger than his bedroom at home. There are four beds in a row, and the room is divided by two desks, back-to-back in the middle. There are four closets built into the walls.

Three faces stare at Chris in disgust and discouragement. The room just got more crowded. Books and clothes and magazines are stacked upon the fourth bed, Chris's bed.

Grudgingly, the three other sailors remove the items from the bed. Chris is allowed to deposit his linen and seabag and start unpacking. He introduces himself clumsily, offering handshakes that are received coolly by the other three. They appear to be more seasoned; their hair is longer and they are wearing civilian clothes, which is permissible after a month at the school.

One asks Chris where he is from, one asks Chris for a cigarette, and the other asks to borrow some money. Chris obliges all three. They warm up to him gradually, because of his gentle and compliant nature. Chris learns they are all southern, one from Alabama, one from Tennessee, and one from northern Florida. They have been at the school for nearly three months and are almost done. They are all headed to ships out of Norfolk; two are going on destroyers, one on a carrier. Chris is jealous and also excited. He is getting close to the real Navy. He asks them questions about what to expect and the places he can go.

After Chris unpacks and makes his rack, his roommates suggest a trip to the enlisted men's club. They know Chris has money in his pocket.

They call him "boot," the term for newly arrived recruits.

They take Chris to the club. It is full of many young men and, again, only a few women. Chris gets very drunk and stands alone while watching his roommates talk to people they know. They don't introduce him to anyone. He will get drunk many times before leaving Pensacola.

He spends over a hundred dollars by the time the evening ends.

After a week, he starts to feel more comfortable, although he is wary of his roommates. He makes one close friend from his own class, a boy named Ben Mahler, who is from Staten Island, New York. Like Chris, Mahler is an outcast back home. Both are young men without current or past girlfriends, non-athletic, and introverted. They drink in the base club and wander to some bars off base, and talk mainly about the future and what the Navy might bring. Chris is fascinated by Mahler's accent, the New York dialect that he has heard in so many television shows and movies. Mahler is obsessed with Woody Allen movies, and he can relate every aspect of his life to a scene in a particular movie. Chris lets him talk, even though he is not in the least interested in the work of Woody Allen. He finds it too cerebral, too weird.

The training isn't effortless. Chris is required to learn Morse code. He learns how to send it and receive it at an increasing speed as the weeks progress. It is tough at first, and some can't do it. They are removed from the school and sent directly to a ship without a skill, or rate, as the Navy calls it. They're the ones on the ships who swab the decks, scrape and repaint the hull, and all the other worst imaginable jobs the Navy has to offer.

Chris pretends that the Morse code is music. He finds a sort of rhythm, tapping his fingers and his feet to the beat of each individual letter. He actually does quite well and is given a letter of merit for being the most proficient in his class.

He had never done well in school as a child. He feels proud in a new way, proud of being tops at something, a feeling that he's never had.

He loves the Navy, the work, the structure, the freedom to do what he wants when off-duty. He loves the look of the uniform. And he loves the thrill of the future and the promise of all the places he will go.

His friend Mahler doesn't fare so well. He can't comprehend the code, and as a result of his frustration, he decides he hates the Navy. He chooses not to conform. He leaves his uniform wrinkled, his face unshaven, and his hair too long. With one week to go of the twelve-week course, he is summarily sent to a carrier out of San Diego as a deckhand. He will probably spend his whole enlistment in that fashion, without a rate, without rising past the rank of a lowly seaman.

Towards the end of school, Chris is promoted to E-2 and given stripes. Finally, his uniform isn't a blank page anymore. He also receives his first duty station. He is disappointed; it isn't a ship. Shore duty. Naval Communications Station, Lutherkirk, Scotland, United Kingdom.

He hadn't given much thought to the possibility of not going to sea. It was pretty much assumed, especially for a first duty station. At first, it leaves him puzzled.

He goes to the base library and studies atlases and encyclopedias and finds the spot on the globe. His future home.is far from Detroit and a lot of other things.

Chris is granted two weeks of leave before he is sent to Scotland. Because it's his home of record, the Navy gives him a one-way ticket to Detroit from Pensacola, and then from Detroit to Scotland.

He will be home for Christmas.

Excited, with just a week left in Pensacola, he calls home to let his mother or father know he is on his way. He hasn't talked to them since he left for boot camp, and though he feels ignored, he still loves them and misses them a little. He wants them to see him in his new uniform. He wants to scan their faces for a look of pride when they gaze upon him.

The phone rings and rings, but no one answers. He makes several attempts over the next few days, but no one answers. He is disappointed, but not surprised. His mother is probably out with god knows who, his brother stoned, and his father lethargic in the basement.

He drafts a letter and sends it priority, hoping it will reach Detroit sooner than he does. He gives them his arrival time, the airline, and all the necessary information they will need to pick him up from the airport.

He gets paid just before leaving, and he is given a travel allowance and the pay he would miss while on leave.

He heads for Detroit with a thousand dollars in his pocket. Suddenly, he feels very adult.

Again, he is thrilled by traveling, even if it is a return to familiar territory.

He dons his dress blue uniform for the flight home. That uniform is referred to as the "cracker jack" due to the similar dress of the character on that box of candy. His uniform bears two stripes and the insignia of his rating, a feather cutting diagonally over radio waves.

The flight to Detroit is interrupted by a change of planes in Atlanta, and Chris nearly gets lost in that very large airport. The shuttle trains and the crowds daunt him.

He makes it to his plane. There is a warm feeling at the base of his stomach as the plane taxis into the gate in Detroit.

There is no one there to greet him.

He scans the cluster of people at the gate, looking for first his mother and then his father, but no one is there. He waits, hoping, assuming, someone will come for him. An hour passes. Dejectedly, he finds the baggage claim and retrieves his garment bag for his dress uniforms and his sea bag, which contains everything else he owns.

He tries phoning his parents' house, but still there is no answer. He rings his uncle, his father's brother, but no one answers there, either. It's four in the afternoon, and he assumes everyone is at work.

For the first time in his life, Chris hails a taxicab outside the airport and heads home. The Detroit airport is west of the city, and Chris lives in a northern suburb. The cab fare is over forty dollars. Chris is stunned at first, but then he realizes he is a man of means. He gives the driver sixty dollars.

There is a for sale sign in front of his house. There is a SOLD sticker splashed on the face of it.

Confused, Chris leaves his luggage on the front lawn, not caring that it sinks into nearly six inches of snow. He looks inside the front window.

Relieved, he still sees the furniture he has known most of his life.

But the house has been ignored. The walks haven't been shoveled; only a footpath beaten into the snow going from the driveway to the front door is passable without feet getting wet.

Chris is wearing his patent leather shoes, and snow has already gotten inside them, saturating his socks. He tries the front door; it is unlocked. As he enters the house, the warm air fogs his glasses. He wipes them off with the bottom of his jumper.

Inside, he finds his mother sitting at the kitchen table, smoking a cigarette, smiling in a way he hasn't seen her smile in a long time. She is not alone; leaning against the kitchen counter is a large, broad-shouldered man in a sweatshirt, blue jeans, and dark, worn work boots. His hair is cut short, almost like Chris's, and he has stubble on his cheeks and his chin. Chris notes his youthful appearance; he would guess him to be about twenty-five.

"Hey, Chris. Sorry about missing you, but I just opened your letter a minute ago. I haven't been here in a few weeks. I've been staying with Nick," his mother indicates the young man leaning against the counter with a nod, "giving that damn father of yours a chance to get his crap out of here. We have until January 3rd to get our stuff out, and he still hasn't done it yet."

Chris turns pale. He knew his mother dated, but not someone so young. Plus, the house is being emptied. His family is obviously moving. He sits down at the kitchen table and doesn't say anything.

"Look, honey," says his mother, a woman of about forty-five, short, slightly overweight with brunette hair that is dyed darker than its natural color, nails manicured, rings on her fingers, bracelets on both wrists and wearing a tight-fitting sweater and tight jeans, "I know you're upset. I was hoping your father would write to you and explain everything, but I guess he didn't, or you wouldn't be here. We hung on as long as we could, and we agreed years ago we wouldn't split up until both of you boys were finished with school. Well, that's happened, and it's time to move on. Your brother moved in with a friend from work a few weeks ago, and your father is moving in with your Grandma and Uncle Steve. Nick and I are moving to Phoenix tomorrow. Detroit is dead; there's nothing here for us. Nick's in construction, and they're building like crazy in Phoenix. He'll get a job like that," she says with a snap of her fingers. She walks over to Nick and leans against him. She holds his hand, letting Chris know that she is bonded to Nick, not to her family.

"I'm sorry you had to see us this way. Your father is in the basement, if you want to talk to him."

Chris starts to head down the stairs, but turns around and walks out of the house, retrieving his bags from the front lawn without bothering to shake the snow off of them.

Shivering because of the cold and his nerves, he clumsily lights a cigarette and starts walking to no place in particular, dragging his luggage in the snow behind him, his sailor suit askew. He looks entirely out of place walking through these suburban streets where no one walks during the winter.

Everyone he knows has a home, in the Navy and otherwise, a place where you can always go back to, an anchor in an often-goofy world. In the Navy, you are required to have a home of record, typically your parents' home or a relative's. Chris no longer has a home. He is truly a child of the Navy, and home is wherever he is required to hang his seabag.

In this instance, home will soon be Scotland.

He remembers the cluster of hotels near the shopping mall a few miles away and starts walking along the busy road. Many drivers strain their necks to see the unusual looking young man.

He checks into a room for the night, blankly staring at the television for most of the evening, not sure how to spend the next two weeks.

When the morning comes, he checks out of the hotel and has the clerk call him yet another cab. This time he finds a Greyhound bus terminal. He purchases a ticket for New York. His flight to Scotland will connect through La Guardia, so he would just as soon hang out for two weeks in a place other than Detroit, and New York is a city he has wanted to visit after hearing his friend Mahler talk incessantly about Woody Allen and all things New Yorkish. He will try to find his friend, who is probably still on leave, before reporting to San Diego.

What would be twelve hours in a car is nearly twenty in a bus. The bus stops at every town and city of size, with a parade of bizarre people coming and going, some carrying no luggage at all, and some their life's possessions stuffed into wrinkled and bulging trash bags.

Again, Chris is traveling, and his glances into the various towns and the landscape of the Ohio Turnpike and onto the rolling hills and low mountains of Pennsylvania provide a welcome relief from the thought of no longer having a home.

Many passengers come and go on his journey; many have occupied the seat next to him. Many try to talk to him, especially because of the uniform, asking him where he's going, where he's been, and where he's from.

Chris answers in one- and two-word responses; he is not in the mood for elaboration or conversation.

The parade of people coming and going off the bus is somewhat illuminating for Chris. Though he didn't grow up wealthy, his needs were met and he lived in comfort. On the bus, some carry trash bags for luggage, some have nicer luggage, some have dirty clothes, and some have clean clothes and dirty hands and dirty faces.

Ultimately, the bus arrives in New York mid-morning, two days before Christmas, and deposits Chris in the Port Authority terminal in lower Manhattan. The vastness of the bus station pales in comparison to the vastness of the city outside. Chris can do nothing at first but stare straight up at all the buildings framing the sky.

Then he turns his attention to the sidewalks, the streets, surging with cars and buses and trucks and people, an overwhelming wave of hurried people.

He is scared, more scared than he ever was in boot camp.

But he is excited. This is the world he longed to see. He feels years removed from high school classrooms and life in front of television screens.

He wanders, staring at the people and the streetlights and all the Christmas decorations in the storefronts. The sight of Christmas at first warms him, but then makes him feel sad. Christmas was never particularly special in his household. His mother would drag him and his brother to his grandparents' house, but as they got older, it was mainly a day for sleeping in and exchanging a gift with their mother.

Even on Christmas, their father never ventured from the basement, and Chris could hear the noise of the television from late in the morning till very late at night.

He decides to try to find his friend Mahler, and knowing he lives on Staten Island, he tries to make his way there.

He tries to catch a taxi, but a taxi is hard to come by in New York at Christmastime.

But because of his uniform and the scared and pathetic look on his face, a cab driver eventually stops and picks him up. He takes Chris through the financial district and drops him off at the terminal for the Staten Island Ferry at Battery Park.

He sits on that boat in a cluster of miserable commuters and tourists from around the world. Chris hears a cacophony of accents and languages. He drops his belongings at his feet, thrusts his hands deep into the pockets of his pea coat, and pushes his sailor's hat down on his forehead, resting it on the top of his thick gold-rimmed eyeglasses.

It is his first time on a boat. He feels at home. The thrill of travel has returned, even though he is not sure of his immediate destination.

The sights from the ferry are at first breathtaking: the Statue of Liberty, that American image that he has seen depicted a million times growing up, the Brooklyn Bridge, the skyline of lower Manhattan with the World Trade Center towers rising majestically over every building

He thinks briefly of his mother and father. He lights a cigarette and looks at the industrial New Jersey shoreline to the west, full of nothing but iron and steel and concrete, and the Brooklyn shoreline to the east, residential, almost bucolic compared to the Jersey shoreline.

After roughly twenty-five minutes and two cigarettes, the ferry deposits him at the north end of Staten Island. The scenery is more suburban, similar to his own native surroundings. He is disappointed. He expected to feel like he was in the middle of a big city.

He walks along the main road and realizes that it is already mid-afternoon and that he hasn't eaten in nearly two days. He stops at a fast-food restaurant, eats without tasting, barely breathing, and continues walking.

Tired, he stops at the first motel he sees, a rather bland building.

He gets his room and peruses the phonebook. There are many Mahlers listed, and Chris is too introverted to start randomly calling people, looking for his friend. Upset, he turns on the television, removes his uniform and neatly hangs it in the closet. He collapses on the bed and falls asleep. He dreams of his childhood, of a camping trip his parents promised him but never took. In the dream, he loves his mother and looks up to his father and brother. They fish from a dock at the campground. They paddle a canoe.

He awakes at dawn the next morning, the day before Christmas, disappointed that his dream did not lead to a reality and that his current reality is a Christmas without a home in a city he doesn't know and a life leading god knows where.

He sighs, retrieves the last cigarette from the crushed pack on the nightstand. He scratches his head and turns up the volume of the television, which has stayed on all night. He can't stand silence. He has not been entirely alone this much in his entire life, and the noise from the television and the brightness of the screen comfort him.

He still has over a week and a half of leave left, time he had planned on spending in Michigan, exchanging gifts with his family, visiting one or two of his friends, returning to his school in his uniform, as he had seen upperclassmen do in previous years.

No one would have known him anyway, he decides.

He thinks about crying but doesn't, thinks about shouting but doesn't, and he shifts his thoughts to how to spend the next eleven days before he is due in Scotland.

He decides to head there early.

He showers, dons his uniform and heads out into the early New York morning, Christmas lights twinkling all around him in that dusky cold and clear sky.

It is a difficult trek to La Guardia, back to the Staten Island Ferry, and then a very expensive cab ride to the international terminal, where he finds the Pan Am counter.

He is able to change his ticket for a flight leaving that day. He checks in his sea bag and garment bag and has seven hours to kill inside the airport. First, he eats a breakfast of a cinnamon roll and soda, and then he purchases some reading material and selects a seat at the gate from which his plane will be departing. He reads the *New York Times* because he is in New York and he feels that's appropriate and worldly, even though he has never really read a newspaper, save the comics on the occasional Sunday. He buys a paperback book, some sort of horror story, but he can't concentrate. He watches the people walking through the terminal, a very cosmopolitan display of people. He has never seen such a variety of cultures and classes, and he finds it fascinating.

And that is how he spends his time: studying the people, guessing where they are from and where they are going.

The late afternoon eventually comes, and he boards the plane that will carry him over the ocean to the parts of the world he has longed to see.

It is the first night home for the baby, a girl named Samantha Marie, born in an Aberdeen hospital to Petty Officer Third Class Frank Beasley and his wife Monica, both from Norfolk, both children of career Navy men. They are a young and handsome and innocent black couple.

Frank is proud to follow in his father's footsteps, performing the same job as is father, and wearing the same uniform.

The baby is brought to their little cottage inside the village of Lutherkirk, a small structure made of stone, heated solely by a coal-burning fireplace. Monica is nervous and scared. Her family is back in Virginia, and there is no one to help her with the baby, no one to give her advice, no one she can talk to, really, except her husband. And it's Christmas. That makes the desolation even more intense.

It is about 2 a.m. and the house is silent, as is the village of Lutherkirk. The pubs emptied hours ago, and the village is asleep. The baby has just fallen asleep, and so, too, do Frank and Monica.

No one in the village hears a vehicle rolling quietly through, searching for the Beasley home.

Nor does anyone see the vehicle's driver and passengers, two young men dressed in black from head to toe, camouflage paint covering their faces.

The vehicle parks about a block away from the Beasley home. The two figures, one portly, the other thin, run to the Beasley home. Each has a can of spray paint. They decorate the front door and stucco exterior of the house with swastikas and "NIGGERS LEAVE" and other vulgarities.

They throw a brick through the front window and dash back to the car before anyone detects them. They have attached a note to the brick:

This is just a warning. Our next visit will end in fatality.
Scotland is not the place for the scum of the earth such as you.
The white race will reign supreme, but not until the lower
races are destroyed. This means you!

The Eastern Scotland Trinity of the
Great White Brotherhood

The Beasleys run out of their lone bedroom and step on the broken glass in their living room. Frank reads the note and hides it from his wife. A few neighborhood lights flicker on and then off. The night is silent again save Samantha crying loudly and the sound of an Austin Allegro speeding out of the village of Lutherkirk.

Chris's journey to Scotland consists of a transatlantic flight from New York to London, with a three-hour layover at Heathrow and a connecting flight to Aberdeen.

He will take a cab the thirty miles from Aberdeen to the base in Lutherkirk.

The flight to London is long, long enough for an in-flight movie. Chris feels worldlier still, vaguely glamorous, traveling long and far enough to be entitled to an in-flight movie, a romantic comedy that Chris really doesn't enjoy, but since he paid three dollars to rent the headset to hear the movie, he suffers through it anyway.

Due to the five-hour time difference between London and New York, it is early morning as Chris arrives at Heathrow. He strains his eyes, trying to catch glimpses of the English landscape through the low and thick early morning cloud cover. He sees nothing but a gray sky and highways and buildings and cars. From the air, it doesn't look any different than the landscape of his suburban Detroit.

As the plane lands at Heathrow, Chris is thrilled with the realization that he has crossed the Atlantic and is now in a country he has always wanted to see, home of so many musicians and esoteric television shows that he watched on late night public television at home.

The walk from customs to the terminal is long. The many tunnel-like hallways are dark, quiet and empty save the recently disembarked passengers of international flights.

The walk through the tunnels ends abruptly at a blind turn that is the entrance to the terminal. Chris is greeted by a throng of faces waiting for loved ones to arrive. He is scrutinized by many, studying him from head to toe, noting his uniform and the country it represents. He was advised not to wear his uniform while traveling overseas, as servicemen had been targets of terrorists in the past, but he never thought to change, nor did he want to. He wanted the world to know he was in the Navy; he wanted the world to know he belonged to something, hang the consequences.

Again, he has time to kill inside the airport, about three hours before his plane to Aberdeen departs.

He converts some money into British pounds and feels cheated when he is given back less than he turned in. He finds a newsstand and buys some newspapers and is surprised at their tabloid appearance. He expects the country to be more intellectual, based on his observations of those whimsical comedies he saw at home.

The contents of the newspapers are meaningless to him. They are laden with stories about politics and places and personalities he has no grasp or knowledge of and the sports pages are also equally dizzying, displaying features on football and snooker and scores and statistics that are difficult to understand.

He returns to the newsstand to find more reading material but instead buys candy with wrappers that he has never seen and cigarettes in odd-shaped boxes with brand names he has never heard of.

So he sits, eating new candy and smoking strong cigarettes, and watches people as they stroll past him. He scrutinizes the young English girls, especially the ones working in the airport, the girls in uniforms behind ticket and gift shop counters. He studies them with longing and wonders if any of them would ever be interested in him.

He thinks about his life, and decides at this moment to never return to Michigan, to never seek out his mother or father or brother.

He is done trying to love anyone who doesn't love him back, and he is resolved to make a life and a family of his own.

He stares at the girls and sighs.

Dear Wife,

I'm sitting here in London and I can't see anything as I am stuck inside an airport and if I had any courage I would wander outside and take a cab and try to see something but I don't so I am just going to sit here and wait for my flight to Scotland, where I am going to be stationed for the next two years.

I am already looking for you, but I think I'll know when I find you, when it's for real.

My mother is basically a slut and I've finally realized it, she is running off somewhere with some bozo and my father is only interested in existing, I don't think he has any feelings and I haven't had a real conversation with him in years. I don't want my screwed up family to have an effect on me throughout my life, I want to be strong, and I want to be loyal to you and the family I want to have.

I want my children to have something to stand upon, not a family that might disappear in a blink and leave them with nothing. That's what has happened to me, but I'll explain more later and you may already know, I may have told you everything before you even read this. Mainly, I want to be a good person, I don't want to be selfish.

Love,
Chris

Father Crowley invites Hinckley and Rodgers to his house for Christmas dinner. There is little Christian about it, but he does prepare a turkey and other traditional food for his young guests.

He makes sure there is plenty of wine and beer on hand, items that he purchases off base, as making alcoholic purchases on base would raise the eyebrows of anyone who witnessed him, the Catholic chaplain, doing such.

He makes sure Hinckley and Rodgers are drinking constantly while he slowly sips a glass of South African cabernet, wine forbidden to be sold in the United States due to the racist practices of the South African government.

Crowley plays Wagner as softly as possible in the background. He feels warm inside as the coal burns in his fireplace and as the young men become more intoxicated. This is his new family. These are his soldiers.

Hinckley and Rodgers are laughing amongst themselves, feeling powerful, befriended by an officer, and enlisted to fight a cause they find easy to believe in.

This violence they have been entrusted with has gone straight to their heads, and they love to boast. Which nigger they're gonna get next. Maybe a spic.

They both have urges to talk to others on base, other young sailors they occasionally drink with in the club.

Crowley, not stupid, well versed in human nature, senses this and instantly hatches a plan to ensure their silence.

Smiling, he offers them more beer and asks if anyone would also like some scotch or rum. Both young men prefer the latter mixed with Coke. Crowley is pleased to oblige. It will be several more drinks before he puts his plan into action.

After dinner, the three sit in Crowley's living room. Hinckley and Rodgers are too intoxicated to notice that the priest is loading a gun. It is an inexpensive Argentine copy of a Glock readily available on the streets of Houston and other cities. It was presented to him by a repentant parishioner, a young man who killed somebody with it. Crowley promised him absolution if only he would give him the gun. This occurred in his last weeks in Houston, and he knew what the weapon could and would be used for ultimately. He longed for the opportunity to use it. He took great care to sneak it into the country with him, as handguns are strictly controlled in the United Kingdom. He traveled to this country wearing his priestly collar, and he was waved right through customs.

Crowley sits quietly as the young men continue to drink and smoke.

He himself has only had two glasses of wine, enough to make him feel serene.

"Gentlemen," Crowley announces, interrupting a one-sided conversation between Hinckley and Rodgers about college football, "let us go for a ride." And donning their coats, the three step out into the quiet evening. It is about 9 p.m. and clouds lighten the dark sky. The motor of the Allegro at first knocks and then grows quiet as Crowley pumps the gas and puts the car into gear. They find themselves on the empty A92 heading south to Dundee, the headlights illuminating the curves and rises in the road.

Crowley tells Hinckley, who is sitting in the front seat, to retrieve a pen and notepad from the glove compartment. The priest dictates a note to Hinckley:

"Scotland is for the Scottish, a noble nation, white and pure. Signed, The Eastern Scotland Trinity of the Great White Brotherhood."

In his travels, Crowley came across a small Pakistani neighborhood just outside the city center of Dundee. It is only a few square blocks with a few restaurants and shops and Pakistanis residing in multiple-family units.

Perfect, he thought upon finding the neighborhood while passing through on a clear and pleasant September evening. In a pub, he asked people about the neighborhood, who the dark skinned people were in Middle-Eastern garb. Pakistanis, he was told with a little disdain by a bent-over old man sitting at the bar, chain-smoking Crowley's cigarettes and drinking slowly from a half-pint glass. Crowley hoped for more displeasure from the man's voice, more disgust from the man's face when inquiring about the neighborhood. He was looking for hate and found only irritation.

He has now harvested hate, and it is traveling in the car with him, driving around Dundee, waiting for the streets to be empty and waiting for the right opportunity.

"Which of you two have gone hunting before?" Crowley asks. He parks the car right in front of a closed Pakistani restaurant. "Kebob House" is written on a handmade sign propped in the storefront window.

Rodgers pipes up and claims to be a marksman, killing rabbits and squirrels on his family property with one shot since he was eight. Not to mention deer and ducks and geese and wild turkeys.

Crowley smiles. "Good," he says. "Then you will be the first participant in our first military exercise." And he reaches towards the back seat and hands Rodgers the gun. "This has rubber bullets," Crowley lies. "We're going to do a bit of target practice and let the good people of Dundee know we're here. I want you to crack the window and watch the sidewalk on the opposite side of the street. I don't want any part of the gun visible, and I will select your target."

They sit in the car on the quiet street for nearly an hour. The windows start to fog and the cigarette smoke becomes suspended and odorous in the cold air.

Crowley spots a solitary man coming towards them from the opposite side of the street. He is a dark skinned, bearded and thin man, wearing a turban and what appears to be traditional Pakistani garb—baggy trousers, a long and loose long-sleeved shirt underneath a wool overcoat.

"Okay, Lee, aim for the head," Crowley commands. "Let's shake him up a bit."

Laughing, the drunk but steady Rodgers aims and fires. He is shocked by the loudness of the gun echoing inside the car, ringing his ears.

He is more shocked by the fallen man, his head bleeding profusely from the shot that went right through his left temple. Hinckley and Rodgers become very sober as they see the blood cover the sidewalk, spilling into the gutter, reflecting the streetlamp light directly overhead.

Crowley drives away, forgetting to leave the note he so desperately wanted to leave, ruining an otherwise perfect situation.

"What the fuck?" says Rodgers. "I thought you said the bullets were rubber!"

"I must have made a mistake." The priest glances in the rearview mirror, looks down side streets. He won't relax until he is out of Dundee, back on the A92 heading north. "I didn't mean to make you a murderer."

Rodgers starts to panic; Hinckley is quiet because of his shock. Crowley makes his point clear. "Silence and devotion to each other is of the utmost importance. If any of us talk, Rodgers will go straight to jail, and I think they have the death penalty in this country." He pauses after this comment for the desired effect, knowing that there is no death penalty in Britain.

"Look, there is no evidence. We will never be suspected. No one will ever think this was done by someone from the base. This is a defining moment in Scottish history. If I had just left that stupid note... The rest of Scotland would see what we are trying to do and they would rally behind us with popular support, never suspecting that we're from across the ocean. We have absolutely no way of getting caught." He pauses again as the car leaves Dundee and passes through the village of Broughty Ferry. Crowley looks in his rearview mirror and over his shoulder for signs of police pursuit, but the Ferry is stark this Christmas night, the buildings whizzing past in a blur as they speed along the highway, and the only sign of life are lamps lit inside the front windows of the elegant homes.

Crowley manages to reassure them some more, but Hinckley really doesn't need reassuring. He is sort of smirking, seeing the humor in the situation, glad that he is part of this accomplishment, having never really done anything distinct in his life.

"Rodgers, you are a saint," Crowley continues. "You have the eye of an eagle, and you did the world a great service: there is one less dirty non-white polluting the white world. I would have rather shot a Negro or a Jew, but we'll take what we can get." Crowley almost regrets shooting a Muslim. Hitler had wished the German people had chosen a more militant, loyal religion, not the soft Christianity that flourished throughout Western Europe. The Muslims would die for Islam; it had been centuries since a Christian had died for Christ.

"I coulda shot a nigger," Hinckley says, "no problem."

"In due time, my son, in due time," Crowley replies. "We will build this temple one stone at a time.

"And Lee," the priest says to Rodgers via the rearview mirror, seeing only Rodgers's silhouette and the whites of his eyes in the darkened back seat, "as a priest, I can forgive you. The Church has not taken that away from me, and our white god, Odin, is smiling upon you, my son. God is smiling."

They return to Crowley's cottage for more drinking. The priest and Brad continually pat Rodgers on the back and compliment his aim, his timing, and his level head. By the time the evening is over, Rodgers no longer thinks of himself as a murderer. He is a soldier.

After midnight, the priest returns the pair to the road just down from the base entrance, knowing now that they won't tell a soul about their activity, or about their friendship.

He is the epitome of an almost dignified Scot, tall and thin, a full head of black hair imperceptibly sprinkled with gray. His face is adorned with pale blue, almost gray eyes and a long aquiline nose on a still longer and red face. Constable Robertson is the lone representative of the Tayside Police in Lutherkirk—a small village with a population of about 300—and has been for nearly twenty years. It has always been his dream to be the man responsible for law enforcement in his native village, and the circumstances in his days upon the conclusion of his police training allowed that to happen for him at a young age.

His is basically a 9 to 5 job, Monday through Friday, and much of his time is spent sitting in his small, one-room storefront office along High Street. His office is very simple, consisting of a solitary desk, a teletype machine, a coat and hat rack, a thin and shallow jail cell, a small refrigerator, and a hotplate for boiling tea on a small table in front of the large picture window, surrounded by a collection of donated mugs used by his frequent visitors, citizens of the village who constantly pop in to say hello.

His day consists of writing his daily reports or reading the police bulletins from across the United Kingdom. He constantly glances out the front window, staring out into the street in case some burglar or murderer from England, one of the U.K.'s most wanted, is passing through.

But all he sees are the same faces and forms he grew up with, people he knows at a glance. And then there are the young Americans from the base, walking along the same sidewalk as the citizens of Lutherkirk but living in a different world, rarely socializing with the Scottish people, except for times spent in pubs or shops. The American faces are never permanent. A face that becomes familiar soon disappears and is replaced by a similar looking young man, with the same sort of homogenous appearance: short hair, blue jeans and tennis shoes. The Americans from the nearby base have been part of the Lutherkirk landscape for all save the very early years of his life.

There is little crime in Lutherkirk, and if things at one of the pubs get out of hand or if a husband gets physical with his wife, the citizens won't hesitate to call the constable at any hour of the night, or even knock on his door, as he lives just a block from his office.

A neighbor of the Beasleys heard their window break. She is an older widow, distrustful of the world—especially Americans, and especially black Americans. She telephones Robertson upon hearing the broken glass, upon hearing the baby scream. She suspects some sort of domestic disturbance, not an act of racist intimidation.

Robertson hangs up the phone and sleepily dons his uniform from the previous day, grabbing his fluorescent orange raincoat with the word POLICE emblazoned on the back. The night damp and frosty, he kisses his wife's red and puffy and barely awake face and promises a quick return.

He walks from one side of High Street to the next, passing his still and sleepy office. The empty street is illuminated by sporadic streetlamps whose lights can be seen twinkling in the moisture-laden air through the low fog that provides a blanket over the entire village.

"Bollocks," he says to himself. His hands are thrust deep into his trouser pockets, the collar of his raincoat turned up to protect his ears as he walks almost hurriedly in his awkward gait, slightly bowlegged with his right foot angling out.

"Nearly bleeping fucking Christmas and I've got to tend to some damn Yanks."

The Americans don't really bother Robertson in the political sense, but he grows irritated when he has to police them. He is paid for by the Tayside government, not the U.S. He feels the Americans that live and wander and drink off base are like children ignored by their parents and left without a babysitter: apt to do treacherous and irresponsible things.

Robertson's approach to the Beasley house is telegraphed by his shoes walking on broken glass and the sound of a baby crying heard through the jagged hole in the living room window. The house is dark save a light from a small lamp on the kitchen table, where Beasley and his wife sit. The wife is trying to breastfeed the baby but the baby can't and won't and all it does is continue to wail quite strongly for such a new child.

Robertson whispers loudly through the broken window, though the immediate neighbors are quite awake. "You there," he says, indicating Beasley with a point and a wave of his hand intended to bring him outside.

Robertson already knows that a black couple lives in the house, a semi-detached property belonging to his wife's uncle, who owned many of the properties rented to the Americans in the area, all furnished meagerly in the thrifty Scottish fashion with furniture bought at estate sales and resale shops. Robertson notes the tattered and worn upholstery. He rolls his eyes and thinks of his wife's uncle, the cheap bastard.

Beasley comes outside in his stocking feet, wearing Navy sweatpants and a Navy sweatshirt. He doesn't look at Robertson but keeps his head down as he tries to step between the shards of glass. He hands Robertson the rock and the note before the constable can inquire into the situation. Robertson squints his eyes and reads the note from the light of the kitchen.

Immediately he thinks of the scruffy looking youths he sees loitering around the city center on his shopping trips to Dundee: young and small and thin men wearing boots and black leather jackets and shaved heads with iron crosses around their necks. He recalls that they're called skinheads, and he fears their influence has spread north to his quiet piece of the Earth. He suspects nothing different and he asks Beasley some obvious questions.

"Any idea who did this?"

Beasley shakes his head while sniffing his nose. His eyes are teary. The tears start to freeze at the corners of his eyes.

"No enemies, no friends on the base that you've rubbed the wrong way?" Robertson continues while staring into the night and through the broken window at the quiet girl trying to nurse a still crying baby.

Beasley shakes his head. Robertson believes he knows nothing. The constable turns his head slowly, nearly 360 degrees, in the hope of seeing a bald-headed leather-clad youth in combat boots traipsing through his village, hoping to solve this crime, this breach of a quiet and almost holy night, this trespass against a young and seemingly harmless family just minding their business.

Robertson continues. His questions are over. This is the first crime he will have to solve where the perpetrator is not some familiar drunk or some abusive husband. "Look," he says, "I'll phone this friend of mine straight away to board up this window, and if you think of anything, you know, anything that might seem relevant to the matter at hand, call me right away."

Beasley nods, sniffles, the tip of his nose growing numb but he doesn't feel it, doesn't feel anything but despair starting to be replaced with anger.

He looks at Robertson, seems to notice him for the first time. "When I know who did it, I'll kill 'em, jail or no jail, Navy or no Navy."

Robertson nods and understands. Anger and vengeance transcend borders and oceans. "Not to worry, lad. I'm on it straight away, and," he adds, "if you or the lass need anything, for yourselves or the baby, you call me. I can be reached twenty-four hours a day." He hands Beasley his business card; he has written his home phone number and address on the back.

Robertson feels sorry for the young sailor, and Robertson is not usually sympathetic. His years of mundane police work have made him sort of callous, but the proximity to Christmas, the new baby and Beasley's obvious youth has touched him. He wants to reach out to this young American.

But Beasley spurns him. "We don't need anybody." He walks inside and Robertson watches him put a blanket around his wife, still sitting at the kitchen table.

Robertson walks the few blocks back to his office and turns on the hotplate upon his arrival. Tea is definitely in order. He telephones and rouses out of bed an acquaintance in the neighboring village to patch up the window in the Beasley house, and then he telephones the sergeant on duty in Dundee, at the headquarters of the Tayside Police. The sergeant is puzzled; that sort of crime doesn't happen in the hinterlands of their region.

"Write a report and send it in," he tells Robertson. "Looks like you'll have a wee bit of police work for a change," he adds sarcastically.

Robertson puts his feet on the desk and waits for the water to boil. He notes the time, not quite 4 a.m. Daylight is still six hours away here in the land as far north as Alaska.

The kettle whistles and he makes his tea, lots of milk and lots of sugar. He plugs in his newly requisitioned electric typewriter and feeds the form used for reporting incidents. He then realizes this is the first crime he will have to try to solve, to find clues and sort them out. He dashes out of the office, leaving the light on and the door unlocked and his hat still on top of the coat rack. He runs to the Beasley house.

"I need the rock and the note," he tells Frank. "It's evidence." He takes the items back to his one-room station. He is not sure what to do with them, but they somehow seem significant.

He finishes his cup of tea and makes another and notes the milkman driving down High Street, starting his day. Robertson feels somehow important; he is the one responsible for maintaining the routine of the village, and an interloper has intruded and infringed upon the tranquility.

He thinks about returning home to catch a few more hours of sleep, waking up to a nice breakfast, sausage maybe, black pudding, a fried egg, but decides against it. He will wait until the detective bureau in Dundee reports in for the day and he will telephone them and ask them to look at his evidence and dust it for fingerprints.

He sits at his desk and taps his fingers, waiting to begin.

The flight from London to Aberdeen is short, perhaps an hour and a little more. The plane is small but crowded. Chris is starting to feel the fatigue of travel and he pays little attention to the other passengers, just listens to the accents of the crew and others talking, his ears sensitive to the differences of inflection from his own native tongue.

He barely looks out the window as the plane flies above the clouds and then abruptly descends again as it approaches Aberdeen.

He expects a small airport and he is not mistaken. The passengers disembark on the runway and are forced to walk across the runway to the terminal. Chris stares at the overcast Scottish late morning sky and he sees many smooth and green low hills with clusters of naked trees and off to the distance, granite colored stone buildings, which he assumes is the start of the city of Aberdeen.

He collects his luggage and walks out of the terminal to a line of taxis waiting outside. He approaches the nearest one and interrupts a driver reading a tabloid-like newspaper. Chris hops in the back seat of the small car, a make of car that he's never heard of or seen, a Lada. He notes the steering wheel on the right side of the car.

"Lutherkirk," Chris says, his orders clutched in his hands. He retrieves his cigarettes from his sock. It is the last of his American cigarettes that he bought in New York. The pack is nearly empty and soggy from the sweat of his skin and the warmth of his sock.

"Aye," the cab driver says. He is a short, heavy man with black rimmed glasses, longish, greasy gray hair, a red nose and a pockmarked face. "Are ya going to the base?"

Chris can't understand a word the driver says. It will be a few weeks before he can tune his ear to the Scottish brogue, much different from the English accent he expected to be universal across the island of Britain.

Embarrassed by not being able to understand, Chris moves his head indistinctly, to be taken as a nod or a shake.

The driver speeds south along the A92, a four-lane highway that hugs the coast of the North Sea. Chris stares out the window and suddenly feels fulfilled.

He has traveled farther in the last forty-eight hours than he has his entire life.

Chris asks the cab driver some questions, in a forthright manner that he has never possessed; he has always felt awkward in new situations, around people he doesn't know. An introvert to the core, he has always been quiet and not the type to ask questions, only giving answers when asked, generally in monosyllable, one-word responses.

But this travel, this distance from home, this need for some self-reliance has changed his nature, so he tries to start a conversation with the cab driver.

"How's the weather been? I don't see any snow." Chris assumed it would be very cold, judging by how far up the curve of the globe Scotland lay.

"Nay, no snow, not much snow, really."

Chris nods, not understanding the words, but understanding that snow is a rarity.

"So, you like soccer?"

"Aye, but we call it football."

Chris gives up. The cab driver tries to talk to Chris, but he can't understand. He just laughs when the cab driver laughs and says, "Hmm" when the cab driver glances at him through the rearview mirror.

Chris looks out the window, studying the oncoming traffic, full of many small cars driving on the opposite side of the road, rolling past gas stations with names unfamiliar to him, road signs of a different shape and colored blue instead of the green he is used to seeing in Michigan and the rest of America, and the hills with sheep standing idly about, almost to the side of the road.

They have been driving just over half an hour when the cab leaves the A92 via an exit ramp and heads west. The cab turns down a paved, unmarked road flanked by tall trees. There is a low brick wall on either side and the road goes down a long incline. Despite the leaflessness of the trees, the growth is so thick that the sky becomes nearly invisible.

After about a mile, the trees thin and the base becomes visible, first the barbed wire fence ringing the perimeter and then the drab brown and dirty green buildings, and then the quarterdeck at the entrance of the base.

The cab pulls up and Chris is disappointed. The base is a blemish on a beautiful landscape, the dreary cluster of buildings, the metal structures used as antennas, the warning signs along the fence.

The cab driver tells Chris the fare and he pulls a wad of pound notes from his front pocket. His wallet is useless in this country; the bills are too large, a third more the size of American currency.

He is not sure what he owes, and the cab driver pulls money from the wad. Chris gives him an extra five-pound note for a tip and the driver says, "Ta" and drives away, the little Lada speeding back to Aberdeen. Chris is once again alone but back in the fold of his Navy family, the only thing he has in the world to fall back on.

After the time and distance of his travel, Chris's uniform is wrinkled and askew, and his white hat is dirty from his clutching it on the plane or whenever he has been indoors. He is also due for a haircut, the tops of his ears just barely covered in blond, wispy hair.

He enters the quarterdeck and the officer on duty is startled and confused by his appearance.

It is Christmas day. No one checks in on Christmas day.

"I'm early," Chris explains.

The officer, a young ensign fresh from the academy and still enthusiastic about his naval career, looks with disdain at Chris, at his dirty white hat, his overgrown hair, and his rumpled uniform. He grabs the orders from Chris's hand, a piece of computer generated paper by now quite wrinkled, and smoothes it out on the counter of the quarterdeck. He looks at Chris. "You're several days early. Didn't you want to be with your family for Christmas?" the ensign asks, longing to be home with his.

Chris shakes his head and stares at his shoes, embarrassed.

"All right," the ensign says, not really wanting to hear Chris explain himself.

"The enlisted barracks are over there." He points out the window across a small field with long-dormant grass and indicates a two-story, brown stucco building consisting of a middle and two wings, shaped in a 'U' with 90-degree angles. "Go in the middle door and you'll find the lounge, and off to the right will be the barracks office. There will be a civilian on duty who will put you in a room. The base opens back up tomorrow. Be here at 0730 sharp to start checking in." He stamps Chris's orders, signs them, and says, "Welcome to RAF Lutherkirk" without looking at Chris.

Chris mumbles, "Thank you, sir." He is somewhat uncomfortable and intimidated by someone with so much authority at an age not much greater than his own.

He saunters across the field, oblivious and too tired to read the prominently displayed "DO NOT WALK ON THE GRASS" signs. He stares around the base and his head is constantly moving left to right and back as he scans the buildings along the narrow asphalt streets. The base is empty and he can't see a single car driving along its streets. No one is walking along the sidewalks, and it is eerily quiet. Chris can hear his breath in quick spurts as he lugs his seabag across the field and into the barracks.

He opens the door into the barracks and finds the lounge inside to be anything but quiet. Many young sailors in civilian dress, mostly young men and a handful of young women, are sitting across several pieces of worn furniture. Chris can hear a television blaring in the corner, but no one is watching it, as most are engaged in easy conversation. There is just an instance of silence as Chris walks in. Heads turn in his direction and then the activities resume.

Chris finds the office. A portly Scottish gentleman wearing polyester pants, a shirt and a tie underneath a v-necked sweater is on duty. He is sitting at a gray steel desk and reading a paperback novel. He stares at Chris and numbly pulls bed linen from a closet and hands Chris a key, recording his name and room number in a green logbook.

"Go up the stairs and make a right. Your room will be halfway down."

Chris only understands "up the stairs." He shuffles off, his linen rolled under one arm, his seabag hoisted over the shoulder of the other arm. He walks up the stairs that go outside and walks along a balcony until he finds his room.

He expects his room to be orderly, as the barracks were in boot camp and in Pensacola: racks always made, the floor free of clutter, all personal belongings stowed in a locker when not in use. He opens the door and turns on the light and sees two beds, one bare and the other unmade, the sheets and blanket twisted in a haphazard way. The floor is carpeted with low, hard institutional carpet and there is a bathroom off to the side.

The room is an utter mess. Chris sees magazines and cassette tapes and food wrappers and drink containers and dirty clothes across the floor and on top of a desk that is pushed into a corner.

Chris is scared; the sight of the room makes him uncomfortable. What sort of person is his new roommate? He worries if the two of them will get along, if the other roommate is a bully. Chris has never been confrontational. He has never been one to speak up for himself if he is being slighted. He senses by the state of the room that the other occupant is inconsiderate.

Chris unpacks and stores everything in the wall locker provided, locking it with a padlock he brought with him from Pensacola, keeping the key around his neck on the chain securing his dog tags. He makes his rack and then takes a shower and pulls on his Navy sweatpants and sweatshirt. It is time for dinner, so he walks to the galley, a building a few yards from the barracks that he saw when he walked from the quarterdeck.

The crowd from the lounge transferred to the galley, as did other people in uniform going to and from duty at the communications buildings. The galley shows no signs of being a military facility; it looks more like a cafeteria that one would find in a hospital, several tables covered with red tablecloths and padded chairs without armrests.

Chris sits by himself as far away from others as possible and eats his meal. He assumes it is something special for Christmas: dry sliced turkey, dressing, and mashed potatoes with gravy. The food is as good as any that Chris has had since his Grandma was alive. He goes back for seconds and drinks several glasses of milk to wash it down.

He studies the faces in the galley, the youthful chatty faces, faces familiar with one another, with the routine of the base, of being in another country. They seem like veterans to Chris. He looks at the girls, the girls in their sweaters and jeans or their dungaree uniform, the working uniform of the Navy consisting of a light blue denim shirt with dark blue bell-bottom denim pants. He hopes to find one that appears to be solitary, perhaps a misfit like himself, a future girlfriend maybe. But he sees no one; the girls are all comfortable, surrounded by friends male and female. Chris leaves the galley with nowhere else to go but to his cluttered room.

He is afraid his roommate may be there upon his return, but he isn't. The sky is now dark and Chris is tired, so he lies in his rack. He tries to sleep but can't; he is waiting for the door to open, waiting for the dreaded roommate to appear. Still, despite his anxiety, he is too fatigued for insomnia, and he drifts off to sleep.

He dreams about his mother, the kind of dream that occurs only in the deepest of sleep. In this dream, she is old, heavyset and crying and destitute. She is sitting on a bed in a nearly empty room with gray walls and a gray tile floor with fluorescent lights coming from a tiled ceiling, like in a hospital or nursing home. She is apologizing to him, for wronging him for so many years. He can't see himself in the dream, but he feels powerful, maybe wealthy, as if a word of forgiveness from him will alleviate her sadness. He is ready to forgive her; despite everything, he loves his mother. He is about to speak but the dream drifts away when the door to his room opens and the lights turn on.

"Shit, I've got a fuckin' roommate."

Chris warily opens one eye just a slit to keep out the light and to maintain the appearance of sleep. He sees a tall overweight young man with blondish hair cut the way the Marines cut their hair (almost bald on the sides, standing straight up on top), freckles, a Nebraska sweatshirt underneath a denim jacket, blue jeans and dirty white leather hightop sneakers. The smell of alcohol is obvious, the odor leaving his pores and his mouth and consuming the whole room. Chris instantly thinks of his brother. It has been a long time since he has thought about his brother, but he doesn't recall him affectionately.

"At least it ain't no fuckin' nigger," the overgrown drunk says under his breath as he turns off the light and jumps onto his very cluttered bed. He leaves his clothes on but kicks off his shoes after he lies down.

He is soon snoring and Chris lies awake, staring at the ceiling, illuminated by the lamppost in the courtyard of the barracks. The joy he felt upon coming to Scotland is now reduced by the prospect of having to share a room with someone so crude.

Chris hopes his roommate's tour of duty is nearly complete. Eventually, he falls back to sleep.

Sitting in his office inside the chapel the morning of the day after Christmas, Father Crowley is hung over from joy. He has no problem killing those of another race, and feels no qualms about dragging others that are younger and less intelligent than he is into his private little army. He dreams the daydream of those who want power based on dogma. He imagines himself addressing a large room with a bevy of devotees becoming tearful upon receiving his words of a white utopia, of the evil and inadequacy of the lesser races. In this daydream, there are no girls or anyone past their twenties, just a homogenous bunch of handsome and athletic young men wearing uniforms of light green pants and light green shirts, a far cry from the imperfect appearance of his two current compatriots. He is frightened of this; it means something, but he doesn't know what. He suspects his longtime fear of some sort of latent homosexuality, which is common in his profession. Rampant homosexuality in the priesthood was common knowledge while he was at the seminary, but it was never discussed.

He has never been attracted to women. When other boys in school were chasing girls on playgrounds, he would sit on a swing and pray and search the sky for angels and saints.

He shakes the thought of homosexuality and contemplates a next potential target, a next action. He stares at the empty walls, walls that the previous Catholic chaplains always decorated with religious art or seminary and undergraduate diplomas. He stares at his bookcase, filled with books of catechism that he has long ignored. He displays them for the mere appearance and for the classes he must teach to the youth of the base, the children of the senior enlisted and officers who are old enough to prepare for first communion. A weekly task that he dreads.

He knows he can't strike on base; he wants any police authority to assume his activities are that of a group of Scots. But he wants to target Americans. It is America that needs the most work. It is America that is the most corrupted.

His mind wanders until about mid-morning, when a young sailor stands at the door to his office. The sailor is be-spectacled with wispy blond hair, soft in the mid-section. He has a once-poor complexion that is starting to recover.

The young sailor is clutching his service record, and it is obvious to Crowley that he must be checking in to the base, going from department to department.

The young man is not handsome or striking, and he appears to be entirely un-athletic, a far cry from the mold of Crowley's daydream, but something in his countenance causes the priest to stir. He searches the air above the young man's head, looking for the white lights that he believes are the angels from Valhalla. In his mind's eye, he sees the slightest twinkling to the right of the young sailor's head.

Crowley straightens up in his chair and produces his best insincere smile.

Chris rises early the day after Christmas and the cloudy sky is still as dark as midnight. He can hear his roommate snoring and smell his sweat, the alcohol from the night before turning stale and pungent before leaving his pores, the pungent odor saturating their room. Chris walks gingerly in the dark, taking care to silence his footfalls. He showers and dresses as quickly as possible.

As Chris is putting on his shoes, his roommate's alarm clock goes off and Chris hears a groan full of phlegm from the bed on the other side of the room. The roommate sits up, and through the dark, Chris can see the whiteness of his vast stomach hanging over his pants and underneath his shirt, which has crept up past his belly button.

His roommate's face turns serious, as if he's recalling something grave. The eyes of that round face see Chris sitting on the opposite bed and stare at him first in fright and then in a sort of bemused surprise.

"This is your room, too?" the heavy young man asks Chris.

Chris nods. "Yep."

"Aw, shit. Did you get here yesterday?" It's clear to Chris that his roommate does not remember seeing him late the night before when he came stumbling into the room.

"Yep."

"Shit." The heavyset young man grabs his head as if it's causing him much discomfort. "I kinda liked not having a roommate."

Chris nods and goes to his locker to grab his pea coat, as he sees frost on the window against the black morning sky.

"My name's Chris. Chris Fairbanks." Chris politely extends his hand, which is ignored.

"Hinckley. Brad," the other replies, head still in his hands.

"You like it here?" Chris asks.

"Nope." Hinckley rises from the bed and puts on his dungaree uniform and working jacket without taking a shower. He puts on a baseball cap instead of the white Dixie cup that Chris is wearing with his dress blue uniform.

Chris walks out without saying anything else. He steps out into the damp morning that is still quite dark and will remain so for several more hours in this land that is so much farther north than Michigan.

In the galley, Chris is surprised to be able to have an omelet made to order. He has it made with ham and cheese, and he gets French toast on the side. He sits down at the empty end of a long table that is crowded on the other end. Moments like this make him feel especially lonely, and he hurriedly finishes his large breakfast. He feels he is being stared at, as if only the odd and the deviant eat alone.

He arrives at the quarterdeck a few minutes early, re-trieves the cigarettes from his sock and smokes. Through the fence of the base, he sees the lights of a farmhouse and the silhouettes of the rolling hills that seem to continue past the horizon. Chris knows he is fortunate to be in a beautiful corner of the world. He could be on a ship out of Norfolk and see only Navy things and a metropolitan landscape no different from what he has known all his life.

As 0730 approaches, Chris enters the quarterdeck build-ing. The base master-at-arms, the head of security, is in charge, and his office is inside this building. The master-at-arms is a chief petty officer; Wilson is his name. Chief Wil-son is a career Navy man and his tour in Lutherkirk is his twilight tour, a nice and easy last tour of duty before he heads off to retirement, where he hopes to be a small-town police officer in his native western Pennsylvania. He spent much of his career at sea. The routine of being aboard a ship is much more rigorous, longer hours and weeks of seeing only the steel of the ship, the blue of the dungaree uniforms, and miles of endless ocean without another ship or sign of civilization in sight.

He has just over a year left of his three-year tour in Lu-therkirk.

He is a tall and large man, muscular, his black hair gray-ing at the temples and through his mustache. He squints at

Chris and studies the shabbiness of his haircut, his scuffed shoes, his wrinkled uniform, and his lint-covered pea coat.

He hands Chris an itinerary of departments to check in to in the proper order. Tomorrow, Chris will report to his department in the smaller of the three communications sites and start to work.

"Hurry up and finish," Chief Wilson says, indicating Chris's itinerary, "and then get a god-damned haircut and square yourself away. If I see you looking like that tomorrow, I'll write you up and you'll go in front of the captain."

Chris nods. Embarrassed, he hurriedly walks out of the building and scurries across the base to medical, dental, admin, the library, public works, the commanding officers' office, the commissary, and the exchange. There are forms for him to fill out and questions for him to answer every step of the way. A spot on almost every form makes him pause:

State your home of record.

The home of record, the residence where you came from, where one or both parents live.

Chris has no home of record. On one form he writes "here" and on the rest he simply writes BEQ Room 11, RAF Lutherkirk, Lutherkirk, UK.

Some who read the forms at the various departments think Chris is being flippant. They raise their eyebrows and demand an explanation. He isn't being flippant; he's being honest. Home is where he is and wherever the Navy and the choices of his life will take him.

He realizes his father's address is just a phone call or letter away, but he has felt so detached from his father for so many years, his father no more than a piece of furniture in the basement, sitting or lying on the couch in a v-necked white T-shirt wrapped in a tattered blanket watching the television at merely an arm's length away for the ease of adjusting the rabbit-ear antennas, and to change the channel without losing his perch on the sagging couch.

Chris's last destination is the chapel, a visit he is not relishing.

Chris is unfamiliar with the insides of the buildings of the holy, and he is uncomfortable upon entering. Inside, the chapel is as quiet as a tomb. Chris walks around the front hallway and glances into the chapel itself. He looks at the small stage with a small altar and enough pews to accommodate maybe seventy-five people.

He looks at the cross on the front of the podium on the stage that he doesn't know is called an altar. He assumes the building is empty in its silence. He is about to leave when he sees an open door into an office by the main entrance. He spies a man in a khaki uniform sitting at a desk. His hands are folded and he is staring at the ceiling. Chris gently taps his knuckles on the open door. At first, the man looks irritated, but then his face lights up when he sees Chris. Chris notes the cross pinned on one collar and lieutenant's bars on the other.

"Come in, come in," the man says, standing up. He is a tall man, pear-shaped and red-faced with reddish hair showing signs of gray. Chris notes that he is a bit old to be a lieutenant.

"Sorry to bother you, sir," Chris says while facing the floor, too introverted to look directly at someone he has apparently irritated. "I'm just checking in." He hands the chaplain his check-in sheet, hoping for a simple signature and not the rehearsed and choreographed welcome he got from some of the other departments.

"No bother, no bother at all. I'm Chaplain Crowley, or Father Crowley, if you share my faith." He offers Chris a firm handshake that Chris returns not nearly as vigorously.

"Sit down, sit down." The chaplain takes the check-in sheet from Chris and places it on his desk, which is barren save a telephone and an empty Rolodex.

Chris sits upon a simple armless chair alongside the chaplain's desk. He has no idea what a chaplain could possibly want to talk about or what he could say to a chaplain.

"So, welcome to Scotland," the chaplain says, swinging his patent leather shoes up on the top of the desk. The posture is disarming, and Chris relaxes in his chair.

The chaplain notes the two lonely stripes on Chris's sleeves and knows he is recently enlisted. "And welcome to the Navy. Now you're in the fleet, as they say." True enough, any duty station not attached to a training command was considered "in the fleet," at sea or on shore.

"Thanks." Chris looks around the sparse office. The walls are empty and the only companion to the desk and two chairs is a small, waist-high bookcase filled with apparently undisturbed books of uniform height and thickness.

"I'm new to the Navy, myself," the chaplain explains. "This is my first duty station, and I'm as tender-footed as you are to the ways of the military."

Chris nods, feeling more comfortable. No one this morning has been as friendly, as personable, as Chaplain Crowley.

"So, what religion is yours?" Crowley asks, the topic turning in the direction Chris dreads.

"I don't have one," Chris says.

"You don't have one, or you don't practice? Surely, you were baptized."

Unsure, Chris nods his head. "I think I was baptized."

"In which church?"

"I think Catholic."

"Aha!" The chaplain pounds his fist on top of the desk and returns his feet to the floor. "Then you're in my club." Crowley beams. "But no matter, no matter, the Kingdom of God is wide open before you, and there are many paths you can choose, Catholic or otherwise. I'm not out to recruit you for Sunday Mass. I see myself here to make sure you're okay on the inside. Where are you from?"

"Just outside of Detroit."

"Ah," says Crowley, unable to expand upon the topic of Michigan. "Well, my son, my door is always open, and if you need someone to talk to about anything—no subject is too remote for me—I can bullshit about anything as well as anybody, so please return. In fact, I even conduct very informal Bible studies at my own home, in case you're interested. Just let me know ahead of time." The priest stands and extends a hand and bids Chris farewell.

Chris decides he may take him up on the invitation as he steps back into the damp Scottish air. The sky is gray and full of clouds thick and low, causing the street lamps of the base to turn on, even though the day is still quite young.

Chris didn't feel so alone in the presence of the priest; he felt warm inside. Maybe church is a place for him to go, as he has no place else to go except his messy room inside the sterile barracks in a country he does not yet know.

He finds the base barbershop and sets about restoring his military appearance.

December 26, 1985

Dear Wife,

I so badly want to fall in love and I don't know if you feel the same way at this point in your life. I've been in Scotland just a day now and I'm looking for you but I don't think you're on this base, I haven't seen a face yet that I'm attracted to or could feel comfortable with. It seems everyone here knows a certain group of people and that's it, if you're not in a group then you're on your own, at least that's what I see from eating in the galley and wandering around the barracks. I never had a lot of friends in school but I always had a few and in boot camp I was never alone and in 'A' school there were guys I went to boot camp with and people I talked to in class and it just seemed different. Here I feel like a leper. I start my job tomorrow and I don't know what that will be like but hopefully I will meet people there.

Do you believe in God? I did when I was real small until I had a teacher in junior high who said there used to be gods for everything. People used to worship sun gods and sacrifice animals and children just to make sure the sun continued to rise, he said there were lots of gods like that and eventually as science grew people learned how the sun rose and of course that meant the end of the sun gods. I saw god the same way, just this thing people used to explain the world, but now I don't know. I think there is something else there and I'm missing it. No one can explain what can happen when you die or why you're born and why there is evil in this world. There must be a god and I think I may only feel this way because I feel so alone. Until we meet.

Chris

It is Friday evening and the new year is beckoning. Friday has become the de facto evening for Rodgers and Hinckley to go to Father Crowley's house, as no one has to rise early the next morning. There is much drinking and dreaming and discussing on this particular night.

Rodgers and Hinckley summon a taxi, one of a small queue that forms outside the base every Friday and Saturday night, waiting to take the sailors to the nightclubs in Aberdeen or Dundee, or to the pubs in Brechin or Montrose.

Crowley is anxious. He wants to strike again, claim another trophy for the advance of the white race. He wants the country and the world to know that a decent white man isn't going to take it anymore, this proliferation of the lesser peoples.

"Now, South Africa," he blurts out while sipping his favorite Boer cabernet after Hinckley and Rodgers arrive. They stare at the fire and drink one of many tins of lager. "South Africa is almost the perfect country. The whites know they're superior. They don't give into that gushy liberalism that has destroyed the West—you know, all men are created equal and all that crap. I don't care what the Declaration of Independence says, Jefferson never meant Negroes; he meant all *white* men are created equal. He owned slaves himself, for Christ's sake."

Hinckley has a vague notion of what the priest is talking about. Rodgers doesn't have a clue; he just hopes he doesn't have to shoot anybody else.

"In South Africa," Crowley says while dreamily staring at his glass of wine, his pale blue eyes almost teary and wistful, "they don't let blacks vote or hold office or even give them good jobs. They keep them in their place because they know they are incapable of taking care of themselves, much less a business or a government. We don't see it that way in the

United States. The politicians and the churches whine about equal rights while the blacks murder each other, while the Mexicans stab each other and all our cities have gone to hell and all the while, more and more white kids listen to black music and every other show on television is about black people. But not in South Africa. In South Africa a white kid goes to school with other white kids and he is safe, and he lives in a neighborhood with other white kids and he is safe, and the blacks live with the blacks and go to school with the blacks, and though they don't know it, they are happier. And if the blacks try to organize—they outnumber the white people there almost fifteen to one—the government goes in and shoots them or arrests them. They make it very clear who is in charge." He drains his glass and refills it from a bottle on the coffee table. He closes his eyes and inhales the aroma of the cork before returning it to the top of the bottle.

"So," he continues, "if I can't make progress and help stimulate some change, we could always find our place in the world in South Africa, where the weather is finer than California and our race is raised to its proper status. "

Hinckley thinks that sounds fine but wonders if he can watch football there. Rodgers helps himself to another beer.

"But I think the gods have placed us here for a reason," Crowley continues, "and I think we should get to work right away. Nothing so random this time. My passion got the best of me on Christmas. Luckily, no mistakes were made, but our work was sloppy and we could have gotten caught."

Almost true. The Tayside Police were puzzled about the murder. Dundee had maybe one such crime every few years, and they were usually acts of passion, not random violence. At first, they thought maybe it was a gang murder, some sort of squabbling amongst the Pakistanis, but they could find no evidence supporting that theory. The victim was a man in his early thirties who was walking home from his dishwashing job in a restaurant in one of the nicer hotels in Dundee. He had just saved up enough money to send for his wife and four children to join him from Pakistan, and they were due to arrive in mid-January. There was one eyewitness account from an apartment dweller above the restaurant where Crowley had parked. They had seen the Allegro parked there earlier, but after the gunshots, the car was gone. Regretfully, no tag number was recorded, and the windows of the car had fogged up and no one was seen inside.

"We have to be very precise, and though it must be tempting, we can never—and I do mean never—strike on base, unless we have to make some sort of point. To show that the blacks and other minorities aren't safe anywhere."

"Well, hell," says Hinckley, "the niggers on base go out every weekend, if they're off. I think they go dancing in Dundee. We could probably find one there, someone from the base."

"Brilliant," says Crowley, who rises from his chair and places his hand on Rodgers's shoulder. "Our little sniper here can pick one off like a clay pigeon. We just have to find a place for him to shoot from."

"Come on, now," Rodgers protests. "I still don't feel good about killin' anybody; let one of y'all do it this time. I don't mind scarin' somebody or beatin' somebody up, but I don't know about killin'. I really just want to go home. I can't stand the Navy and I hate this god-damned country."

"Listen," says Crowley and he prepares to talk to Rodgers as he would talk to a small child, "you have been given a talent, and it would a shame for you to waste it. Nothing has been gained by just scaring people. The Klan has been doing that for years, and now the blacks run the south. Pretty soon, they'll run Missouri, too. You don't want that. Your family doesn't want that."

Rodgers agrees.

"And if for some reason things get too hairy for us, I can use my authority as a chaplain to have you sent home. I can come up with some sort of family emergency, you know, like a death in the family. I can help you... You just have to help me."

Rodgers reluctantly agrees and feels a glimmer of hope at the possibility of his returning home. Nothing would make him happier. He would agree to almost anything that could get him home sooner.

"Now Mr. Hinckley, back to your idea." Crowley stands up and walks back and forth in front of the fireplace. "Do we find someone in particular, or do we just wait outside a nightclub and seize the perfect opportunity at the first shot we get?"

"Well, I think we should take the best shot we see at any nigger walking around Dundee."

"Excellent, excellent," Crowley replies. "Do you know where they go? Do you know which clubs?"

"Yeah, I hearda this one called Angel's. I think it used to be a church or somethin'. A lot of them go there—you know, pick up on them bloke girls."

"I hate bloke girls," Rodgers pipes in. "They all smoke and drink and wear ugly clothes and they're fat."

Hinckley and Father Crowley both ignore Rodgers.

"You two spend the night here, and tomorrow morning we'll drive to Dundee and scope out the situation, see where we can park. This time, I want to leave a note. We have to leave a note." Crowley sits down on the couch, too close for both Hinckley's and Rodgers's comfort. "Hinckley." Crowley pours more wine. The bottle is nearly empty, save half an inch covering the bottom. "You write the note again. Take time to be creative and make an impact. Let those of the lesser races know who we are."

Hinckley nods. "No problem."

Crowley retires upstairs and leaves the living room and several dusty blankets that came with the furnished house to the two young men. Hinckley and Rodgers drink and talk. Hinckley feels important; he has been trusted to write the note, to be the spokesman for their group. He rubs his hand over his hair and thinks about shaving it off, almost bald, the way the skinheads that he has heard so much about do. But he decides Father Crowley wouldn't like that; it would draw attention to him. Rodgers, nervous about firing another shot, complains to Hinckley.

"Don't ya think it would have been better if the South won the Civil War?" Hinckley reasons.

"Well, yeah."

"Look at it this way: you're finishing what the Confederates started. You're kinda like Robert E. Lee."

Rodgers swells at the comparison. His thumbnail knowledge of history is mostly of the Civil War. He is at peace with the decision to be the shooter, and the possibility of returning home early is enticing. He drifts off to uncomfortable, drunk sleep in the priest's sagging armchair and he dreams of walking through his father's fields hunting for geese in the fall, his black Labrador retriever that died in his early adolescent years wagging his tail at his side.

Friday, a few days after Christmas, Chris is assigned to the smallest division in his department and is put on a shift schedule. The shifts are called watches, as they are known at sea, and they are divided up among four sections. Two twelve-hour day watches, then 48 hours off, two twelve-hour midnight watches and then 72 hours off. Chris goes to his site in the morning, this time in his dungaree uniform that he took the time to iron properly the night before.

The previous afternoon left him with nothing to do and no place to go. He had his hair cut so short and close that a cowlick stands up on the back of his head. He constantly licks his fingers to unsuccessfully flatten his hair.

Chris arrives at his department early in the morning to check in. He meets the division chief, Lassiter, a short and heavyset man with a double chin and glasses. He sits in the chief's small office, a room barely big enough for a desk and two chairs.

Chris sees the sum of the chief's career spread across the walls. There are letters of commendation, certificates of advancement, a signed letter from the President for bravery in Vietnam and many plaques indicating completed courses of training.

Chris wonders if he will ever achieve such things. He wonders if he'll ever go to war.

The chief tells Chris about the division. They relay messages from the Atlantic Fleet headquarters to ships and submarines in the North Atlantic and those on exercises going into the Barents Sea, just by Russia, tempting the Soviet border. The job is highly classified but routine, mainly monitoring signals and making sure they're intact and the lines of communication stay open. He will be trained on all functions of the equipment and the proper sorting of printed messages. He is permitted to read but to never reveal the contents of the messages, as the information is classified.

Chris has been granted a top secret clearance, the Navy having conducted an investigation on his very unremarkable background, interviewing teachers who barely remembered him and neighbors who seldom saw him or paid him much attention. He was a shoo-in for a clearance.

He is given a badge with his laminated photograph attached to it, permitting him access to the building, past the guardsman, who is British and a member of the Ministry of Defence Police, or MoDP.

The British own the buildings and protect and maintain them, but it seems to Chris that the Americans are more than in charge.

Chris listens to the chief. The chief tells him what is expected of him, now that he is in the fleet and not in school. He is responsible for himself now, getting to work on time and sober. If he comes in hung-over, he will be written up. The chief expects him to advance his rank in a timely manner while he is here.

And, Chief Lassiter adds, he should get off base and try not to become a barracks rat, someone who never leaves the base and spends all his free time in the barracks lounge drinking beer from a soda machine and playing pool or watching Armed Forces Television.

Chris will start that night. Chief Lassiter tells him to hit the rack and come back at 1730 to start the shift that begins at 1800 and ends at 0600.

"And forget everything you learned in Pensacola," the chief says. "It won't mean shit here. It doesn't mean shit out in the fleet. The equipment is different and the mission is different. The mission is always different, depending on the game they're playing."

"'They'?"

"The commie-pinko-faggot hippies." He pauses, waiting for Chris to laugh, but Chris doesn't. "The Russians, who do you think? I'll see you tomorrow morning and I'll talk to you and your supervisor and see how you did. Go hit the rack." The chief looks down at his desk and says no more. Chris walks away.

This gives Chris just six hours to get some sleep after being awake less than that. He had slept well the previous night, as his roommate was gone until the wee hours of the night and apparently returned sober as he entered the room and put himself to bed noiselessly.

To kill time, Chris goes to the base bookstore, which is a little Quonset-style hut full of paperback novels and magazines from the States and several days-old copies of *USA Today* and the European edition of the *Stars and Stripes* newspaper.

Chris buys a novel, a book about World War II, and a copy of the *Stars and Stripes*. He eats a hurried lunch in the galley and returns to his room; he knows his roommate is at work and the room will be vacant.

He strips himself down and climbs into his bed, where he smokes and reads the newspaper. It is almost propaganda and is mostly about army bases in Germany, where most of the newspaper's readership is stationed. There is a smattering of current events: the latest diabolical activities of Muammar Qadaffi in Libya, backing terrorists who hijacked a plane over Italy and killing an American serviceman and supporting an airport attack in Vienna. The possibility of the Americans retaliating is strong and Chris swells with pride at the harsh words of President Reagan, telling the nation that the United States will be bullied by no one and that the U.S. has the finest servicemen and women in the world. Chris is proud to be a part of it.

The paper also contains a smattering of sports, stories about the upcoming football playoffs and the ongoing basketball season. Chris couldn't care less, so he puts the paper under his bed and tries to read his book about American prisoners of war in Germany during World War II who manage to escape and sabotage the Nazi plant where atomic bombs are nearly being completed.

Libya, Russia, and earlier, Germany... Chris wonders why it's always the Americans fighting evil.

He reads several chapters of the book and grows restless; his mind and body are too awake to sit peaceably in bed, so he smokes and thinks about his upcoming job and the messages he will read.

His thoughts then turn to his family, who never completely escape his mind. He wonders about his mother and contemplates trying to find her address from a relative and sending her a letter. He decides against it as he recalls those evenings in boot camp that seem so long ago, memories of letters never received and the anguish it caused.

He hates his mother, but deep down, he needs her. He subconsciously desires to be loved. Since he's been on his own, he feels mature and independent, but his heart feels desolate and his mind can't define it, can't find words to describe this emptiness. He stares at the ceiling and then retrieves his Walkman from the bottom of his locker. Because he is feeling melancholy, he foregoes his current favorite cassette by a band called U2 and decides to listen to the radio instead. He flips the switch to FM and finds nothing and then switches it to AM and he finds a cornucopia of talk and sounds and music that he hasn't heard. He lingers on each station for a while and finds it fascinating and eventually identifies the local station, Radio Tayside. He listens to a news program about local politics and sports. He finds himself feeling a bit more of a part of this refined but somewhat rugged nation of Scotland that lies on the other side of the barbed-wire fence surrounding the base.

He vows to find himself in this country; he promises himself that much. He also guarantees that he will fall in love. He imagines a Scottish girl somewhere over that fence who is pretty and kind and smart and who will allow him to make love to her. He isn't shallow, but he is a young man and his virginity is killing him. His nineteenth birthday is in mid-February, and he fears he will be (if he isn't already) the oldest virgin in the entire Navy.

The last hours of the afternoon quickly pass. He showers and dresses and goes to the galley for a dinner of ham and mashed potatoes. He foregoes the milk and drinks cola for the caffeine, as he knows he will be tired.

He then walks nearly a mile underneath a rapidly darkening sky across the ancient and potholed concrete runway that was used during World War II to the far side of the base where the communications buildings stand. His stomach suddenly becomes upset as his nerves get the best of him. He trembles and sighs as he presents his badge to the Scottish sentry who guards the building that only a cleared American can enter.

They rise before the sun on this damp Saturday morning as mist falls upon the hard ground outside Crowley's house, saturating the un-raked leaves, which are starting to crumble and decay.

Into the Allegro they go without showering. Rodgers smokes a cigarette to combat his hangover, but the bumpy ride in the back seat of such a small car curving along the North Sea coast is more than he can bear. He gets sick before he can roll the window down.

They breakfast in Arbroath, halfway between Dundee and Lutherkirk. They pull into a little restaurant along the highway aimed at lorry drivers. They park clumsily and leave the window open to allow the vomit and body smells to escape the car.

The breakfast is simple, greasy and bland: fried eggs, links of sausage, a slice of tomato, and black pudding (only Crowley knows what black pudding really is, dried blood and oats). Crowley takes tea with milk and sugar the way the British do; the other two ask for cola. They eat in hung-over silence and stare out the window facing the east, watching the invisible sun lighten the cloud laden sky over the deep and black and cold North Sea.

As the night turns to dawn and the dawn turns to day, they hop into the car and proceed to Dundee and to the favorite nightclub of the sailors of Lutherkirk. They are there on a scouting mission, Crowley tells them.

The landscape lends itself to their task. Across the street from the club is an ancient and small urban cemetery. The haphazard tombstones are leaning and faded with age, and some are being lifted from the ground by the roots of the large oak trees covering the entire ground.

They park the car and enter the cemetery and look across the street. There are no obstructions between the graveyard and the main door, and no streetlights to illuminate the cemetery grounds.

Crowley walks through the cemetery and reads what tombstones he can: McGregor and MacLeish, Wallace and Scott, and he makes out the faded years in the crumbling white markers, born in 1792 and dead in 1852 or '53. Crowley feels this resting ground of white souls is holy, a blessing of the task they have given themselves.

Beyond the cemetery is an alley and beyond that is West Bell Street, with many passages through the buildings leading to the sidewalk and the presumed getaway car.

Crowley maps it all in his mind. The plan is obvious to the other two. Rodgers crouches behind the largest tombstone and peers over the top while eyeballing the club. Hinckley thrusts his hands into his Navy pea coat, his only warm coat, and searches the sky and the street and the alley beyond. Crowley taps an oak tree and decides that is where the note will be tacked, announcing to the world who committed this act. Let the cleansing begin. A warm feeling erupts from the base of his stomach and spreads to his chest.

They attempt several practice runs; Crowley parks in the street behind the cemetery, Hinckley stands in the alley, a stage whisper from where Rodgers takes his post. From the alley, Hinckley can see the graveyard and the nightclub and the street on the other side, in case Rodgers can be seen. Rodgers makes a pistol of his index finger and thumb, fires and turns and walks slowly and follows Hinckley across the alley, through a passageway between a small pub and a dress shop, and they calmly climb into the waiting Allegro.

It is lunchtime. They are satisfied with their progress, and they eat lunch in the same small pub that flanks the passageway. They order fish and chips laden with vinegar and salt and drink a pint or two of lager. It is just 11:30, and the pub is nearly empty. They sit at the bar a few stools over from a bent-over and solitary older man. The man hears their accents as they order their food and drinks and accuses them of being American. Crowley puts on his best smile and says, "Ah yes... we're guilty, but we're really the same, you and I, from the same line."

Crowley continues to engage himself in conversation with the nearly toothless man. Crowley is expounding on his not-too-offensive theory that the planet would still be in the

Dark Ages if it weren't for the Industrial Revolution and the innovation of the Western Europeans. The man merely agrees and thoughtlessly says, "Aye." Crowley buys him a drink and leaves him his phone number, in case he ever wants to talk about the history of man.

The trio leaves. The stage is set. They make plans as they drive back to Lutherkirk and Crowley's stone cottage.

Rodgers cleans the gun and loads it. Hinckley considers the note and then starts to write, his tongue sticking out of the corner of his mouth as he concentrates.

Crowley merely sits in his tired armchair with his eyes closed and his head tilted back, his fingers tapping the armrest in time with the Wagner recording on his turntable.

When he senses the two young men are done with their assigned tasks, he opens his eyes and levels his gaze. Hinckley hands the priest his note, which the priest reads quickly. He smiles.

"Excellent, excellent. You possess a talent, Mr. Hinckley."

Hinckley's face turns red. No one has ever really complimented him on his efforts before. He stares down at the dirty shag carpet and thanks Crowley.

"So, Friday?" Crowley inquires of both sailors.

The young men nod in concurrence.

"Excellent, excellent. If either of you need to talk, I can be found in the chapel all day tomorrow and of course throughout the week. I think for today we shall separate, as I think Mass tomorrow will be especially difficult. My heart isn't in it at all, with what we're proposing to do next weekend. So I think I will retire early and send you two back to base." Instead of driving them back himself, he calls for a cab and hands Hinckley a five-pound note.

Crowley hugs both young men as they make their way down his crooked driveway to the main road to wait for the cab. "I love you both," he says, with a bit of melancholy that neither Rodgers nor Hinckley has seen in a grown man.

"That was weird," is all that is said between the two as they return to the base and back to the barracks and their late Saturday afternoon ritual of playing pool in the barracks lounge and then supper in the galley before heading off to the enlisted club, where there will be more playing of pool accompanied by loud music.

They won't talk about Crowley; they won't talk about their other lives. They will spend the evening in drunken ignorance of the responsibility of the shameful deed they have put in front of themselves.

Without admitting it to the other, each young sailor is feeling the pangs of regret, but they are fearful and in awe of Crowley. Someone of his rank and stature and age can't be all wrong.

Chris's job proves to be very different from what he trained for in Pensacola. He had to spend hours of frustration mastering Morse code, and it was all for naught. All codes and signals are deciphered here by monstrous computers standing monolithic in their own climate-controlled room.

Chris has only one co-worker, his supervisor, a female petty officer second class. She is thin and bespectacled; the long brown hair that she sweeps up while in uniform is revealing wisps of gray, and her long and narrow and sallow face seems tired, with crow's feet forming around her eyes. At first glance, one would guess her to be chronically unhappy, but Chris sees a kindness in her face. She smiles vaguely as she shakes his hand upon introduction. He notices that she could have been or could be pretty, in a different set of circumstances, out of her dungaree uniform.

"Freeman," she says. "Petty Officer Freeman, but on mids, you can call me Karen."

"Fairbanks, Seaman Apprentice Fairbanks," Chris replies.

"I know. I saw your orders a week ago. We didn't expect you so soon."

She proceeds to explain all the pieces of equipment in their small and cramped and poorly lit working area, which consists of two desks, a row of four teletype printers and four or five computer monitors with black backgrounds and green characters that Chris will spend many hours staring into, retyping messages that he rips off the printer. The workspace is flanked by two offices, one for Division Chief Lassiter and one for the division officer. A division as small as this requires only the lowest ranking officer; it is the same ensign who welcomed Chris to Lutherkirk.

After an hour or so of explanations and demonstrations of how their job is done while a few messages trickle in and are retyped, Chris gets the idea, sees how the work flows, and is amazed at the simplicity.

Freeman leaves Chris on his own. She picks up a book, and he stares at her in disbelief.

She understands the stare and explains: "It's a mid, and no one is around. The chief doesn't care as long as everything gets done. Some mids are busy, but if there are no exercises and the Russians are being quiet, then we just kind of sit here, so why not? You can do the same, as soon as you get the hang of what we do here. Days are different; the chief and Ensign Hughes are around. He's a little son-of-a-bitch, and we usually work non-stop, but mids... It's hard to stay awake sometimes."

Chris merely nods and continues to stare at the printers, waiting for messages to arrive. An hour goes by and then two, but all is quiet. He is desperately trying to stay awake. He drinks coffee after coffee from the older-style percolating coffee machine inside the chief's office.

The hours between midnight and 5 a.m. are brutal as Chris tries to stay awake and the printers remain silent. Karen continues to read and smoke cigarettes and drink coffee and Chris taps his fingers and thinks about home and how he would much rather be on a ship than chained to a desk with nothing to do in the middle of the night, stuck inside a dark room in the middle of a windowless building surrounded by antennas and satellite dishes. The work is not as intriguing or stimulating as he had hoped or imagined it would be.

Again, it is Friday. Snow flurries spend the day flying through the air in no particular direction and never seem to touch the ground, which is perpetually shiny and white from frost.

The end of the working day is preceded by an uneventful sunset. Father Crowley drives home after locking the chapel, just before Seamen Hinckley and Rodgers eat a hurried dinner in the galley and meet a cab outside the gate and proceed to Crowley's house.

The two young men have donned black garments underneath their pea coats: black jeans and black sweatshirts and their Navy-issue black watch hats. The cab driver regards them with suspicion as he drives them in silence across the back roads in between Lutherkirk and the A92, but forgets about them as soon as he drops them in front of Crowley's house. He decides their appearance has something to do with the general oddity of those from across the ocean.

They enter Crowley's house through the back. The small kitchen is the only room lit in the house. From outside, the two can hear a scratchy recording of Wagner, though they don't know the composer. The music is heavy and loud and bombastic and it reinforces the feeling that they are about to take part in a very grave ceremony.

Crowley is not dressed unusually at all. He has on typical Scottish middle-aged garb: gray trousers, a pale blue oxford shirt underneath a burgundy v-necked sweater. His tam is at the ready on the kitchen table next to his bottle of Boer wine along with several tins of beer for the boys. He enjoys the affluence that a naval officer's salary brings, far exceeding that of a parish priest.

"Welcome, welcome." Crowley embraces the two and kisses them each on the cheek, giving Rodgers the shivers and irritating Hinckley. "Something to eat?" He points to a pot on the stove containing what appears to be canned franks and beans. Rodgers refuses, but Hinckley grabs a bowl from a cluttered cupboard and a spoon from the dish rack alongside the faded porcelain sink.

"I think we should do this later rather than sooner," says Hinckley. "People are gonna be more drunk, you know, and move a bit slower."

"Quite right, quite right," agrees the priest, staring at a corked bottle of wine on top of the fridge. He decides to take it down and open it up.

Hinckley grabs a beer from the refrigerator. Rodgers is about to do the same, but Crowley stands in front of the refrigerator and wags his index finger in front of the thin man's face.

"No," he says. "We can't afford stray bullets. You have to be as sober as, well, a priest." He laughs heartily, so heartily that his double chin starts to shake.

Rodgers looks dejected, more hurt than angry. In an attempt to boost his morale and to make sure he stays a part of the team, Crowley becomes conciliatory.

"Look, after it's over, we can come back here and you can have all the beer you want. You can take a bath in it, for all I care, but for now, you of all people have to be clear headed and focused. Brad and I will just have one drink, okay?"

"Okay."

One side of *Das Rheingold* is complete and Crowley hurries into the living room to flip the record before the needle works itself to the center of the disc and travels across the paper label in the middle. He returns to the kitchen as the scratchy preamble of the needle working its way to the music concludes and the bursting and heavy music again fills the house and the air outside.

"No American composer could ever hope to compare," Crowley says, nursing his glass of wine. Hinckley's beer is long gone and he is tense and fidgety, as he wants another, needs another, the one beer not even lightening his mood in the least. But the priest said one, and he isn't about to challenge Crowley. He lights a cigarette and leans against the kitchen counter, trying to ignore his craving.

Rodgers is also smoking, sitting on the dirty kitchen floor, staring down between his knees, trying to figure a way out of this situation. He decides that after the shooting, he will ask the chaplain to send him home. He is elated at the thought of returning to Missouri. The memories come in waves: the sight, sound and smell of him driving his truck, listening to the radio, a girl—any girl—sitting next to him on the seat driving towards the sunset over the hilly roads on a late summer evening as the sun turns the sky orange after a good day of working in the fields.

Crowley talks about race, about history, about the smiling gods of the North, about the closeness of their Valhalla, about the future, but neither young man really listens. Hinckley is too wrapped up in his craving for another beer, and Rodgers is trapped in a daydream of Missouri, chain-smoking all the while.

A few hours pass. The clock strikes eight, and Crowley allows himself another glass of wine and Hinckley another beer. The priest offers Rodgers a beer, too, but Rodgers is indifferent. He refuses by pretending to be noble; he will wait until his task is complete.

Another half hour passes and out of restlessness, they decide to go. Hinckley hands the note he has composed to the priest, who reads it while smiling broadly. Rodgers checks the gun, making sure it's loaded. He puts the safety on before he tucks it into the front of his pants between the waistband and his undershirt.

They are silent as they drive to Dundee. None of them are drunk. They are not familiar with one another sober, only inebriated or suffering from a collective hangover.

After an eternity, they find themselves in Dundee. The city is not as empty as it was on that Saturday morning a week before; the sidewalks are crowded with couples lost in adoration and groups of young men and women banded together by age.

This does not deter them. They drive in front of their chosen club several times and circle the city center, discussing their plans, recalling the previous week's rehearsal.

They decide that Rodgers will hide behind the same headstone and wait, no matter the minutes or the hours that elapse. Hinckley will wait in the alley behind the cemetery and cover Rodgers's back. Father Crowley will park on the opposite street, in front of the same pub. They drive until the space becomes available, circling and circling the block until nearly an hour passes; the congested street shows no sign of lessening its density of cars or people. They decide that Crowley will circle the block and watch for the arrival of the young men in black, Hinckley on one corner and Rodgers on the other.

Crowley drops Rodgers off in front of the nightclub, which looks less like a church in the evening than it did in the daytime. The music from inside can be heard from the sidewalk and all the way into the heart of the cemetery. Rodgers enters the cemetery unnoticed and takes his post behind the tallest of the headstones, a faded white marker bearing the name Rammage, born in 1822, passed away in 1873.

Crowley drops Hinckley off at the end of the block. He stealthily walks down the narrow alley, where he assumes his position, turning his collar up to soften the cold wind, stuffing his gloveless hands into his pockets. There will be no smoking no matter how long he stands. There will be no evidence save the shell of the discharged bullet and the note, claiming responsibility and letting the people of Scotland know that they, this alliance of disparate souls, are fighting on their behalf.

On his way to the alley, Hinckley tacks the note inside an envelope to the trunk of a large and ancient oak tree. Its branches cover the entire cemetery, the evidence of its leaves still on the hard and frozen ground. He places the note at eye level, ensuring that someone will see it. It is addressed to the Tayside Police.

Crowley assumes his route of circumnavigating the block. He is not nervous at all; in fact, he is tapping his fingers to a tune, a silly children's tune that he recalls from his youth. He doesn't remember the words, just the melody, just the rhythm.

He smiles broadly underneath his tam, and he feels as giddy and excited as the morning preceding his first communion.

An hour passes slowly for Rodgers, who is watching the comings and goings from the club, people running up the steps, people staggering down. Not one black person so far, not even an American, as far as he can tell; the stature and the dress and the gait of most indicate that they are Scottish.

"Fucking blokes, get out of the way," he thinks to himself.

The time goes even slower for Hinckley; he has nothing to divert himself, nothing to really concentrate on. He stands in the shadows on the edge of the graveyard, looking down the alley, and occasionally studies the silhouette of Rodgers's thin and bent-over frame, his head appearing to cap the gravestone.

His thoughts turn to football and the news he read in the recent *Stars and Stripes* and the *USA Today*. Nebraska losing in the Fiesta Bowl to Michigan, 27 to 23. He pictures his grandfather in Omaha wheezing in his armchair, cursing at the television, and it is one of the few times he has ever been homesick.

Crowley drives, staring at the people, comfortable in his small car, the window slightly open with the night air refreshing his face, the coolness tempered by his automobile's cabin heater set on high. He enjoys the scenery, the collection of pale faces walking underneath the streetlights on wide sidewalks in front of very old buildings with detailed architecture, carvings set in stone in every facade, done in a way he would never see in Houston, and especially not in rural Minnesota.

Eventually, as the hour nears eleven and the night is starting to thin of pedestrians and cars, three young black men walk out of the club with what appear to be three Scottish girls. Lee recognizes the tallest of the three black American sailors. He is a petty officer third class, one of those communications types that he despises so much. He can't recall the name, but he remembers the payday of November 15th, this same petty officer called him stupid through the windows into the disbursing office because he handed him a check belonging to an officer on the base with the same last name. Rodgers has always felt especially awkward when chastised even in the slightest, and he felt that all the people in line waiting for their checks were laughing at him because of his mistake. He fumbled around for the rest of that morning, passing out checks without looking anyone in the eye.

So just as the sailor reaches the last step and stands alone on the sidewalk as the rest of his party trails behind, Lee fires what is supposed to be just one shot, but his recalled anger has him do it in four, firing the gun faster than the victim can react. The first shot strikes him in the shoulder, the second in the stomach, and the third and fourth in the face and in the forehead. The young man collapses on the sidewalk, the remains of his head splattered against the cement stairs. Rodgers can see the blood coursing from the body and spreading to the gutter. Everyone coming in and out of the club drops to the ground, their arms covering their heads. No one looks to see where the shots are coming from.

Rodgers calmly walks away and finds an agitated Hinckley, who was only expecting to hear one shot. They walk in between the buildings and hurriedly out into the next street. Each young man walks to opposite ends of the block. The sound of sirens fills the air, joining the commotion and panic and screaming coming from the next block.

Crowley has kept his window cracked open to listen for the gunshots. His glee turned to anger and later fear as he heard the gun continue its firing. He was almost afraid to pick Rodgers and Hinckley up; he was sure someone could see the flare of the gun as it was fired so many times. His anxiety subsides as he approaches Hinckley; no one is giving him a second look.

He picks up Hinckley and says nothing as they traverse the block and see Rodgers waving his arms vigorously, drawing attention to himself, drawing looks from spectators in passing cars and those few pedestrians still on the sidewalk, exiting the pubs in drunken bemusement or melancholy.

Crowley decides to drive on but changes his mind. He can't risk Rodgers being caught. Crowley realizes it will be some time before they try something like this again. He will need to introduce a certain sort of discipline into this Trinity. He might have to replace Rodgers.

Because of his indecision, Crowley has to slam on the brakes. His tires squeal as the car skids past Lee, who runs up to the car and flings the door open.

He is out of breath as he takes his seat. "I shot that nigger good! If you could have only seen it, Father Crowley! I shot that nigger good!" He claps his hands loudly in a swiping fashion, the left hand going up while the right hand goes down. "Damn! I shot him good. I didn't want to shoot nobody, but damn, I shot that nigger good! He was a real son-of-a-bitch, and I fixed his ass good." Rodgers feels more powerful than he has in his entire life, and a vague memory enters his mind, a remote recollection of rabbit hunting as a young adolescent early one winter with just a dusting of snow on the ground. There is a small forest behind his house of poplar and pine. He shot a rabbit as he chased it through the woods, a younger rabbit, male and small. The first shot, in the leg, only mangled it, and the rabbit was still alive, running on its three remaining legs. Instead of killing it instantly, he continued to maim it, shooting off the legs one by one, and then the ears, and then the nose. He felt like a god as he controlled the rabbit's remaining moments. With a powerful scream that echoed in the grove of trees, he shot the rabbit completely and the snow on the immediate ground turned to pink.

That's how he feels tonight—like a god. He thinks of Thor from Crowley's speeches on Norse mythology. He feels like a giant, a great and mighty ancient giant, deciding who remains on this earth and who doesn't.

Crowley listens to Rodgers's exuberance, and then chastises him. "Listen," he says, his teeth starting to clench, "we agreed on one shot. No one can tell where one shot came from, but you decided to wake up the whole city of Dundee and draw them a sonic map with your gunfire. I still can't understand why the police haven't pulled up behind us, you idiotic child. We have come too far and are going to go further; we don't need you to desecrate our sacred mission, to turn the hands of progress back any further than they've already fallen. I would be very careful, if I were you... You better hope no one saw you." Crowley says this in a calculating matter, glancing at Rodgers inside the rearview mirror, waiting for his reaction.

"Nobody saw nothin'." Rodgers's excited mood turns somber, and the joy and pride he felt just moments ago vanishes. "They was all too scared to look my way. They just ducked and covered their heads. I don't think they knew where what was coming from. So I shot that nigger. I shot that nigger good."

They drive on to Crowley's house in silence, the A92 black and only scarcely lit by a smattering of oncoming headlights. Crowley constantly looks in the rearview mirror, waiting for sirens to approach, but the receding landscape remains black and silent all the way to his farmhouse. He is satisfied that no one saw them take flight; no one saw Rodgers scramble out of the cemetery. If the note was placed where Hinckley said he put it, he knows the Tayside Police are reading it by now. He hopes there is a silent cheer from the heart of the white officer who reads the note.

"Sweet Mary, mother of God," says the freshest-faced of the two young constables who are the first to arrive at the steps of the club where the sailor lies dead, his blood reflecting the streetlights and the moonlight straining through the clouds.

"Sweet fucking Mary, mother of God." He vomits profusely into the gutter, taking care that his throw-up doesn't taint the evidence; only his shoes and the cuffs of his trousers are spoiled. He continues to wretch amidst the confusion, the hysterical and shocked passersby who witnessed the brief carnage, and the sound of sirens coming from all directions asserting their gravity upon what had been a typical and cheerful Friday evening.

The ambulance arrives as the constable wipes his mouth with the back of his sleeve. The taste of the take-out curry from four hours previous is still with him, but now it is not so appetizing.

The ambulance's arrival is pointless. No one else is injured, and the young sailor is long past mortality. Still, they check his pulse and his breath before closing his eyes with rubber-gloved hands. The young constable tapes off the scene while his companion takes statements from witnesses. No one saw anything—no suspicious looking people, no shooter. It is quickly surmised that the victim is an American from the base in Lutherkirk.

"Did he have any enemies?"

No.

"Did he have a go at it with some of the lads in the club?"

Again, no. He had spent the evening with his friends drinking and dancing with the three local girls who are still hugging each other tightly on the sidewalk, the fog of their breath intermingling before it rises into the damp and cold and crystal night. They are interviewed. They are too intoxicated and upset to give any information, but what they say is still recorded by young police officers with damp notebooks.

The inspectors arrive after a quarter of an hour, having been yanked from sleep or drink by frantic calls or pages. The one in charge, Chief Inspector Holliday, is a veteran of many Dundee crimes, but nothing like this. A Pakistani murdered the previous month, and now this. His instinct tells him the two are related.

He is a very obese man, and his obesity is driving the department to retire him this coming spring, still at the tender age of forty-nine. He isn't sure what he will do with his time or how he will supplement his pension, which won't keep him in the comfort that he has grown accustomed to. He has dreamed of spending his twilight years on the lonely and peaceful Isle of Skye, miles away from the urban decay that has crept into Dundee. He envisions himself stretching out his pension living a simple life alone in a cottage on a treeless and windswept shore on a cliff overlooking the sea. He longs to spend his retirement days fishing and reading and drinking and maybe even find a nice shepherd's daughter or widow with whom to pass the time. He could lose the weight and prolong his career and increase his pension; a loss of about three stone would make him more acceptable in the brass's eyes, but he's never been one for discipline. He's more of a connoisseur of comfort, an aficionado of ample food and endless pints after the end of the working day or working night.

On this night, he had been at his desk late, surrounded by cartons of Chinese take-out, writing a report about the Pakistani, leaving the case unsolved, chain smoking all the while. He received a hurried tap on the shoulder from someone in uniform and drove the short distance across the city center to the scene, where he now stands in his dirty shirt and wrinkled tie underneath a fluorescent yellow police-issue raincoat. He is short of breath and wheezing as he studies the scene. He sees where the bullets ripped the body—an uncommon sight in a country where guns are a rarity and even the police patrol the streets unarmed.

"An American?" he asks the nearest uniformed constable.

"Yes, from up on the base."

Holliday nods and lights a cigarette from a white box. He offers them to the patrolmen, but they all refuse.

Holliday studies the huddled Scottish girls and the shocked and confused friends of the dead American. His instinct tells him they have nothing to offer him, no information that could be relevant to this crime of intentional brutality. He stares at the club and down the sidewalk and then across the street. He rests his gaze on the cemetery.

"He shot from there." Holliday points to the darkened cemetery. "I want that taped off, too, and the grounds combed." More uniformed officers arrive and they walk across the street with more yellow police tape and flashlights. It isn't long before they shout and beckon Holliday over. He waddles across the street and sees the envelope tacked to the tree. He gingerly rips it down. He doesn't open it there; he doesn't want to risk the contents getting wet from this damp night. He drives back to the station and proceeds upstairs to the long and low office. He sits at his desk and carefully opens the envelope. He has long assumed that nothing can cause him alarm; he feels he has seen it all in the course of his twenty-plus years of police work, but his imagination could never take him to something like this, and the contents of the letter anger him. He takes it personally. Someone was murdered in his city, and on his watch.

He reads:

This is the beginning of a war. We are out to get rid of the lesser races, any non-white, they don't belong in Scotland. We will continue until they have returned back to their native lands. Scotland is for the Scots, not for blacks or Asians or foreigners of any kind. The purge will continue unless our demands are met.

Signed,
The Eastern Scotland Trinity
of the Great White Brotherhood

He recalls hearing something of a hate crime just before Christmas, up in Lutherkirk, a note being left and signed by this same group. Each victim has been a black American, someone from the base. He checks the computer, a new piece of equipment that intimidates him, and searches the United Kingdom for hate groups, hate crimes, especially violent hate crimes, but he finds nothing related, just random acts of broken glass and football hooliganism. No murders.

He dances his fingers through the worn out Rolodex on his desk and dials Constable Robertson in Lutherkirk. The reason is twofold. First, Holliday is looking for information about the incident that occurred the previous month, if anything unfolded in that investigation. Robertson is embarrassed, but no, he has found out nothing. He interviewed the mother of every school-age boy in his village, he has interviewed every young adult that lives on the dole, and he has interviewed anyone who might be angry enough to hate so much, and he has uncovered nothing. Everyone in the village has an alibi of sorts, and no inclination of racism. There is a dislike of Americans that has long existed, but nothing based on race.

The second reason Holliday calls Robertson is to ask him to inform the Americans about the passing of the sailor. Someone will have to claim the body after the autopsy and make all the arrangements.

Robertson asks the inspector if he has a hunch who the murderer may be.

"I suspect they're American. If you ask me, they must be American. Theirs is known to be a racist lot... There's no Klan in Scotland, and our lads don't go in for that sort of thing, carrying guns and wearing hoods, but I could be wrong. I'll be in touch. I think we need to talk to the Americans and tell them there is a racist targeting their sailors and we can't rule out that it's one of their own. It could be some local lads, gone over the edge a bit. There have been some hard cases in Arbroath, but nothing like this; they've only been stealing cars and smoking hash. I can't rule out one of our own, but this whole thing feels American to me; I can feel it in my stomach. If you can, ask the Americans if anything suspicious has happened on the base—you know, tension between the blacks and whites living in the barracks. Anything would be helpful."

"No problem," says Robertson, who has been brought from that first edge of sleep by Holliday's phone call. "I'll phone you after I talk to the Americans."

"Cheers."

Robertson dials the number to the base; he has long since memorized it from the years of reporting drunken sailors in his cell. His phone calls are usually routine, but not this one. He reaches the officer on duty and relays this heaviest of messages.

M onday comes and the news of the murder has spread across the base, cloaking the atmosphere in gloom.

Constable Robertson had contacted the base's duty officer-of-the-day, who in turn woke up the commanding officer, who immediately contacted the base master-at-arms, Chief Wilson. He tells Chief Wilson of the Scottish police's suspicions, and he is angry. If something is going on on the base, Wilson had better know about it, and if something isn't, he had better be able to prove it.

The master-at-arms is flabbergasted. He assures the captain that nothing is going on. There have been no signs of trouble from the barracks, and the only thing that ever really happens is the occasional fight at the enlisted club, but the confrontations are never racially motivated.

Chief Wilson feels that the bloke police are trying to shed responsibility. They're not mentally equipped to deal with a crime of hate in this country, which is so pastoral compared to the United States.

Maybe, maybe, the captain agrees. But since one of their own is dead, travel to Dundee is temporarily forbidden, and Dundee is added to the list of places that sailors are not allowed to visit: Northern Ireland, Libya, China, virtually every Eastern European country, and Dundee, Scotland.

The announcements are made at the various Monday morning quarters, informal meetings administered by division chiefs or officers, though word of the murder had already circulated through the enlisted barracks late Saturday night and early Sunday morning. With the travel restriction, there is a sense of fear that disrupts the mood of an otherwise very pacifistic existence on the base and in this serene country. Dundee is the nearest city of any size; many shopping trips are ruined and many plans of leisure are indefinitely delayed.

Rodgers, as Crowley has always feared, talks.

There is hushed and sorrowful talk among the handful of enlisted sailors in the disbursing department, sitting in a row of desks inside a crowded room inside the base personnel building. Everyone had some claim of friendship to the dead sailor, even if they just spoke to him in passing. Rodgers isn't mournful like his co-workers.

"Maybe he deserved it," Rodgers says, not quite under his breath. He is met by a roomful of arched eyebrows and open mouths attached to bodies frozen in motion.

"How can you say such a thing?" someone asks.

He shrugs his shoulders. "I dunno. Maybe God decided it was time for him to go. He was always acting uppity, anyway. I never did like him, and I don't know why you all are pretending like you did. I don't think none of you knew him, anyway. I'm tired of his kind here, playing their music so damn loud in the barracks and dancing and carrying on and such. I'm glad he's dead."

The personnel officer, a young and pretty female ensign, hears of Rodgers's remarks, as there is obvious disharmony in her department. She pulls Rodgers into her office to find out what he meant.

"I just didn't get on with him too well, ma'am; I figure he shouldn't be dead. I'm sorry for what I said." Rodgers knows what he said was foolish.

Crowley hears of Rodgers's comments. He shares a table at lunch with the young personnel ensign in the separate room for officers in the base galley. She is talking to another officer as he sits at the opposite end of the long table by himself, as he usually does. His day is already miserable from a working point of view, though he is joyous at the weekend's success. He has been assigned to eulogize Hughes in a memorial service. Hughes happened to be a Catholic, and although his body will be shipped to his native Baton Rouge upon the conclusion of his autopsy, the captain thought it would be prudent for the base to have a service in the chapel. Crowley has always hated funerals. He could never feel remorse at the passing of anyone, except for his mother. His prepared eulogy for Hughes is generic and deeply impersonal, as all his eulogies have been.

His heart stops a beat as he listens to the thin, blonde ensign speak of Rodgers's comments. She is disturbed and wonders what kind of sick mind the young seaman has to have to say something so callous. She concludes what each of Rodgers's co-workers has known all along: he isn't very bright and he has a tendency to speak without thinking.

The priest doesn't finish his lunch; he picks up his tray and walks back to his desk in the chapel as fast as his pear-shaped frame is able, his body leaning forward at the waist, as if he is bent by the wind. He telephones Hinckley in the supply department and instructs him and Rodgers to come to his house immediately after work.

This they do, both expecting praise from the priest, not wrath.

Crowley's reception is not as warm as usual. He offers no drink or food, and disappointed, they sit at their usual places on his couch, staring at the freshly lit coal-fire inside the dirty fireplace.

"Listen to me," Crowley begins, his attention turned to Rodgers, "you are very, very, stupid. I heard what you said. I bet the whole godforsaken base has heard what you said about the heathen deserving to die. You two have to be above board all of the time. I suggest you stop hanging out together for a time. Stay in your rooms, go to the gym, do whatever, but no more hanging out in the club. You can come here Friday, but take separate cabs. There may be extra attention on you right now, Lee, and we can't drag Mr. Hinckley down with you. Hopefully no one has noticed that you two are friends.

"We will lay low for a while; we will lull the enemy into an artificial respite."

The pair nod, glad they don't have to do anything, that the violence can maybe go away for a while.

"Lee, I want to talk to Mr. Hinckley privately. You should go back to base."

"I ain't got no money for a cab."

"Then walk," Crowley says tersely.

Rodgers slumps out of the room, his head down, his hands in his pockets. He walks out into the darkness of the late afternoon. He didn't bring a jacket, and he is shivering before he even leaves the house.

When Rodgers is gone, the priest brings Brad a tin of beer and slides the ashtray on the coffee table towards him, indicating that it's okay to relax.

"We can't keep him with us," Crowley says. "He is too stupid to be a part of our Trinity. We have to do something with him. We have to replace him. That is your task for the next couple of weeks. Find a friend. Find a replacement. Distance yourself from Lee as much as possible. Don't eat with him, don't walk with him. Don't do anything with him. By Friday, I'll know what to do."

Hinckley remains for an hour longer. Crowley tells him they did the people of Dundee a favor; there is one less dirty creature in their midst.

He gives Brad a five-pound note for the cab ride back to base.

Chris is starting to slip into a routine, though it is a lonely one. He is no stranger to loneliness, but still, he doesn't like it.

When not at work, he spends time lying on his bed, listening to his Walkman radio, the local stations a beacon from the world that exists outside the barbed wire and guarded gates of the base. He has still not ventured off base, his mind and body too weary from the changing shift schedule to travel even the shortest distances. His off-time is absorbed by eating, reading and sleeping, with the odd load of laundry done at the oddest of hours.

He likes his job, likes the importance of it, the vigilance of it. The messages must keep flowing; if they don't, the Russians have an edge.

He wants to learn more about his supervisor and sole co-worker, Petty Officer Freeman, and he wonders about her throughout the watches. He starts to reveal himself to her during the long and quiet solitude of the midnight watches. She doesn't reciprocate.

He tells her about himself at first, with a candidness out of his usual character. He is comfortable with her, as there is a certain amount of intimacy that comes with being inside such a small room for several hours at a time. He tells her how he came to join the Navy, the frustration of life with his parents, and his need to escape from Michigan.

She gives him only the vaguest and simplest of answers to the questions he poses, but is interested in what he has to say. He learns that she has been to college, with a degree in history, and that she is from Maryland and lives off base in a flat above an ironmonger's shop in Brechin, another nearby village that is much larger than Lutherkirk.

He asks her why she joined the Navy, and if she has a degree, why isn't she an officer? She just shrugs her shoulders and stares into the blankness above his head. He feels that there is something that happened in her past that forced her to the Navy, and this something is what makes her seem so perpetually sad. He wonders who she is and how she came to be here.

There is a void that Chris feels while not at work, a void that the cigarettes, radio, and books can't fill. An emptiness made all the more intense by his loneliness. He thinks of the priest who checked him in at the base chapel. He recalls the kind and pale face shrouded by the almost unkempt red and gray hair. The face seemed sort of paternal to Chris. Maybe he could find some comfort in the company of the priest, inside the walls of the chapel.

He decides to go to church.

Friday night comes, and as Rodgers arrives alone at Crowley's house, he expects the type of reception that came with most of his previous visits. He is disappointed. He is offered a beer, which he takes, but he is not greeted with a smile. He notices this right away.

The priest is nice enough to open the can and pour it into a glass.

A moment later, Brad arrives, his arrival telegraphed by the whining motor of the little Fiat taxicab that brings him hurriedly down the driveway, the gravel complaining underneath the tires.

The priest greets Hinckley warmly, an affable arm put around his shoulder. Crowley gently slaps him on the cheek with his open hand. He, too, takes a beer and they retire to Crowley's sitting room, neither Hinckley nor the priest looking Lee in the eye.

"Well, Lee," begins the priest almost nonchalantly, "how would you like to go back home?"

"Really?" Rodgers's face lights up and he looks hopefully at the priest. "Hell yeah, I'd like to go home. When? How?"

"Soon, but it is going to be tricky, and it will take some courage on your part. Do you think you can handle it?"

"I can handle whatever takes me out of this back-asswards country. I can handle whatever puts me back in Missouri."

"Fine. First, I want you to write a note." He offers Lee a pen and a sheet of plain white paper.

"Okay. What kind of note?"

"A pretend suicide note. Write whatever you like. Brad here is going to find the note in your barracks room, but by the time he does, Sunday, you'll be landing in St. Louis. The Navy won't bother to look for you because they'll think you have wandered out into the North Sea or shot yourself. Pretty slick, huh?"

The priest shows Rodgers a Pan Am envelope. The envelope contains the tabs of Crowley's original tickets to Scotland, but Rodgers thinks the envelope contains new tickets for him.

"Whatever you say, sir." Rodgers begins to scribble furiously: *I hate the Navy and I hate this country and I can't take it anymore, good-bye world.* He signs his name the way a small child does, slowly and deliberately, each character of his name very distinct.

The priest stands up and dons a raincoat.

With thoughts of home, Rodgers's vision is starting to blur, and all he can see is the priest's face smiling at him. The rest of the room melts away into a multi-colored haze. He sees the priest whisper something in Brad's ear. Brad takes another sheet of paper and starts writing.

Rodgers collapses. His beer had been laced with crushed Valium tablets from an ancient prescription that Crowley had confiscated from a parishioner with a drug problem years before.

Rodgers falls into a deep sleep, his mouth open and smiling, a look of complete serenity written on his face, as if an arduous task or long hard journey has been completed.

Hinckley rewrites Rodgers's suicide note. It takes several efforts to match his characters to the simplistic ones on Lee's letter, but he succeeds. The match would only fail the most severe handwriting analysis.

Dear all,

I had to do what I did and I hope you will forgive me for ending my life and understand why I did what I did. This world has become too corrupted by the niggers, the Asians and all other non-whites. I thought I could kill them off one at a time but I can't and it's too much. I can't take this world no more. A white working man like me don't stand a chance. I want to leave before there is none of us left.

Love,
Lee

They shove the letter in his left hand and crumple it up. Donning thick leather gloves, Crowley places his revolver in Rodgers's right hand and raises his limp and wispy arm so the nozzle of the gun is at his right temple. The priest squeezes Rodgers's finger and the gun fires.

Even though the noise is expected, Hinckley and the priest jump from the startling and loud report of the gun. The shot is not as clean as expected. Rodgers's head is a mess; the bullet didn't pass through the temple without leaving a bloody and fleshy wake. There is blood splattered everywhere. The priest's raincoat and his face is covered with blood, especially his mouth.

Gingerly, he steps out of the raincoat and licks his lips; he has always loved the taste of his own blood, white and ancient blood, and he treats it as some sort of communion. Rodgers's blood is also white blood. It is holy. The strength of Rodgers will enter him through his blood.

Crowley goes to his washroom and washes his face and rinses his hair. He examines himself closely in the mirror.

Hinckley is in shock, but he understands that the task was necessary for his survival.

The priest goes outside and throws his raincoat into a trash bag and then into the small hatchback trunk of his Austin.

Tomorrow, before dawn, he will go north on the A92 to the seaside village of Stonehaven and throw the same trash bag weighed down with rocks into the bottom of the North Sea. He will do this standing on a cliff in the shadow of the gloomy, majestic Dunnottar Castle. He will stand shivering in the wind and wait for the arrival of the sun, the same sun that arrives from Norway and Sweden and the lands of the gods.

He will then breakfast alone in a little café in Stonehaven Harbor, tea and toast with gooseberry preserves, maybe some eggs.

But on this Friday evening, he has some acting to do, and as he is without a conscience, it is easy for him to prepare for his role as confessor and performer of last rites.

"Get out!" he barks at Hinckley. Hinckley wanders off into the night and walks back to base. He will go to the club and drink and try to find new friends.

Crowley calls the quarterdeck on base and reaches the duty officer-of-the-day, a young lieutenant, junior-grade.

"This is Chaplain Crowley. I need to report the suicide of a sailor in my home."

The officer jumps up from his desk and his heart sinks. "What? Who? Where do you live?"

"Off base, just outside of Lutherkirk, on the road going to the castle."

"You need to call the bloke police. I'll call the skipper. Who's the sailor?"

"Seaman Rodgers, from disbursing. I think we found our Dundee killer."

"Really?"

"Really. I'll fill the captain in, but let me get the authorities notified. I have a corpse in my living room, and it is starting to become unpleasant."

"Keep us posted."

As the officer hangs up the phone and goes to dial the captain, he is struck by how calm the priest was. Someone just killed himself in his presence and he was as calm as anyone could be. Almost insensitive. The duty officer's hand shakes as he dials the captain's home.

Crowley decides to clean up his living room, emptying ashtrays and picking up beer cans and any and all signs of activity not befitting a priest. He drinks some of his wine directly from the bottle and calls the police.

Constable Robertson arrives at his home minutes later, and an ambulance from the hospital in Brechin is close behind.

Crowley welcomes the constable. There are tears in the priest's eyes; he apologizes for his appearance. He points to Rodgers's lifeless body on the couch, and the constable removes his hat and sets it on the coffee table.

"He shot himself?"

The priest nods.

"With a gun?"

The priest nods and points to Rodgers's right hand.

"How in the bloody hell did he get a gun?"

The priest shrugs his shoulders. "He came to my office on base this morning, just before the lunch hour, and said he needed to talk. I said sure, anytime, my door is always open and we could talk then and there or whenever he liked. He said no, he didn't want to talk on base. He didn't want to risk anyone hearing what he had to say. He had some grave confession to make, or so I gathered, so I said okay and gave him directions here. I was not prepared to hear what he had to say."

"Go on," says Robertson, removing the gun from the limp right hand and the crinkled note from the left. He realizes he should take pictures, but the only dead bodies he has ever seen have belonged to those more elderly Lutherkirk residents who die peacefully in their homes of old age or illness. Never a body in this state or under these circumstances. He reads the note and squints at Crowley.

"He said he had shot the sailor in Dundee a week ago, and some Eastern individual the previous month. I'm not sure who or where."

The Constable turns to Crowley and stares quite open-mouthed.

"He said he was going to kill every person of color, especially the blacks, one at a time if necessary. He felt that they looked down on him ever since his basic training. He never grew up around them, he said, but he was inspired by the memory of some great-uncle who was in the Ku Klux Klan, if you are familiar with that organization."

The constable nods, and the thought occurs to him that the whole of the world knows more about American culture than Americans know about the rest of the world. Their programs are on television almost every night. Their movies are at the theaters and the video shop. Their music flies through the airwaves of virtually every nation. Except in the East, and in the Soviet Bloc, but then who could be sure about that?

"So he was inspired in some way to start killing. He was going to continue and not finish until they were all gone. He realized this would be an impossible task, and he felt like he was going to get caught. He also had feelings of remorse; he didn't want to be a murderer in the eyes of God. So he confessed to me, looking for absolution. I told him God forgives unconditionally, but he still had to take the responsibility for his actions and turn himself in. He said that would be impossible, and as I stood up to put more coal in the fireplace, he pulled the piece of paper from his pocket and the gun from the small of his back and shot himself. There was nothing I could do. And then..." Crowley pauses as if the memory is too painful to recall. He turns his head down and rubs the bridge of his nose with the index finger and the thumb of his right hand.

The ambulance arrives, the sirens breaking the still of the early evening. Robertson nods at the body through the front door, which has remained open since his arrival. The two young paramedics squeeze Rodgers's wrist to check his pulse and listen for his breath, but they hear nothing. They both notice the peaceful look on the young man's face. They load him onto an ancient gurney and cover his body with a sheet. Crowley follows the body with his eyes as it leaves his living room and is loaded into the back of the ambulance. He feels as if a great burden has been lifted from his soul, and he relaxes a bit more as the ambulance travels slowly and peacefully down his driveway.

"And then I immediately ran over to him, made sure he was dead, which was obvious to me. I gave him last rites. I hope his soul heard me; I hope it hadn't left. I know our Father looks down upon suicide, but he also knows the pain inside the human heart." Crowley now stares into the corner of the room, his gaze focused on nothing in particular. "Only the lord knows what's in the heart. Sometimes sin is a necessary act of service, of devotion. And he sees that, as he sees everything."

Robertson has been writing everything the priest has said into a notebook, but he skips these last few sentences. He sits down in the sagging chair and looks at Crowley, his pencil in his mouth.

"Well," the constable says, as if in conclusion, "it seems pretty cut and dry to me. The lads in Dundee, from CID, may want to talk to you. I'm sorry for what you had to go through, but I feel somewhat vindicated, as I'm sure the police in Dundee will."

Crowley looks at him quizzically.

"Well, we always suspected the shooter in Dundee was an American; there were too many connections with the base. There was also some vandalism done to a sailor's house in Lutherkirk, with the same sort of note signed by the same group. It's more like your lot to be violent in that way. That and our lads don't usually have handguns such as this." The constable waves the gun in its plastic bag.

Crowley is shocked. He had thought no one would suspect an American, and he is sure he took care of Rodgers at the appropriate time. He is disappointed, and he knows he will cease activity for a few weeks or even months. He will then continue. He must continue.

Robertson rises to leave, and he shakes Crowley's hand. Crowley walks him to the door and wishes him farewell.

As the door closes, Robertson sees the swastika on the mantel.

He will phone Dundee straight away.

Crowley grabs a bottle of wine from the top of his refrigerator and collapses on the couch, where the blood has just started to dry. He doesn't care. Tomorrow is going to be a tortuous day. He is performing the memorial service for Petty Officer Hughes and it is a task he will not enjoy. He wonders if he will be tapped for a service for Rodgers, but he doubts it. His death will be quickly swept away and his body will be sent home to his devastated and simple family in Missouri. He will be mentioned as little as possible. Crowley will call Hinckley Monday morning. They will strategize. His gun is now gone, and that is part of his plan. The police will run a ballistics test on it, and they will find conclusively that it is the same gun that shot Hughes and the Pakistani, and they will look no further. They will be lulled into a calm. And then Crowley will strike again.

He lies awake for several hours. He remains in the dark waiting for the white and smiling lights to appear, to give him some sign, to lead him in a certain way. He sees nothing except the dying embers in his fireplace. The room goes cold as he falls asleep, fitfully.

He dreams. A beautiful Valkyrie arrives from the northern sky and floats into his living room. She takes Rodgers's bloodless body from the couch and flies away into the northern heaven. They are off to Valhalla. Crowley awakens, and he is jealous.

Robertson returns to his little storefront station, turns on the light, and boils water for tea. He inserts a blank sheet of paper into his typewriter and telephones Holliday in his home in Dundee's southeast corner, where he can see the motley boats docked in the quay from his living room window.

He tells the inspector that his suspicions were correct; the racist killer was an American, an American of the most pathetic sort, a wispy young man who, judging from the contents of his suicide note, was none too bright. He tells him of the priest's house, a dark and cluttered and smoky place, and of the swastika on the mantel.

"Well, it's no crime to own a swastika... Very, very odd for a priest, I must say, but not a crime. However, I doubt your little American was capable of pulling off these acts by himself; it took some sort of an effort. The letters were signed by the Eastern Scotland Trinity of the Great White Brotherhood. Trinity means three, you know—the Father and the Son and the Holy Ghost."

"True," says Robertson, "but this priest seems to be a pleasant bloke, and I would have thought nothing ill of him if I hadn't seen that swastika."

"Did it seem to be a suicide, a genuine suicide?" the inspector asks.

"Yes, as near as I could tell. I've never seen something so gruesome in my life. But yes, I saw the gun in his hand, and the hole where his temple used to be."

"Where in the bloody fucking hell did he get a gun? I hate to imagine there are several hundred Americans walking around up there with bleeding fucking guns like in the Wild bloody West. That is a separate matter I want the Americans to answer for, but as far as the question of suicide, an autopsy will tell us more—powder on the fingers, the trajectory of the bullet—it will give us evidence one way or the other. We won't close the book on this one yet, won't call it a suicide just yet. The body should be in our morgue directly. I'll have a look." The inspector coughs a phlegmy cough into the receiver and Robertson hears him light a cigarette and inhale deeply, the cigarette burning audibly across the thirty miles from Dundee to Lutherkirk.

"Did you contact the Americans yet?" Robertson hears the inspector wheeze.

"No, I wanted to give you a ring first. I will, shortly."

"Good, but don't mention the swastika. Don't mention any sort of suspicion of the priest. Give them the impression that we don't doubt the suicide, and that we have no doubt that the question of the murders in Dundee has been laid to rest. Let the priest explain himself to the Americans. If they think we suspect him of something irregular, he may be suddenly 'transferred' back to the States. If he is guilty of something—and my gut tells me he is—then we want first crack at him. I don't need those damn Yanks spoiling it."

Robertson has seen Americans suddenly sent away when they have gotten in too much trouble outside the base, where they would be in grave trouble with the Scottish police, transgressions such as domestic assault, more than one drunk driving offense, and shoplifting. They tended to disappear just as the British courts had their cases built against them. The Navy would whisk them back to Norfolk or San Diego and assure the British judicial system that their crimes were not ignored in the Navy's eyes.

The Americans have never wanted the embarrassment of one of their servicemen sitting in a foreign jail.

"I'll drive up tomorrow evening, and we will come and visit the priest. I'll meet you at your office at about half past six; I suspect he will be home then. Enjoy the rest of your evening."

"You as well," says Robertson, and he hangs up the phone. He calls the base and reaches the duty officer. He tells him just the basic facts; he tells him of the apparent suicide in the priest's home and that the recently deceased left a note implicating himself in the murders in Dundee. The young American officer patronizes the constable.

"Isn't it our say, where the body goes? Maybe we don't want it autopsied. I think it should be sent to Washington. After all, the body is property of the U.S. government."

"Regretfully, you have no jurisdiction outside that wee little base of yours, regardless of the citizenship of the victim. We are sure it is a suicide, but there are procedures we must take, and we are concerned that he had a gun. We don't allow handguns in this country... I don't suppose you can explain how he came to possess one?"

There is silence on the other end. Robertson continues. "Tell your security department that we'll be in touch. I'll alert the Ministry of Defence Police myself. Have a good evening. Cheers."

Robertson hangs up the phone, props his feet on his desk and waits for the teapot to whistle. He notes that every passing year, the freshest of the crop of Americans becomes more arrogant. Not like in the old days, when they smiled politely in the street, had you over for supper, would buy you pints in the pub. Now, they've become clannish and boorish, as if their life of large television sets and hi-fis and washing machines and refrigerators and large cars make them feel like giants in this country. Wee-minded giants, the constable thinks. He makes a cup of tea and leaves the bag in the mug as he types his report of the trip to Crowley's cottage on his old and comfortable typewriter.

An empty heart and a lack of anything better to do causes Chris to rise early on Sunday. It is his first day off. He breakfasts and then heads to the chapel for the nine o'clock Mass.

He is dressed in one of the two pairs of civilian pants he brought with him to Scotland, a pair of gray jeans and a white button-down shirt with long sleeves that he purchased in a mall in Pensacola.

He lacks a decent pair of shoes. He dons the same grubby high-top tennis shoes that have been with him since the start of his senior year in high school.

He finds himself alone in a pew. The chapel is more empty than full. Some older sailors who are married and have children are in attendance, the children bored and wandering in the pews, and there are a few solitary faces that Chris has seen around the barracks and the galley and the exchange. He knows virtually no one on the base, so he doesn't feel awkward in this situation, unlike the crowded galley, where no one eats alone. The chapel is still and quiet and empty. No one speaks.

Based on his amicable conversation with the priest, Chris expects the atmosphere inside the chapel to be more buoyant and relaxed. He assumed those in attendance would be smiling, as people did in his memories of church as a child, but there is a tension in the air that he can't define. The chapel seems gloomy.

A recording of an organ plays from behind the altar as the priest walks down the center aisle of the chapel. He is wearing a robe with a large cross on its back. Chris thinks he looks much less comfortable than he did sitting in his office in his khaki uniform.

As the priest starts to speak, Chris watches the other members of the congregation. He imitates their behavior.

He kneels as they kneel, he stands as they stand, and he crosses himself a step behind the other members as they cross themselves.

The sermon is brief. The priest talks about the gift of life, how each day is numbered, and he uses the passing of the sailor in Dundee and the suicide of the other sailor as examples. Chris had just heard about the suicide from Karen the evening before, and learned that it occurred in the priest's home.

The priest tells the passive devotees that they should treat each day as if it's their last, because it could be, and they may never get the chance to do the things they need to do. The words ring true enough for Chris, though he feels miles away from mortality. He just realizes it's yet another day in a string of lonely days. He hasn't met a girl, he's still a virgin, and he feels as desolate as ever.

The homily concludes and the priest prepares the Eucharist. He invites everyone to sing a hymn accompanied by the tape recording. Chris finds the words in the hymnal and mouths along: "Lamb of God, you take away the sins of the world. Have mercy on us." He wonders what God was doing with a lamb.

Chris stands in line for communion, which is something that he's never been prepared for or invited to do. Every member of the forty-strong congregation stands in line, so Chris does too. He watches those ahead of him in line carefully, so he can imitate their actions. He finally stands in front of the priest. Crowley recognizes him and smiles. Chris notices the priest's hand shaking as he deposits the wafer on his tongue. "Take and eat," the priest says, "the body of Christ."

Dear Wife,

I have just gone to church for the first time since I was very small. It was about how I remembered it, but I remember people being happier. A lot of it I didn't and still don't understand. It seems as if there is a lot of emphasis on certain types of ceremony, rather than any sort of message. It was quiet like I remember, and I wondered while I was sitting there how different my life would be if my parents brought me to church, and how different their marriage would have been. I think, if it helps, that you and I should take our kids to church. It can't hurt. I remember kids' parents getting divorced all the time while I was in school, but I don't remember any of them talking about going to church. I wonder if there is a connection. Maybe you have a different religion, you could be Jewish or Muslim for all I know and I don't care. I don't understand Jesus well enough and I was baptized as a Christian. I think we should be something. I've already figured out that life is too crazy to do things by ourselves. We need help.

Love,
Chris

Robertson is waiting for the inspector. He has heard of him, has known him for his work, but they've never met. They've both been in the force for years. Both are nearing the age of being put out to pasture, but their careers have taken different paths. Holliday is a man with the keenest sense of intuition and vengeance for the victims of crimes, be they petty or large. He always wants to be challenged, and he longs to be recognized for meeting those challenges. He was promoted through the ranks very quickly when he was younger and slimmer.

Robertson is a man with honor but no ambition; he is exactly where he wants to be, doing his job perfectly to the letter, but having no desire to leave his piece of the world, to leave his village in the valley that is surrounded by rolling hills that in the spring and summer look like a massive and wavy green carpet that rises above the clouds and stretches past the horizon.

Robertson stands in the storefront window of his station, drinking a cup of tea. He has his coat and his hat on, and he is ready to go. His heart races; never has he gone to question someone with the intent of implicating him in something as sinister as murder.

The inspector pulls up in front of the station in a car that Robertson doesn't expect, a 1970-something white four-door Ford Cortina. When the inspector steps out of the car and into the empty street, Robertson sees why he needs such a large car. He is a massive man, average height but thick in the legs, thick in the chest, broad in the back and shoulders, with a gut of tremendous size. Robertson wonders how he chases the thinnest of thieves through the alleys and neighborhoods of Dundee.

They shake hands without introducing each other. Silently they step into the inspector's car and Robertson gives

him directions as they drive past the dark and stony ruin of
Lutherkirk Castle to the priest's cottage.

There is a light in the window, and they can hear music
pouring out of the house.

They tap softly on the front door, and there is no answer.
They knock louder and the music stops. The priest answers
the door in his bathrobe. Robertson fears he is naked underneath.

One fact is obvious to both men of the law: the priest is
drunk. They can smell it on his breath, can smell it coming
from his pores.

The priest smiles his best disarming smile. Crowley recognizes the constable, and though he is smiling, Robertson
can see irritation in his eyes, the same drunken anger he has
seen in the eyes of husbands whose wives have called because
they've taken to knocking her around a bit after a night out
with the lads. Eyes that say they're being bothered and you
are a nuisance, Mr. Policeman.

Robertson introduces the priest to the inspector. As
promised, he says, someone from Dundee would like to have
a word.

"Hello, hello," Crowley says. He invites the two men in.
He offers them a drink, wine, beer or sherry. Robertson declines because he is on duty and he's not much for drinking
on Sunday. Holliday takes a glass of sherry.

The living room is cluttered, as it was when Robertson
came on Friday. A thin and worn sheet with a pattern of
flowers in between stripes is thrown over the couch. "To
cover the blood," Robertson says to Holliday as the inspector's gaze lingers on the couch.

The priest opens cupboard doors, searching for the
sherry and an appropriate glass. Peering into the lighted
kitchen, Holliday sees stacks of dishes in the sink and others
strewn across the counter. The garbage can in the kitchen is
also overflowing, and the old and yellow tiled floor is dirty.

A bit of a pig for a priest, Holliday thinks to himself. But
not too piggish to take a crack at innocent blokes coming
out of a club on a dreamy Friday night, or minding their own
business on Christmas day.

They sit down, the policemen on the covered couch and
the priest on his sagging armchair. Holliday is direct, leaving

no time for pleasantries. He points to the swastika on the mantel. "Father, what is that doing there?"

Crowley sips his glass of wine. His body betrays nothing, but Robertson sees his gaze follow the inspector's chubby finger and rest on the black miniature swastika on the iron pedestal.

There is fear in Crowley's eyes. He doesn't look up until puts his smudged wine glass back on the coffee table.

Despite his apparent inebriation, Crowley's mind quickly summons a lie. "My first job out of seminary was as a parish priest outside an Indian reservation in Arizona. There was a conference of community churches and tribal leaders, and a Navajo medicine man gave it to me. He said that it's a Navajo symbol for peace."

Impressive, thinks Holliday, but he doubts the sincerity of the story. He decides to ask about Rodgers instead—was he a churchgoer, how long had Crowley known him, and if he wasn't a churchgoer, why had he confided in Crowley?

Crowley answers each question with either a "no" or an "I don't know." Holliday and Robertson both know that he will reveal nothing to them, but a seed has been planted in the priest's ear. He now has a face to the otherwise faceless Scottish law, a law he has so callously and carelessly ignored.

"Well, it must have been disturbing, seeing a lad blow himself away like that," concludes Holliday. "But you've got the Holy Father to lean on, don't you? In times like this."

Crowley stares at the fireplace and thinks a moment before answering. "Yes, it was—and still is—disturbing. Sometimes our Father leaves us more questions than answers, and then some of us stop looking for answers."

As they leave, Robertson and the inspector say farewell to the priest without shaking his hand. Crowley stands in the open doorway and remains there until the white Cortina disappears down the driveway. He closes the door and leans against it, studying his living room.

He thinks he has fooled the police and his tracks are sufficiently covered. He takes one of his few remaining Valiums. He lies on the couch and feels the pleasant narcotic effect. He thinks about the newly arrived seaman who attended Mass earlier in the day. He seems lonely to Crowley... Maybe he can come out with Hinckley, if the two already know each other. He has nice features, the priest thinks, blond hair, pink skin, and he seems somewhat intelligent; the eyeglasses intimate and perpetuate that stereotype.

The priest falls asleep again on the couch and soon begins to dream. He is standing in a field, a green and purple Scottish field full of heather and thistle. The sun is shining in an azure and bright summer sky. The sparse and wispy clouds are high above the hills and mountains and he is standing on the shore of a loch, facing the water. He is wearing a white robe, the warm but forceful wind ruffling the skirts and the fabric of his sleeves. A knotted wooden staff is in his right hand. In front of him with their backs to the water stand Hinckley and the new seaman. In his dream, he remembers the name Fairbanks. They are wearing brown robes, the waists tied with ropes, like novices in a monastery. Past them, he can see his reflection in the still, pure water. His hair is long and gray and his face, unusually thin, features a full white beard.

He looks to the sky and calls to Odin, speaking in tongues in what he guesses is ancient Icelandic. He raises his staff to the sky, which quickly darkens. Thunder roars. From a newly formed cloud, a lightning bolt strikes his staff. A current of electricity binds the three of them together. He receives their energy, and they receive his wisdom and his desire.

The priest awakens. He is sweating and smiling. He ambles up the stairs to his musty bedroom. He had been dreading Monday, but now he can't wait for the day to begin.

It is the heart of winter, and Chris goes a whole week without seeing the sun. It is dark when he goes in for his mid-mid-watch and dark when he finishes. The same holds true for the day watches; the sky is perpetually dark. He doesn't see the sun until his day off.

February comes. Chris has been in the Navy for six months. His days in Michigan seem distant, and the members of his family become more and more blurred as they drift into the recesses of his memory. He seldom thinks about them anymore. If he does, he becomes sad and then angry.

During Monday morning quarters, a Monday when Chris has a day-watch, Chief Lassiter singles Chris out and calls him in front of the half-dozen people who make up the day-staff of their division. He shakes his hand and presents him a patch consisting of three stripes and the insignia of their communications rating. He is being promoted. His face turns red and he feels a giddiness in his chest. He has made it to E-3. The chief points out to those witnessing the event that not everyone makes it to E-3; some get promoted to civilian, and this shows that Seaman Apprentice Fairbanks is an asset for the Navy.

After a few announcements germane to the functions of the base, Chris and his supervisor return to their work area, and there is work to do. The printer is printing constantly. There is a Soviet exercise in progress, and it appears that a good chunk of the Northern Fleet is leaving Murmansk, as it would do in a war. The Americans respond by sending naval fighter jets scrambling out of Keflavik, Iceland, and the Air Force sends jets from bases in England and Germany. It is exciting and somewhat tense as Chris watches the events unfold via the messages coming on the printer. He feels very important; he has just earned more stripes and the security of the United States is passing through his hands.

Petty Officer Freeman has seen all this a hundred times before during her six years in the Navy. She sees it all as a giant chess game between the two superpowers. She stifles a yawn while Chris constantly rips paper off the printer and types into the computer.

The activity wanes as the day winds down. Chris asks Karen a tentative question, one that has been on the tip of his tongue since he met her.

"What kind of job can you get with a degree in history?"

"Nothing, really. Teaching, that's about it."

"Were you a teacher?"

"Yes," she replies, without looking at him.

"Why did you stop?"

She looks up from her desk where she has been writing the details of their watch in a green logbook. Her eyes tell Chris that she doesn't like his question, but she smiles slightly. "Because I joined the Navy." She returns to the logbook, and Chris knows not to ask her any more questions.

He has filled in a detail of her life. She was a teacher. He can't picture that. In his still adolescent mind, teachers still possess a place of authority and sometimes veneration. Many teachers, good and bad, still affect his behavior, as they assume part of his recent memory. Teachers were more influential than his parents. Even though he was a mediocre student, he liked some of his teachers better than either his mother or father.

He respects Karen as a supervisor, but he can't picture her melancholy and pretty face standing in front of a classroom. He can't picture her in anything but the dungaree uniform and blue working jacket that she constantly wears, as she appears to have a perpetual chill.

She has become even more enigmatic.

Quietly, the Americans' ban on travel to Dundee is lifted. Almost instantly, the population of the base forgets about its recently deceased fellow sailors. The clubs in Dundee once again host a bevy of young Americans, Americans who don't worry about their safety in the slightest.

The killer is dead. The Navy, the captain of the base, and the master-at-arms all sigh in relief. They quickly vilify Rodgers and don't question Chaplain Crowley's role in the suicide at all. In fact, the captain apologizes to him. He states that it was only out of the kindness of the chaplain's heart that the young and disturbed man ended his life in the chaplain's presence. It was above and beyond the call of duty for Father Crowley to invite the young man into his home to discuss his troubles, and he is sorry that the result of that extension of compassion and kindness resulted in such a pathetic tragedy. It would have been better if he had turned himself in. The families of the victims would have been able to feel a sense of justice.

The Tayside coroner did not find enough evidence to rule out the assumption of suicide. The coroner did find the Valium in Rodgers's blood, but it was not a lethal or even a particularly large dose, and he could have gotten it anywhere. For all they knew, he may have been taking it recreationally for several weeks or even months. There was no strange skin or debris under his fingernails, as there would be if there had been some sort of struggle, and there was powder on his fingers, indicating his hand was holding the gun when it was fired.

Holliday alerts the coroner of his suspicion of murder, with the priest possibly having a hand in it. He wants the coroner to agree and say that murder is still a possibility. His requests are pointless; the inspector's superiors quickly and tidily wrap the case up. The murders now stand solved, and if there are more Americans involved in predatory racist behavior, they probably won't do it again. Not now, not after they've been under scrutiny. Leave the sick American buggers to the Americans; let them sort out their own. Spend the people's money locking up criminals who victimize the Scottish people.

Holliday is furious when he telephones Robertson and tells him Rodgers's death was ruled a suicide and that no further investigating will be done of the murders in Dundee.

As a personal favor, Holliday asks Robertson to keep an eye on the priest, to drive by his place as often as possible.

"You know I'm a one-man outfit here," replies Robertson.

"I know it," says Holliday, "but if this priest thinks he got away with something, he'll be apt to try it again. If he is the leader of some wee group, then he's an arrogant bastard. He probably thinks he's smarter than we are. Just do what you can. Drive by when you can, ask his neighbors, ask people up in that cute little village of yours if they notice anything peculiar going on at that bloke's place. He will do something again, and I don't want to miss him. My gut has never been wrong, not on something as big as this. That, and I just don't like him. I know he came off as being pleasant when you first met him, but when you and I went to see him, he was drunk off his ass. What sort of priest gets drunk on a fucking bloody Sunday?"

The inspector pauses long enough to light a cigarette that has been unlit in the corner of his mouth for the entire conversation. Robertson remains silent and doesn't answer his last question.

"Do what you can, that's all I ask. I'm sure we'll be talking about this sooner than later."

"I will, Inspector, I will. You look after yourself, and I hope our paths cross under more pleasant circumstances."

"Cheers, mate, but in our line of work, I don't think they will."

Crowley calls Seaman Hinckley in the supply depot. Eye-brows are raised among his co-workers when he is sum-moned to the phone. It is an odd occurrence for Hinckley to receive phone calls; he is not known to be sociable, and now he is even more of an outcast because of his past association with Rodgers. He was interviewed by Chief Wilson and the supply officer after Lee's surmised suicide. They found him to be without suspicion. He said that he and Lee were only drinking buddies. He knew Lee didn't like blacks, but he didn't know about any killing. Nobody pressed him too hard for details. The command was fearful that Rodgers didn't act alone, and they didn't want to know about any further in-volvement. They took Brad at his word and told him to choose his friends more carefully.

The priest is direct. "Come on out Friday evening. Don't eat at the galley; we will drive into Dundee and eat there."

"Okay..."

Crowley hangs up.

Friday comes and Hinckley takes a cab out to the priest's house. He is quiet and not his usual brash self. Lee was his friend, and he had a hand in his murder. Guilt and sadness have been consuming him for the past week.

He misses his friend. He has been eating in the galley by himself, spending his evenings in his room in the barracks if his roommate is working, or in the lounge watching Armed Forces Television if his roommate isn't. The Armed Forces Network mainly offers reruns of the less racy American sit-coms, major sporting events, or news of the social and good-will activity of the various branches of service stationed throughout the world.

He has gone through the week mindlessly, barely making himself presentable in the very casual dungaree uniform.

Crowley senses all this immediately upon Hinckley's arrival. He offers him a beer. Brad declines. This concerns the priest. He herds the young man into his car and they head to Dundee. They drive in silence. The priest attempts some small talk; he even asks about football.

"The season is over," replies Hinckley. It's the only comment he makes during the half-hour drive into Dundee.

They stop to eat on the edge of town at a gloomy pub along East Dock Street, an establishment preferred by the men who work the boats. It is dark and plain and somewhat dirty. They sit at the bar and eat fish and chips. Brad, in this atmosphere, drinks one pint and then another and then his mood lightens and he forgets about the previous week.

He realizes he is with his other friend, the priest.

"Why was he such a dumb son-of-a-bitch?" Brad asks the priest suddenly.

"I don't know, I don't know," answers the priest, who knows a little bit about mourning. He knows Brad misses his friend and is feeling guilty. Even though he is and was a bad priest, he has a sort of intuitiveness for human nature. He was himself a sensitive young man. His sensitivity didn't erode until his latter days in Houston when his heart became filled with so much hate.

"He is better off where he is now, I assure you. His acts were seen in heaven, and the gods want us to continue, they do. I had a dream that a beautiful maiden flew down from the sky and took Lee into her beautiful alabaster arms. She held him against her breast and flew into heaven. She was a Valkyrie and Lee was given the honor of entering Valhalla, our white heaven, as a fallen warrior. We had to do it. He would have talked and then you and I would not be sitting here right now."

Brad nods and he feels reassured by the priest's words.

"He wasn't nearly as intelligent as you are, not nearly," Crowley continues. "He didn't sense the importance of what he was doing. He didn't see the big picture, unlike yourself. You know our task is holy and right and necessary. We must continue, but we will do so differently. We need another member. Two of us just aren't enough. There is magic and strength in the number three, in a Trinity. There must be three of us, three of us bonded by blood and courage."

Hinckley is flattered by the priest's compliments. No one has ever complimented him on his intelligence. He was considered slow in school and slow by his mother, who raised him in front of a television set. He often spent the late afternoon and evening hours after school by himself, watching cartoons and game shows, as he waited for his mother to arrive home from whatever restaurant or tavern she was working in at the time.

She would leave him bags of potato chips and soda for dinner if she was going to be especially late coming home. If she returned at a more reasonable hour, she would bring him something from work in a Styrofoam box. Homework was largely ignored; she would only pay attention to his grades when he came home with a dismal report card. She thought he was dumb, and there wasn't much point in trying to develop him academically. She felt he was happiest in front of the television set. So be it. He would have to work for the rest of his life, so what was wrong with a little childhood slothfulness?

He became obese by the age of eleven, and was pushed through to the next grade each fall even though his teachers knew he shouldn't be. They didn't want him back in their classrooms the following year, finding it too hard to teach a child when there is no structure at home, no continuity of the orderly school day.

He learned his predicament by the time the fall of his senior year approached. He heard other kids talking about jobs and college and potential careers. He had never thought about his future after school, other than being miles from his grandparents' neighborhood in Omaha and in a place where there were no black people. He dreamt of a sort of Utopia where college football is played all year. (The fact that several of the Nebraska football players are of African descent has been of no consequence to him. That fact, he has always conveniently ignored.)

He knew he needed some sort of vehicle to propel him towards adulthood. He knew his childhood had not prepared him to take care of himself. He didn't want to keep following his mother around—nor was he welcome to do so. Many of her boyfriends looked at the chubby child and then the tall and fat adolescent with disdain. Life with his grandparents wasn't appealing, either; aside from watching football with his grandfather, life in their home wasn't too pleasant. He didn't like sitting in the dark and small living room with bottles of pills on a television tray. He didn't want to fall asleep each night listening to his grandfather wheeze while attached to an oxygen tank.

So he was led to the military, and because of his late and unknown father, he picked the Navy. The recruiter was straight with him. "If you want to get in the Navy, you need to lose the weight, most of it, anyway. You won't make it, looking like that."

He lost the weight. A lot of it, anyway.

Through sheer willpower and starvation, he deprived himself of food after seven in the evening and didn't eat lunch in school. He hid in the school library during the lunch hour and pretended to do his homework while his stomach ached for food so badly that his hands started to shake. He wanted out of this life badly, and a certain discipline that had not been evident in him for his entire life took over and he succeeded. He still looked like an overweight young man. Some would call it baby fat. His stomach still hung over the waistband of his pants, but in appearance, he looked respectable enough.

His success in losing weight gave him confidence, a sense of pride that he had never possessed. He passed his physical during the summer after graduation, and he was sworn in and sent to boot camp late in September of 1984.

And at that moment, all the discomfort of being ignored by his peers because of his weight or color vanished. His life was presented with opportunities he thought would never come. Better still, his life was presented with a plane ticket from Omaha to Chicago, and boot camp in Great Lakes. He flew away from an existence he knew was pathetic.

He had hoped to find some sort of acceptance in the Navy. He thought everyone would form a sort of clique of the type he had observed as an outsider all through his childhood days. He thought a common uniform and a common occupation would cause all his fellow sailors—in boot camp and beyond—to be a sort of fraternity. A family.

He found this to be untrue, as he has never really developed any sort of friendships. He didn't know how friends should act. He became obnoxious, almost a bully. He made fun of the more inept and smaller recruits in boot camp. (He did well. He was able to follow the directions of the company commanders, and he managed fairly well with the physical training, despite his girth.)

He remained friendless throughout basic training and throughout the storekeeper school conducted on the other side of the base at Great Lakes. He remained obnoxious, loud mouthed and opinionated in the classroom. His friendlessness caused an emptiness in his heart that he was not able to identify. He didn't know that his loneliness bothered him, as he had grown callous from the years of watching endless television programs wrought with violence and betrayal and casual relationships. He thinks that's how the world is. Every man for himself.

He was equally miserable when he arrived in Scotland fresh out of storekeeper school, and he found another outcast in Lee Rodgers. He found the first real friend he had ever had in his life. When sober, they talked little. While drinking, they talked a great deal.

Then Father Crowley comes along and he feels as a part of a family; he feels the camaraderie he hoped for and subconsciously expected the Navy to provide. He finds himself a member of an exclusive club. He is a member of the white race. He is descended from supermen from the north, descended from the gods of fire and ice.

He is comfortable in the priest's house, in front of the fireplace, drinking beer and smoking cigarettes, comfortable talking about the inadequacies of the races, and how the white man should and shall reign supreme.

He feels vindication for those Omaha days, those days of fearing his classmates and the passage along crooked sidewalks through the crumbling neighborhood going to and from school.

To be bonded by blood and courage.

These words continue to ring in his ear, drowning out the noises of the small pub, the noise of conversation, the din of drunken humanity that resonates through the establishment.

He lets the priest's words resonate inside his cluttered mind. He stares at the barely perceptible veins traversing his wrist and the back of his hand.

Blood. White blood. It is holy blood—chosen blood—that is traveling throughout his body. He decides that the misery he felt in Omaha wasn't his fault. He is an Aryan, a supreme being, never meant to mix with the lower races. Anyone else growing up in his situation would be miserable and destined for failure.

But not Brad Hinckley. The world owes him too much. He is a warrior, and he will continue to fight.

"We can't stop," he says to Crowley after the fish and chips are exhausted and the pint glasses reappear full of lager. "Two or three of us, we can't stop."

"I agree, I agree," the priest says, "but we shall lay low for a while, maybe avert our attention towards another sphere. There is a small Jewish population in this country, one that hasn't been dealt with yet. They are too comfortable here. We can change that."

Brad has never thought about Jewish people before. As far as he knows, he has never met one, nor has a Jewish person ever done him any harm.

He only knows Judaism as the religion that doesn't believe in Jesus, the religion of Israel, that faraway nation from the evening news that is fighting Palestinians in southern Lebanon, which is now a nation of scarred and bombed out buildings. He has never given any thought to the Jewish people. The blacks were an enemy he could identify, could summon up the sufficient anger to fight.

"I think that the bloke police suspect me of something. They came around after Lee's suicide. They have nothing on me. I never fired a gun, and, unfortunately for you, I never wrote a letter. If I'm to direct any operation, I have to do it cleanly. The head of the Trinity, as the head of an army or a state, must never fall. With no evidence against me, I will never fall."

Brad suddenly feels betrayed by this information. He hadn't noticed before that the priest's hand never did get involved in any of their activities.

The priest senses Brad's sullenness. He places his hand on Brad's shoulder. "Look," he says, with an intonation of tenderness, "I never had you fire a gun, did I? You are special. You will always be my lieutenant, my right hand man. I won't let you fall, either."

He returns his hand to his pint glass, drains it halfway, and continues.

"I want no attention drawn to me right now. If anything occurs in this country, any sort of violent behavior against minorities, the bloke police will pay me a visit. There are some indoor projects we can work on, and these we can do with just the two of us. No one will know."

"What's that?" Brad asks, his third pint glass now empty. Alcohol-induced joviality streams through his body, and his face and stomach and heart feel warm.

"In due time, in due time," the priest says. "Meanwhile, stay away from my house for a few weeks, or even a month. Make some friends, meet some girls—but don't get too involved with girls. They will weaken your will. We need a third member, and I want you to find one. Once you find one, let me know. Bring him over, and we shall see. We have to have someone to do the dirty work."

Chris learns of his roommate's association with Lee Rodgers by doing what he's always done best: he listens to the conversations of others.

He sits in the galley for dinner before a mid-watch in the days after the word of Lee's suicide has fanned across the base, along with the news that he was the one who murdered the sailor in Dundee for purely racial reasons.

Across the base, Rodgers is recalled with disgust and loathing by all who claimed to have known him. His co-workers, those who frequent the club and the barracks lounge, all speak of him lowly, all saying they knew something wasn't right. But they didn't know he was racist, not until his remarks after Hughes was shot. They thought of him as dim and crude, but not a racist with a propensity for the most severe form of violence.

Rodgers is characterized as a misfit and a loner on the Scottish radio, and Chris has heard as much about him that way as he has on the base. There were countless phone calls during a phone-in show on Radio Tayside about Rodgers, and then the conversations led to Americans in general. Some of the callers' brogue was so thick that Chris could barely understand them, but their point was clear: the Americans should leave. Especially now.

Chris overhears a typical conversation about Rodgers. A cluster of young men is congregated at the opposite end of the long table he is seated at. The group is almost done eating. They sit and talk idly, glancing at their watches to see if they have enough time to continue their chatter before their own mid-watches start.

"He hung out with that fat kid in supply—you know, that goofy one with the buzz-cut that wears Nebraska shirts all the time." One of the young men says this knowingly, working a toothpick between his teeth.

Chris feels his heart stop. He recognizes the description instantly, and knows the fat goofy kid is his roommate.

He now remembers Rodgers. On the few times Chris would return to the room unexpectedly, there his roommate would be with Rodgers, as if they were getting ready to go somewhere. Chris could hear them talking quietly through the closed door, but as soon as he opened it, their conversation would cease and they would leave. That was okay with Chris; he never felt comfortable with his roommate in the room. He felt tense, as if every move he made was irritating, and as if he were being watched with disdain. Hinckley's stature and almost constant sneer make him intimidating to Chris, as he is much slighter and shorter, and with a personality more curious than confronting. He has always hated confrontation, even as a child. Chris spent hours hiding under his bed with his hands over his ears during the weeks and months when his parents' marriage became unraveled. He was maybe ten or eleven and didn't want to be in the middle of the skirmish. He is not necessarily a coward, but he prefers people to get along in his presence.

Several days after hearing that conversation, Chris has finished his string of watches and he is entering his period of three days off. It is now mid-February. The days are slowly starting to lengthen; a hint of sun is visible in the sky during the afternoon shift change.

His first full night off is Saturday, and he knows he will be up all night; he slept most of the day, having worked the previous night. His roommate is absent throughout the day, occasionally popping in to quietly grab duffle bags of laundry. Chris barely hears his roommate; he is surprised at the consideration Brad is showing him. He refused to accommodate Chris's schedule prior to this, making an equal amount of noise whether Chris was asleep or awake.

He goes to the galley for supper shortly after waking up. It is five in the afternoon and the sun is nearly faded; only a gray light breaks through the dark and cloudy sky. It is a typical meal: spaghetti, garlic bread and glasses of milk with cake for dessert taken from the revolving glass dessert carousel next to the milk dispenser.

He is quite full and content and looks forward to a cigarette and an evening of reading and laundry as he returns to what is usually an empty room, especially on a Saturday night. Chris sees light coming from the bottom of the door leading into his room and is surprised that he left the light on. He didn't. He finds his roommate sitting at the desk they share, the chair tilted back on its two rear legs and Brad's feet on top of the desk sporting dirty and unlaced high-top sneakers with the tongues pulled out and folded over.

"I thought you might be off tonight," Brad greets Chris. "Whatcha doin'?"

Chris is taken aback. His roommate has never asked him a question, never treated him any differently than a piece of furniture.

Confused, Chris shakes his head. "Nothing."

"Cool." Hinckley reaches into the small refrigerator that came with their room and retrieves a six-pack of canned and stale American beer that he bought in the base commissary. "I figure we'll have a couple of cans of the good stuff, and then we'll hit a pub somewhere, and then we'll have to drink the bloke beer. It won't taste so bad, though, after we have a couple of these in our guts."

Chris is thrilled at the sight of beer; he hasn't really had any since Pensacola, as there has been no one for him to drink with. The thought of drinking alone somewhat disgusts him, and the prospect of drinking is a pleasant one. Even if it is with someone he is afraid of.

Chris takes the beer and is indifferent to the poor taste. He drinks the can hurriedly and the warmth from the alcohol works rapidly, spreading across his body. He feels as much at ease as he has in the longest time.

"Well, look at the thirsty one." Hinckley laughs and tears another can from a plastic ring and hands it to Chris. This beer, too, he empties quickly, and he now feels lighter than air, an intense joy. The joy comes from the sudden show of friendship from his roommate as much as it does the alcohol.

"Ya got bloke money?" Hinckley asks Chris. Chris checks his wallet and pulls out his entire paycheck. He has hardly spent any of it except on magazines and newspapers and cigarettes and soda, nor has he thought to save it. He has never had a bank account and he has stared thoughtfully at the branch of the Bank of Scotland on base while walking by.

"Yeah, I got like twenty-five pounds."

"Well, I got about fifteen, so that should be plenty. Where do you want to go?"

Chris shrugs his shoulders. "I don't know," he says. "I haven't been anywhere yet."

"I noticed that. You've always been the stay-at-home type. I want to go where we won't see none of these idiots from the base. I like to go where the blokes go—you know, somewhere off the beaten path." His reasons for this are twofold: he wants privacy while talking to Chris, and he feels like a bit of a pariah. He is stared at constantly across the base, and he knows people whisper as he walks by. "There goes that friend of that one guy—you know, the racist killer. He was probably in on it, too."

They leave their room after the six-pack is a memory and walk across the courtyard to the main gate of the base, their breath visible underneath the floodlights that shine on all the sidewalks and roads of the base. It is perhaps seven in the evening, and there is a queue of cabs outside the base.

"Brechin," Hinckley says to the cab driver with the veteran air of someone who has directed many cab drivers.

The cab driver recognizes Hinckley; he has taken him to the priest's house in the past. "Aye, where's your mate? Where is the lad you usually run with?" The driver is referring to Rodgers in a friendly manner, not knowing what Rodgers did. Hinckley gets nervous and looks at Chris, to see his reaction to the cab driver's question. Chris is too drunk to notice, too drunk for the words to resonate any more than the sound of the radio.

"He's gone," Hinckley says.

"Aye, back to the States?"

"Yeah."

The conversation ceases as the cab drives the six or seven miles into the village of Brechin, a pretty town with maybe five thousand souls, providing shopping for the farmers and smaller villages—such as Lutherkirk—that lie in this northeast corner of Scotland's Tayside region.

Though it is a small town, it supports perhaps thirty pubs of varied size and pleasantness. The more modern and larger ones are favored by the Americans, as they more resemble bars back in the States.

Hinckley found some of the off-beaten-path pubs with his friend Lee in their jaunts they took together before they met Father Crowley. They would sit and drink and stare at the girls and look down upon the Scottish people that they saw, complain about the beer and poor choice of food. Hinckley would somehow manage to talk about Nebraska football, and Lee would talk about Waylon Jennings or Johnny Cash or Hank, Jr. and how the South would rise again.

The cab deposits them in the center of town, per Brad's instructions. He is not quite sure which pub he wants to go to, so they walk through the windy and damp night air along Brechin's High Street, which winds in several curves and goes up and down three low hills over several blocks before it reaches either end of the village center. The center contains simple shops: an ironmonger, a chemist, a small appliance store, a bakery, a butcher, a small supermarket, a storefront department store selling everything from records to tennis shoes, and there are a few more specialty shops, all surrounded by pubs.

As they walk, Chris constantly circles around looking at the faces of the stores and the faces behind the wheels of the cars that drive by. He has never been off base, and he feels silly for not having ventured off sooner.

They veer off High Street to a small street that lasts only half a block before dead-ending into the wall of what is an auto repair shop. They find a pub that Brad has been into once in the past. It is small, perhaps four tables and a bar large enough to accommodate only six stools.

It is dark when they enter, and smoke from many exhaled cigarettes hangs in the air like so many low flying clouds or an early morning fog. Each face in the pub shines in the light of two bulbs hanging in solitude from the ceiling, which is fairly high for such a small room. The rest of the room is dark, the walls covered in artificial wood paneling, the floor carpeted in a low and dark gray rug decorated with various stains and burns. The crowd of mostly men grows quiet as the two walk in, as it is obvious that they are American and don't belong in their intimate circle. They are ignored, however, and the scattered conversations resume. The sight of Americans in Brechin is an everyday occurrence, and one or two even occasionally wander into this simple pub.

They sit at a rickety table that is bare save a half-full ashtray sporting the Tenants Lager logo and some empty pint glasses left by a previous patron. Brad and Chris quickly light cigarettes, and Brad goes to the bar and brings back two pints. It is Chris's first sample of a beer that isn't American, and the aesthetic thrill of drinking out of a pint glass inside a dark and gloomy British pub brings back that feeling of worldly conquest that he lost upon his arrival at the base in Scotland. He realizes now while sitting in the pub with beer flowing through his blood that the previous six months were emotionally draining and he probably holed up in his room because he was too depressed from his loneliness and because of his all but lost family. He figured he had two years in this country, plenty of time to explore, as two years is still a big chunk of life for someone his age.

Additionally, his division is small, the smallest on the base, and most people work with several other sailors and make friends through work. He works with a shy and secretive woman. She is pleasant, but she has made no overtures of friendship. She lives in Brechin somewhere, and he thinks momentarily about finding her.

He and Brad remain silent as their first pints disappear. They have little to talk about, as they don't know each other. Brad is thinking about Crowley, wishing he were spending time with him instead of his quiet roommate, who so far is quite boring.

Chris studies the women. There are perhaps half a dozen or so in the pub, all with their husbands or boyfriends, covering the spectrum of adulthood. They are sort of homogenous looking, short and heavyset, all smoking and drinking. They don't drink pints like the men; they choose cider or beer in half-pint glasses or mixed drinks. The women are almost identical; the clothes are similar, the style of overly-treated hair is similar and the only distinction is the advance of years. This is his first impression of Scottish women, and though it is a false one, it is also a permanent one. He is disappointed; he expected to find a sort of purity in the Scottish women. He expected them to be small and thin with dark hair and skin like ivory. He thinks about his wife. Maybe he won't find her here after all.

Chris breaks the silence between him and his roommate abruptly with a question that has been burning in his mind for the entire evening but he has been too timid to ask. The alcohol has eliminated any trepidation. Brad has gone back to the bar to retrieve two more pints.

"Were you really friends with Lee Rodgers?"

Brad receives this question as he comes back to the table, gingerly carrying the two pint glasses that are filled to capacity with lager, taking care not to spill any.

"Yeah," he says, while sliding his chair back into the table. He offers no more information.

"Well," Chris says almost cautiously, "did you, you know, know he was a racist?"

Hinckley's face changes from the affable drunk that Chris has been spending the evening with to the same face that Chris has known for the past couple of months: an unfriendly, stern face with the constant ghost of a sneer.

Hinckley nods at his pint glass and then turns to face Chris. His expression causes a return of Chris's inner trembling that occurred every time Brad was in their room. Uncomfortably, Chris drinks his beer and lights a cigarette.

"I didn't know he wasn't." Hinckley takes a cigarette and lights it. He inhales deeply. He makes a face upon tasting the cigarette.

"You like these menthol things?" he asks Chris. "Me, gimme a Marlboro red anytime or give me shit." He violently stomps out the cigarette in the ashtray at the center of the table. This angers Chris. A whole cigarette wasted, and on base, a pack now costs just over a dollar.

This time, Chris goes to the bar and orders two beers. "Two pints of lager," he says with a veteran air, as if he has ordered several pints in several pubs over several years. The bartender snickers at him. He thanks Chris but is otherwise unfriendly and doesn't appear to be too happy, as if life itself is a burden. Chris wonders about the man. How can someone not be happy working in a pub with all the beer and people?

Chris returns to the table, unsuccessful in his attempt to carry the beer without spilling it. His hands are soaked by the time he sets the glasses down, and Brad laughs at him, as his glass is half an inch short of beer.

They sit in silence, smoking cigarettes and staring at the other people in the pub. Everyone else seems to know each other. Although they are spread across several stools and tables and their bodies are facing a variety of ways, the conversations appear to be part of the same one, as though they all arrived together. They talk over and around Brad and Chris, and Chris is envious. He is here with Brad, but he feels the same loneliness. He is not part of the larger group. He doesn't fit in.

"I suppose you think I'm a racist, too, dontcha?" Hinckley asks.

Chris shrugs. He is too afraid to answer truthfully, despite the pleasant effects of the lager. He assumes and somehow knows without being told that Hinckley is a racist, sharing his late friend's sentiments.

The subject of race is one that Chris has never dwelt on, except on his travels to the city of Detroit from his blue-collar suburb just north of the city. Detroit was always a different world to Chris, like crossing a border into another country. Even though it was less than five miles away, every journey into Detroit consisted of locking the doors and rolling up the windows as he drove down streets with names he didn't know past stores with iron bars in front of the windows. There was genuine fear in the vehicle, whether he was riding with his mother or father or a sober version of his brother. He and his friends would infrequently drive into the city early on Friday evenings to buy beer. No one was ever carded, and they assumed the Detroit Police wouldn't care. They were probably too busy bagging dead bodies and chasing drug dealers down boulevards of broken glass. Kids from the suburbs buying beer would be of no consequence. They were always successful in their beer purchases, sometimes frightened and harassed by drunks hanging out in front of the various liquor stores trying to bum cigarettes, money, or a can of beer. They would always quickly oblige the requests and then run away and hop behind the wheel of a parent's car that was borrowed for the evening. They would drive home, to one of their houses if their parents were gone, or to a park (no matter the weather) and sit on the darkest park bench, as far away from the street as possible.

"Well, I'm gonna tell you something," Hinckley continues. "Everybody is a racist, even you."

Chris shakes his head.

"Where did you say you were from?"

"Just outside of Detroit."

"Perfect. Detroit, that's a big city, ain't it?"

Chris nods and softly says, "Yes."

"Probably a lot of black people, ain't there?"

Chris nods again.

"And I bet there's parts of Detroit a little white fellow like yourself don't feel safe in, parts where you don't stop the car for nothin', parts where you keep the doors locked and windows up even in August and the air conditionin' don't work."

Chris recognizes those scenarios, and they do ring true.

"Now," says Brad, "do you drive that way because the people are black or because of the way the area looks? And I bet it looks like hell, too."

Chris shrugs his shoulders. "Probably because the neighborhood is poor—you know, a lot of boarded up buildings."

"Really?" asks Brad with a hint of skepticism. "I want you to think about this next question and answer me honestly. If Detroit was all white, and still looked the way it does, would you be as afraid? Would you still roll up the windows and lock the doors?"

Chris shrugs. The pleasant effects of the alcohol are fading away, being replaced by a subtle headache.

Chris thinks about the question and his mind travels back to drives down Woodward Avenue, that vein that runs from the northern suburbs all the way to downtown Detroit, ending at the Detroit River, the sight of Canada beckoning beyond. The avenue changes considerably as one heads into the city. In the suburbs, Woodward Avenue is lined with restaurants and shopping centers and every kind of business establishment imaginable. In the city, it is quite different; the broad avenue is the home of adult movie theaters, of many boarded up storefronts and houses and apartment buildings, an infinite number of party stores (stores that sell beer and wine and a few groceries at an extremely high markup) and quite a few churches of the fundamental kind. The scenery remains bleak until the Downtown, the skyscrapers and stadiums that project the image of the city. Chris only took a few such journeys in his life, trips to Tiger Stadium with his father in his pre-adolescence years and more recently, the trips to party stores that he made with his friends. "No," he says, staring at one of the lights hanging from the ceiling, slightly swaying from the breeze of human commotion on the floor below. "I wouldn't be as afraid. I never thought about it that way." His thoughts turn to his two friends; he wonders what their lives are like, at college, making new friends, maybe even meeting girls like they talked about over beer on Friday nights. Girls and the future and the places they would go and the things they would do was all they ever talked about, more fluidly after the beer took effect. He misses his friends now that the alcohol is flowing in his blood. His present company is too challenging and not drunk in a happy sort of way at all.

Hinckley breaks Chris's brief reverie. He slaps his open palm loudly on the table, loud enough for the entire pub to turn and briefly stare. "Exactly!" he says. "Ya see, I knew it. Everyone is a racist. Most won't admit it, but everyone is. People like to be with their own kind. Black, white, yellow or red, they stick together. It ain't natural any other way."

Chris had never thought in those terms before, and in this subdued level of consciousness, Hinckley makes a little bit of sense. He hasn't the mental resources or the education to intellectually think of any challenges to Hinckley's generalizations. He assumes what Brad says is true: the races aren't supposed to meet.

"If you look back in time, all the wars and that, they were all fought because of differences in religion or color. Look at Israel. You got those damn Jews who think they run the place and you got the stupid Arabs living among them trying to get rid of them but they're too damn stupid to do any damage to the Jews. They all live together in a small country, and it don't work." Brad searches his memory for more of Crowley's proselytizing remarks. "Try to think of parts of the world where the people live well, where all the streets are clean and there ain't hardly any crime.

"Here," Chris says. "As near as I can tell, they live okay here."

"Yeah," Hinckley says. "These blokes are stupid, but there are hardly any niggers here to mess things up, so yeah, hardly any crime, just ugly women and bad beer. Most of Europe is the same way; the Germans live among Germans, the Scandinavians among the Scandinavians, and they all live well and all live among the white."

"Canada, too," says Chris, recalling the trips through the tunnel under the Detroit River to Windsor, Ontario on the other side. Windsor seemed like a different world compared to Detroit. An urban setting with many pedestrians walking fearlessly, clean streets and buildings standing without abandonment.

"You're god-damn right, Canada, too," agrees Brad, "Canada is too damn cold for anyone but whites to live up there. They don't have the murder the U.S. does, or the ghettoes, or any of that stuff."

Their beers are empty, and Chris can tolerate no more. He gives Brad a one-pound note and Brad goes to the bar and fetches a pint for himself. Hinckley barely seems drunk, Chris thinks. He has a full-blown headache and is feeling queasy. The room tends to spin.

"The only country that works with a mixture of race is South Africa, and that's because there's no question of who is in charge. The whites take no crap from the blacks. There's none of that equal rights bullshit, no Jesse Jackson running around causing trouble. If a black gets out of line in South Africa and doesn't stay in his appointed place, then bam, he either goes to jail or he gets shot, and that's it." Hinckley takes another cigarette from Chris, this time not complaining about the flavor. His own cigarettes are gone.

"I bet if you asked a nigger—or anyone who isn't white— I bet they would rather live amongst themselves, not with whites. You don't have to be white to be a racist. You just have to be human."

Another question burns in Chris's mind, one that he fears he now knows the answer to, in light of Hinckley's current sermonizing.

"But killing, like Rodgers did. Did you know he was killing, shooting people like that just because? That isn't right, is it?"

Brad is silent. He turns his stare back to the table after Chris's last question. He isn't ready to reveal that information just yet, and his conscience is still somewhat troubled by his duplicity in murder, despite his outward callousness.

Hinckley considers his answer carefully. "Hey," he says, "he did what he felt he had to do. I can't judge him for it. I don't know what was in his heart. I know people on base look at me funny, but I'm not responsible for what Lee did. He made his own choices."

Chris is satisfied with his answer. The conversation exhausted, they find a taxi along High Street and go back to base. Chris vows to himself that he will get off base more often now and see what exists outside the fences, beyond the rolling hills.

He collapses onto his rack back in the barracks, as does Hinckley. The room spins for Chris, in part because of the beer, and also because of what the evening has introduced into his mind. He is confused. All he has been told about black and white throughout his childhood has now been tampered with, and he isn't sure what to believe. He has never thought of himself as a racist, but now he is not sure where his heart lies.

The days of inactivity turn to weeks, and the monotony becomes gradually irritating for Father Crowley. He tempers the boredom by drinking wine while sitting next to his turntable enjoying the evenings with the operas of Wagner and Verdi, and when his mood is livelier, the music of Schumann or Beethoven. He averages a bottle of wine a night—South African, no matter what. He saves the empty bottles in cluttered rows on top of his kitchen cabinets, as if they are trophies of conquest. Despite the boredom from a lack of battle, a lack of plotting with his young friend Hinckley, he enjoys the loneliness and the freedom found only in solitude to conduct himself as he wishes. He often sits with his bathrobe open. He looks prayerfully out the window, admiring the leafless elm and oak trees hovering high above the uneven ground still strewn with fallen leaves. He feels the leaves are resting on holy ground, ground defended by Celtic blood, blood once pagan and pure, not diluted by the myth of Christianity. Blood not too different from Nordic blood. White blood. On occasions of inebriated reverence, he will wander outside his front door and kiss the ground through the brown and decaying leaves, the odd passing set of headlights from the main road just catching the faintest glimpse of a portly bath-robed man kneeling in his garden.

Besides Mass and other chapel activities, the weekends offer a return to his old habit of driving around the country, mainly through that swath of coastal land stretching from Edinburgh in the south to Aberdeen in the north.

He shops occasionally, mainly at bookstores in fruitless searches for separatist literature, and most of these trips include stops in pubs. Small pubs, mainly, the type found on the edges of city centers, in the grimier parts of Edinburgh or Dundee, or in the least quaint and affluent of the smaller villages. Pubs surrounded by a sea of dirty gray tenement houses, pubs without windows, pubs without charm. That's where dissent will ferment, he thinks, in the realm of the working poor. Hitler appealed to the lower-class Germans, those who had no hope for the future from the government that led Germany to economic ruin in the years after World War I and prior to Hitler's elevation to Chancellor.

He tries to engage the locals in conversations about race. The fact that he's an American always draws attention. The pubs he frequents are worlds away from the base and even farther from the paths of tourists. The fact that an American is in their midst is always an interest for the Scots who cross his path. He usually starts with a half pint, entering the pub with the claim that he became lost and felt the need for a small drink. He then stands at the bar and stares at the tiny television next to the bartender, or the dart game in progress. He will attempt small talk, which he is somewhat adept at from the years of parishioners sitting in his office presenting him their problems petty or disastrous. After perhaps a quarter of an hour, as the usual questions about America become exhausted, he will exclaim nonchalantly: "What a pleasure it is to enter a saloon and not be surrounded by blacks or Mexicans like I see back home."

That comment usually solicits silence and then the nodding of drunken heads who claim to sympathize with Crowley's dilemma. Aye, they say, no Negroes here, maybe in London, but no Negroes here. Then, without fail, the conversation turns to black American athletes, their size and prowess, and invariably someone mentions Muhammad Ali.

Crowley knows little about sports, and frustrated, he politely takes his leave of whatever pub he is in. On to the next pub, on to the next village.

After about a dozen such trips spread over a month of Sundays and the occasional weeknight, Crowley gives up. He had been hoping for a Scottish member for his Trinity, and perhaps to expand his little group. He realizes he will not find members for his Trinity amongst the Scottish. He will have to settle for Hinckley and whoever the gods put in his path.

He does maintain periodic contact with Hinckley, calling him at work once a week, saying hello, asking him if he's made any friends.

"One, maybe. My roommate," Hinckley tells him. "We went drinking, got along okay. We'll go again. I think he may feel the way we do, but I'm not sure. I didn't want to ask him too much and I didn't want to tell him too much, not yet. I have to be careful, especially about the Lee thing, you know. That can't get out."

"What's his name?"

"Chris, Chris something, starts with an 'F'. New here, from Detroit."

"Fairbanks?" Crowley asks.

"Yeah, that's it."

Crowley recognizes the name belonging to the young man who attended his Mass a few weeks prior, the young man who checked in with him. He was taken by the young man, and he remembers the giddy feeling. That feeling returns upon the memory of Chris's face.

"Excellent," Crowley says. "Excellent."

Crowley's appetite for battle is whetted by a visit in his office one Sunday morning late in March. A young, white female seaman, obviously several months pregnant, arrives in his office with a young, black male seaman who appears to be her boyfriend. Crowley notes there are no rings on either of their hands.

The girl does the talking.

"We want you to baptize the baby," she says, "when it comes, this summer."

Crowley is sickened, but he doesn't show it. He keeps his constant smug grin throughout the conversation. Another dilution of the white race, he thinks. Another mongrel, another cursed child.

"Sure," he says, and asks if they are married.

Embarrassed, the girl softly answers no and looks down at the floor. "We want you to marry us, too—soon, as soon as possible."

"How old are you?" he asks.

"Eighteen," she says, "but he's twenty." The young man nods, looking at the floor, too uncomfortable asking a priest for a favor, fearing that the priest will judge him harshly for having intercourse outside of marriage.

Crowley could care less about that, and would expect no less of him. He feels he deliberately stalked the girl, a white girl, as part of his instinctive drive to conquer the white race and to improve his own.

"Well, I can marry you, but we have to do pre-marriage counseling, you know, things the Church requires, but you don't have time for that." Crowley points to her stomach. "So we can bypass all that and you can be married when you like."

The girl is confused but smiles and thanks Crowley. He invites them to his office during the week to set a date.

"How long have you been in Lutherkirk?" Crowley asks as they rise to leave. He prepares to put on his robe for Mass.

"Six months, both of us," the girl says.

He says nothing as the two walk away. He sees them in the pews during Mass. He watches them sit listlessly during the entire service, neither one paying attention during his homily. He speaks about being true to your beliefs and not being hypocritical.

The sight of the mixed couple sickens him, and he follows his own advice. The battle must be resumed; the enemy has quickened its pace. Scotland must be liberated, and if Scotland can be liberated, the rest of the white world will see Scotland's example and the other whites will follow suit and arm themselves and repatriate the lesser races to their ancestral homelands. They will return to the impoverished Africa, the crowded Asia, and the miserable Eastern Europe.

That night he has a dream, a wine induced dream. He is met by the god he recognizes as Odin, his image occupying the entire sky above the base as it might appear on a sunny spring afternoon. He recognizes the long white beard, the thin and narrow and wizened face, the tall and wide brimmed hat pulled far enough down to cover his missing eye, his one remaining eye shining brighter than the sun.

Odin does not speak to Crowley in this dream, but this god of war, this god of death, this god of poetry and wisdom, draws Crowley a picture in the clouds. He draws an image of the Star of David with his long and crooked finger, and then blows it away with a mighty breath. He then draws a picture of a cross, and over the cross, he draws another picture of the Star of David. With a breath, he lights both on fire, and they burn slowly as the clouds turn to smoke and the entire sky turns black save Odin's one eye, shining above all.

Crowley gets the message.

He awakes in a sweat. Odin is the Norse god of warriors and kings, not of the common man, and this reaffirms Crowley's sense of self-importance. Odin doesn't appear to just anyone. He has been chosen by this call from Valhalla, and he knows he is blessed and what he believes in is right. The Jews must be dealt with; they too must be driven from Scotland, and then the rest of the West will follow Scotland's example. The blacks are far inferior to the Jews, he thinks, and if the Jews go, the blacks will leave of their own accord. The blacks do the Jews' bidding, do the grueling tasks to upset the good white sense of security.

The cross signifies something else, something he has believed for the longest time but never seriously until Odin reminded him: Christianity is a fictitious religion started by the Jews to ensure their grip on Israel, to remain the chosen people in a competing religion that they somehow knew would grip Europe. Jews wrote the Bible, they created Jesus and St. Paul, they created the Beatitudes, they created the cross. Lies, all lies. Odin told him so. His heart has long felt this, but now he is sure.

This confirmed belief angers him. He has spent a good chunk of his life in service of this myth, of this false religion led by a figure who has never existed. He is glad he has found the one true religion that belongs to his race.

He lies awake in bed, thinking of a course of action. His gun is gone, and this cripples him somewhat.

An idea forms in his brain and his mouth draws slowly into a smile. There is a way to deal with the Jews. He can picture it clearly.

Hinckley needs to bring Fairbanks into the picture—and soon. He will help Brad in that endeavor.

He realizes that he has just over two years of duty remaining in Scotland, and precious little time to waste.

Chris and Hinckley do not become the closest of friends, yet Hinckley's overture of friendship has made Chris feel more comfortable in the room. They do occasionally dine in the galley together when their schedules coincide.

As they eat, Chris can't help but be aware of the loathsome glances cast in Hinckley's direction. The less disparaging looks are given by the lower enlisted and even more hateful are the stares from the chiefs and officers. They look at Chris, too, and assume he must be trouble for dining with such a pathetic creature as Hinckley.

Chris is conscious of those stares. They make him feel awkward, but he would rather feel awkward this way, dining with a friend, instead of eating alone.

A few weeks after the night out in Brechin, they venture to Aberdeen in search of American fast-food restaurants, in search of pubs, in search of beer.

There is still some daylight as they summon a taxi and venture north with the sun receding in the west and the moon starting its ascent in a relatively clear but leaden sky over the North Sea. Chris stares out the window and is quite glad to be seeing things again, to be venturing outside of the base, which is like a stifling and miniature America, save the British cars, the direction of the traffic, and the lack of rock and roll stations, which Chris is starting to miss. That may be the only thing of America that he misses; there is no other memory tugging at his heart.

Chris hadn't seen the center of Aberdeen, its elegant downtown a mixture of low and old granite buildings intermixed with modern semi-high rises along the River Dee.

The people, too, look different, different than they did that evening in Brechin. Chris can't pinpoint the difference, but there is a certain provincial air in the countryside and the villages surrounding the base that is neutralized by the oil-wealthy city of Aberdeen.

Chris and Hinckley eat pizza at a Pizza Hut and expect the pizza to taste as it would at home, but it doesn't. It is more bland, less doughy, and disappointing. They proceed to a pub, a more modern one frequented by younger, more affluent Scots, and Chris and Hinckley are even more out of place than they were in Brechin.

After a pint, Hinckley starts rattling about race. Chris had almost forgotten their conversation from a few weeks prior; on base, Hinckley had never brought the subject up again, not even in the privacy of their room. They talked mostly about trivial things, Hinckley asking Chris which sports teams he follows and what his favorite sport is.

It's as if there are two Hinckleys: one a simple boy from Nebraska and one a drunken, hell-bent racist.

Chris is not a huge sports fan, but he glances at the Detroit teams' standings in the back of the *Stars and Stripes*. His favorite sport is baseball, the season still remote, even though spring is about to dawn.

Hinckley scoffs at Chris's comments and lauds Nebraska football and, to a lesser degree, Nebraska basketball. He doesn't care for professional sports, as there are no teams in Omaha. He doesn't mind watching the Kansas City Royals on the summer nights, but nothing compares to Nebraska football.

They even occasionally venture to the club during the week, opting to eat there instead of the galley. Hinckley used to go there nightly with Rodgers, drinking until closing time, but not anymore. He had stopped going there altogether after Rodgers's suicide, too nervous to go there alone, too uncomfortable under the stares and whispers. Now that Chris is his companion, the stares and whispers aren't as bothersome, and they are starting to subside. Still, no one on the base is especially pleasant towards him.

Chris is a little too quiet for Hinckley's liking, so he has been looking forward to the opportunity to travel off base with him and get some beers down his throat, to get him leaning more towards his way.

Father Crowley has called him. Crowley needs him and Chris, needs them for battle.

"I want you to bring him out here. Give whatever reason you wish. We have to introduce him slowly; we don't want him to shy away from us—and we don't want him to talk about us. Tell him you come here for comfort, as a place to get away from all your problems. Call it Bible study."

Hinckley, like Crowley, is growing bored. He doesn't really like Chris; he prefers his company to be more abrasive, somewhat like himself. But they need a third to make their Trinity complete.

Hinckley, too, is ready to do battle, to carry the white man's burden. He misses the company of Crowley and the thrill of war. He misses the flattery that the priest lavishes upon him.

The night in Aberdeen is uneventful except that they do manage to get drunk in the pub in front of a television screen displaying a soccer match.

In between comments about the superiority of the white race, Hinckley exclaims that soccer is the most boring sport in the world.

Chris somewhat agrees, but he admires the zeal the patrons of the pub display in regard to the game. He notices their intense concentration, their boisterous exclamations when a shot on goal is attempted, and their constant, seemingly intelligent observations of the game.

"All they do is run around the field and try to kick the damn ball," Hinckley says. "There ain't no strategy, not like football. Just a bunch of damn little blokes running around trying to kick the ball. Hell, there ain't no tackling or anything, and these bloke fellers get all worked up over a bunch of men running around in shorts. I hate this country. It's white, but I hate it."

They return to the base as the pub begins to empty. The sky is unusually clear and the northern night is thick with stars. Chris stares straight up while waiting for a taxi to pass by, noticing constellations that he never saw before in the perpetually hazy suburban sky of his youth. Hinckley knows the stars; he saw them so many times over the Nebraska prairie. He thinks Chris is odd, odder than he thought before.

Chris had ignored Hinckley's diatribe on race and the inferiority of Scotland. He expected Chris to go along with what he said, to agree with him, to show enthusiasm. All

Chris did was stare at the people in the pub, watch the soccer match, drink beer, and smoke cigarettes.

Brad realizes that he misses Lee, someone apt to follow
his lead. But Crowley needs a third and no other candidates
have presented themselves, and he noticed that Chris was
friendless, not unlike himself.

A Sunday morning comes, a hangover laden Sunday after Chris's night in Aberdeen. He manages to rise early, and he awakes to the sound of Brad snoring in his rack, asleep on top of the sheets and still fully clothed. He is curled up in a sort of fetal position, with his back to Chris, and through the darkened room Chris can see the paleness of Brad's lower back and the top of his fleshy buttocks as his pants sag beneath his waist.

Chris turns away and decides to leave the room and start the day. He showers, gets dressed as neatly as he can in his constant gray jeans, white shirt, and high-top sneakers. He enters the galley as it opens and, despite his queasiness, eats a large breakfast consisting of an omelet with ham and cheese and onions and green peppers, hash browns smothered in ketchup, and a Coke. He dines alone, but as it is Sunday and the galley is nearly empty, this doesn't bother him. He doesn't feel as conspicuous.

He eats slowly and thoughtfully and decides to go to church, to Father Crowley's nine o'clock Mass. He enjoyed it his previous visit, liked the peacefulness of it, and he thinks Father Crowley must be a very nice man.

And there must be something more to this life than drinking beer and waiting for a girl to come along.

He arrives at the chapel a few minutes before nine. He smokes a cigarette outside, shivering because he forgot his coat. Only a handful of people approach the chapel. The pews are even emptier than they were during his previous visit, so empty that the tape recorder playing organ music echoes off the low ceiling. There may be fifteen people in the church. Chris sits in the darkest pew in the back.

Crowley enters, and at first Chris thinks he looks irritated, but his face brightens as he stands behind the podium that serves as an altar. He sees Chris and smiles, and his gaze doesn't leave him.

"In the name of the Father, and of the Son, and of the Holy Spirit," Crowley begins, and the congregation responds by crossing themselves. Chris does this in imitation.

The service is brief, a few hymns sung along with the tape recorder, Crowley's voice rising above the collective voices of the congregation. Chris sings very softly, almost only mouthing the words.

It is the season of Lent, and that is what Crowley's homily pertains to. He talks quickly about sacrifice and the importance of giving up the things that interfere with what you believe in. He doesn't mention Jesus; he doesn't mention the great sacrifice that is the cornerstone of Lent and the upcoming Easter holiday. He talks vaguely about personal belief and the strength that comes from discipline in that belief. He then dispenses with the Eucharist. After just half an hour, the Mass is over.

Crowley is waiting by the door as Chris leaves, and he invites him into his office. Uncomfortable for being singled out, Chris obliges.

Crowley pulls off his robe as he and Chris enter the office. He is dressed casually but neatly underneath, corduroy pants with a burgundy hue, and a yellow long-sleeved collared shirt. He retrieves a burgundy cardigan from the closet after discarding his robe.

Crowley sits at his desk and indicates the other chair. Chris takes the chair. He looks at everything in the room except for Father Crowley.

Crowley props his feet up on his desk, and this casual gesture puts Chris more at ease.

He wonders what the priest wants, and he half expects him to say he doesn't want Chris to attend service unless he's a serious Catholic.

"Well, well," Crowley begins. "I am surprised to see you here—especially twice."

Chris shrugs his shoulders.

"Usually, young single men aren't exactly the churchgoing type. Do you know what I mean?"

Again, Chris shrugs his shoulders.

"If I had to guess, I would say that people like you come to church because they were brought up that way, and they come out of habit or obligation. I know this isn't the case with you. Or they come because they're looking for something, some answer to the deep mysteries of life, some alleviation from a kind of pain, or some redemption to soothe a guilty conscience."

He pauses, takes a bottle of wine from one of his desk drawers, and pours it into a dirty coffee mug on top of his desk.

Chris is shocked but also impressed in a way. An officer, a figure of authority, who drinks. Very cool, he thinks, very cool.

"I always celebrate a Mass that goes off without a hitch with a bit of the blood of Christ. If I had another cup, I would offer you some, but I don't. If you really want some, you can drink out of the bottle."

Chris declines politely with a shake of his head.

Crowley does not take the wine in celebration. If Chris were able to keep his gaze from the floor or the ceiling, he would see the priest's hands trembling, and trails of sweat running down his forehead. Chris somehow sends the priest's heart racing. There is something attractive in the innocent look on Chris's face, his air of no worldly experience, and this bothers Crowley. He drinks to deny the emotion, to kill the nerves.

Additionally, he wants Chris as the third member of his Trinity, and he wants him to be sold on his personality unequivocally.

Crowley empties half his cupful of wine and wipes his mouth with his sleeve. "People such as you come to church for one of those reasons that I described. And I would say—most assuredly, as I have studied your face—that you come for fulfillment. Life isn't leading you where you want to go, and you think there should be something more, something that maybe only God in heaven can offer. Am I right?"

"Maybe," Chris says, having to clear his throat from the minutes of silence.

"So I thought, so I thought," Crowley says warmly but triumphantly. "What, may I ask, are you looking for? What of this life do you feel that you have missed? What hasn't been put upon your plate? I have answers, my good young man. I have answers to some of the great questions of life. Ask, ask away!" Upon this last statement, Crowley pounds his open palm on the top of his desk, hard and loud, so loud that Chris slightly jumps, so hard that Crowley's hand rings.

Those questions stir so much emotion in Chris. What does he want out of life? What does he feel he's missed? Images of his mother and father and brother and lonely days on playgrounds and classrooms and cafeterias dance and twirl in his brain.

He starts to cry.

"I don't know," he says, trying to turn his head in a way so that the priest doesn't see his tears, but Crowley does, and the sight of tears rolling down Chris's pale and pimply cheeks endears him to the young man even more.

Father Crowley is no stranger to tears, and he is not uncomfortable in their presence. The years of dealing with parishioners' trauma have left the sight of tears and raw emotion as mundane an event as the brushing of teeth. Wisely and tenderly, he pats Chris on the back. "There, there. I didn't mean to hit a nerve. Please, I insist, take a swallow of wine." And Chris, doing anything to distract from his tears, takes the bottle and swallows vigorously, emptying almost a third of the nearly full bottle. The wine works almost instantly; his body starts to feel warm inside, and the effects of last night's lager drinking start to subside.

Chris wipes his eyes and his nose with his shirtsleeve. Crowley puts his hand on his shoulder.

"You know, I've heard it said that tears are merely poison leaving the body, so you should feel much better. Cry more if you like."

Chris shakes his head and he composes himself. Embarrassed, he again wipes his eyes and his nose with his sleeve. "I don't know why I did that."

"Well, you're obviously looking for something. There is an emptiness in your heart that causes you pain. However," Crowley continues, "I don't think you will find fulfillment inside the stuffy confines of the Church. You'll learn some songs and some prayers, but I'm afraid, my dear son, that there are no answers here that will satisfy your longings."

Chris is shocked, and the look he gives the priest indicates as much.

"I know, I know, not the sort of answer that you expect to hear from a priest, not the rah-rah line that other men of faith live by and answer everything with. We live in an imperfect world, my young friend. This is an imperfect Church, and I am truly an imperfect man. The Church leaves me with many unanswered questions, and I know you won't find what you're looking for here."

"I'm not even sure what I'm looking for." Chris stares at the bottle of wine in hope of an invitation to drink some more. "I guess I came because you were nicer to me than anyone else when I checked in to the base. I was curious, mainly, and I have nothing else to do here. I have no friends and I've been too afraid to leave the base very much, though I want to. I want to travel, see Europe, the rest of Scotland, London, maybe. I don't know if I'm looking for anything particularly. I believe in God, I just don't know much about him."

"Your answer tells me exactly what you're looking for."

"It does?"

Crowley pours another glass of wine and offers Chris the bottle. Chris takes a drink and waits for the priest's answer.

"You are looking for the same thing that every intelligent man has been seeking since the dawn of time. You are looking for peace."

"Peace?" Chris asks, thinking of the word only in the context of international relations or the absence of war.

"Peace of mind, a comforted heart, a clear conscience. Contentment. Satisfaction. You need to know that your life is on the right path, that what you are doing is worthwhile. You need to be loved, and you need to love someone back. That is peace. A calmness in your heart that prevails no matter what calamity befalls you. And peace can only be brought by faith, not by a church, not by a book, not by a set of rules."

Chris can identify with what Crowley tells him. Peace. He has never thought of his life in relationship to his personal contentment. It seemed more like a long and hopeful journey, with hopes of love and experience awaiting him. He never thought about why he wanted love, or why he wanted experience. He now realizes by Crowley's illumination that it is all a subconscious distraction to his one true aim. Peace.

Chris nods, his mind and his outlook on life much different than it was just an instant before. "Maybe," he says, "but if I can't find the answers in church, where should I go?"

"Most people in your predicament attend church for

weeks or months or even years spanning the rest of their lives. They sing the songs and pray the prayers and participate in all the sacraments and they still long for more. So they find other avenues: they drink, they gossip, they overeat, they cheat on their spouses, or whatever. The Church simply misses the mark. Fortunately for you, I am an expert on this matter. As a priest, I too felt the need for peace. The Church wasn't providing my soul the sustenance it so dearly craved. So I too went seeking."

"But you're still a priest?" Chris asks, somewhat confused by Crowley's repudiation of the Catholic Church.

"Yes, yes, I'm still a priest. I still sing the songs and pray the prayers and perform the sacraments. It's what I do. I'm not exactly employable in any other profession. There are worse things to do, and the answers I have found sort of lend themselves to the priestly life."

"What have you found?"

"I turned to history. Everything you need is already written and foretold in the history of the world. These things I will tell you in due time. I have a sort of informal study at my home on Friday or Saturday nights. When might you be off one of those nights? We tend to talk for hours—and I like to drink—so it is best if you don't have to work the next day, either."

Chris runs his upcoming schedule through his brain. It will be several weeks before he has another weekend off.

"I can't," Chris says, "not for another two weeks."

"We'll make it a date, then." Crowley writes the date down on a piece of paper inside a cluttered desk drawer. "Please, continue to come to church. I would like to see you." He says this affectionately. Chris notices the softer tone of his voice, and this makes him feel at ease.

Chris stands. "I will." They shake hands. Chris leaves and Crowley empties the bottle of wine completely, this time not bothering with the triviality of using a glass. He feels very satisfied, very hopeful. He has accomplished in a matter of moments what Hinckley has not yet accomplished after being friends with Chris for over a month, after living in the same room with him for a quarter of a year.

He closes his eyes. He enters a daydream that involves much smoke in the sky and fire on the ground. Out of the fire, he rises like a giant white phoenix.

The next set of day-watches is busy, and Chris and Karen barely have time speak to one another. The day staff is busy scurrying about the operations floor and the printers are spewing messages incessantly and Chris types so much and so fast that his fingers hurt and his wrists start to cramp.

He has things he wants to talk to Karen about, as there is no one else he can talk to. He wants to talk about Hinckley. He wants to talk about his conversation with Father Crowley.

He is anxious about both potential friendships. He knows Hinckley is a drunk racist, but he seems friendly enough. No one else has been. He is afraid that if he digs into his life too deeply he will find that he had some participation in the acts that Rodgers committed. He doesn't want to know; he wants to maintain the status quo.

As for Crowley, it isn't common for an officer to befriend an enlisted man. In fact, it is discouraged if not forbidden. Even though he is still a novice in the Navy, he has heard the term 'fraternization' bantered about. Seeing Crowley socially probably would fall under that category.

He needs reassurance from a neutral party, someone to tell him the friends he's chosen are okay, even though his heart makes him wonder.

The mid-watches finally come and there in the darkened quiet and the relaxed solitude that comes from being in a room alone with someone for several hours at a time, Chris tries to reveal to Karen, slowly and innocently, the things that he's done, the places he's been, and the friends he has started to make.

He approaches first the subject of religion. He tells her that he's been going to church.

He tells her this in the first hour of their watch, her nose already buried into a book, and she looks up at him with a curious glance. "Why?" His statement comes entirely from left field; he has never mentioned religion before, and they have never discussed anything philosophical or lofty.

"I'm not sure," he replies. "I guess I want to see what God is about. I want to see what the big deal is, but I'm not really sure."

She gives a slight smile, charmed by his innocent curiosity. "And did you find Him? Do you know more about Him than you did before?"

"No," he says, looking down at his feet underneath the table they share as a sort of desk. "I sang songs and repeated prayers, but none of it made any sense to me." He returns his gaze above the table and stares at her without looking in her eyes. "Do you ever go to church?" He asks this question in another attempt to unravel the mystery of his supervisor, to find a detail about her life that he has been forbidden to learn.

Her faint smile disappears. "I used to go to church," she replies. "Years ago."

"Why did you stop?"

"Because," she says in a way that is meant to end the discussion, and she returns to her book.

Chris persists in a fashion unusual to him. He wants to know why she quit going to church. He poses a question in the same forthright manner a young child would. "Because why?"

She looks up from her book, her mouth closed as small and tightly as possible, her forehead wrinkled in a frown. She lets out a deep breath. "I became angry at God."

This statement intrigues him even more. "Why?"

She is starting to surrender. She even puts her book down. "Because he took something very important away from me."

"Oh." The tone of her voice lends itself to no more questions. Her face looks even sadder than usual, and he senses that her constant listlessness has something to do with whatever God has taken from her.

He changes the subject. He tells her of the pub he went to in Brechin and the pub in Aberdeen. He asks her if she knows where the pub in Brechin is.

"No," she says. "I only live in Brechin. If I have the time or money, I'm usually gone."

This surprises him. He has always pictured Karen as a sort of homebody, someone who never ventures outdoors unless it's absolutely necessary. He pictured her in some small two-room flat above a store with a sparsely furnished sitting room with a few trappings of femininity: the odd potted plant, a vase of flowers in the middle of the coffee table surrounded by magazines, and bright pictures on the wall. He sees her sitting on the couch, her nose in a book, just as it is on this night. He sees her alone, wrapped in silence.

"Where do you go?"

"It depends," she says. "It depends on how much time I have or how much money. Even though I get an extra allowance for living off base, it doesn't go as far as you think. I have to pay rent every month and I have to buy groceries. In between the days and mids, I may find a castle nearby that I haven't seen. I love castles. On the longer breaks, after the mids, I may spend a day or two in Edinburgh, or Newcastle or Glasgow, and sometimes I just get in my car and drive, and I see where I wind up."

She does what Chris had hoped to do before he arrived in Scotland, what he had hoped to do before joining the Navy, and he is jealous.

She continues. "You won't see the country from a barstool. You won't get a feel of the people or the land in the bottom of a glass of beer. If you want to sit in a pub, you might as well be back home. Alcohol is the same in the States as it is here."

"You don't drink?" Chris asks, assuming everyone drinks.

"No." She makes a face as if the thought of drinking makes her nauseous. "I think alcohol is a sign of weakness. I think it ruins lives." She gets a far-away look in her eyes. "I know it ruins lives." She returns her glance back to her book.

"Oh," says Chris. "I never thought of drinking that way."

"Well," she says, "you're young and naïve. You're apt to do what those your age tend to do. But do yourself a favor—go out and see what you can. Before you know it, your time here will be up and you probably will never return. Life won't present this opportunity again." She puts her book facedown on the table, spread open to mark her place. "Life is relentless," she continues. "If you don't take care of the moment, it doesn't return, and time keeps moving. We grow older and start to recall the past with regret. Don't let that happen to you."

He nods his head.

"In fact," she says, "on these next days off, I'll take you somewhere. You can chip in for gas and we'll find a castle, maybe a city. Edinburgh for the day wouldn't be bad. I haven't gone to Inverness yet, been meaning to. I don't know. We'll see what the day brings."

Chris is excited. "Really? You'll hang out with me?"

She smiles, albeit slightly.

"Sure," she says, returning to her book. The conversation ceases until the next night, the next mid-watch, when they decide where to go.

Dear Wife,

I have been in Scotland now for almost three months and at first I was disappointed, all I did was sit around the barracks or go to work and I wouldn't leave the base. I couldn't and didn't make any friends. Do you have a lot of friends? I never have (I think I told you that already). I don't know why. I'm not a jerk. My brother has a lot of friends—he used to anyway—and he's a jerk. He borrows money without paying it back, he says mean things and he uses people. Still, he has a lot of friends. The most popular kids in school were usually the most obnoxious. I don't get it. I try to be nice.

Anyway, I'm starting to do more things now. I've been hanging out with my roommate more. He was mean to me at first, kind of inconsiderate. He doesn't seem to have many friends either. He had one friend, but he killed himself. A complicated story that I don't like to think about too much. I may explain later.

I have gone to church a couple of times. I've gone to the Catholic Mass here on base. I was baptized Catholic but we never really went to church as a family. There is a lot I don't understand. I don't know if I'm going to church to find God or to maybe meet friends. I may find you there, but I don't know.

I try to pray, I hear that's important, but I don't know how you're supposed to do it. I think you just close your eyes and talk to God in your brain, tell him what you need. But doesn't He already know everything?

The priest after Mass talked to me, trying to find out what I was doing there. He's very nice, as nice as anyone has been to me here. I trust him. He told me church wasn't for everybody, and to basically not take it so seriously. Very confusing. If a priest doubts what he's teaching then there must be something wrong. Maybe there is no God. They didn't teach religion in my school, but I think they should have. This world doesn't always make sense to me.

I'm going on a trip with my supervisor. She is going to show me some castles. I didn't know there really were castles. I thought they were just from fairy tales or the movies. She says there are a lot of them. All over the country. She too is nice, but she doesn't always seem that way. She is very quiet and doesn't always talk, so I don't know if she is angry with me, or just sad. She seems sad, like something terrible has happened to her that she can't get over. She's older, I think she said she was in her early thirties, and she used to be a teacher, a history teacher. Why would someone who was once a teacher become an enlisted person in the Navy? I would think maybe an officer, but not enlisted. It doesn't add up. Maybe I will write more later, but I haven't had much to write about, just hanging out in my room and going to work. Work is pretty cool, but sometimes there is nothing to do and it can be real boring. It's classified, what I do, so I can't really tell you. The communists might see this, you know, the Russians. If I tell anyone what I do that doesn't have a clearance I go to military prison. They say it is in Leavenworth, Kansas. I want to travel but Kansas is one place I don't want to see.

One more thing I want to tell you about me. I read a lot. Horror and war stories mostly, anything to take me away. Do you read? I imagine if you're going to be married to me than you probably do. But if you don't then that's okay too.

Take care, and until we meet.

Chris

Chris and Karen agree to meet outside the base gate early in the afternoon following their last mid-watch. The passing of the hours of the morning gives them enough time for minimal sleep without wasting the day.

The day is unusually warm and the sky is a cloudless and brilliant blue as Chris waits outside the gate minus his coat, smoking a cigarette with his pale face turned towards the sky, his skin absorbing the warmth of the sun.

Karen pulls up in her car that he has already seen parked outside of their work site, a late 1970s Austin Mini, brown body, beige top. The car itself is no taller than the base of Chris's sternum. He gets in, surprised at how low to the ground he is sitting, as if his rear-end will feel every bump in the road.

He doesn't recognize Karen at first and he is shocked at her appearance. He has only seen her in the dungaree uniform, her thin body continually clad in denim and hidden underneath her blue working jacket. Her long hair has also always been put up into a sort of bun to keep it above her collar in accordance with Navy regulations.

Today she is wearing blue jeans that are slightly fashionable and an argyle sweater, fitting her figure much better than her uniform. Her hair is also down, and she is wearing just a hint of makeup.

Chris sees her as an entirely different person, and despite the difference in years, he finds her attractive. He is as attracted to her as he has been to anyone else in his life.

Still, he sees that same trace of sadness written in her eyes, as if nothing in this world can make her truly happy.

She says hello without taking her eyes off the road. It is Chris's first time in the front seat of a car for quite some time, and the view is quite different from that of the back seat of a taxicab. The road is spread out before him. They head south on the A92.

"I thought we'd see Arbroath Abbey first," she says. "It's close and cheap and there is a bit of history there, fairly important in relation to Scotland."

They drive in silence. Chris studies the nearby hills and sporadic trees aching to return to the color of green. The same hint and smell of spring that he encountered in the Michigan air is present here. He can feel the world trying to awaken upon the conclusion of the dark winter. Far away, just before the horizon to the west, the higher hills still have a smattering of white on top.

Arbroath is perhaps a twenty-minute drive along a mostly empty highway save the occasional farmhouse or cottage along the road. Chris again looks longingly at the North Sea. Despite the warmth in the air, the sea itself looks very cold.

They arrive in Arbroath, a town not much different in size from Brechin. Karen navigates the narrow streets through the city center confidently and they arrive at the abbey.

It is an enormous and majestic ruin. Chris learns that it was founded in 1178 by King William the Lion. He can't comprehend an age so far back; his knowledge and imagination cannot perceive the breadth of the elapsed years.

They walk through the grounds, past the walls that are mostly intact, though the roof has long since decayed. Karen speaks indirectly, as if to a classroom, though Chris is her lone listener.

"This abbey," she says, walking along a wall, her index finger casually grazing it, "is a significant part of Scottish history. The Scots then—almost as they are now—were subject to English rule. Early in the fourteenth century, Robert the Bruce secured Scotland's independence with a series of victories over the English, but the English king, Edward II, still claimed Scotland as part of his kingdom. The pope then had jurisdiction over all such matters in the Christian world and summoned Bruce to Avignon. Bruce ignored the pope and around 1320, a group of nobles signed a letter and sent it to the pope, stating that they would never again be subject to the dominion of the English. That, of course, changed."

Chris understands very little of what she says, though he does learn more of the distinction between the English and the Scottish, realizing that they are indeed two separate nations, not like different states in America.

They drive south again.

Chris asks Karen questions about the country, about the things she's seen. He notices that her mood is as light as it has ever been since he's known her. She almost seems happy driving through the countryside, briefly illustrating the history of the Arbroath Abbey.

"Do you like it?" he asks while lighting a cigarette and cracking the window and enjoying the novelty of being a passenger in what would be the driver's side of an American car. "Do you like it here in Scotland?"

"Yes," she replies, "as well as anyplace I've been stationed."

He knows she has been in the service for almost six years and has never thought to ask her where she's been. Now he does.

"The first place I went to was Guam. The weather was good, but you can only travel so far on an island, and only see the sights so many times. I'm not big on beaches, anyway, you know, laying around and trying to get tan, never my thing. The next place I went to was Adak, Alaska. Miserable, and thank god it was only a year and a half. It's this little tiny island at the end of the Aleutian Islands that is treeless and windswept and as bleak as the moon. I read a lot there, took some college correspondence courses, but quit. That part of my life is over. I know I won't teach again..." And on this last statement, her voice trails off and the trace of happiness she just recently displayed starts to fade.

"After Alaska," she continues, "it was time to re-enlist or separate. My four years were up. The Navy offered me my choice of duty stations, so I looked on a map and my eye caught the British Isles. I asked if there were any bases in this country and I was given quite a list, more extensive than I imagined. All the way from the northern tip of Scotland to the shores of the English Channel. Even though I wasn't happy in Adak—it was the longest eighteen months of my life—the possibility of going back to Maryland was even more disturbing. So I re-enlisted, with the condition of being stationed somewhere in the United Kingdom. So here I am." The faint smile again returns.

They approach the city of Dundee, coming in along East Dock Street, past the cargo ships alongside mighty docks, the tenement towers rising in the distance. Chris is excited at the sight of a city. But they don't stop; they circumnavigate the city center and continue southward. Chris is burning with curiosity. What was so terrible in Maryland? He is still too unfamiliar with her to ask, sensing that if she wants him to know the privileged details of her life, she will tell him.

The afternoon starts to recede as Chris glances at Dundee in the rearview mirror.

"Where are we going?" he asks, starting to feel very far away from the base, though they are still less than fifty miles away.

"I don't know," she says. "I'm just driving. It's kind of nice not driving alone for a change." She too lights a cigarette and the drive continues. They approach the town of St. Andrews and park in front of large and ancient and luxurious building with a vast beach leading to the North Sea behind it. Chris can make out a golf course surrounding the building, a dull green and bleak and treeless golf course. Even the low grass seems to perpetually bend in the wind.

They get out of the car and stand shivering in the wind, the day much cooler now than it was when they started. "Do you golf?" Karen asks Chris.

"No, I never have." Golf is a sport Chris has given little thought. He has always thought it to be the province of the rich. No one in his family has ever played golf.

"Well," Karen relates with a little tinge of disappointment, "this is where it started." And she sweeps the golf course with her hand.

"Really?" Chris says with an equal tinge of interest. This is a bit of history he can understand, standing in the birthplace of a sport.

"But if you don't golf, then there is very little to appreciate." She climbs back in the car and they drive up a hill leading into the center of St. Andrews, a picturesque university town, the main street laid in stone, the older and ornate gray buildings well maintained and warm looking.

They find a Chinese restaurant. Karen tells Chris that most of the fast food to be found in this country is either from Chinese restaurants or kebob houses run by families from the Middle East. Chris is surprised to learn of the foreign presences in Scotland. He assumed only America was a country of immigrants. He thought the rest of the world consisted of its own ethnic enclaves: Italy only home to Italians, Russia home to only Russians, Japan strictly Japanese.

He tells Karen of his surprise upon finding a Chinese restaurant, especially with employees that appear to be solely Chinese.

"The Chinese are across the world—Europe, North and South America. The world is smaller than you think."

Chris orders a Szechuan meal, chicken and rice, and Karen eats something similar. It is spicy, spicier than the carryout storefront Chinese restaurants of his childhood in suburban Detroit. He drinks glass after glass of water and orders soda, the Coca-Cola cans much smaller than those in the States. The can fits neatly in the palm of his hand. The daylight still persists as they leave the restaurant, an almost fancy establishment with cloth napkins, the tables pre-set with gleaming silverware and crystal glasses.

Chris still needs to see a castle. The solution is easy; Lutherkirk supports such a structure. They head north back to the base and Chris feels fulfilled somehow, the day being wrought with experience and a sort of friendship that he didn't expect and Karen taking on a less gloomy countenance than he expected.

Still, her past, her personality, remains a mystery. The conversation they have as the Austin Mini points north centers on their common workplace, the idiosyncrasies of the chief and the ensign, their poor leadership, the disorder of the message center, the permissible laziness of the other watch members, who constantly leave piles of messages for Chris and Karen to sort and deliver, even after the most quiet mid-watch. Their complaints are common, no different from any other insubordinate in a situation that can't help but be bureaucratic.

As the signs loom on the A92 indicating that the village of Lutherkirk is near, Chris asks Karen a simple question. "Why did you join the Navy?"

She is silent for more than a moment. Lighting a cigarette, she answers, "I was married, once upon a time, and then, all of a sudden, I wasn't. I hated my job, I had no special place in my heart for the state of Maryland, nor was I especially close to my family or my former husband's family. I saw an ad in the back of a magazine. It was a glossy sort of ad, you know, an aircraft carrier steaming off into the sunset, a Mediterranean port with whitewashed quaint buildings in the background. I thought 'Why not?' I love to travel, I love a challenge, so why not? Of course, they wanted to make me an officer, suggesting that the enlisted life is somewhat sub-par to that of an officer, but I would have had to wait for an opening at Officer Candidate School. I didn't want to wait. I wanted to go right then or not go at all. So I signed the same stack of papers that you did, took the oath, and away I went. It was less than a week between my first visit to the recruiter's office and my trip to Orlando."

They turn off the main highway and travel on a secondary road that forks, one fork leading to the base and the other going to the village of Lutherkirk. The road is unmarked and shrouded in trees. Karen turns her headlights on as the dusk becomes even more imminent on this road that is always in the shadow of trees.

Despite being only a few miles away, it is Chris's first visit to the village that the base is named after and is inexorably linked with.

Karen continues her thumbnail sketch of her entrance to the Navy, which leaves Chris craving more information.

"At first," she says while exhaling a cloud of blue cigarette smoke that splashes against the windshield of the Mini, "I regretted my decision. Boot camp was not fun, as you know. The barracks stank with the scent of women. Having been married, I know that an unhygienic woman smells more than a sweaty man. Hopefully you will never have to endure that smell, but take my word for it, it's bad." She draws on her cigarette and Chris studies her lips adorned with lipstick that he has never noticed before, her eyes squinting shut as the smoke enters her lungs. "I had never been thrust into the midst of so many different types of people. I expected something like college, more like a dorm, you know? But college put me with girls like me, girls who grew up the same way I did. But boot camp, they came from all over, and I realized more fully than any cross-country trip had ever taught me how vast and different our country is from state to state and region to region. After the shock wore off, I stopped looking down my nose at everyone and decided to fit in as quietly as

I could. I made a few friends, girls I smoked with outside when the smoking lamp was lit, but I chose to remain somewhat anonymous. It was hard. I was older than everyone else in my company, and the company commander kind of singled me out. She probably wasn't much older than me, a first-class boatswain's mate, and she looked it. She was tough. She was from New England somewhere, I think, because of her accent, probably Boston. She hated me. She knew I went to college and I think she resented me, figuring I was a loser for joining the Navy relatively late in my life, as if I couldn't handle it in the outside world. Which is somewhat true."

"What happened, if I can ask, to your husband?"

She doesn't answer. The car pulls in front of Lutherkirk Castle, a well-kept ruin, the courtyard adorned with manicured hedges, the face of the castle lit with floodlights as the twilight approaches.

"I don't know much about this castle. It's always been a little too close to home to be interesting to me, maybe not glamorous because no real drive is required and no decisive moment in this country's history took place here, at least not that I've read about."

She doesn't get out of the car. They sit facing the castle as the Austin idles loudly. "The best time to come here is in the summer," she continues, "not now, when all the flowers are dead and the grass isn't really green. The garden here is fantastic, very colorful for a country that always seems so dreary." Chris nods, feeling awkward that his question remains unanswered. He won't ask anything about her past again. He notices that she no longer looks at him while speaking during her brief monologue about Lutherkirk Castle. She stares blankly out the window and he realizes how good it made him feel to have her looking at him while she talked, even while driving, casually glancing at him with a smile on her face, looking him in the eye.

He misses that, even though it's only been gone for moments.

No woman, not even his mother, has ever looked him in the eye in a friendly way, as if there were interest in his attentiveness. He has never seen feminine eyes twinkle in response to his gaze, to his questions.

He feels something in his stomach that he has never known upon recalling that sensation. A fluttering in the base of his stomach that is more intoxicating than any beer he has ever drunk. Butterflies. His lack of experience doesn't know what to call this feeling.

He does know that he is maybe in love. Maybe. Infatuated, definitely. And this emotion surprises him. Karen has always been a figure of authority, not unlike a teacher, and though she is not nearly old enough to be his parent, she is maybe twelve years older than he is. The space in years seems vast, as if a lifetime separates them.

Still, he realizes he has developed a sort of crush, but different from the ones he had in school. In school, the girls were unapproachable and probably didn't even know his name. He stared at them across cafeteria and library tables and from lonely desks in classroom corners. Never has a girl talked to him so candidly and intimately.

Maybe this is the start of finding peace, Chris thinks as Karen reverses the car and heads towards the base.

She drives Chris all the way to the barracks as the Ministry of Defence Police at the gate wave her onto the base.

"We'll have to do this again," she says while extending her hand.

Chris takes her hand to shake it. "Yes," he says. "Thanks. Thanks a lot." And he leaves his hand in hers until she takes it away.

Chris is miserable in the first hours of his separation from Karen. The day has been exhilarating and he feels somewhat clean for having done something leisurely without resorting to drinking, and he actually learned something in the process. His vision of the world has increased by a little more.

He returns to the barracks just after the galley has closed for the evening. He finds Hinckley moping about in the room, wondering where Chris has been. He knows Chris's schedule and expected him to be back when he got off work so they could eat supper together.

"Where ya been?" Brad asks Chris, who enters the room with a silly grin on his face. His tone is confrontational.

Chris senses Brad may be jealous if he realizes Chris has befriended anyone else.

He lies.

"I was at the site, studying some of my job qualification requirements. I want to be ready, you know, to get promoted." Hinckley is satisfied with this explanation. "Ya eat yet?"

"No, have you?"

"Yep, but if you want to go to the club, I'll go with ya."

Chris isn't really hungry. He ate a late lunch in St. Andrews and he is too gleeful to eat, but he agrees anyway and they wander off into the early evening darkness.

At the club, Chris absentmindedly eats a burger and fries and Hinckley slurps a milkshake loudly, sucking the straw obnoxiously as the cup quickly empties.

Brad prattles on about his usual subjects: football, the poor quality of life on the base and in Scotland, and his hatred of the Navy.

"Any damn fool can make it in the service," he says. "Black, white, yellow or brown, you can make it. Shit, even me."

Chris ignores him. His thoughts are on the past day and Karen. The next day watch is still two full days away. He glances at the clock above the bar and calculates the hours.

He asks Hinckley a question, an abrupt one, and it takes him by surprise.

"You ever have a girlfriend?"

Hinckley doesn't answer. He swirls his straw in the empty milkshake cup.

"Well, yeah, sure, of course." And Chris knows he's lying. There is a certain air and lack of confidence that tells Chris that like himself, his roommate has never had a girlfriend.

"Really, who?"

"Well, hell, lots of them." He forgoes the empty cup for one of Chris's cigarettes. He lights it somewhat nervously between two of his chubby fingers. He stares at the table.

"A couple, ya know, in school. Nothing serious, just had some fun."

"Really?"

"Yeah, really."

"What about since you've been here?"

"Naw," Hinckley says. "I can't stand them damn Navy women. They all act like they're good looking when you know damn well that where they ain't surrounded by like eighty guys for every girl they'd be nothin' special. But here, even a fat ugly chick can get a date; they do all the time. And them bloke women..." He gives a dramatic shiver. "Well, they're just plain ignorant."

"Have you known any?"

"Don't have to. I can tell by lookin' at 'em."

Chris lights a cigarette and stares numbly at two young sailors playing pool at a table in the corner of the club. They chalk their sticks incessantly and Chris wonders how hard of a game it is to play. There are two girls watching them play, two girls Chris has seen on the base. He wouldn't call them ugly. He is jealous of the four; they are smiling, enjoying life, and seem quite at ease.

Chris inhales his cigarette. "Don't you ever wish you had a girlfriend, you know, instead of hanging around me?"

Brad is taken aback by the candor of Chris's question; he has never had anyone ask him about how he should feel.

"Shit, I don't know. I guess, hell... I never thought about it."

There is silence almost a minute.

"Well, I want a girlfriend," Chris says. "I think this sucks, watching other people with girls. No offense against you, but I'd rather hang out with a girl."

Hinckley can only nod. He has never talked about girls with anyone before.

Chris finishes his cigarette and they wordlessly rise to leave. Brad suggests a beer and Chris declines. He doesn't want to blemish that pure feeling he has enjoyed all day. He wants it to remain clean. He wants his mind to remain clear as he falls asleep and thinks about Karen.

They go back to the barracks and silently get ready for bed. Hinckley simply pulls off his jeans and socks and grabs a t-shirt and climbs into his rack. Chris brushes his teeth and puts on his Navy-issue sweatpants and t-shirt.

His body is somewhat tired, but his mind is wide awake as he stares open-eyed at the barely visible ceiling. There are two days before his day watch, and he wonders how he can pass them. Hanging out and reading in the barracks won't quite do; he knows that he won't be able to concentrate on words.

He enters the nocturnal world through daydreams. He envisions himself as Karen's boyfriend and feels silly for feeling so in awe after just one day of friendship. But something inside him stirred, some emotion that he never thought he could feel.

It must be love, he decides.

He sees himself living with her in her tiny apartment in Brechin, spending quiet evenings at home together, both reading silently and then eating together.

Sex, the thought of sex, doesn't enter his mind just yet. He is a virgin, and this is something that causes him anxiety. He knows she was married, so she must have a measure of experience. But how much? And why isn't she married anymore? And is she truly not married in her heart?

An hour, maybe more, passes in this sometimes blissful, sometimes agitated daydream.

Then Hinckley interrupts the silence. Chris assumes that he's been asleep all along, but he, too, has been thinking.

"I hear you're going to Father Crowley's next weekend."

Chris is shaken upon hearing his roommate's voice in what is otherwise an extremely quiet night. There is no sound of traffic or any civilization, quite unlike the night-time noise of his suburban childhood, the constant roar of expressways and electric lights and industry and civilization.

"Yes," he replies, after a moment's hesitation. "How did you know?"

"Just do," Hinckley says. "I've been meaning to talk to you about that, just didn't know when. I'll be there too, when you go."

"I've never seen you in church."

"Don't go to church. I met him over in Lutherkirk. We got to talking."

"Oh... Really?"

"Yep. I'll talk to you about it more tomorrow."

Chris hears Brad roll over on his side, and Chris continues to stare at the ceiling. He feels somewhat betrayed or maybe jealous. He thought he was the only young man to have bonded with the priest. He is curious about what the priest and Brad could have talked about. He doesn't see Brad engaging in any sort of theological discussion.

Several more moments of confused thoughts occur, and finally Chris falls into a troubled sleep. He dreams about the priest. Instead of Karen driving him around the countryside, it is the priest, and this too makes him happy. He has a friend, an older friend who takes an interest in his state of mind, unlike his mother or father.

In the dream, Brad drifts in and out of the back seat of the priest's car, but he is silent, not his normal obnoxious self.

Chris wakes up. Hazy sunlight comes from behind the drawn shade over the picture window. He peers behind the shade and looks through the damp and foggy window. The buildings of the base are now a darker shade of their true color against a grayish sky as they have been painted by a soft and cold steady rain.

Brad has gone to work. Chris gets his bearings. His first waking thoughts are of the priest and his dream.

Then he recalls the previous day with Karen. His thoughts of the priest vanish in an instant.

The time is 10 a.m., according to the clock radio that he bought at the exchange. He turns it on to Radio Tayside and hears the voice of who he now knows to be Margaret Thatcher, a name from the news at home that he couldn't connect to anyone or anything.

She is talking about unemployment, how there are record highs in Great Britain, and what her government will do to alleviate the situation.

Industry, she says, has to grow.

Chris showers, the plans of the day unsure. He dresses slowly, the AM radio playing statically in the background. He hears a Thompson Twins song that was played incessantly on Detroit radio his last year in high school. Despite not being fond of the song, he finds his feet tapping rhythmically to the music and his lips silently mouthing the lyrics. He feels light, despite the dreariness outside, the specter of loneliness that shrouds his life, and the fact that his family has all but abandoned him.

The world, this life, is wrought with possibility.

The galley is closed. It won't open for lunch for another two hours.

He finds his billfold and counts his money. Thirty pounds and twenty dollars. He decides to go off base on his own.

He walks to the lobby of the barracks and calls a cab. He will go to Brechin.

He puts on his Navy pea coat over his civilian clothes and walks towards the gate while staring at his feet, his breath visible and cloud-like in the chilly and moist air.

Walking past the chapel, he looks up, getting the feeling that someone is watching him.

Father Crowley is standing inside the doorway with his arms folded across his chest. As Chris looks up, Crowley's face brightens with recognition. He waves to Chris and beckons him in.

Chris shakes his head and points to his wrist, indicating that he has a time commitment.

The priest's face is immediately crestfallen, as if Chris has distressed him greatly.

This look of disappointment concerns Chris, but he forgets about it as he spots the taxi already waiting for him outside the gate.

He climbs in and instructs the driver. "Brechin."

"Aye, where in Brechin?

"I don't know... Somewhere in the middle, I guess. Someplace I can eat."

The driver nods. He thinks Chris is peculiar, but a fare is a fare. Silently, they ride the ten minutes past farms and pastures and cottages and woods until they approach Brechin.

Chris is deposited in front of a storefront café, and he enters and studies the very short menu. Too early for lunch and too late for breakfast, he sits at a rickety table with a linoleum top and orders two sausage rolls, as that is all that is being offered at the present time. The café is nearly empty save an older man in a dirty overcoat who stares at Chris grimly over the rim of a tepid cup of tea. The waitress is friendly and aloof and doesn't cater to Chris the way he is accustomed to in the restaurants in Michigan.

The rolls are greasy but relatively palatable, and he thinks he will eat them again if the opportunity arises. His eyes never leave the picture window; he watches the activity of High Street, studying the cars and pedestrians as they pass by.

He is hoping to see Karen's Mini, or Karen herself, drive or walk by.

He leaves the café and wanders around Brechin, much the way he and Brad did a few weeks prior.

This time it is different. He is looking for someone. The whole point of his trip to Brechin is the possibility of seeing Karen.

He wanders along the narrow and clean sidewalk. His Americanism is made even more obvious by his choice of outerwear. His hands are thrust into his pockets, and his collar is upturned to keep out the wind and the cold and gentle rain that is now falling sideways.

He looks up, studying the windows above the businesses that look like they may have apartments inside. He makes several trips up and down the four blocks that make the center of Brechin.

He wonders what he will say if sees her, standing in a window or on the sidewalk.

Would he let her know he was looking? Or would he make it seem happenstance? Or would he be too happy to think? He may be too happy to talk.

He decides to put that situation in the hands of fate and continues to look up and down along the sidewalk, picturing how his day would go if he does indeed run into Karen. They could have lunch again, and maybe he would tell her about his family at home. Maybe she would invite him to her apartment. He could sit next to her on her couch and watch television in the comfortable manner that he suspects happy couples do.

His neck is craned in futility; he doesn't see Karen anywhere. After nearly an hour of walking up and down High Street and its adjoining side streets, he decides to surrender his search. He eyes a pub and ventures inside.

He drinks a pint but does it quickly, as he is quite alone in the crowded pub, belying the lack of people outside. He returns to that awkward feeling of being alone in a crowd, merely a listener in a room chattering with animated conversations.

He finds a cab in a queue just uphill from the pub.

The cab driver doesn't even ask Chris where to go. He knows.

Chris returns to his room, lies down on his bed and stares at the ceiling. He will do little else except venture out for food until it is time to go to work.

Though his search for Karen was fruitless, he decides it was a good thing to do, to strike out on his own, to see a little bit of the country.

The middle part of the week is the happiest for Father Crowley. There are no Masses to prepare for or suffer through, and no church related activities. No one comes to the office to discuss a spiritual crisis on Tuesday or Wednesday; the requests for answers to life's problems usually come just before and just after Mass, when he is usually ambushed by tense faces with eyes full of expectation.

He hates those kinds of faces because they expect him to act a certain way.

They expect him to act priestly.

But Tuesday and Wednesday nights are his. He can sleep without dread and relax the entire evening, drinking wine, listening to records.

On this Wednesday night, he takes a large map of Scotland and places it on the wall above his sofa. Underneath that map, he affixes four smaller maps depicting the city centers of Dundee, Aberdeen, Glasgow, and Edinburgh.

He stands on the couch, naked underneath his bathrobe, his right hand occasionally pulling at his penis, his left hand holding a sterling silver goblet of wine, a vessel that he found at a resale shop in Dundee during one of his travels. Odin probably drinks wine this way, he thought as he greedily snatched it from a dusty shelf.

He stands with his legs slightly apart for balance, as the coach is old and sagging, and his body rocks back and forth. He feels like a general mapping out his strategy. In his mind, the scenario is clear: first, some low-level sorties, some indications of warning to let them know they're here and they mean business. And then the final blows, dealt in such a fashion that their effects will be heard around the world.

First, we take Scotland, he thinks, drinking the wine in an undignified fashion, the excess liquid running down the corners of his mouth, streaking red on his fleshy chin.

Then maybe England, and after that, who knows? He calculates that he has just under two years left on his tour. After that... He could end up anywhere if he stays in the Navy. He doesn't want to waste any time at all.

He needs to replenish his Trinity, to make his triumvirate complete.

He thinks of Chris. A week from Friday and he will be here, in this house.

Crowley will pull out all of the stops: steak, maybe prime rib, beer—plenty of beer—perhaps ice cream, whatever, whatever Chris wants.

He wants Chris to feel like family.

He will use the same approach that he used on Rodgers and Hinckley, one of paternal friendship. His years of priestly discernment tell him that Chris is hungry for that sort of attention, for an older man to take an interest in his life.

He steps down from the couch and goes to a kitchen drawer and rummages through a clutter of utensils and small tools and finds a red felt-tip pen. He climbs back on the couch and places a solitary dot on the Aberdeen map as well as one on the map of Dundee.

He places several dots on the maps of Glasgow and Edinburgh.

He then takes the pen and draws a swastika on the face of the Scotland map. He takes a long drink of wine in triumph. A twinkling of light above the map tells him that the gods are pleased. He can feel the faces in Valhalla smiling upon him.

Chris eats breakfast in the galley quite hurriedly on the morning of his first day watch signaling the end of his long break.

The break has been brutal, especially the last day, hanging about in his room or in the barracks lounge, watching the television, perpetually tuned to the Armed Forces Network. The same propaganda over and over again—news broadcasts depicting servicemen and women doing honorable things—with just a little real news thrown in and the occasional and very mild sitcom from a few years back shown for laughs.

But his mind was anywhere other than the television. He was deciding how he would act with Karen the first day back to work. It would be different. The last time he saw her at work, she was merely his supervisor.

Now she is the object of much emotional—and maybe a little physical—desire.

Various scenarios play through his head, starting with not speaking to her at all. He could act totally aloof and maybe a little obnoxious. Girls in school always seemed to go for the obnoxious sort.

One problem—he doesn't know how to act obnoxiously.

Then the other extreme. This fantasy allows him to confront her immediately and tell her how he feels and that he is deeply and madly in love with her. In response, her eyes become teary and she presses her face against his and they kiss passionately.

One problem—he doesn't know how to kiss, at least not more than a peck on the cheek.

He puckers his lips while watching the television, not caring if anyone else in the lounge notices. He shapes his lips, first tightly, as if they kissed on the outside, and then more openly, as if his lips would surround hers.

In this daydream, his lack of experience haunts him, and he favors it with an approach a little more subtle.

He will be himself and try to be kind and maybe a little more amiable, not as morose as he can sometimes be. He also expects her to act differently, too. She may not feel the same about him as he does her, but they did form a bit of a bond that day. Surely, she will look at him differently, not as some lowly seaman.

He eats only a bowl of cereal poured from a small cardboard box of the same kind he took on his few camping trips in northern Michigan with his Boy Scout troop. His career as a Boy Scout was short lived; his parents weren't exactly encouraging and he grew embarrassed at showing up at functions that required the attendance of parents. Typically, neither of his would show up.

Thoughts of those days in early junior high are with him as he crumples the empty box violently, but then they quickly fade. He is seeing Karen today, and all those people and memories are many years and miles away.

He arrives at the site early, twenty minutes before his shift begins. The pair that he is relieving eyes him with curiosity. He wants to be at work early, to be in place as Karen arrives.

He receives the pass-down from the seaman that he relieves, a thin sailor with two years of seniority on Chris who always fails to be promoted due to marginal behavior, fighting in the club because of alcohol, late for work, out of uniform due to the length of his haircut. He is referred to as a burn-bag by Karen and by members of the day staff of their division. A burn-bag is merely a brown paper bag that one would find in a grocery store where classified documents are disposed of until the bag is full and then stapled shut before being taken to an incinerator to be burned. A burn-bag is a generic term for any sailor in the communications field whose military bearing or performance is sub-par.

Chris strives to avoid that label; he makes sure his hair is cut and his uniform clean and wrinkle-free. He is always on time; he has always hated being late. Being late makes him tense.

Chris reads the entries in the logbooks; the mid-watch had been a quiet one. There are only two entries, and little concentration is required. He assumes his station and stares at the door with much anxiety.

He is shaking.

The hands of the clock move very slowly as he alternates his glance from the clock on the wall to the door. He is waiting for 6 a.m.

She arrives just as the hands of the clock are exactly opposite one another.

Chris is sweating.

She smiles upon seeing him and then turns her glance toward the supervisor she is relieving. He tells her little and she sits in the desk assigned to the supervisor and sifts through a pile of messages, sorting them here and there. She doesn't look at Chris.

He stares at her and is ready to cry. He was hoping for her to say something, so he wouldn't be the first to speak, as he is not sure he can summon his voice.

But an hour passes and the printers start to print and the day staff starts to arrive. There is work to do, and still she doesn't talk to him except for words relating to their work. There is no mention of their day together or any future plans.

He is sad, but as the day progresses, he gets angry with himself for getting so worked up over someone who could never possibly be interested in him. Almost as rapidly as the flame of attraction was lit, it starts to fade until there is nothing left but smoke. Chris is exhausted from the emotional journey.

Their shift turns out to be quite busy, and they barely have time to eat.

The activity of the day winds down and the day staff starts to leave around 4 p.m. Chris and Karen have the workspace to themselves and the same sort of familiarity creeps in, as they are the only two who belong here and they belong alone after spending so many hours sitting at opposing desks from one another.

While making entries in the logbook, Karen speaks. "Well, did you have fun the other day?"

His irritation disappears. "Yes," he says. "I did, thank you."

She looks up from the logbook and smiles directly at him. He is struck at how different she looks without makeup. He notices the lines around the corners of her eyes and mouth. Suddenly, she seems much older than she did the other day.

"Good," she says. "Maybe we'll do it again."

He nods and asks suddenly, "How old are you?"

She gives a nervous laugh. "Why?"

"Just wondering."

"Well, I'm thirty-three, and you? Eighteen? Nineteen?"

"Nineteen. Just turned nineteen."

"Well, happy birthday," she says. "You're younger than me, but I'm still not old enough to be your mother..." Karen says as her voice suddenly fades away.

"Thank you." He starts to feel a little uncomfortable with the attention, and a little guilty, as if something he said made her voice change so suddenly. It subconsciously reaffirms his opinion that women do not find him the least bit appealing.

She returns to her papers. "So, what did you get?"

"Get?"

"Yeah, for your birthday. What did you get?"

"Oh," he says, realizing that most birthdays are celebrated in some fashion, but his have passed unceremoniously for a number of years. "Nothing."

"Nothing? Not even from your parents?"

"Nope."

"Well, surely they sent you a card?" She looks up from her stack of papers.

He shakes his head. The loathsome feeling he has for his family returns. Petty Officer Freeman can tell by his eyes that there is pain in response to her questions.

"Maybe next break we can do something for your birthday."

"Really? Like what?"

"You know, maybe we'll go to the McDonalds in Dundee or something. Nothing big."

"Okay," he says. The spark of passion has returned but not as fiercely as before.

The short break in between the day watches and mid-watches arrives, and Karen makes good on her promise. On a Monday afternoon, she picks up Chris outside the base and drives him to Dundee and takes him to McDonalds. He would rather try something different, something more un-American, but he knows not to question the kindness of others.

The thrill of going somewhere, anywhere, is still exhilarating, especially with Karen.

He tells his roommate the truth as Brad watches him get dressed. His supervisor is taking him out to eat. Chris feels bad and Brad gives him the third degree, questioning who his supervisor is and where they are going and at what time will Chris come back. Chris answers the questions as honestly as he can.

The restaurant looks the same on the inside as any back home, except it may be a little smaller. Instead of being a stand-alone building like all the fast-food places he has known, it occupies a storefront in the center of Dundee, tucked in between a pub and a bookseller's with a simple sign across the face of the building above the door, instead of the monstrous roadside signs that signify their presence in America.

The food is quite the same.

They drive in silence and barely speak until her car is parked in a multi-level garage. They walk the few blocks to the restaurant.

"How much do you want to bet that someone from the base will be here?" Karen asks.

Chris shrugs his shoulders.

"There's always someone from the base here. It's like some kind of gastronomical pull, you know? I have a weakness for this stuff. That is one thing I miss about home, the food."

Chris nods. "I could use a good pizza."

"Well, you can't find that here, not even at the Pizza Hut in Aberdeen."

"I know."

They enter the restaurant and stand in a long line in front of the counter. True enough, there are several people from the base, and though Chris or Karen don't know any of them by name, their appearance indicates their nationality. They study Chris and Karen in return, they too being obviously American and from the base.

After a quarter of an hour, they sit down and eat the unremarkable food. Chris is almost shocked at how heartily Karen eats. She notices him watching her. "I'm sorry," she says while chewing still in between bites. "I love this stuff. I can't help it."

He nods. "It's okay." She has become more human, not the same occupant of the pedestal of superiority that she once was. Unceremoniously, and rather quickly, they leave. The twilight approaches and the setting sun and low buildings cast shadows upon the pedestrian-only street.

Chris assumes they are going back towards the base, but Karen just stands there and bites her lip. She asks, "How about a drink?"

"Sure," Chris says. "I didn't think you did that."

"I won't, but you can. I'll grab a soda or something."

"You don't have to do that. We can go back."

"No, no, I insist. I have nothing else to do, and it is your birthday, sort of."

They enter the pub next to McDonalds. It is very clean and modern, much cleaner than the pubs Chris has visited in Brechin. The bar is wood with brass trim and the booths are padded comfortably. The establishment is very well lit, not like the dark pub that masked the drunken squalor in Brechin.

Chris has a pint of lager and Karen orders a soda-like beverage called Irn-Bru. She makes a face upon sipping it. "I've always wondered what this stuff tasted like. I guess I should have kept wondering."

They sit opposite one another in a booth near the front window. Chris faces the street, watching the people walking by. Most are happy and most are with someone else. Seldom does he see anyone walking alone. Most of the faces that he catches merely in profile as they pass quickly in front of the window are pale and smiling. People with lives, he thinks. He realizes that he, too, is starting to have a life. Never in any daydream from his schooldays would he have ever pictured himself sitting in a pub on the other side of the world with a woman almost a generation older than himself.

"So," Karen says, abandoning her drink for a cigarette, "I guess you're not close to your parents."

"No, not really." He drinks his beer slowly, taking only the smallest of sips. He wants these moments to last. "I guess you could say not close at all."

He has told her in the past of the emotional distance of his parents, but he's never been too specific. On this day, he tells her about their living arrangement. He describes how his mother lived upstairs with the run of the house, and his father's existence in the partially finished basement, coming and going solely through the side door that led directly to the basement stairs. His father's presence was always visible, but seldom was he seen. When Chris would go down to talk to him, even just to say hello, his father would never look at him. His gaze would never leave the television.

He starts out slowly and starts retelling his family's problems, as though he were an outside observer and not a part of the situation. His voice is flat and emotionless, but as he continues, his voice changes and he feels pressure behind his eyes that he knows is the start of tears. By the time he tells Karen about finding his house for sale and his mother running to Arizona with a much younger man who didn't say two words to him, tears are running down his cheeks, but his voice is still steady. However, by the time he tells her of his days and nights without mail in boot camp, he is out and out bawling, too sad to feel embarrassed.

Karen reaches over and pats his shoulder. He is grateful for the contact. He has had no human contact for such a long time. No one has shown him any affection whatsoever, and that probably hurts the most. Everyone needs a hug and Karen placing her hand on his shoulder is the closest he's ever been to someone—save the tears in Father Crowley's office—since he was a small child.

"How awful," she says. She orders him another beer, even though he still has most of one left. "Drink some more. It's your birthday and you've missed too many."

To distract from the tears, he quickly drinks the remains of his first pint in a fluid motion, as if he is an experienced drinker, which belies his youthful and innocent appearance.

"You know," Karen says, "there are people who have children that could care less about them. To them, having children is no different than having a dog, if not less than a dog. And there are some people who want children more than anything and they can't have them, or God takes them away. It makes no sense."

Her face too, shows signs of strain as if she might cry, but she doesn't. She stares into space, looking above Chris's head. She lights another cigarette. Chris does, too.

He is in love with her, but not as fanatically as he was before. And he realizes from her last statement that another piece of her puzzle has been exposed. At some point in her life, she either wanted children or couldn't have them, or she or someone she knew lost them.

Still, he is afraid to ask. Her face and something in her mannerisms still don't invite questions about her past.

In silence, he finishes his second beer, and in silence, they drive back to the base. The afternoon started on a happy note, but the emotional downturn has made them both tired and not in the mood for conversation. She drops him off at the gate and gives him a hug in the cramped confines of the Mini.

The hug makes him very happy. And though he hasn't cried over his mother or father, it somehow feels therapeutic. His heart feels much lighter, and the burden of near-abandonment that he has been carrying isn't nearly so cumbersome. He finds his room, his bed, and falls asleep, just moments after the sun disappears.

Dear Wife,

I think I always assumed you would be my age or probably younger. I think I've thought that because I always assumed I would be too immature or inexperienced for girls
my age. All through school the girls my age have always
seemed older, especially in high school. They started to look
like women, a lot of them, and I looked the same since junior high, not a speck of facial hair, but maybe more acne. I
would listen to girls talk in class among their friends or with
different guys, you know, the more popular ones. They always seemed to have a lot to talk about, and me, I never
could say much of anything. They talked about parties and
movies and gossiped about different kids in school. Who was
dating who, who was sleeping with who. I always pretended
to ignore them, during those moments in class when the
teacher would be absent or in between classes just as the bell
would ring. Those moments were always torture for me. Everyone seemed to have someone else to talk to and I would
put my nose in a book without really reading it. Now I know
the difference between me and them, my memory has a way
of making sense of the past sometimes. They had been living, I now realize, leading lives, having and making friends.
Enjoying life. Maybe they found peace? I don't know. I pretended to hate everybody but I now know I was jealous. I
hadn't and still haven't done much living, not as much as I
would like to or need to.

Anyway, you could be older than me. Maybe a lot older.
I think that would be okay. You may have gotten to a point
in your life where looks aren't everything and love is more.
You could look past my looks, my inexperience. I would
cherish you. Maybe you have been married before and it
didn't turn out so well. I won't ever get divorced, especially
not with kids in the picture.

Well, not much else to tell you. More when I have time.
Until we meet.

Love,
Chris

Crowley has been collecting. During his spare evenings and early on Saturdays and late on Sundays he is rummaging through chemist shops, ironmongers and agricultural supply stores through the Tayside and Grampian regions. He is looking for and finding gunpowder, saltpeter, charcoal, fertilizer, cans of gasoline and any rag that can be used for a wick. He is saving all his empty wine bottles. He stores everything in his kitchen, in the cabinet underneath the sink or on top of the table, and what doesn't fit, he shoves underneath his bed.

On a Monday after work, he decides to drive to Edinburgh, a little south of his usual realm. He telephones the barracks and has the Scottish man on duty fetch Hinckley and bring him to the phone. He asks Hinckley if he wants to go to Edinburgh; he does. The priest instructs Hinckley to meet him down the road a quarter of a mile from the gate, so no one will see him as he picks him up.

Crowley asks Hinckley where Chris is.

"He went to Dundee with this bitch supervisor of his. They went to eat or somethin'."

Crowley is silent upon hearing that news. He rubs his chin as they turn onto the A92 and head south on the road that will take them most of the way to Edinburgh, an hour and a half south.

"You need to discourage that," the priest says. "Do what you can to stop it. We don't want him to have friends away from you and eventually me. In fact, in the future, you must stop it. As an officer in the Navy, I command you. Do what you have to do—bring him to my place, go and get him drunk, but in the future, if he talks about spending time with anyone else, you need to stop it. Do anything except tie him down. You got that?"

Hinckley nods, forgetting that the priest's status in the Navy has absolutely nothing to do with their personal desires.

Crowley becomes somewhat cheerful. "Enough of that, enough of that. We had it wrong before, my good young man," Crowley explains. "We were attacking the blacks, which is just what those Jew bastards wanted us to do."

Brad looks at him, confused. It has been a while since he has seen the priest and had a conversation of this nature. The last time they talked, blacks and other minorities were the enemy, enemies he could discern at a glance. He has hated blacks since school, and it is an anger he can easily summon. But to direct his anger against the Jewish people? He has never known any, as far as he knows. He doesn't know what they look like, and he doesn't have any reason to hate them. The only thing he knows about the Jews is what he learned during a few visits to Sunday school as a small boy—they don't believe in Jesus. But neither does he, not really, and neither does Father Crowley.

Crowley notes the confused look on his young colleague's face. "To finally win a war, you don't succeed by killing off the foot soldiers... You must get to the officers, and kill the generals. The blacks do the Jews' dirty work. In case you didn't notice, any neighborhood that is black used to be Jewish. The blacks follow the Jews."

Brad has never noticed.

As they drive south, the priest continues to talk vaguely about the evil of the Jews, how they have started the decline of the world with the creation of Israel, how they control the banks of the world and hold power over all people via a sort of economic slavery.

"Why do you think Hitler attempted the Holocaust? Which is in fact only partially true, but I'll explain that later. Even here in Britain, in England, really, way back in the late thirteenth century, the Jews were expelled. They entered England from France and quickly set themselves up in the banking business, as they were allowed to lend money with interest and Christians were not. The lending of money for usury was considered a sin. Of course, the interest payments caused as many problems then as it does now, and much of the country experienced financial difficulties. Many went deep into debt while the Jews' wealth increased exponentially. Rightfully so, the Jews were blamed for the financial difficulties many of the English were facing, and as a result, the King expelled them from the country. Of course, they came back—they always manage to resurface—and again, as they still do today, they wrestled control of the nation's wealth."

In silence, they skirt Dundee, the city of so much memory and activity of their recent months. Crowley shakes his head the entire time the city is in view, and Brad lights cigarettes, one after another, until the city disappears in the rearview mirror. Crowley had thought of Dundee first for this visit, but he doesn't want any reason to appear in the field of vision of the Tayside Police. Edinburgh is both far enough and near enough.

The country south of Dundee is new for Brad, but he is disinterested, not caring for what the landscape has to offer or the names of towns that he has never heard of or seen.

Crowley continues his rant just as the tallest of Dundee's tenement high rises disappears from his rearview mirror as they descend a long rise in the road. "You know, I must tell you," he says, now more relaxed than he was when their journey started, "if one were to examine the wealth of the industrial nations of the world, and examine their banking systems, one would find that almost exclusively, Zionists are at the helm. And at whose expense? Who pays?"

Brad shakes his head, not really understanding the question.

"You do, I do, and our families do. The honest white people do."

Brad nods, too afraid to show he doesn't understand.

"Tell me, Brad, you grew up in Nebraska, correct?"

"Sure did."

"Would you say you or any of the people that you grew up with were wealthy? Wasn't your mother a waitress?"

"We were poor, but not starving. Blue-collar, I guess you would call it."

"Right, no shame in that, no shame in that. Now tell me, were there any Jewish people in your neighborhood, or in your school or anywhere in your community?"

"No, can't say that there was. In fact, I don't know if I've ever seen a Jew anywhere before."

"Exactly!" The priest slams his hand on the dashboard in triumph. "While you and your family were scraping by, making ends meet and working hard living in what I guess to be small houses or trailers or apartments, the Jews of America were living in mansions and comfort, probably owning the banks where your mother cashed her check, or the drug company where your grandfather gets his medication, or his doctor may even be Jewish, making sure he never gets well. They are in control—and the blacks do their dirty work. The Jews use the blacks to keep the whites agitated. If the good white people of America are worried about being robbed by a black man while walking down the street, they won't worry about being robbed by a Jew the next time they go to the store, or buy property, or take out a loan. The Jew robs much more stealthily; he robs and you don't even notice. It is time for men like you and me to lead the way, to light the path to the gods of our ancestors, and stir the Viking soul of all white people in North America and Europe, before it is too late."

Brad understands most of that last statement, except for the references to the Norse religion, but he does understand that he is among the despised and the downtrodden. There is something about being on the underdog team that stirs up his emotions, and he suddenly understands what the priest says. The same anger that he was able to summon up in attacking blacks can now be pointed towards the Jews, especially if they were responsible for his meager upbringing.

Edinburgh approaches. The empty fields and lonely hills make way for a series of smaller towns that run together. Finally, they find themselves in traffic stuck at stoplights and fending their way through a series of roundabouts.

Crowley is not used to the traffic. He has not driven in so much congestion since Houston. Even Dundee, though it hosts over a hundred thousand souls, has very little traffic, and it doesn't last long. Here in Edinburgh, it seems to snake for miles, leading all the way to the city center, where they eventually find themselves.

Crowley is seldom taken in by objects of beauty, but the heart of Edinburgh is indeed striking. The ancient downtown, a collection of castles and other medieval buildings, the narrow cobblestone streets all accented with a large civic park and a vast collection of people walking back and forth.

They park the car in a garage and wander briefly, stopping in a pub that is obviously more cosmopolitan than any they've visited in Dundee or in the vicinity of the base. They sit quietly in the pub, where they are taken for father and son American tourists. They don't offer the fact that they're American servicemen.

However, they are not here on holiday. Crowley finishes his second glass of red wine, and as Brad finishes his pint, Crowley whispers that they must be off.

Crowley is in search of a neighborhood that hosts a small Jewish community clustered along Salisbury Road. He learned of its location during a visit to the base library. The Scottish librarian employed by the Navy recognized him, though he didn't know her. The library was empty save a sailor's wife and her two small children, who were behaving badly. The mother tried to read them a story in the corner of a library with a rocking chair and a small collection of toys and stuffed animals, ostensibly the children's section of the library, a very small and drab establishment containing mostly westerns and science fiction novels, with a small reference section. Crowley found what he was looking for in a travel guide. The librarian watched him the entire time and tried to engage him in conversation, asking if the Church of Scotland was really different than the Catholic Church. He said no, not really. She inquired about the practice of exorcism and if Catholic priests really perform such feats, and if he had done one himself. He said yes they do and no he hasn't, and he asked her to kindly leave him alone. Shocked, she sauntered off behind her desk and pretended to rifle through papers. He smiled. Seldom has he ever had the heart to annoy a middle-aged woman. He used to feign respect for those who were older than him, but these days, he doesn't really care.

The priest summons a taxi and they are transported from the near magical heart of Edinburgh to a neighborhood that looks as unremarkable and typical as any in Scotland that he's seen so far. They are deposited on Salisbury Road and Crowley walks with his hands in the pockets of a black leather coat he purchased before he left the States. Never before has he worn leather, and he thinks of the World War II movies he saw as a child. The Gestapo always seemed to wear black leather.

He spies a small gray building with a Star of David over the front door. He is disappointed by the size of the synagogue. The building appears to be empty. He walks around it, counting the windows and doors. There is one door in the front and one in the back, which leads to an alley that is shared with a bakery, a jeweler's, and a small fruit market. There are only four windows, all facing the street.

This will be simple, he thinks.

He leads Brad to the front door. The priest takes a small penknife from his pocket and pricks the index finger of Brad's left hand. He squeezes it until blood starts flowing. He takes Brad's finger and traces the image of a swastika on the front door in blood. And then he signs: THE TRINITY.

"I suspect that will get the neighborhood talking." Crowley laughs and Brad thinks what he has just done is very cool. "We'll be back, my young friend. We'll be back." The pair walks down Salisbury Road, waiting for a taxi to come along. They return to Lutherkirk, feeling quite satisfied.

"How did you know I was going to see Father Crowley tomorrow?" Chris asks Brad on a Thursday evening, realizing that tomorrow he is going to the priest's house. He had forgotten their nocturnal conversation of a few weeks past. So much has been on his mind, Karen and the world that is being shown to him.

Hinckley is taking off his uniform and rummaging in the bottom of his locker for his cleanest dirty sweatshirt and jeans. The galley is serving supper, and he and Chris are on their way.

"Oh, I talk to him from time to time," Brad says without looking at Chris. "You know, he was there when Lee did what he did, and... I just know him that way."

"I was going to say, I've never seen you at church, and you're usually sleeping when I go."

"Naw, I don't have time for that crap. Father Crowley says it don't matter if you go or not, it don't make any difference. It's a crutch, basically, for those who need it. I talk to him now and again, you know, we're both on the support side of the base, not out at the communications sites. I run into him or I go to his office, and we talk about stuff, life, you'll find out some of it tomorrow. I used to go to his place. He'll treat you real good, all you can drink and eat, and you can smoke, if you want. He ain't like any priest I've ever known. He's basically a regular guy."

Chris is confused and maybe a little jealous. He thought the priest had only befriended him, that their relationship might be somewhat exclusive. But nonetheless, it is a new friendship, and he is excited about what the evening might offer.

They walk to the galley in air that is still cold but less frigid than it has been during the previous weeks and months. The trees are starting to show just the slightest trace of green.

"So you'll be there tomorrow?" Chris asks.

"Yep, I'll be there. He asked me to go. He figured out that I knew you and thought you might be more comfortable if there was someone there that you knew."

The galley is buzzing, and there is much animated conversation, especially among those who have just gotten off their shifts at the communications site. The atmosphere indicates that something significant just happened. Though Chris and Hinckley are basically ostracized, Chris asks someone a few chairs over, a petty officer third class, what happened.

"We're at war, buddy," he says with glee. Chris is taken aback; the word war instantly makes him think of the Soviets, which would certainly lead to nuclear annihilation, a threat that looms over the free world that he is now so proud to defend.

"War?" Chris asks while Hinckley works on a mouthful of food, almost disinterested.

"Hell, yeah. We just bombed Libya. We're gonna take that damn Qadaffi out. It's about damn time we did something; we can't let those A-rabs push us around anymore. We're the United States and that's all there is to it, and if you try to push us around, there'll be hell to pay. I think we got a carrier group right off the Libya coast. Gonna blow Qadaffi right out of his socks."

"Wow," Chris says. He knew that the Navy patrolled many fronts, keeping an ever-watchful eye on the Soviets, the Chinese, the North Koreans, and the Cubans. But there were also constant rumblings about the Middle East, the Palestinians being pursued by the Israelis in Lebanon and the ever-troublesome Colonel Qadaffi in Libya.

Under his breath, Hinckley says, "Notice how excited everyone is because of fighting?" The chatter and animated faces make that fact seem obvious.

"Yes." Chris scans the diners in the galley.

"They're happy, ain't they?"

"I don't know if they're happy, but I'd say they're excited."

"Same difference, but sure enough, they're happy. And you want to know why?"

"Because they're patriotic, and the United States is defending itself, that's why."

"Maybe yes, maybe no, but I think people like to fight. They need to fight. They need to take care of their own. Just remember that, that's all. They're happy because the group that they're a part of, the United States military, is fighting, and it makes their life a little more worthwhile. It gives them peace."

Chris is startled by that last sentence. He knows where Brad first heard it.

An elderly man clutching the *Evening News* and walking along Salisbury Road in Edinburgh is the first to notice the red and runny swastika. He walks to the synagogue's door to examine it more closely, and is chilled by its striking appearance. The dark red blood is in stark contrast to the ashen door. "Bloody fucking hell," he says to himself, barely audible above his breath.

He quickly walks home to his flat a few blocks away and telephones the police.

Two PCs arrive, dressed in bright yellow rain gear, as a light early spring rain comes out of a barely sunlit sky. After examining the door, they summon an evidence technician, who arrives very directly to scrape part of the swastika from the door.

"Blood," the evidence technician says, a plain looking woman on the cusp of early middle age. Her hair is cut just above the shoulders to stay within police regulations and it is not styled at all; it lies flat and straight. The early evening rain causes mist to form on her thick and dark rimmed spectacles, which she wipes on the sleeve of her yellow slicker. "I imagine we'll find out this is blood." Her face indicates her disdain, though her years on the job leave her shocked by precious little.

The two constables take pictures, as does a reporter from the *Edinburgh Evening News* who keeps his ear glued to a home model police scanner and chases the reports that may be of human interest. He often arrives at the scene as officers converge, and his face is known by most. His presence is acknowledged with a semi-friendly nod by the evidence technician, who waves and says hello.

The rabbi of the synagogue comes a short while later, a short and thin man imported from England, who is dressed rather neatly in a simple black suit with a white shirt and black tie, an unremarkable yarmulke perched neatly on top of his head. In his private thoughts, he hates Scotland and longs for the scholarly life he led in London before taking this job in the bitter north. He puts his hands on his hips and stares at heaven but doesn't interrupt the police as they take their pictures.

The reporter approaches him. "You must want some sort of explanation, don't you, Rabbi?"

The rabbi turns to face him and the reporter snaps his photo, with the door and the swastika in the background. "No," the rabbi says with irritation. "God will reveal who did this... Whoever did this can't hide from God."

"Very noble of you, Rabbi. Any idea who might have done it?"

The rabbi shakes his head. "Whoever claims to be the Trinity. A skinhead group, I suspect. Never heard of them before. We get crank calls all the time, so this doesn't surprise me terribly."

One of the constables interrupts and tells the reporter that he's asked enough. They ask the rabbi the same sort of questions and get the same answers. They write everything down, unlike the reporter, who can commit such details to memory. The police tell the rabbi that he can clean the door and they will be in touch with him. They tell him to please be careful. The rabbi nods and enters the synagogue. The reporter runs away and hops into his rickety Vauxhall and drives away to the office. He knows the picture of the bloody swastika and the grim rabbi will make the front page of the next edition.

Back at the station, an Inspector Parlabane is given the case. He looks at the Polaroids of the door and studies the name 'Trinity'. This all seems familiar, and he feeds information into the national crime computer and waits for the printer to laboriously print out a smattering of pages. He glances at the reports and immediately picks up the phone and dials the headquarters of the Tayside Police in Dundee.

It is Friday and Chris and Brad share a taxi for the very brief ride to Father Crowley's house from the base. The taxi drives by the ruins of Inverhaven Castle through the twilight as the castle eclipses the nearly descended sun. Chris can see the tulips of the vast gardens starting to bloom and he recalls his day with Karen. He smiles as broadly as he ever has in his life.

Crowley—while waiting for the two—is anxious. He left the chapel half an hour earlier than normal, telling the Protestant chaplain that he needed to go the home of a despondent sailor off base. When Chaplain Lambert questioned him about who he was going to see and the nature of the crisis, Crowley replied that it was confidential, between himself, the sailor, and God.

Chaplain Lambert didn't respond. Crowley took his silence as approval, but he knows Lambert is suspicious of him, ever since the death of Lee Rodgers. The priest has felt that Lambert doesn't regard him as a peer, but more of a nuisance, a monstrous nuisance.

Crowley sped home. He laid the table as garishly as possible with a somewhat dusty linen tablecloth that is part of the furnishings that came with the house, using polished silverware that he purchased from a resale shop and wineglasses that also came with the house, rather offensive wineglasses with frosted impressions of flowers against a glass that is tinted red.

He has his goblet in his hand, and he has nearly drained a bottle of his favorite South African wine. He constantly checks himself in the bathroom mirror, smoothing out his clothes and his hair, tucking and un-tucking his oxford shirt, which he wears underneath a thin sweater now, as the evenings aren't quite so chilly. He splashes water on his face and checks his eyebrows and nostrils for renegade hair. Finding several, he plucks them by hand and somewhat enjoys the pain.

He will start to prepare the food when they arrive, simple dishes: spaghetti, garlic bread, salad. He will lean on a well stocked refrigerator full of tins of varied British beers.

The cab pulls in front of the house, and as he watches Chris pay the cab driver, Father Crowley removes the swastika from his mantel and hides it in a kitchen cabinet. He doesn't want to reveal too much too soon. He could tell that Chris is more intelligent than either Hinckley or Rodgers, and knows he will probably be alarmed by the sight of the swastika.

He watches as the two young men approach his cottage, Brad in front, swaggering with the familiarity of entering this house, and Chris walking timidly behind him, looking around, studying the elm trees that are starting to show signs of life.

Crowley swings open the front door as they approach.

"Welcome, welcome," he says, and he is quite jovial.

The sight of Chris without a window or desk between them makes him tremble.

"You got beer, Father?" asks Hinckley. He pulls off his jacket and places it in a stuffed and disorganized front closet.

"Of course, of course. Help yourself." Crowley reaches for Chris's coat and stores it in the same closet. He hangs it with care, as if it has just come from the dry cleaners.

Hinckley returns from the kitchen with two tins of beer. Chris is impressed by the size and takes one gladly.

"Sit down, sit down." Crowley points at the couch. "You two fine gentlemen sit down and relax, and I will prepare dinner." He walks into the kitchen, and asks Hinckley to retrieve coal for the fireplace from the bin outside. Hinckley grabs a tin pail next to the fireplace and walks outside. Chris is alarmed with the familiarity that Brad seems to display with the workings of the priest's house.

The house isn't what Chris expected. He thought it would be light and clean and somewhat cheerful based on the conversations he had with the priest. Instead, he finds the house dark, even though the sunlight has just started to wane and is still streaming through very dirty windows. It also seems damp, and Chris feels a chill that is intensified as the beer first hits his throat.

Brad returns quickly, straining from the weight of the coal-laden pail. He sets it down on the ash-covered hearth and feeds the fire, which shows only embers. Chris feels heat instantly and the chill he felt dissipates. He starts to feel warm inside as the beer starts to affect him.

"I told ya he was cool." Hinckley sits down and quickly drains his beer in just over three swallows. He crushes the empty tin with his hand and asks Chris if he is ready for another. Chris hurriedly finishes his and nods, handing Brad the empty tin.

"Like I said," says Brad as he returns from the kitchen, "he's a real nice guy, not like a priest at all. He makes you feel like you're at home."

Chris can't help but agree. Even Karen hasn't invited him to her home, and here is this priest—an officer no less—having him over, giving him beer, making him dinner.

After a few minutes, the priest summons them to the table and gives them their salad, and then arrives with their spaghetti and a bottle of wine. He fills their wineglasses nearly full. "Eat and drink, and drink and eat as much as you like. You're in a house of family, so to speak. I want you to feel like you're at home here."

Chris appreciates the gesture. He does feel like he belongs.

They all sit down. Chris expects the priest to say some sort of blessing, but he doesn't. He pushes up his sleeves and attacks his pile of spaghetti with a certain vigor.

They eat mostly in silence, but the priest talks of current events: the bombing of Libya, the threat of nuclear war, which he feels won't last forever, and the problems in Israel, between the Palestinians and the Jews. "That," he says of the latter, "should worry us more than the Russians, and in a while, I am sure you will see why."

"Yup," says Brad, "you surely will." The priest stares at Hinckley with mild irritation, as if he intends to be the lone speaker for this evening, and interruptions won't be permitted. Brad feels the stare, sees the mirth in the priest's eyes, and in embarrassment, quickly drains his glass of wine.

The things Crowley will use to lure Chris into his realm are different than what he used on Hinckley. Hinckley was very simple, just alcohol with a little rage. With Chris, he knows his approach will be with alcohol, and food for the intellect. Chris may be enticed by the Nordic gods, and learn how a Caucasian fellow such as himself can only find happiness with the only religion nature ever intended him to have. He has never discussed such things with Brad more than briefly.

Chris eats slowly, but Crowley and Brad eat quickly. The priest notices with growing irritation that his pants are constantly getting tighter. Chris tries to eat neatly, taking care to place a napkin on his lap the way his mother taught him when in the presence of company. He rolls his spaghetti tightly on his fork, in contrast to the priest and Brad, who slurp the noodles almost directly from the plate, using the fork more as a prop than as a utensil.

Crowley brings out an apple pie that he bought from the freezer section in the base commissary, along with vanilla ice cream, which he scoops liberally onto the pieces of pie that he takes right out of the oven. This is one of Chris's favorites, and this he eats not so casually. The priest offers coffee, but Chris and Brad refuse in favor of beer, which they drink while Crowley cleans the kitchen rapidly with little regard to perfect cleanliness.

Chris and Brad retire to the living room while Crowley finishes in the kitchen. Brad wordlessly piles more coal on the fire. The extra warmth makes Chris realize that he is indeed intoxicated. But the feeling is not at all unpleasant, and he feels as comfortable as he ever has at any point in his life. It feels almost like Christmas at his grandparents' in northern Michigan so many years ago, when he was just seven or eight. They had a fireplace and he remembers feeling very safe as the wind and the snow swirled outside the window as he and his brother opened presents in their pajamas that had feet sewn in while in front of the warm fireplace, and his parents and grandparents were all smiling, casually sipping steaming mugs of coffee.

He feels that way now, as if he is in the cradle of someone who cares. The fireplace reminds him of that scene so many years ago. By the following Christmas, his parents had stopped smiling and his grandfather had had a stroke. His grandparents moved closer to Detroit for access to doctors and clinics. They spent their remaining years in a walk-out apartment in a cinderblock building designed for seniors.

Crowley enters the living room, the goblet in his hand. He smiles at Chris and then briefly studies a fresh set of maps above the sofa.

"Well, Chris," he begins as he sits down on the sagging armchair that Brad knows is reserved just for him, "was the dinner good?"

"Oh, yes, sir, very. Thank you."

"We're off base now, my good man. You can dispense with the 'sir's. Call me 'Father', as I am used to it and will be sure to answer, or you can call me Alex, whichever you prefer."

Hinckley is jealous. He has always called the priest 'sir', and had never been invited to refer to him in any other way. He didn't even know that Crowley's first name is Alex.

"I think I would feel more comfortable with calling you Father, if that's okay."

"Yes, yes. Absolutely, absolutely, whatever you like and whenever you like."

"Thanks," says Chris.

"Now," the priest begins, rubbing his hands together, "I promised you something when I invited you here, didn't I?"

"Yes, I think so."

"If I can recall correctly, though it was several Masses ago, I think I told you how you could find peace, the kind of peace that most people spend a lifetime searching for."

"Yes," Chris says.

"You're still interested?"

"Yes, very much. I've been wondering lately, about God, you know, the meaning of life, why I'm here, what all this means, this stuff that I've been through, you know, what life is supposed to be about."

"Well, some of those questions, I am afraid, will have to go unanswered, at least for the time being. But I can tell you the answers won't be found in the Bible, the Koran, or the Torah. I should know; I know all the works intimately, especially the Bible." Crowley sips his wine, wiping his mouth with his sleeve.

"I only know about the Bible," explains Chris. "I've never heard of those other ones."

"Not to worry," says the priest. "They're not worth knowing about. The Koran is the holy book for Islam, the

Torah is for the Jews, and they're all dribble. They're all rubbish, and so is the Bible."

Chris stares at the priest wide-eyed. He knows little of the Bible, except that it is divided into the Old and New Testaments. He does know, and has always felt intuitively, that it is a book to be revered and never bad-mouthed. He has always had the impression that to talk ill of the Bible was a sin in and of itself. He recalls some of the black recruits from the south in his company in boot camp. They gave their little pocket version of the New Testament its own revered place in their footlockers. Nothing could be placed on top of it. They showed the book that much respect.

Crowley notices Chris's look of morbid confusion. "I fully expect you to be shocked by what I have to tell you. It is information that is not easy to digest, but as it all becomes clear, you will feel like a great fog has been lifted from your eyes and the order of the world—the nature of predisposition, and the reason for many of life's mysteries—will be revealed to you. That revelation will give you an incredible sort of power that a mere mortal can hardly contend with."

Chris likes the sound of that. He has felt everything but powerful throughout his life. Even though the Navy has given him more freedom than he has ever realized, he is as near to the bottom of the ranks as is possible. The weight of the entire Navy stands above him. He has no power, no authority over anything or anyone, except his own destiny and the course he wishes it to take.

"Any questions so far?" the priest asks.

"No, Father, none."

"Very well, but first let me refresh my drink. Beer, anyone?"

Chris declines and Hinckley asks for another tin. The priest goes to the kitchen to refill his goblet. He returns to the living room with a freshly opened bottle of wine. He does not bring Brad a beer.

"Now," he continues, "where do all three of the major religions have their origins?"

"I don't know," Chris says.

"The Jews come from Israel," inserts Hinckley, starting to feel starved for attention.

"Very good, Mr. Hinckley, very good. I didn't think you would know that, but looks can be deceiving," he says, paying Brad a compliment followed by a back-handed insult. The insinuation is lost on Hinckley.

"Yeah, I knew that, and Jesus was Jewish, and the Christians probably came from Israel too?"

"Yes indeed, yes indeed. Christianity did spread from Israel. And Islam, where do you suppose it started?"

"I don't know." Chris's conscience has been bombarded with images of Palestinians across countless television screens and photographs in newspapers and magazines, throwing rocks at Israeli soldiers. He knows the Palestinians to be Muslim, and he also knows the Libyans are Muslim, as is the rest of the Middle East, a region of the world that he regards rather darkly, based on his impressions of current events. "I guess the Middle East, somewhere in there," he says, not entirely sure of his answer.

"That is correct. Saudi Arabia, to be precise, is where that religion took wing, fairly recently, actually. In the grand scheme of things, it's a mere babe compared to the other religions, especially to the one I am going to introduce to you shortly."

Chris lights a cigarette, and Brad, without asking, takes one from Chris's pack, which is set upon the coffee table.

"Now, unless I am entirely mistaken, I would say you're a Caucasian, a white male, one hundred percent, not a drop of black or red or yellow or Arabic blood in you. Is that correct?"

"Yeah, sure, of course," replies Chris.

"And so is Mr. Hinckley and so am I, which is why we're all here, together, in this house, without the company of blacks or Hispanics or any other lesser race of man."

Chris notices the use of the word "lesser" in reference to minorities, but his mind is too intoxicated to take offense.

"Where do people of our race traditionally hail from?" asks the priest, enjoying the flow of this conversation, of this instruction. Every statement he has made has been unchallenged, and he feels smug in his intellectual superiority.

"I guess we all came from over here somewhere, you know, Europe."

"Right, mainly northern and central Europe, to be more specific, but not the Middle East, wouldn't you agree?"

Chris nods and sips his beer.

"Now, I can tell you most assuredly that Europe was civilized and populated long before the birth of Christ, long before the Zionist spread of Christianity. You see, those religions—the three big monstrosities—weren't designed for people like you and me. We had our own religion, a library of beliefs and gods that were natural to us, given to us, and meant for us alone. It is blasphemous for people of our race to worship any god other than what was intended for us. You, my kind young sir," he points at Chris, "are a descendant of pure and noble and superior European stock, and your ancestors were born under the all-knowing and illuminating eye of Odin.

"Our true religion, mine, yours and anyone of European descent's, has a written history going back some eight thousand years, long before that lousy little Jew was born. The religion is called Odinism, and our Father is a god called Odin, who sits right now in his hall in Valhalla, smiling upon us. He is the father of all the gods, and also the god of magic, the god of poetry, the god of death, essentially all that is beautiful and ugly in this world. We are all a result of his union with the goddess Frigga. She is the mother of all the gods, as well as the goddess of marriage, goddess of birth and the goddess of the dawn. She is the Earth, Mother Earth, and Odin is the sky, Father Sky. And their union, their marriage, if you will, is responsible for the conception of all of us and our world, a world not meant to be intruded upon by false gods and prophets and the blood of lesser races. You see, Chris, have you ever noticed that there are so many different churches in America, but all supposedly Christian in nature? I should know—I am a part of one of the biggest. Yet there is so much conflict between them, differences of opinion, and you know why? Because each follower has an organic doubt and instinctive knowledge that what they're hearing in church and reading in the Bible is not true—certainly not for them. They are born of a higher god, and his reason resonates in their soul.

"Simply put," Crowley continues, "it is against your nature to believe in Jesus, just as it would be against your nature to live in the water like a fish, or in a tree like an ape. Did you go to church as a child?"

"Yes," says Chris.

"Me too, sometimes," says Hinckley.

"And did you enjoy it?" asks Crowley, still talking exclusively with Chris.

"No, not really."

"Exactly. Even at a tender age, it is obvious that Christianity requires a slavish devotion, a denying of oneself, everything that goes against human nature. It is a religion that plays on guilt and doubt. Your Father in heaven loves you, therefore, don't disobey, and one doubts where his soul will land when his life is over. It is a religion with a figurehead, a religion that has it all mapped out for you in a convenient little package over a thousand pages thick, vague enough to be interpreted a thousand different ways, causing a thousand different cults to arise from it, because that's all the Christian Church is—a giant tree of cult—with countless branches twisting and turning away from the same basic trunk.

"And the good thing about your natural religion is that there is no guilt. Surely common sense does prevail—you shall not kill your brother, say, or sleep with his wife. But other than that, well, I shall reveal to you further. Is any of this sinking in?"

"Yes," says Chris, "I think so. But can I ask you, if you hate Christianity so much, why are you a priest?"

"A bit hypocritical of me, isn't it? Yes it is, yes it is. Well, first of all, this is all I know, and I have a lot of training and time invested in it. I am not exactly employable in any other occupation, at least not one that could provide me with any sort of living. And most importantly, there is a certain amount of privilege being a priest. I can meet people such as yourself, and I can typically do no wrong. My actions are seldom questioned. Even the harshest of policemen tremble in front of a priest. Villains tremble before a priest. So, in order to do what I must do, I need to hide behind the collar of the clergy. In due time, if all goes well, the collar will no longer be necessary. Are you interested?"

"I think so." And Chris is somewhat interested. A religion that is not too bureaucratic does have a certain appeal. And if someone as nice as Father Crowley is a part of it, then it can't be all bad.

"Excellent. I knew you would be, but first, I must get to the bad news. As you know, growing up in Detroit, there is an assault of the white race going on in America, and, unfor-

tunately, it is spreading throughout the world. This is done by the Jews. Our mortal enemy."

Chris looks puzzled. "What do you mean?"

"Just as it isn't natural for you to have a religion other than what is innate, it is not natural for the races to live and work amongst each other. I have never been to Detroit, but I can only assume that the suburb where you lived was virtually all Caucasian, and the city is all black?"

"Yes."

"And tell me, can you tell me if there is a neighborhood or suburb where the races meet, where they live side by side, where they live in harmony? Can you?"

"No," answers Chris, and he now knows where Brad has learned his point of view. He originally thought Brad was capable of his own thinking and forming his own values based on his life experiences. He now realizes that it isn't true; Brad has learned much from the priest.

"Same way in Omaha," says Brad. "Niggers stay on their own side of town, and if a white kid like me moves in, let me tell ya, it ain't cool."

Crowley acknowledges Hinckley. "See, the voice of experience. It is against your instinct to co-exist. Brad can tell you, it doesn't work, and seldom do you see it. I will grant you, and I've noticed it since I've been in the military, there is a rash of mixed marriages going on. The reason is simple. Whoever the white party is in a mixed relation has had one of two things happen: the person of the lesser race has put them under some sort of spell, or there is some sort of possession, evil or demonic, if you will, and surely, their souls will perish. Have you ever been attracted to a black woman?"

"No," Chris says, starting to feel slightly swayed by the priest.

"Exactly. You probably wouldn't even look at one twice, and, naturally, a black girl wouldn't give you a second glance, either."

Chris nods his head, thinking that no girl will probably ever give him a second look.

"Well then, are you now willing to proceed down the path to everlasting inner peace and a fulfillment that can't be extended by any other belief, religion, or way of life?"

Life has had no better offers, so Chris thinks for a moment, a little uneasy about the xenophobic views of the priest. But no other hands of masculine or paternal friendship have been extended to him. Karen is a lukewarm companion that he happens to work with, and though he does find her beautiful and intelligent, he doesn't think he has a shot in hell of ever forming a relationship with her, at least not the kind he desires.

He nods. "Sure, why not?"

"No, no," says the priest, "there can be no equivocation on your part. You either want it or you don't. If you don't, that's fine, may the gods bless you and lead you their way at another point in your life, but if you accept, I can only tell you that I will guide you like a son."

This last statement makes Chris's heart tremble. His father has never even called him "son". In fact, he barely uttered his name in Chris's recent memory.

"Okay," he says. "I want it. I want in. What do I have to do?"

"There is a bit of initiation. Brad here has gone through it. A harmless prank, really, no different than what you might expect in a college fraternity or something like that. Grab your coats and take some beers. We're going on a trip."

Quickly and with some confusion, they don their jackets, as does the priest, grabbing his leather coat from the back of a kitchen chair. He stands on the couch and rips down the map of Aberdeen, studies it, and haphazardly folds it and places it in his pocket.

Each of them stumbles as they walk out of the warm house and through the front door into the cold night. It is still early, not quite 10 p.m., and the sky is as clear as Chris has ever seen it since he's been in Scotland. The black and cloudless night is filled with a multitude of stars, so thick and clear that the outline of the Milky Way, a thick white ring, can be seen arching across the sky.

The priest opens his Austin Allegro and looks at Brad and points at the back seat. Brad frowns and climbs in the back, his oversized body very cramped and uncomfortable as he squeezes himself behind the pushed-up driver's seat. He sits amongst a pile of debris, paper and wrappers and food containers. The priest has never bothered cleaning out the car since he purchased it.

Chris climbs in the front and slowly the car starts as Crowley pulls the manual choke and then returns it to the running position as the car begins to idle smoothly. He wipes the inside of the windshield with his sleeve; their breath has already cast a fog upon the glass.

Quickly he drives away, causing the tires to spin on the gravel driveway as he accelerates towards the main road out to the A92.

Something suddenly comes to Chris as he stares out the passenger window, searching the now empty and black fields that during the day contain sheep and farmhouses and trees, interrupted by the occasional side road leading towards another village.

If Crowley tends to have racist views, no matter what his justification, what was his role in the treachery of Lee Rodgers? Chris shivers. He fears what he has gotten himself into.

He is afraid to ask, but he must. He had asked Brad in the past if he knew about Lee, and Brad had said no, but he was skeptical even then and didn't enquire any further for fear of having to know the truth. But now he must, as he has made a sort of commitment, willingly, with the priest, as if he has become a part of a family, a bizarre and macabre family more closely knit than the one from his past, who are now scattered from Scotland to Michigan to Arizona or god-only-knows where.

"Umm, Father Crowley?" Chris asks, retrieving his nearly empty packet of cigarettes from the shirt pocket of his best button-down shirt, his Sunday church shirt.

"Yes?" Crowley replies, knowing that he is too drunk to drive but also sensing that the angels from Valhalla, his white angels, are twinkling in the night sky and swirling around the Allegro as it cuts through the evening, speeding north several miles faster than the legal limit. Crowley is not concerned in the least, not worried in the least about the police who heavily patrol this highway, which is the main thoroughfare for Eastern Scotland. He now feels the white lights are elves known as the Alfar, the holy elves who reside in the uppermost part of heaven and who do Odin's bidding, traveling to Earth to guide him and to protect his chosen ones.

"Well, no offense, but I know that Brad here and Lee Rodgers were friends, and I heard you were with him when he committed suicide. I heard about what he did, and from what you've told me tonight, you know, it just seems..."

Crowley is prepared for the question, and he fields it the same way he dealt with the halfhearted inquiries from his commanding officer, from Chaplain Lambert, from the base security department, and the easy questions asked with doubtful eyes from Chief Wilson, the master-at-arms.

"It must appear awkward," Crowley replies without hesitation, "especially in light of my faith, but I assure you," and he turns to glare at Hinckley, as this is a topic they didn't think to address before bringing Chris into their fold, "that Lee acted alone. I wouldn't condone such careless actions. I knew what he believed, and that in itself wasn't bad, he just went about it the wrong way. Neither Mr. Hinckley nor I had any idea about what he was up to, but we did have discussions—you understand, discussions only—about the topic of race and the injustice the white man receives in American society, and how that injustice is especially amplified in the military, where there is no natural separation of the races. They are all forced to live together, unlike in the States, where people have instinctively settled amongst their own kind. Lee was a disturbed young man indeed, and what he did in Dundee and his suicide later can be marked as one of the most cowardly acts I've ever seen in all my years as a priest. I will agree with the Church on one score; suicide is indeed a most blatant act of selfishness, and a sign of weakness. Our religion tells us that weakness makes us vulnerable to attack, and whatever hardships we face only can make us stronger. Lee was faced with hardship. He had a deep sense of guilt and an even deeper fear of being caught and arrested for murder. He could have been a shining example for our faith and for our race. Instead, he chose to flee, in a most permanent way. Neither Mr. Hinckley nor myself had anything to do with his demise. Brad lost a dear friend, and I lost a potential student of the faith."

Chris is satisfied, mostly, with Crowley's answer. He opens a can of beer. He drinks it greedily, as the effects of the alcohol previously consumed are starting to recede, leaving a dull headache in its wake.

"Okay, good. I was kind of wondering, you know, because of some of the things you said tonight and all that stuff he did. It seemed kind of like, you know, you could have been doing things with him. I'm sorry for doubting you, Father."

"No need for apology. I suspected you may ask about that situation, a situation I wish to discuss no further." Again he turns to glare at Hinckley in the back seat, who already has a collection of empty tins of beer gathering at his feet. "Leave in the past what belongs to the past. Life moves forward, not backward."

"Okay," says Chris.

"I will say this," Crowley says, scratching his cheek. "Lee did give me an idea for our initiation rite tonight. This I will reveal to you as soon as we arrive in Aberdeen."

The rest of the drive is silent in the smoking of cigarettes and the drinking of beer while Chris stares at the moon, which hovers full over the ever turbulent North Sea. Chris stares at the sea and wonders about the life on the other side. Crowley stares at the sea and longs to be on the other side, Norway, where he knows there are many adherents to his faith and he could find friendship in between the fjords and the mountains and the infrequent cities.

As Aberdeen approaches and the signs loom indicating the turn-offs for the city center, Crowley retrieves his map from his pocket and unfolds it on top of the steering wheel, causing the car to swerve and causing the cars traveling in parallel lanes to sound their horns, but he is oblivious to their irritation. He is in deep concentration and in frustration hands the map over the seat to Hinckley. "Find me Dee Street, and get us there."

Hinckley takes the map and flips it over several times, unable to detect in the moonlight and the now present street lamps which way the map should be read.

"Hell, I don't know," he says, too intoxicated to focus on the seeming irrational lines of the map. "I don't know where the hell we're at now."

"Chris?" Crowley looks at Chris, and Chris understands that he is looking to him for help. Chris takes the map. He knows they have just entered the southern edge of the city along the A92. The light is better in the front seat than in the back, and the lights from the buildings along the edge of the city provide even more illumination. Chris quickly finds Dee Street. After a quarter of an hour, they cross a bridge over what must be the Dee River and find the street they're looking for.

Crowley slowly drives down the street. A line of cars forms behind Crowley's Allegro, and again the sound of horns slices through the night. He is looking for an address, number 74, and all his attention is focused on the numbers on the buildings, which are hard to distinguish, as many of them are only seen in recessed doorways.

Finally, he finds the building and speeds up to drive around the block. He points to the building and things start to make sense to Chris.

It is a synagogue.

Crowley parks the car illegally a few streets over, in front of an institution of some sort, perhaps a school. The sign indicates they are parked in a fire lane, but Crowley ignores it. He instructs Brad to stay in the car, to keep an eye on it, as he and Chris have business to conduct.

They step out of the car and walk back towards Dee Street, the Friday night sounds of downtown Aberdeen audible nearby. Chris can feel the edge of the oncoming spring in the air, a feeling that he has always enjoyed, even as a child. The air has a warm and damp quality, and the odorless chilly air gives way to an air that carries all the smells of its surrounding earth, soil, and the grass and flowers and trees that are about to enjoy a reincarnation.

"Chris, you are a lucky young man indeed. Very few are initiated so quickly into our faith. Often, months of study are required, but I can tell you're an apt pupil, and time is wasting. We have a war on our hands, and you are about to enter into the fray." Crowley says this as he walks hurriedly down the street, Chris's shorter legs working hard to remain in a walking stride to keep up with him.

The initiation rite that Crowley is about to administer is a fictitious one, one he made up on his recent trip to Edinburgh, but the idea came to him as an epiphany as his mind raced throughout the week to come up with a way to quickly indoctrinate Chris—and a way to make him culpable also, at least to make him think he's culpable, for whatever they may attempt in what is the very immediate future.

They approach the synagogue. Crowley is disappointed that so many cars are streaming by and their actions will not go unobserved; the doorway to the building is quite well lit underneath the high streetlamps and the harsh moonlight.

But as they approach the front of the synagogue, Crowley rubs his eyes and there he sees dancing in the streetlights and in the air above the door and walkway of the synagogue the white and flickering lights he has come to know and love so well.

"Alfar," he says, and Chris looks at him. Crowley points into the air. Chris follows his finger and sees nothing, just a long sidewalk going uphill in front of shop windows and cars parked in the road.

"Don't you see them?" asks Crowley, hoping that Chris, too, has been deigned significant enough to be given that glimpse of the hand of Odin.

Chris shakes his head. "Do I see what, Father Crowley?"

"Never mind," replies the priest, sighing with a certain gravity. "The emissaries of Valhalla are here, here for your initiation."

"Really?" Chris asks. He believes Crowley is sincere, as the man seems very spiritual to him, as if he is gifted with an extra sense of the world unseen, the world of spirits and realms and principalities that Chris has read of in many of his horror books, but has never known.

"Yes, really." Crowley loses his fear of being seen by any passersby. He feels again somewhat invincible, and he removes a safety pin from the pocket of his leather coat. The coat seems phosphorescent as it reflects the artificial light of the illuminated night.

He grabs Chris's right hand and says nothing in a sort of mock Icelandic, a language he longs to speak but is too lazy to attempt to learn, and his mind is too pre-occupied with the scope of his own private race war to devote any additional intellectual energy. The artificial Icelandic is for Chris's benefit and deception; it is meant to lend credence to this mock ceremony and to help ensure Chris's belief in Crowley's spiritual prowess.

He pokes Chris's right index finger quickly. Chris can barely feel the prick, as the air and evening breeze mixed with the alcohol of the beer serve as a sort of anesthesia. Crowley squeezes the finger until the blood comes in a current. Still holding his hand, he leads him to the front door of the synagogue, a darker door than the one in Edinburgh, but this does not discourage the priest. He takes Chris's hand and with his index finger leads him to draw a swastika, though a vague and sloppy one, and again signs it "The Trinity".

Crowley is still holding Chris's hand he steps away from the door to get a look at their work. Satisfied, he turns and walks away. Chris shakes his hand loose and reluctantly, the priest loosens his grip.

"There, there," the priest says. "There is no turning back now. You've just committed in blood."

"What did all that mean?" asks Chris solemnly. "Why the swastika? What is the Trinity?"

"Well, the swastika is quite intimidating to the Jews. As you know, it is a symbol for the German Nazis, who were on the right track, I must say. The Trinity is you, me and Mr. Hinckley. You indeed are one of us now. We were 'The Trinity of the Great White Brotherhood of Eastern Scotland', but the name is too grand sounding and a bit bombastic. I—we—simplified it. The Trinity is much neater sounding, more precise. Holy. It's a name that can mean different things to different people, but it carries a certain power."

"Oh," says Chris, not sure of what certain power the priest is referring to.

A god whispers in Crowley's ear, and the white lights swirl around his eyes. "Don't trust the boy."

He is startled. This is the first time a god has spoken during a conscious moment. The voice in his ear was powerful yet old. It spoke with a certain authority that causes Crowley to feel fear for the first time since his father was alive.

I've just heard the voice of Odin. Instantly, a plan is hatched in his brain and he thinks the inspiration is Odin-sent. His mouth forms words that come from nowhere in mind, but deep, deep from the caverns of his much-blackened heart.

"Now, Chris," the priest says, inspired by the voice as they approach the car, where an unconscious Hinckley is slumped in the back seat, "there is no turning back now. You're with me one hundred percent. Ours is a faith not without discipline, and it will require a certain amount of devotion and a certain amount of work. All religion has a cost. I suggest strongly that you keep no other friends other than Brad or myself or whomever we let in. Our secrecy must be maintained, and the risk of compromise is too great."

This the priest says without looking into Chris's eyes, unlike the rest of the evening's conversations, as he has constantly kept eye contact with Chris throughout every verbal exchange.

Chris thinks of Karen, and already he can feel her slip away. This gives rise to a certain amount of anxiety. In his mind he can see her waving farewell to him, as if all they have shared would now only be a memory and not an active friendship or relationship that he longed for. However, Chris realizes that she doesn't feel for him the way he feels for her, so he can justify the severing of his longing and transfer that emotion to the priest and whatever the priest requires.

The priest's words do cause a certain amount of fear; there is a finality in what he says, in his call for unequivocal devotion. Chris feels like he has just stepped off of a deep ledge and he is feeling terror for the first time in many years, perhaps the first real fear he has ever felt.

They approach the car. Hinckley is unconscious in the back seat, a collection of empty tins of beer surrounding him. Chris thinks briefly about leaving on his own and severing his ties with the priest as quickly as possible, but he doesn't. He climbs into the front seat and resigns himself to fate.

C hris returns to work on Monday, the thought of what he has become in the back of his mind.

Subconsciously, he knows there is something wrong with the priest's beliefs and his own acceptance of those beliefs. He rationalizes it consciously with the fact that the priest is the only adult to show him any sort of respect, as if his opinion and well-being were of value. The priest also invited him to be his friend, and the priest is not a nobody, unlike the only friends he ever had in his past, a small collection of boys that he spent most of his schooldays with, a collection that found itself in the margins of the school-age society.

He is not sure what approach he is going to take with Karen, as the priest has all but forbidden him from having friends other than him or Hinckley. This makes Chris anxious, and he is trying to decide if he should act the same or if he should treat Karen with indifference, perhaps avoiding conversation with her as much as two people stuck in a room for twelve hours together possibly can.

He decides to act much the same as he has in the past, but this idea is discarded when he sees her and their watch begins. He doesn't feel the same, so it is difficult for him to act the same.

He adopts a sullen approach and doesn't speak to her for the first hour of the shift, a time when they usually engage in small talk while reading the reports from the previous watch and updating the logbook.

Karen notices this but doesn't take offense. She is not unversed in human nature, especially the nature of young men. She writes it off as a mood swing that men are prone to suffer, though the fact that women are notorious for this trait always strikes her as sexist.

They spend the watch in near silence. Chris doesn't look her in the eye once.

The second watch in the string comes along and again, Chris's behavior is unchanged. Karen is now concerned and wonders if it is something she said or did that is affecting him so much. She searches her brain and recalls their previous conversations—the words exchanged and the mood—and she can remember nothing unsavory. She is also concerned because he may be hurt in some way, regardless if she offended him or not. She wants to help him.

This is puzzling and somewhat disconcerting for her. She is not sure if her concern for Chris is maternal instinct or something she fears even stronger: her attraction to this boy.

When the watch is nearly a quarter complete, Karen can stand it no longer. After a few attempts to goad Chris into their normal flow of conversation, she asks in exasperation, "What the hell is the matter with you?"

He stares at his computer screen. "Nothing." He doesn't turn to face her, but he can see her reflection staring at him in the illuminated blackness of the blank monitor.

"Bullshit."

Chris is startled by her unusual use of profanity. His gaze remains on the computer monitor, and he can see her forehead and her eyes crease in what appears to be anger.

"You haven't said shit to me in two days, and I can't help but wonder if I've done something to piss you off."

"You haven't." He revolves in his chair to face her, but he avoids looking in her eyes. He wonders for the first time about her ancestry, her darkish hair, her brown eyes and the shape of her nose, which he has never considered before. He notices she is of a darker complexion than he is, and he knows from somewhere that those of Jewish origin appear darker than the garden-variety Western Europeans from whom he is descended.

Freeman. He runs her name in his mind. German? English? Jewish? He doesn't know, and he realizes he has never wondered about another's ancestry before, but suddenly, in this semi-confrontation with Karen, it becomes of some importance.

"I just have things on my mind, that's all."

"I thought so. Jesus Christ, you've been a moody little son-of-a-bitch. Is there something I can help you with? Whatever you're going through, I've probably been through it myself."

"No, I don't need help," he says. "I'm just thinking about myself, my life, where it's going."

"Well," she says, "you're too young to have a mid-life crisis, so snap out of it. It's boring enough being here for twelve hours at a time. We don't need to make it any more miserable than it already is."

He agrees and is less despondent as the watch progresses, but he still doesn't smile at her. She seems very far away to him now. He is still attracted to her, but she is unattainable and now off-limits, and his immature mind is trying to distance himself from her.

As the watch concludes, Karen wonders what Chris will be like when they meet again in forty-eight hours. She knows he isn't being truthful, that there is something causing the change in his behavior.

She plans to find out what.

With synagogues in Edinburgh and Aberdeen being desecrated, the investigations by the Borders and Lothian Police in Edinburgh and the Grampian Police in Aberdeen have all resulted in phone calls to Inspector Holliday, who in turn calls Constable Robertson in the quiet solitude of his office in Lutherkirk.

There is a common thread—the racist nature of the crimes and the use of the word "Trinity"—that links the attacks on the synagogues instantly with the murder in Dundee earlier in the winter.

"Our friend is at it again," says Holliday. Robertson immediately recognizes his voice. The two haven't spoken for several months. Their paths haven't crossed; the cares of Dundee are many miles from the bucolic life of Lutherkirk.

Holliday fills Robertson in on the details of the crimes in Aberdeen and Edinburgh, and the bloody signature left on each door. Evidence technicians reveal nothing. The fingerprints are unknown, and the blood on each door is of a different type, indicating the activity of more than one person.

"Well," Robertson replies, "I have driven by the priest's place now and again. Haven't noticed anything unusual, you know, no signs of gatherings or anything, though he is a peculiar bloke. I've seen him standing about in his garden wearing nothin' but a bathrobe when it's cold enough to see your breath. Maybe this is just a recent act of imitation; maybe some lads got the idea from what happened in Dundee and decided to have a go at a few synagogues, just for laughs, you know. No damage has been done, just graffiti, not murder, like what happened in your town."

"Maybe," replies Holliday in a brogue much less thick than Robertson's, his pronunciation a little more urbane. "Still, most lads apt to copy something like that would have been brought in before, and their prints would come up.

You're right, there are a lot of blokes who don't like anyone but Scots, and they don't even care for *them* most of the time. Maybe it is an imitation, but my gut tells me different. This priest is testing the water, stirring the pot, seeing what kind of ripple he comes up with."

"Worth paying him a visit?"

"Absolutely. Even though nothing has happened in Tayside, there is no law against knocking on his door and seeing if he's home. I'll be up there tomorrow."

Holliday and Robertson agree to meet the following evening, a Saturday. Robertson will find out what time the Saturday Mass is and plan accordingly. They will drive to the priest's house as the afternoon approaches evening. If he's not in, they'll wait.

"You're off again this weekend, aren't you?" Brad asks Chris as they sit alone eating supper.

The galley is nearly closed, and the sound of the dishes being sprayed and the cutlery being sorted in the scullery echoes in the nearly empty dining room.

"Yes."

"Good, I thought so." His voice lowers to a whisper. "Father Crowley called me this afternoon. He wants us to go to Glasgow on Saturday, early. He has to be back in time for evening Mass. Have you been to Glasgow?"

"No." Chris shakes his head, excited about the prospect of travel to Scotland's largest city. "What are we going to do?"

"Not sure. There's something he wants us to look at. He wants to take the first train because he doesn't feel like driving this time. He'll pick us up at the gate at 0700. You'll have to make sure I get up."

Chris rolls his eyes. His roommate is not an early riser on the weekends and often sleeps through breakfast.

"Sure, no problem," Chris says reluctantly. "Where do we catch the train?"

"Montrose."

"Cool." Chris has never traveled by train.

On Saturday, Chris tugs Brad out of bed. Due to the constraints of time, they forego breakfast and wander out the front gate of the base and walk a quarter mile down the road, past the eyes of the suspicious MoDP officer posted at the gate.

Chris can hear the Allegro before it is visible. It arrives followed by a cloud of blue smoke that hangs thick in the foggy morning air that hovers over the crystal and dewy ground.

"Good morning, good morning," Crowley says quite pleasantly. "Beautiful morning for a train ride, wouldn't you say?" He points to a hole in the clouds over the rim of the valley, sunlight trying to inch its way across the sky.

"The car's acting up, and I don't want to risk taking it on such a long trip," explains the priest. The car shows its own evidence, as it tends to hesitate all the way to Montrose, fifteen miles to the east of the base, a larger town on the North Sea.

Crowley purchases their tickets and they walk out onto the barely covered platform, where a collection of Scottish people of various ages wait for the next southbound train.

Chris, in his excitement, cranes his neck around the bend of the track, looking north, waiting for the train to come.

The fog has now lifted and the sun is nearly risen. A northeasterly wind blows the scent of the sea Chris's way, and he inhales the dampness and the salt and feels worldly again. He is traveling across the country, and though it is only two hours away, it is still across the country. He is going to a big city. He recalls the thrill he felt upon spying the edge of New York, its seemingly infinite number of skyscrapers jutting out of the lower end of Manhattan between what he knew from his television-provided education to be the Empire State Building and the World Trade Center.

He is looking forward to that thrill again, and feels it is much better to travel with company. If he were traveling alone, he would feel scrutinized by all those unfamiliar faces staring at him on the platform. Now, in the strong presence of the priest, he barely notices them. They are just part of the landscape, like the train tracks themselves.

The train arrives and Crowley and Chris board, armed with paper cups of steaming tea from a vending machine on the platform. Hinckley foregoes tea and buys a small can of Coke with 30p he borrowed from Chris. The car, marked Scot Rail, is somewhat shabby on the inside but more comfortable than Chris expects. They sit in a berth not unlike a restaurant booth, cloth benches on either side of a white linoleum table.

They sit as far as possible from the other passengers, and talk in near-whispers.

The train rolls away and Chris looks out the window as Crowley begins to speak.

"Now, I suppose you want to know what we're doing today." Crowley has a sports bag on his lap, which he hugs as if it were as dear as an infant. Chris spies the word "Umbro" on the bag, and knows the priest purchased the bag in Scotland and rightly assumes it is a bag used by soccer players.

Chris nods and Hinckley smiles. Chris senses from his smile that Hinckley already has an idea about what they're going to do.

"Well," he says, smiling as broadly as Chris has ever seen, "we're going to extend an invitation for the Jews to leave Scotland." He pats the bag and scans the car, to make sure no one can hear him.

He unzips the bag and motions for Chris to lean over the table and take a look inside.

Chris moves his cup of tea close to the window and arches his body over the table. He looks inside the bag. He can smell gasoline, and he sees short pieces of pipe with wicks sticking out of them and four or five corked wine bottles wrapped in rags with a thin and dirty liquid inside them.

Chris understands it all in an instant. He sits back as Crowley zips up the bag.

They ride in silence. The towns roll past, and as they go south and west, the scenery changes. The landscape is a bit more lush; the trees are starting to show green on the edges. The train rolls across high bridges over rivers and valleys with names Chris does not know. He stares out the window, trying to understand what Crowley has planned exactly, unsure what role he will be required to play when they disembark in Glasgow.

The train stops in Stirling, and Chris can feel the edge of Glasgow approaching, the lack of empty spaces visible from the train window, the endless array of power lines and telephone cables. They enter a cavern and emerge in the middle of the illuminated labyrinth that is the Glasgow train station.

Upon disembarking, Chris spies the multitude of trains, the growing throng of people, the large clock on the wall at the focal point of the station, and he feels he's stepped into an old black and white movie.

They scurry up some stairs leading outside the station and step out into the heart of Glasgow.

Chris expects to see a city not unlike an American city, towers of glass and steel shrouding wide avenues, but not here. The scene is more like an overgrown Aberdeen or Dundee, blocks of low stone buildings barely casting shadows on the concrete and pavement underneath.

They enter a cab from a long queue outside the train station. The cab is unlike the Ladas or Skodas or Vauxhalls that buzz around the base. Again, he feels like he steps back into an old movie as they enter a black taxi that looks like an old car, like he imagines a Packard or Studebaker would appear, with large doors, a high roof and a rounded hood.

Crowley's face is serene as he clutches the duffel bag against his chest. Hinckley nervously smiles and lights a cigarette, even though the priest looks at him with disdain. Chris looks out the window, studying the would-be skyline.

The driver assumes the odd trio are tourists, a father and two sons, perhaps. "So you here on holiday?" he asks, staring at the rearview mirror. Chris can barely understand him, as his brogue is even thicker and bit more lilting than the dialect spoken around the base. From his travels, Crowley's ear is more in tune with the sounds of Scotland, and he answers right away.

"No, no," replies the priest. "We're here to rescue Scotland." He looks out the window and taps his bag to make sure its contents are still intact. "Please take us to the Newton Mearns Synagogue, Beech Avenue, please."

"You Jewish?" the cab driver asks. "You don't look Jewish, none of you"

"No, no," replies the priest. "We're not Jewish, but thank you for the compliment." He laughs, and the cab driver laughs with him. "We're going there to take care of some unfinished business from the thirteenth century."

The driver looks in the mirror and stares at Crowley, a look of confusion plain on his face.

"Read up on Edward I at your library, and then watch the news. You'll know who we are after that." This the priest says with pride, and Chris is alarmed. How can Crowley advertise what he's planning? What if the police get involved and the cab driver comes forward somehow? He will recognize them, and though Chris himself hasn't spoken, he is traveling with the priest. He is culpable.

Crowley looks at Chris and can read his thoughts by his expression. He winks at him. He pats Chris on the knee in reassurance and allows the hand to linger there for longer than necessary. Chris is reassured and realizes the priest knows what he's doing. He is comforted.

The cab driver clears his throat. "I'm a quarter Jewish, on my mother's side. She came from Warsaw just before the war."

"Oh." The priest squints as he stares at the rearview mirror and studies what is visible of the cab driver's face. Chris watches as the priest scrutinizes the dark hair, the pale but ruddy face behind a normal sized nose, which supports a black-framed pair of spectacles. Chris can see the accumulated dirt and smudge marks on the cab driver's eyeglasses, as if they haven't been cleaned in some time.

"Well, that is interesting, that you're Jewish. I wouldn't have guessed that. You're not a practicing Jew, are you?"

"No, Church of Scotland I was raised, but, you know, I always pull for Israel. Every time I hear about a squabble in the Middle East, I always cheer for them, sort of like rooting for the home side."

"There is nothing wrong with loyalty to your ancestry." Crowley looks out the window as the cab rolls to a stop.

"Here you are. That'll be ten pounds," the cab driver says with a bit of cheer, the change of conversation somewhat refreshing. It's not every fare that dares to talk about something as occasionally cryptic as religion.

"I'll take care of that." Crowley hands his bag to Hinckley and tells the two young men to wait outside, to walk towards a cemetery that is next door to the synagogue, a drab building along a fairly wide avenue for European standards.

As Brad and Chris walk away, the priest pretends to search for his wallet, watching Brad and Chris walk until they're out of earshot. Impatient, the cab driver turns to face Crowley.

"Sorry, I should have it here somewhere." He pulls the wallet triumphantly from the inner pocket of his black leather coat. "Ah, here it is. How much did you say the fare was?"

As the cab driver turns to read his meter, Crowley grabs him from behind and in an instant puts one arm around his neck to choke him. With his other gloved hand, he manipulates the driver's head until his neck snaps.

It is the one lesson he kept from his father, who taught the young Alexander self defense all through junior high, as he was sure he would be picked on later in life.

The cab driver dies instantly. His head slumps down, and he looks as if he's taking a nap.

Crowley reaches over the seat and turns off the ignition.

"Cheers." He leaves the taxi and goes to find his two young protégés.

They are standing at the gate of the Jewish cemetery attached to the synagogue. Chris is standing with his hands in his pockets, shivering from the still cold morning; it is not quite 10:30 a.m. Brad is holding the bag just as Crowley did, with a tremendous amount of delicacy.

"Excellent, excellent," the priest says, surveying the cemetery, which is perhaps only an acre, with a wooded rise in the middle, providing a shelter from the view of the motorists and pedestrians who may happen along the wide boulevard and narrow sidewalk.

Crowley reaches into the duffel bag and pulls out a manila envelope containing a handwritten letter, another letter done by Brad per the priest's instructions over the phone on the previous Friday. He attaches the letter to the granite face of the cemetery gate with a roll of tape that he has in a pocket of his jacket.

He will reveal the contents to Chris later, when circumstances deem the knowledge necessary.

They enter the cemetery, Crowley walking in the front, Chris and Brad walking behind him side by side. Crowley leads them to the center of the cemetery.

He points to a spot of bare ground next to a flower-strewn headstone, and Brad gently deposits the bag. He then grabs the two young men and tells them to form a circle with their hands. Awkwardly, they do, and Crowley looks to the sky and asks Odin to guide them and protect them as they do his bidding, returning the northern part of Europe to its rightful heirs and banishing all interlopers from Odin's realm.

Chris shudders as a passing cloud covers the sun at the conclusion of Crowley's plea to Valhalla, as if Odin is acknowledging the priest.

Crowley opens up the bag and retrieves the wine bottles. He deposits them haphazardly around the trees that provide them shelter. He then takes his crude pipe bombs, made with the material he has been collecting, and deposits them next to the bottles.

Slowly and deliberately, he ties them all together with a 60-yard spool of ignition wire that he managed to buy through the mail from a granite supply company in the States, the kind of wire quarrymen use to tie dynamite caps to blast rock.

The company wouldn't ship explosives overseas. He did inquire.

He connects a wick to each of the four pipe bombs and places gasoline soaked handkerchiefs in the tops of the wine bottles, to serve as crude wicks for those as well. He then takes a leftover wine bottle and pours gasoline on the trunks of the nearby trees.

Chris and Brad stand by wordlessly and watch him. They know from observing his clumsiness that he is a novice in the realm of pyrotechnics.

Brad lights a cigarette. "You want to blow us all up, you common idiot?" Crowley barks, and Hinckley immediately stomps out the cigarette. He keeps stomping until even the smoke is extinguished.

Finally, the pipe bombs and wine bottles are arranged to Crowley's satisfaction. They have been in the cemetery for half an hour and Chris can hear the Glasgow roar, the cacophonous sounds of traffic that don't quite overpower the collected voices of the pedestrians that drift over the cemetery from the sidewalk.

Crowley douses the Umbro bag and leaves it in the center. It is now empty, and he no longer has any use for it. He walks with the spool of wire trailing behind him, making a path towards the cemetery gate. Brad and Chris hurry along beside him, too afraid to stay behind him, in case they, too, somehow become ignited.

The spool runs out just inside the gate, and in the full view of passersby who take no notice, Crowley asks for Brad's lighter. Brad fumbles it out of his pants pocket and hands it to the priest, who holds the end of the wire in his right hand.

"No," says the priest. "You want to be part of this, you light it."

Brad lights the wire. Chris is shaking. He notes that Hinckley is as calm as bathwater.

The wire hisses and they follow Crowley out of the gate. Chris wants to run, but Crowley walks as if he were walking down the aisle during the opening procession of a Mass.

They are just ten yards away when they hear the pipe bombs go off, a near deafening roar. The pedestrians freeze, but the automobile traffic moves on. The pedestrians only stop for a moment as they write off the noise as just another sound of urban civilization.

They are almost a full block away when they turn and see the smoke rising from the cemetery, and a block and a half away when they hear the sound of sirens.

Crowley grins broadly. He walks between Brad and Chris, his arms around them.

Constable Robertson arrives in his little storefront station half an hour before Holliday is due to arrive.

He turns on the lights. The fluorescents hum and seem so out of place in the century-old building. Robertson plugs in the hotplate and takes a mug and rinses it out in the sink and readies it for a cup of tea. It is Saturday. His office is usually closed and calls are forwarded to the station in Brechin, but he does come in on occasion if there has been a bit of trouble the night before or if there are reports to write or follow-up calls to make.

The kettle whistles after what seems an eternity and he pours the tea. The steam from the clean but stained mug rises and ends at his furrowed brow. He bobs the tea bag up and down and discards it in the lined wastebasket next to his desk, pours some milk and adds more than his usual amount of sugar, as he is trying to build up the energy and maybe a little courage to confront the priest.

He goes over to the teletype and rips up the accumulated paper. He scans the items line by line and looks for what is germane to his part of the country.

He sees the word "Trinity" and stops. He reads of the murder of the cab driver, of the fire in a Jewish cemetery in Glasgow, a city that seems worlds away to him, full of industry and commerce and pestilence. It is not known if the murder of the cab driver is related to the desecration of the cemetery, but it is assumed, and the investigations are intertwined. There is mention of a note left on the cemetery gate, and that is where the name "Trinity" is drawn from, but the contents of the note are not printed for the rest of law enforcement in Great Britain.

Holliday will know, thinks Robertson. He'll have all the details on the tip of his tongue, have them as part of his intimate knowledge.

He is somewhat comforted by the fact that the crimes occurred on a Saturday, making it unlikely that Crowley is indeed responsible, as he has Mass to perform Saturday afternoon. That would take the problem away from his attention, and his life and work would return to normal, as leisurely as a cup of tea with someone he has known for years stopping in at the station.

He checks the time on the report, approximately 10:45 a.m. He sighs. There was plenty of time for Crowley to return to Lutherkirk, plenty of time to perform Mass.

He looks out the window and sees two Americans walking down the street, a husband and a wife, older, senior enlisted, he guesses. The man doesn't have the slender or genteel look of an officer. He is slightly pudgy and mustached with silver-rimmed glasses. They live in the village. Robertson has seen them about, but they occupy that parallel universe of America that floats through the Lutherkirk air. He doesn't bother to memorize their names, as they will be gone suddenly, transferred to another part of the world. The man sees Robertson in the window and smiles and waves. He has seen the constable before. He recognizes and respects the uniform.

Typically, the constable would return the smile and the wave. But not now. He has developed a subconscious resentment for Americans. If the Americans weren't here, none of this vileness would have happened. There would have been no murders, no rocks thrown through windows, no grotesque suicide in a cottage just outside his wee little village. Life would have progressed with nary a ripple.

He pretends not to see the Americans. He looks at the top of his desk and shuffles some papers.

Holliday arrives as the sun sets. His white Cortina pulls up in front of the station and he parks not quite parallel to the curb.

"Wouldn't dream of doing that back in Dundee," he says. "Kind of nice to be up here in the country and not have to worry about such things."

"No, we just have racist priests sailing around the bloody country leaving a bloody wake in their trail," Robertson says with a hint of a smile.

Holliday laughs, and coughs as he loses his breath in a guffaw. He wheezes for a moment and his face turns red, but in an instant, his composure returns. "As soon as I retire, I'm giving up the fags." He points at a box of cigarettes tucked into his shirt pocket. He is wearing a tweed jacket that at one time fit him quite nicely but now hugs him at the waist and in the shoulders and it is too short in the sleeves. He is wearing a striped and faded blue shirt and a wide maroon tie. None of the three articles of clothing match his gray trousers, but the disorder of his attire is just part of the overall essence of the inspector, so he doesn't really come across as looking peculiar at all.

"Tea?" asks Robertson, pointing to the kettle on the hotplate next to his desk.

"That would be fine," replies the inspector. "We had better develop a plan of attack before going to see this priest bloke." He looks at his watch and sits in a chair in front of Robertson's desk, crossing his legs and making himself as comfortable as possible in a padded metal chair.

Robertson plugs in the hotplate and rinses another mug for the inspector. He returns to his desk. "I suppose you know about Glasgow?"

"Yes, I do. I think our friend is getting nasty again."

"But we have no proof."

"Correct. We have no proof."

"I'm a bit out of my league here. How do we get proof?"

"Well, usually someone has to tell us something. The last time we visited our good American priest, he seemed to like to talk, but not about the truth. So we talk in his fashion—not dishonest, but misleading."

"How do you mean?"

"Follow my lead when I talk, and you'll see, but I want you to remain as close as possible to the door, just in case."

"If he bolts?"

"Yes, or if someone else comes in."

They are silent as the kettle comes to a boil. Robertson stands to make the tea, but Holliday puts up his hand, telling him to stay seated, that he will fend for himself. The inspector stands up and re-hitches his sagging pants as far over his vast stomach as possible. He makes himself tea. A little milk, a lot of sugar.

He sits down, retrieves a cigarette from his pocket, and offers one to the constable.

Robertson shakes his head and slides a clean ashtray across the desk for the inspector to use. "You know," says the constable, "he may not be involved. To go all the way to Glasgow on a day he normally works—granted, he doesn't work until late in the afternoon—would be a bit unusual. Unless he knew what he was going to do, and had it planned to the minute. What did the note say, by the way?"

"Oh, yes." Holliday pulls a wad of paper from inside his jacket. "An old friend of mine in the Strathclyde department called me. They have armies of racists in that bloody city, but the armies don't have a wide number of targets to choose from. Just some Pakis, some Turks, a few blacks, you know, transplants from the West Indies, no large population. Never, ever, has he seen something so randomly violent as this." Holliday relays more information to the constable, the crude pipe bombs and wine bottles, the discarded athletic bag, the cab driver murdered and the letter, a chilling and worrisome letter, promising more things to come.

He reads:

To the wretched Zionists who deign to call Scotland home,

This is an invitation to you who so want to undermine the white race and subject it to perpetual slavery. We know who you are, and what you've been up to throughout the ages, the financial slavery of those who are genetically superior. You had the foresight to control the wealth of nations by owning its banks and printing paper money you established control that has yet to be wrestled, even in this modern and evil world of which you truly reign supreme. But you don't control us. We are whites of European stock, indigenous to this part of the world. You belong in Palestine, in that wretched part of the world. This is your invitation and opportunity to leave, we give you a month. If you don't, the blood of your wives and children will be spilled on the streets of this fine, white country. When you leave, the Asians, and blacks, and those from the Middle East who follow your dollars will leave also, and Scotland will once again be the strict domain of one of the most ancient white races on this planet. The month starts today.

The Trinity

"And they signed it in blood," concludes Holliday, folding up the wad of paper and placing it back in his pocket. "That may not be word for word, mind you; I scribbled as he talked, but in our profession, as you know, we learn to scribble rather quickly."

"I wouldn't know," replies Constable Robertson. "I can barely type, let alone take notes." He sips his tea. "So since the young American died in the priest's home, the focus of attack has gone from blacks to the Jews. Why?"

Holliday shrugs his shoulders. "Dunno. Maybe this is an imitation. Maybe the shootings in Dundee gave birth to an idea already fermenting in Scottish lads. I dunno. But that priest was peculiar, and most people don't have swastikas on their mantels. I don't care if it's some Native American mumbo jumbo, it's not normal. I have a vast and experienced gut," he pats his stomach, "and my gut tells me that this priest is more than involved."

"Should we talk to the Americans? Ask permission to investigate?"

"We don't need permission to investigate. If I'm not mistaken, the base is British property, through and through. The MoDP can pull in whoever they want. I would have thought you knew that?"

"Something like this has never happened. It's all new."

"Right. Well, we don't need permission, but we would need their cooperation. Through the years, what has been your experience with the Yanks? As far as them keeping troublemakers around?"

"They usually ship them back to the States or god knows where."

"Right. We need to try on our own first. You ready to go?"

"Yes."

They climb into the inspector's white and vaguely rusty Ford and drive to Crowley's cottage.

The priest isn't home.

So they wait.

Crowley's performance of Mass is an anticlimactic and pathetic end to what otherwise has been, in his eyes, the most glorious of days.

He is more than pleased with the success of the events in Glasgow. He was especially cheerful on the train ride back to Montrose. He was so happy that his joy was contagious, Chris and Hinckley both engaged in laughter.

He asked them about future plans, after their work is done and the Navy scatters them across the globe. He asked them what they want out of life.

Their laughter subsided but did not disappear. Over the rumble of the train, Hinckley said, "I just want to know I made a difference, that I've done something worthwhile. I feel like that now, though, that I'm making a difference, making the world a better place. But I'd like to go home, back to Nebraska, get me some land, maybe have a little lake on it or a pond, stock it with some fish, I don't know. I think I'd be happier back home. Maybe I can clean up Nebraska, like we're doing here."

"Excellent, excellent," replied the priest, proud of his first protégé. "And you, Chris? What about you? Where do you see yourself in a few years?" This he asked as the train rolled to a stop at Arbroath, the end of their journey drawing near.

Chris did not hesitate. "I want to be in love, maybe have a wife," he said, quite candidly.

His reply shocked and dismayed Father Crowley. He didn't think Chris thought about such things. He hoped he would be more like him, his heart and mind focused on only the higher things.

"I see," said the priest, and he considered his response carefully. He rubbed his nose, looked out the window, and again there was the North Sea under a partially sunny sky, the waves of black water churning even though the trees stood still. "You know, the sort of life we lead, warriors for the white race, doesn't lend itself to a traditional lifestyle. It's hard to maintain that sort of commitment when you're committed to something much greater. I'm not saying it's impossible, but I would recommend against getting your hopes up, at least until we've made some headway."

"But what's headway? What will satisfy us?" Chris asked, as the priest has never outlined anything. He has only taken Brad and Chris from place to place, conducting little acts of vandalism—or in this case, murder, though they don't yet know it—without making clear to them what his goals are.

"We will be satisfied when all non-whites and Jews leave Scotland, which I think we can accomplish fairly quickly, with the right pressure. Having succeeded with that, we will concentrate on England, but by this time I guarantee our numbers will have swollen, as other decent white people who have been too afraid to act will take up our cause and do the dirty work for us. We can sit back and direct, like the executive of a big company, and reap the benefits and accolades. We are like the Founding Fathers of the United States. We are rebel soldiers, except our battlefield is much larger, and we answer to the gods of Valhalla. After Great Britain comes Northern Europe, and after that, America, and our friend Mr. Hinckley can return to Nebraska in peace and live out the rest of his days fishing and drinking and watching football and not have to worry about blacks robbing him or the Jewish banks controlling his money and lending it to him at a ridiculous rate of interest. So, girls are out of the picture." He coughed, cleared his throat, and lowered his voice even more. "I am a virgin. I too have never been in love. Someday? Maybe. As a priest, I of course took a vow of celibacy, and when I discovered the great lie of Christianity and the truth of Odinism, I took another vow. I vowed to wage war against the lies of Zionism and to shun all other influences. The fairer sex is definitely an influence and an avenue I don't have the time or inclination to explore." He knows this last is partially a lie. For years, as an adolescent, in college and in the seminary, he successfully prayed to stifle a latent homosexuality, which re-emerged upon meeting Chris. He has never been interested in girls and as a child had a hard time understanding what all the fuss was about on playgrounds, boys chasing girls, girls chasing boys and trying to kiss them. He had a subconscious hope for he and Chris, and in his most depraved thoughts he envisioned himself and Chris, occupying a throne just underneath Odin, in an earthly kingdom, stretching from the north of Europe to North America, the rest of the world sectioned off, fenced in, and left to fend for itself.

As disappointed as he was in Chris's statement, it was a reality he expected, and he wants to keep Chris happy and content to be in his fold. He forms a plan, a carnal reward that he will present to Chris later.

They have given the Jews thirty days to clear out. He knows they won't and he hopes they won't, because the repercussion will ring around the world, and indeed, the world will know that there is something very powerful and white in the Scottish lowlands.

"Still," Chris said, "I wouldn't mind finding somebody. I'm kind of tired of being by myself." And his time alone is long for someone his age, feeling the pain of a lack of nurturing going all the way back to early childhood.

"In due time, in due time, my fine young friend," replied Crowley, patting him on the shoulder and allowing his hand to linger.

"You know," chimed Hinckley, in a moment of uncharacteristic and brazen honesty, "I'm tired of not havin' a girlfriend, not ever," a fact he had previously denied in front of Chris. "I like girls, better'n football, better'n scaring niggers and Jews. I always kind of figured I'd wait till I got back home, out of this Navy, and find myself a good Nebraska girl, not like one of these tramps here in Scotland or in the Navy. A wholesome girl, loyal, you know, a good churchgoer."

Crowley rolled his eyes, but decided that although Brad would never go astray, he needs some kind of reward too, like a training treat for a dog, to encourage him to stay the course.

The train arrived in Montrose in the middle of the afternoon, giving him time to drop off Brad and Chris, with instructions to meet at his house during the middle of the week, in the evening, for drinks and dinner and discussion.

He returned home and showered briefly, removing the sweat of travel and the smell of gasoline and gunpowder. He drove to the base and performed Mass with a pasted grin and a listless emotion. Easter is drawing near, and he speaks briefly and by rote of Jesus's march through Jerusalem, carrying his cross to his crucifixion, and how each man has his own cross to bear and it's up to the individual to deal with it. No man can bear the burden himself. He needs help from up on high, and the sooner he realizes it, the happier he can be. He will be at peace.

Now he is driving home. The Austin backfires as it exits the base, and the MoDP sentry on duty at the gate shakes his head as the priest who always seems very strange and secretive drives away.

Crowley has his evening plans made. It will be an evening of relaxation. He looks forward to tearing off his uniform and donning his bathrobe. He will eat a can of soup warmed up on the stovetop of the ancient oven in his kitchen. He will drink wine from his goblet. He will listen to Wagner. He will fall asleep with visions of Valkyries carrying him off to Valhalla, in celebration of his achievements yet to be realized.

However, his plans are interrupted abruptly as he sees a white Ford Cortina in his driveway, parked horizontally instead of vertically, blocking his passage all the way to the house. The car looks familiar, and he searches his memory for where he saw it. It looks out of place, large enough to be a mid-sized American car, monstrous in this country.

The shape of the figures who emerge from the car as he pulls up are also vaguely familiar, one large shadow, nearly grotesquely obese, and one tall and thin shadow, standing behind the larger one, the subservience visible in the near-dark.

As he exits his car and walks towards the pair, their features become visible, and he instantly recognizes them. The members of the Tayside Police, one the local constable he disregards as a bumpkin, and the suspicious inspector, whose appearance is somewhat troubling.

But not unexpected.

He knew they would be back as soon as the work of his Trinity resumed. He rehearsed various scenarios in his brain, construed likely alibis, alibis that couldn't possibly be verified. And he adopted a mantra, something he repeats now under his breath, nearly audible as he extends his hand first to the larger inspector, and then indifferently to the constable.

They can't arrest me for what they can't prove. They can do nothing if I give them nothing. I will give them nothing.

He brings a smile to his face that appears sincere but is far from it, and he reaches down deep and pulls out an old persona, that of the humble and pious priest, a personality he has known but with which he has never felt entirely at ease.

"Gentlemen, gentlemen, how can I help you?" He acts surprised but pleased to see the two policemen.

"Good evening, Father." Holliday discards a cigarette on the edge of the gravel driveway, where the sparse grass starts to grow. "Quite sorry to bother you, but some nasty business has come up, and we think you can help us."

"Whatever I can tell you, I will," Crowley replies readily.

"Very well. What's the Trinity?"

"Well, the Father, the Son, and the Holy Spirit—"

"No, no," says the inspector. "I am referring to the activity of the young man whose life ended in your home. Lee Rodgers. Wasn't that his name?"

Crowley makes the sign of the cross and a look of melancholy comes across his face. "May God forgive him and give rest to that troubled soul," Crowley says, with almost a trace of an Irish accent, trying hard to play the role of a good priest. "In all my years in service to our Father, never— *never*—have I had to witness something so unpleasant."

"Right," says Holliday, his exasperation evident. "When the sailor was murdered in Dundee, there was a letter left in the cemetery, signed by the Trinity of the White Brotherhood of Eastern Scotland. I take 'trinity' to mean three, meaning Lee didn't act alone. Did he tell you who he was with?"

"No, no, he seemed very much a loner. I think he had one or two acquaintances on the base, as I've gone through with the commanding officer and the base master-at-arms, but he seemed to act alone. I think he had an overactive imagination and may have led a fantasy life, thinking he was part of a movement larger than himself. Hence the word 'Trinity.' He also had a perverse sense of Christianity, obviously, to do what he did. He intimated to me that the blacks weren't chosen by Jesus, only the white race. Therefore, he could have come up with the name that he did. He didn't seem that creative to me, just sort of fanatical."

"I see," says Holliday. He ignites a cigarette and offers one to the priest and the constable. Both decline. "Well, here's the troubling part." He tells Crowley about the synagogue door in Edinburgh, the desecration in Aberdeen, and the arson in the cemetery in Glasgow, and though it can't be assuredly related, the murder of the cab driver just outside the cemetery gates.

Crowley acts surprised and horrified. He makes the sign of the cross and says a quick prayer for the cab driver.

"And Father?" asks the inspector.

"Yes?"

"A man fitting your description was seen outside both the synagogue in Aberdeen and the synagogue in Edinburgh. You weren't alone. There were two others with you."

The priest hesitates ever so slightly, reaffirming Holliday's conviction of his guilt.

But his hesitation is interrupted; he wasn't in Edinburgh with two others. Chris wasn't there, and he realizes it is a ruse to try to ensnare him.

"Inspector, I do travel to the places you mentioned. I am a bit of a bookworm. I frequent bookstores—and if I can be truthful, I am a fan of your pubs. As they say, wherever you find four priests, you'll find a fifth." Crowley laughs. The constable smiles a little, but Holliday's face remains like stone. "I like my pints, no sin in that, and it isn't appropriate for a chaplain to drink on base. Therefore, I travel. I meet new people, sample different pubs, and drink my lager. But I do it alone. I daresay, go to any pub from Aberdeen to Dundee with a picture of me in hand and ask if I've been in. If I have, ask them if I had companions, and they will say no."

"Father, I'm talking about incidents outside of pubs, three incidents specifically. You are the only link we have to the activity of Lee Rodgers, and I have not been entirely satisfied with your explanations. May I ask where you were this morning?"

"Here, Inspector, relaxing before Mass, going over my notes. This is Lent, don't you know?"

"No, I don't know. Can you prove you were here?"

"No, I live alone. Can you prove I wasn't here?"

"Not yet. I suggest you make yourself available to us when necessary. Thank you for your time. We'll be in touch."

The two policemen shake hands with the priest. Robertson notices that the priest's handshake isn't firm like most, but nearly anemic, as if he were shaking hands with a small boy. No grip, no firmness. In order to avoid hitting the priest's car, Holliday drives onto the grass along the driveway, leaving tire marks in the still brown, perpetually unkempt lawn.

Crowley walks inside. He knows he should be nervous, but he isn't. He will just be careful. He feels in his heart that his intellect is superior to anything the police can offer. The angels and elves of Valhalla will not let him down. He is to succeed by fate. It is his destiny.

He sighs with relief that the two policemen did not come inside. He sees the maps of Aberdeen, Edinburgh, Glasgow and Dundee above the couch, the locales of synagogues and cemeteries clearly marked. He would have been done for if they had come in. Even the bloke policemen could have figured him out, putting two and two together. He sees it as a sign of the intervention of Odin, intervening in a way that Jesus never did for all those years and years of devotion.

He smiles and removes his clothes right in the middle of the living room, leaving them in a pile on the floor. He walks naked to the bathroom, where his musty bathrobe hangs from a hook inside the door. He puts it on without bothering to tie the waist. He puts on a record. Beethoven for a change, the inspiring Ninth Symphony, the slow beginning, the furious conclusion. He drinks glass after glass of his Boer wine, grows quite drunk and mulls over his plans. He has no fear. Odin is here, and he can be as brazen as he wants.

"**B**ollocks." Holliday slams the door shut and drives down the lane towards Lutherkirk. "I could have had him. I would love to have him at the station, just the two of us alone in a room. I would beat the piss out of him." Robertson looks at him, shocked, not believing that things such as confessions gained by force ever actually occur. He thought it only happened on television shows and movies.

Holliday sees the constable's face and waves his hand at him. "Aye. I'm an honest cop, but please, he had duplicity coming out of his pores. I could smell it. Couldn't you?"

"He did seem a bit startled when you said he was seen by the synagogues. I noticed that, but otherwise, no, he seemed very natural, very sincere."

"No," says Holliday, "he knows something. I think maybe Scotland Yard should get involved with this one, if they aren't already up here sniffing about. Maybe more pressure is needed. I'd like to interview some of the Americans on the base, talk to some of Rodgers's coworkers, maybe any mates he might have had."

"Didn't he have only one?" asks the constable.

"Yep, the Americans and the MoDP cleared him. They said he had nothing to do with it. I'm sure the Americans didn't want to dig too deep. One murderous sailor on their hands was enough; they couldn't stand two, certainly couldn't explain three. Rodgers, the priest and the third lad, I forget his name."

"But Rodgers is dead," thinks Robertson aloud.

"Right."

"So if our theory about three being involved to make a trinity is correct, then Rodgers has been replaced. Or are we barking up the wrong tree?"

"Ah," says Holliday, "a detail I've overlooked. I would venture to say that Rodgers has been replaced. I'm sure it's not hard to find another gunman on a base full of cowboys from Texas or Rambos from New Jersey. The Americans seem to go for that, guns and violence and the like. I can't stand American movies. I get enough violence from life. I don't need to be entertained by it. So if there is a third, who is he? And how do we find out?"

"I'll watch Crowley's house. But I'll need help."

"I'll try to get it."

They agree the only way to tie up Crowley is to catch him doing something, see where he goes when he leaves, and who comes to his house.

That night, Robertson kisses his wife on the cheek after dinner and tells her he is going on a stakeout. She is confused, as he never has had to do anything like that in all his years of police work. He explains, briefly, about Crowley and Holliday and their suspicions.

"Well," she says, "I'll bring you a thermos of tea in a while, maybe some biscuits, too."

He drives off, past the castle, and parks his car by the rim of the ditch that runs along the side of the narrow lane that leads to the priest's house. He parks just a few yards from the mouth of the priest's driveway, the stone cottage visible through the still bare, sporadic trees.

He sees nothing for several hours, sees nothing all through the evening as he dozes in and out of sleep. At about midnight, he sees the priest walk out of the front door, his body swaying as if the wind moves him, although the air is calm. Constable Robertson can see the priest is naked underneath the bathrobe, the paleness of his flesh almost luminescent in the hazy and moonlit sky. He watches as the priest kisses the ground and looks towards the moon.

He realizes now that the priest is indeed very peculiar.

Sunday morning, Crowley drives with a hangover the few miles to the base for Sunday Mass.

He sees the constable pulling away from his driveway. This doesn't surprise him. He has developed an alternative plan.

Per his instructions, Chris and Brad are both at the morning Mass. They share the last pew and sit nearly a yard apart. Chris listens attentively. Hinckley stifles yawns.

The Mass is attended even less than it was when Crowley started on the base. Only the very devout remain, and they are disappointed every Sunday. But his Mass is the only game in town, and they are left without alternatives. His Masses have become furious in their brevity; he even talks rapidly to conclude them as quickly as possible.

After the chapel empties, Brad and Chris enter the priest's office. His mood is somber, and they adapt theirs to match his.

"Scotland's finest seem to have me under observation, which is fine. It's actually to our advantage. We will give them nothing." He removes from his desk two manila envelopes. Each envelope contains a letter identical to the one attached to the cemetery gate in Glasgow.

Chris still has no idea what the letter said.

"Take these and read them. Go ahead, open them." The priest hands Brad and Chris each an envelope. Brad reads his, his mouth moving slowly, and upon conclusion, after all the words are digested, he smiles.

Chris reads his quickly, staring open-mouthed at the end. "What does this mean?"

"Well, it is identical to the letter I attached to the cemetery gate in Glasgow, and I wish for similar letters to be posted on or near the synagogues in Aberdeen and Edinburgh. Dundee has a synagogue, too, but we will stay away from there for now. That synagogue will be special."

The priest hands each of them a fifty-pound note. "Today, I want you two to travel to Aberdeen and Edinburgh, by whatever means necessary, and deliver these letters. No smoke, no fire, no bombs, just a note. One hundred pounds should be plenty for train or cab fare, and maybe some extra for a few pints along the way."

"Father?" Chris asks.

"Yes?"

"Do you really think they—you know, the Jews—will leave Scotland in thirty days, just like that?"

"No, of course not." Father Crowley smiles.

"So, after thirty days, what do we do?"

"I can only reveal to you things on a need-to-know basis and as Odin reveals them to me. I have a pretty good idea what we'll do. It may not be on the thirty-first day. It may have to wait until the moon is full and Valhalla tells me the time is nigh. All I will say is that the Jews of this country and the world will think of the Holocaust and wish they hadn't fabricated such a story."

"What do you mean?" Chris plays with a book of matches, desperate for a cigarette. The priest intuitively slides an ashtray across the desk.

"The Holocaust was created by the Jews to gain sympathy around the world and to finagle Israel from the British and the United Nations. It never happened. It was a lie."

"I heard that before, Father. My grandpa said something about that one time, but I wasn't sure what the Holocaust was," says Hinckley.

"Your grandfather was correct. I knew you had some knowledge in your genetic makeup." He pats Hinckley on the back, and the passive compliment and affection causes Brad to smile and straighten up in his chair.

"How couldn't it be true? Millions of Jews died. I've seen all kinds of movies, and in school, I learned about it in history. American soldiers liberated concentration camps and saw them. It is true."

The priest shakes his head with a bemused smile and glances at his watch. "America has long been dominated by a Jewish elite. Jews control the media and Hollywood. Their political influence reaches deep, all the way from the White

House to what America's children learn in school. You have been taught a lie; you have been entertained by a lie. They claim six million Jews died. Hogwash. If that were true, the number of Jews in the world would be scarce, and as you can see, they are all over the planet, in Detroit, in Omaha and in Scotland. Additionally, the Nazis weren't capable of containing that many Jews; they did what they could. I don't necessarily espouse a holocaust, though if the races aren't separated—and the lands of the whites aren't left for the whites—then we should proceed by any means necessary. This is a war, and the stakes are very high."

"Hell, yeah," says Brad, moved by the priest's sermonizing.

Crowley smiles. "I suggest you get moving. It is early, but you have a lot of geography to cover in a short amount of time."

Wordlessly, Brad and Chris go to the quarterdeck. There are no taxis queued this early on a Sunday morning. They use the payphone outside the quarterdeck, a yellow British Telecom phone inside an old-fashioned red phone booth with multiple panes of glass. It looks very peculiar amidst the drabness of the uniform buildings of the base.

After nearly half an hour and three cigarettes each, the cab arrives and they ride in silence to Montrose and board a train first for Edinburgh and then for Aberdeen. Brad directs Chris to Salisbury Road and amidst the pedestrian traffic, Brad puts the letter in the mailbox of the synagogue as people turn to stare. Chris keeps his head down, his eyes on the sidewalk.

They then take the train to Aberdeen, a long trip. Chris stares at the scenery in the dim sunshine of the early spring day. He has brought his portable radio and he finds a news program. He and Brad exhausted their reserves of small talk hours and months ago, and their mission at hand cannot be discussed, as the train is nearly full.

The newscaster makes mention of the rash of anti-Semitism that has plagued the country. A rabbi from the synagogue in Edinburgh is interviewed. Chris can tell immediately that his accent is not Scottish, but more of an aristocratic English, of the kind he heard during those programs on public television back home. An accent that he imagined the whole of this British isle would speak. "Ours is a religion that is used to suffering, to persecution. We will not be frightened," the rabbi says.

Then there is a reference to the cab driver, murdered outside the cemetery gates. The body of the deceased was discovered when a fire truck tried to get the cab to move, as it was parked in a fire lane. It of course could not.

And Chris makes the connection with horror. His heart starts to beat very fast and his palms perspire. He recalls in an instant how the priest remained in the cab for more than a few moments while he and Brad stood on the sidewalk outside the cemetery.

He knows now that the priest murdered the cab driver.

In a panic, he rips off the headphones, as if being caught listening to the story would associate his guilt. He whispers in Brad's ear.

"The cab driver—remember the cab driver in Glasgow?"

Brad turns and stares at Chris, irritated by the fact that Chris has disturbed a daydream. He notes Chris's even paler face, his trembling hands and lips. "Yeah, so?"

"He killed him. Father Crowley killed him! Strangled him, the radio said."

Brad removes his gaze from Chris and plops the back of his head against the cushion of the seat. "Yep, I know. Didn't mean for you to find out, but Father told me about it when you was in the bathroom or somethin'. Collateral damage. He could've recognized us. That's why Father picked a cab driver that was kinda little, so he could overpower him if he had to. Plus, he was a quarter-Jewish. What are you gonna do?"

Chris is ready to throw up. He is as nauseated by Brad's casual air about the whole thing as he is about his proximity to the act of murder itself. The priest has always talked about wars and blood and things of that nature, but he never thought these things would mean anything literally. They have. He now knows that the sailor in Dundee was probably ordered dead by the priest, and god only knows the whole truth about Rodgers.

He has always dismissed these things as coincidental impossibilities. The priest had always seemed too kind, too softhearted to do anything heinous. He is still nothing but paternal to Chris, and Chris admires him. But murder— murder is too much.

Or is it? After the initial shock of the brutal realization, after his heart slows down and his hands and lips stop quivering, he somehow rationalizes it all. He likes his life now, more than before. He has friends, places he goes. He has some semblance of a life. To run away from the Trinity, to ignore the priest and Brad, would lead to a return to his old life of days and nights in the barracks, looking forward to work to disrupt the tedium.

Besides, he hasn't killed anybody. He didn't see it happen. He's done no more than what could be interpreted as harmless pranks, some graffiti here, a little arson there, nothing too incriminating.

Still, he doesn't feel good. Before the train arrives in Aberdeen, he retires himself to the lavatory and vomits.

Without emotion, he deposits the letter in the mailbox of the synagogue that he visited with Father Crowley in what seems so long ago. He was different then. Innocent, his mind unstained by the horrific.

Crowley drives home from Mass slowly. He is happy but nervous about the task he has just sent Brad and Chris on. Neither of them have traveled so far in this country without his guidance, and he knows what a parent feels like when a child ventures far away from home for the first time.

But the gods are watching. The white lights were dancing over Brad and Chris's heads while they sat in his office. He knows they will be fine.

As the thermometer has now reached fifty degrees, he rolls the window of the Allegro down as it sputters through the village of Lutherkirk.

He will have to get the car's poor idle fixed before the thirty days expire, before he decides the fate of the Jews of Scotland.

His Sunday will be a solitary one: wine and records and sleep, interrupted only by frozen dinners from the commissary that he has stacked in his freezer.

He sees the car belonging to Constable Robertson outside his driveway, a pale blue Fiat 1100. His car stalls right next to it. It restarts after several seconds. He honks his horn and waves at the constable as he drives onto the gravel and rolls in front of his cottage.

Robertson, knowing his cover is blown, returns home. He tells his wife the bad news and drinks some tea morosely.

The constable calls Inspector Holliday almost immediately and tells him about it.

"Nay bother," replies the Inspector. "We haven't been granted the manpower to watch him, anyway. It would have been impossible—and exhausting—to do it yourself. At least he knows that we are watching him. If you can, just drive by once every few hours. See if he's home or not. That way, if something happens, we will know whether or not he was home. Make sense?"

"It does," replies the constable, who is embarrassed at his failure but somewhat heartened by the inspector's reassurance. "You have a good day, Inspector."

Wordlessly, Holliday hangs up the phone. Robertson drives by the priest's cottage several times on this day. The car is in the driveway. The curtains are drawn. Robertson wonders what a single man can do home alone for several hours at a time. The loneliness must be agonizing.

Not for Crowley. He is joined by angels from the North. He hears the poetry of Odin floating through the air of his house, louder and clearer with each goblet of wine that he consumes.

Later that evening, as the constable and his wife conclude their supper, his phone rings.

It is Holliday, telling him that two letters in manila envelopes were found sticking out of the mailboxes of synagogues in Edinburgh and Aberdeen. Each letter was identical to the one found in the cemetery in Glasgow.

Robertson reports to Holliday that the priest has been home all day and he last checked less than an hour ago. As there were Jewish services on Saturday, the letters had to have been placed today. Crowley couldn't have done it.

Holliday is irritated by this discovery. "I guess we wait thirty days, and may God bless the Jews"

Crowley takes his car to the lone garage on High Street in Lutherkirk. He leaves it for two days. Two hundred quid later, he retrieves his car, which is worth little more than that. He has felt affluent, but two hundred pounds is nearly four hundred dollars. It hurts, cutting into money for wine and war.

He has three weeks to recover his losses, three weeks during which he will have to deal with Easter and all the ceremony required of him as the ranks of his congregants swell an additional third. He will see the part-time Catholics looking bored and lethargic in the pews, awkwardly taking communion, not sure how to receive the body, loudly sipping the blood.

During this time, he waits for a common weekend between him and Brad and Chris. He still wants to reward them.

On a Thursday night, he drives his car the forty minutes north to Aberdeen. It is a city he doesn't know well, not like Dundee, whose industrial side, its grayer buildings, its working class air, has always attracted him more. He can feel the wealth of Aberdeen. During his recruiting days, he knew his ranks wouldn't come from the haves, only the have-nots.

He must still avoid Dundee.

He finds a pub on the highway to Aberdeen, just as the city approaches along the A92. It is somewhat tawdry on the outside, down and out dingy on the inside. He receives some wine in a dirty glass and finds a ripped stool at the bar, electrical tape covering the tears in the vinyl covering and holding the padding in.

He chooses a seat next to a very slight man, perhaps in his forties, his black greasy hair combed to the side. The thin man's slacks are made of polyester, his gray sweater is of wool, which he wears over a once-white t-shirt. Its yellowed neck protrudes just above the neck of the sweater.

Crowley can smell the history of the man. The stale smell of alcohol and sweat comes out of his pores and hangs over the air of the bar; he hasn't showered in days. He is an out and out drunk, and that's why Crowley chooses to sit next to him. Drunks, he believes, are honest. Their reason is destroyed by alcohol. A drunk will not be condescending, and that is important in his current search.

He is looking for prostitutes, his reward for Chris and Brad, the carrot he wants to dangle to keep them happy and looking forward on their quest.

They are both shamed by their apparent virginity, especially Chris. Shame is a distraction, an emasculation. He needs them to feel full of vigor. He knows human nature; nothing bolsters a man's ego more than satisfying a woman.

Directly, Crowley asks the man, "Are there whores in this town?"

Unflinching, the man says, "Aye, my wife is one."

Crowley laughs. "No, I meant for hire, prostitutes, or whatever you call them here."

"You're an American," the man says, accusing the priest of his nationality.

"I am. So how about it? Are there any here?"

The man directs Crowley to the Aberdeen harbor, specifically Clarence Street, in between Church and Wellington, and there the lasses will be, after dark. Sometimes there are twenty and sometimes only two, but there they will be.

"How will I know if they're prostitutes or not?" Crowley asks.

"I hope you'll be able to tell," replies the man.

"Thank you," says Crowley. "Buy you a drink?"

The man nods and Crowley beckons the bartender. "Whiskey for my friend here."

"Make it Glenmorangie, will ya?" the man asks, taking advantage of Crowley's benevolence.

Crowley walks out, and though he doesn't know Aberdeen, he makes the car hug the sea. He drives around until he sees a roundabout, which points him to Clarence Street.

He sees them, sure enough, these girls of the night. They are not as garish as he expects, not as garish as they are portrayed in American television programs and movies, nor are they as destitute as the ones who have crossed his path, pockmarked addicts seeking confession, which he always obliged, imposing the stiffest penance he could muster.

No. The half-dozen girls he sees as he drives slowly down this industrial road are indeed fuller-figured than he would imagine, and more modestly dressed. It's the makeup and hair that gives them away, the heaviness of the eye shadow, the dark scarlet of their cheeks, and their hair large upon their heads. As he drives the block several times, their attention becomes rapt and they follow his car with turns of their heads, their eyes sizing him up. The car is unfamiliar, and under the streetlamps, the figure he cuts behind the wheel is very much unlike a cop. He seems to be just another punter.

He stops. A girl approaches him, speaks to him in a thick brogue that he tunes his ears to understand. He tells her she wouldn't be for him, but he wants her for the following evening, her and a friend. She tells him that would be expensive. He says that doesn't matter.

"What's your name?" he asks.

"Jane, and yours?"

"Alex. Can you get to Montrose? I'll pay you extra for the cab fare."

"Sure."

He scribbles the name of the George Hotel on a piece of paper that he retrieves from the floor of his car. The George Hotel is an elegant looking place that he has poked into once or twice. It has a nice bar and restaurant downstairs with hotel rooms upstairs. He will let two for tomorrow evening. He also gives her two fifty-pound notes, promising the balance tomorrow upon the conclusion of her duties.

"You're not some sort of pervert, are you?"

"No—not the kind you need to worry about." He tells her the situation; she is only needed to terminate someone's virginity.

"That's it?" she asks. "I really don't like virgins. It's so awkward and painful, and they always need directions." She rolls her eyes, which are barely visible underneath the bangs of her dark brown hair.

"That's it," he says, disinterested in her commentary on virginity. "Be at the George around eight o'clock tomorrow night. Who's your friend going to be?"

"I dunno. Margo, maybe, but she's not here. See you to-morrow?"

"You will see me tomorrow, but just for a minute. I have no interest to stay and watch."

With that, he drives away, back to his cottage, back to his wine and records.

Friday morning comes and Crowley discusses the use of the chapel for Easter services with Chaplain Lambert. That is, Lambert tells him his needs for the Protestant services and Crowley works around him. Crowley barely speaks more than a word in reply to Lambert's questions. His mind is elsewhere. There are just two weeks until the deadline arrives. The Jews must leave Scotland or the sky will be hazy from the smoke of Jewish flesh and the streets will be red from Jewish blood.

Lambert watches Crowley's face change, smile and scowl, smile and scowl, entirely out of context with their conversation.

"Lieutenant, is there something I'm saying that you find amusing?"

Crowley's mind returns to the chapel. "No, sir. I was just recalling past Easters. There are a lot of memories, always a wonderful time for the Church." He is lying. He hates Easter, as he hates Christmas. In his youthful, zealous days, he prayed constantly throughout the Lenten season. Not only would he deny himself meat; he also abstained from sugar, caffeine, and watching television.

They return to their respective offices after the chapel schedule is set. Lambert's desk is covered in paper, his desktop calendar in appointments and notes.

Crowley's desk is nearly bare, save a cup full of pens and pencils and a single yellow legal pad with unblemished pages.

Quietly, Crowley calls Hinckley in the supply depot and instructs him and Chris to take a cab to Montrose this evening, to the George Hotel, and to be there before 8 p.m. He tells them to wear nice clothing. Their years of waiting are over.

"Waiting for what?" Brad asks.

"You'll see. Remember—Montrose, the George Hotel, before eight."

Brad finds Chris in their room when he gets off work. Chris is sitting on his bed, reading the *Stars and Stripes* and listening to his radio. The sound of news always causes some anxiety, in case there is talk about the attacks on the synagogues or the murder of the cab driver.

Brad tells Chris about Father Crowley's phone call and tells him to be ready. Chris is concerned that there may be another task for them to do, but Brads tells him no, they're laying low until the deadline.

They shower and get dressed in silence and hang out in the room for an hour without really talking. Chris is thinking about what he's been waiting for years for. Only one thing comes to mind: a girlfriend.

"No, that can't be it," he thinks to himself, and as the hands of his watch arrive at seven, he and Brad walk across the base to the gate. They find a row of taxis in Friday night formation.

They are deposited at the George Hotel, as elegant an establishment as Chris has ever been to in his life. Most pubs he's been to have been cloaked in semi-darkness, but the bar area of the hotel is well lit in soft light, exposing clean upholstered booths and a wood bar with brass trim.

They find Father Crowley alone at the bar, drinking a glass of red wine with an uncorked bottle at his elbow. He is wearing black slacks that Chris or Brad have never seen, a black turtleneck, and his black leather coat, which he leaves on to hide his pear-shaped body and his protruding stomach.

"Gentlemen, gentlemen, sit down. I suggest you start drinking right away. You will need to be as relaxed as possible within a few hours. I would hope."

"What's going on, Father?" Chris asks, clearing his throat.

"You shall see, you shall see." He pats Chris's shoulder and allows his hand to linger. Brad and Chris take barstools on either side of the priest. They receive their pints and Brad asks Chris for a cigarette. Chris takes an unopened pack and throws it on top of the bar. Brad helps himself without saying thank you.

Father Crowley removes two keys from his coat pocket, each with a keychain indicating a room number. Crowley points upstairs and hands Chris and Brad each a key.

"For later. For the end of an era in your lives."

They drink in silence. Chris starts to feel the alcohol. Again, he gets that peaceful and warm feeling, drinking with friends across the world from home. At this moment, he is at peace, the threats to the Jews far from his mind.

They remain at the bar until quarter past eight. Crowley's bottle is empty and he doesn't replenish it. He checks his watch constantly, and his face grows tense.

Then suddenly as he checks the front door, his face softens and his forehead smoothes.

Two girls walk in. One is Jane, whom he met in Aberdeen, and the other, similar in appearance except for hair that is frosted blonde, is Margo.

"Hello, hello." Crowley offers the two girls stools, Jane next to Chris and Margo next to Brad. He chooses to stand in the center. "Drink?" he asks, tilting his empty hand toward his mouth.

"Vodka and fresh orange," both girls say, nearly in unison. The bartender shuffles off, eyebrows raised. Not the usual Friday night crowd assembled in front of him.

The bar is nearly two-thirds full, containing mostly members of the Montrose elite. The Americans don't belong, and the girls look entirely out of place. The fact that they are not from Montrose is obvious to all the patrons.

With a wave of his head, Crowley walks outside, indicating that Jane should follow. He shakes hands with Chris and Brad. "Do what comes natural and do what feels good. That is what life is all about." Just a few years ago, he never would have dreamed of uttering those words.

Brad has a goofy and awkward and sporting grin, as if he is just understanding what is supposed to happen.

Chris looks pale and terrified. He *is* terrified. He wants his virginity to end, but not in this fashion, not at what seems like gunpoint.

Crowley and Jane go outside and walk down the cement steps, clutching onto the ornamental stair rail. He hands her another two hundred pounds. "If I hear all goes well, I will find you and give you more. I will be in Aberdeen during the week."

She takes the money without comment. She snatches it from his hand and places it in her purse. Crowley watches her walk up the stairs and back into the George Hotel. He can't take his eyes off her large, jiggling buttocks, stretching the skin-tight black pants that end just above her ankles. He finds her repulsive. He scratches his head as he has all his life about the base attraction men feel for women. He hops in his car and drives to a pub that stands alone on the road between Montrose and Lutherkirk, where he will sit ignored by all as he watches two young men compete in snooker, a game he can't comprehend. He will return to his cottage of near perpetual solitude and get lost in his current recurring daydream, a fantasy where he is lauded in Valhalla as the Valkyries carry him on their elegant wings after plucking him from the field of battle that he imagines to be somewhere outside of London, as his conquest for Britain comes to a close. Odin welcomes him with open arms, his solitary eye twinkling through the shadow of the brim of his hat.

Jane returns to the bar, where she finds Margo and Brad and Chris sitting in silence. And that's how the remainder of the hour will go, save casual small talk initiated by the girls. They ask the two where they are from and how big America must be and aren't they homesick?

Chris does try—after his tongue is set loose by a few pints—to make conversation. He asks Jane her age, as he can't tell behind her makeup, which makes her look like something out of a science fiction movie.

"Nineteen," she says. Chris thinks at least they have that in common.

"Why do you do what you do?" he asks.

She shrugs her shoulders. "Why do you do what you do?"

Brad, too, after the passage of time and alcohol, becomes verbally freer, but in an obnoxious sort of way. "Do you really fuck for a living?" he asks Margo, who sits as far from him as possible. She nods. "And Father paid you to do me?" She nods again.

"Is he your father?" she asks. She receives no answer.

"See, Chris? I told you he was all right!" Brad shouts over Margo's head. Chris nods, embarrassed.

There is more drinking and small talk and a few more crass remarks from Brad, but somehow he manages to swing the conversation towards Nebraska football, and he tells

Margo, who understands nothing of it, the long and success-ful tradition of Cornhusker football.

"I see me playing ball someday," he says to Margo, mean-ing to impress. "After I go to school when I get out of the Navy, I can walk right on the team."

"That's grand," she says. She asks Brad for a cigarette, who in turn gets two from Chris.

"Well, then," says Jane, staring at the clock above the bar. Although Crowley has retained her for the night, she knows her presence won't be necessary long after the ritual is performed. "Are you boys ready for bed?"

"Hell, yes!" Brad slaps the bar.

The bartender presents them with their tab.

"I thought Father took care of it," Brad says to Chris. "I ain't got no money. Can I pay you back in the room?" Chris nods, wondering where Brad's money goes.

They walk up the red-carpeted stairs to the lone hallway that contains all the rooms of the George Hotel. Their rooms are adjoining. Sheepishly, Chris unlocks his door. Brad opens his in a rush.

Chris finds the light switch. The appearance of the room is somewhat surprising. It is a stark contrast to the elegance of the establishment downstairs. The walls are plaster that has yellowed with age; hairline cracks are visible throughout, like so many spider webs. The lone light in the room is a bulb that hangs from a cord from the center of the ceiling, cracks fanning out from the fixture. There is a desk that ap-pears to have been taken from a child's room, wicker that could have once been white but is now stained with the ex-haust of a thousand cigarettes.

The bed, the focal point of the room, is against a wall. It is too small to be a full-sized bed, but wider than what Chris knows as a single bed. The mattress sags in the middle un-derneath a thick down bedspread.

Jane deposits her purse, an oversized bag made out of something that could be moccasin leather, on the desk. De-spite the glare of the unsheathed light, she undresses as casually as she would drink a morning cup of tea.

Chris stands open-mouthed and afraid, a cigarette smol-dering in his hand.

She undresses down to her bra and panties, plain white things exposing a soft and fleshy stomach, large thighs pockmarked with cellulite that that fans out across her buttocks.

This is not how he pictured this moment.

She pulls down the sheets and looks at him. "Well, are ya just going to stand there and toss-off, or are ya getting into bed?"

Shyly he unbuttons his white shirt, pulls off his gray jeans and sneakers, removes his glasses and places them on the desk. He climbs into the bed, unsure of how he is supposed to proceed. He thinks of movies and television programs where couples climb into bed. So he does what he's seen: he starts to kiss her.

She doesn't return the affection. "You don't have to do all that," she says, pushing him away, giggling. "You just have to fuck me."

The vulgarity of that last sentence is like a cold shower on his already limp organ.

He rests his head on the pillow and stares straight at the ceiling.

After a moment, she grabs his penis and starts moving her hand up and down. He becomes semi-erect and decides that now is the time to proceed. He rolls on top of her, pulling down her panties awkwardly. He has trouble getting them down past her knees. She has to remove them herself. She guides him inside her, and it isn't what he expects. He is unsure of the required motion, so unsure that he can't keep himself inside her. He goes up and down and he pulls himself too far out, so far out that he can't stay inside her. He goes limp, and he knows the exercise is pointless. She knows this, and takes advantage of the situation.

"You all done?" she asks, feigning tenderness.

"Yep, I'm done." He turns his back towards her.

"Well, I have to wait for Margo. Do you have a cigarette?"

He leans over and retrieves his shirt from the floor, removing the cigarettes from his shirt pocket. He takes two and gives her one, lighting it for her. He realizes he has never done that before—lit a cigarette for a girl.

They don't have to wait long for Margo. They hear a loud pounding on the door.

"Let's get the fuck out of here, Jane!" Margo shouts through the closed door. Jane rapidly stands up and opens the door.

Margo is standing in the hallway naked. She has gathered her clothes in bunches around her, and her hair is askew.

Through the heavy makeup, Chris can see a swelling above her right eye.

"That fucking Yank tosser hit me," Margo says, still quite excited. As she pulls on her clothes, standing in Chris's room, she tells Jane how the strike occurred. Apparently, Brad ejaculated just as they started, and Margo laughed. He called her a bitch and she told him to fuck off. Then he hit her, open handed, on the side of her face.

Without saying goodbye, the two leave. A clothed Brad, minus shoes, steps out into the hallway, shouting so loud that Chris is sure people in the bar can hear.

"Go to hell, you fucking whore! You were the ugliest piece of ass I ever had in my life!" Brad returns to his room and slams the door shut.

Chris returns to the bed, still undressed. He closes his eyes as his mind tries to decipher the events of the evening. He isn't sure if he's still a virgin anymore. He decides that physically he isn't, but emotionally he is. He recalls with agonizing disgust the crudeness of the entire evening. Tears well up behind his closed eyes.

Chris returns to work, still unsure of his technical status among the ranks of virgins or non-virgins, a group that he knows is much larger.

Ultimately, he decides he is still a complete virgin, though he may have more of a clue about what's going on the next time he is close to a woman. He had always expected that he would feel different after his virginity ended. He imagined that his whole essence would somehow change, and the change would resonate throughout his whole being. He imagined he would strike others as manlier, more adult, and that his personality would also change. He would feel more confident, more secure, and not like the misfit that he has always pictured himself to be.

However, as he enters the building to commence a day watch that he is about to begin on very little sleep, he feels no different at all.

He wants to talk to Karen about it, and get her opinion. He feels somewhat ashamed for sleeping with a prostitute, and maybe wants someone besides his roommate to tell him that it is okay. A thousand rationalizations go through his mind, how prostitution is in the Bible, how it is the oldest profession, and how he's heard it's legal in the state of Nevada. It can't be so bad then.

But his conscience can't be reconciled. He feels ashamed, and his self-worth sinks even lower.

He chooses not to tell Karen, and they talk very little during the two day watches. He is afraid he won't stop talking if he gets started. He is afraid his tongue will leap from the account of the prostitute to the accounts of his anti-Semitic activity with Father Crowley and Brad, acts for which he also feels various degrees of shame, but he can't emotionally deal with being friendless. So he remains quiet for the string of day watches, but his mind can't keep still.

Dear Wife,

A lot has been happening so I haven't written much.
There are some things happening that I don't feel comfortable writing about. They're not exactly legal, and I'm not exactly proud of them and they're also too painful to think
about more than necessary. Let's just say it has to do with
race. I've only been around white people like myself all my
life, I didn't know anyone different before, and there were
no black or Jewish kids in my school. White Christians like
me, though I have to wonder about the choice of the word
Christian. No one I knew ever went to church. The blacks in
boot camp made me feel uncomfortable, and I don't know
why. I've met someone here, a priest, but not really a priest.
He explained to me why I feel uncomfortable around blacks,
and it made sense. At first. But he wants to do things to
keep the races separate, things that I can't even imagine.
When I meet you, I think I will still be a virgin. I have
had an opportunity to end my virginity, but I couldn't do it.
That experience is also too painful to mention. If you're not
a virgin when we meet and I still am, that's okay. I would
hope that you haven't led as boring of a life as me, maybe
you've enjoyed life enough when the time comes, that you
know you will be happy and satisfied with me. More later.

Love,
Chris

Crowley has not seen any sign of the police around his home, so early in the week, at the conclusion of Chris's day watches, he summons his two young friends to his house.

He has yet to hear their account of the activities at the George Hotel. The time of their deadline is drawing near. The Jews of Scotland will have to be dealt with, one community, one synagogue, at a time.

Brad and Chris arrive at his house and don't speak until spoken to. They have decided previously not to reveal the truth about the events at the George Hotel. They don't want to disappoint the priest; they want him to feel good about his generosity.

Brad wants to do it again, and have another chance. Chris wants none of it.

So they thank him and tell him the night went well. No mention of women being hit, no mention of impotence caused by disgust.

"Well, then, you truly are men," replies Crowley. "More men than I am, I must confess, but maybe someday..." His eyes wander as he contemplates his own virginity.

He pours out a large measure of wine into his silver goblet and returns the bottle to the coffee table. He points to the refrigerator in the kitchen and tells Brad to grab some beers. Brad returns, and Crowley commences his agenda for the evening.

"Just after Easter, our day of reckoning will come for our enemy. We have to decide how we will proceed, how we will rid them from this country once and for all. I must tell you, it will be a glorious day, because as the Jews leave, so will the Asians, the blacks and any other minority you can think of. The Jews have always blazed a trail for the lesser races, the subservient races. They always drag someone along to do their dirty work and to drive a wedge against the whites. Anyone have suggestions?"

Chris remains silent. Brad mentions shooting them, one by one, like Lee did in Dundee.

"That would be fine, but time consuming," replies Crowley. "We also don't have a gun, and the Jews have imposed strict gun-control laws in this country. Even the police don't carry guns. It would be very difficult to acquire a gun here, without having to go through a lot of red tape."

Crowley has inquired in the past about obtaining a gun illegally, without the notice of the authorities. As he has gone from shabby pub to shabby pub across this part of Scotland, he has asked, casually, about what it would take to find a gun. Every inquiry is met with indifference; no one he encountered had ever given any thought to buying a gun.

"No, no. A gun won't work. Any other ideas?"

Chris remains silent. Brad mentions pipe bombs, not unlike the ones they used in Glasgow.

"Well, in order to be effective, we have to have a large number of Jewish people in one place, like in a synagogue, correct?" Crowley asks in response to Brad, but he looks at Chris, to make sure he is interested.

Chris nods, just to go along with the priest. He can sense where this conversation is heading, and he is quite uneasy. He had hoped all along that they would grow tired of targeting synagogues, and just spend their days drinking and driving around the country in a harmless idyll.

No, the priest has an agenda and conviction darker than Chris can realize, and Brad's suggestions of various forms of murder are quite chilling.

"No, no. It would take several bombs to be effective inside a synagogue. We would have to get them inside, ignite them, and get away without being detected by a large room full of people. Impossible. Any other suggestions?"

Chris remains silent and motionless. Brad shakes his head after a moment of thought. His well of inspiration has gone dry.

"Let me offer one idea that I think would be the most plausible. Our gods have given us four elements to command as men. Can anyone take a guess as to what they are?"

Chris's mind harkens back to his junior chemistry class. He knows a lot of elements, but still, he remains silent. Brad vigorously shakes his head.

"Earth, fire, water and air," Crowley says. "We have command over all four. They are a gift from the gods that have been used since the ancient days when the likes of Thor walked among us." He is referring to the Norse god of war, a deity he will draw upon often in these final days.

"I think fire would be the most useful element in our endeavor," he continues. "We can manufacture it on our own, and it will cost very little. Plus, its power is hard to counter. Let's think of some ways we can use fire. Suggestions?"

There is a pause. Chris shakes his head. Brad looks thoughtful and his eyes roll upward as they search his brain for an idea. "Well, I bet if we get a bunch of them inside their church, synagogue or whatever it's called, and start the inside on fire, we could somehow block their way out. They would go in the fire."

Chris shudders. He is amazed that someone can think of setting another person on fire.

"Excellent, excellent. I think we are on to something here. Brilliant, Mr. Hinckley, brilliant." Crowley, too, has had the same idea all along, but he wants his two young companions to feel like they're participants in the whole process.

The paleness of Chris's face and his silence disturbs Crowley. He is concerned that a member of his Trinity may be tempted to drop out.

"Chris, what do you think?"

Chris answers, too afraid to be singled out for being noncommittal. "Yeah, fire would work, I guess, as well as anything. What exactly are we trying to do, though?"

"Isn't it obvious?" Crowley asks.

Brad laughs and the priest joins him.

"Look," says Crowley, seeing Chris's obvious squeamishness, "this is a war, and the stakes are high. We have to defend our culture and our race before it is absorbed into the mess of blacks and Jews and god knows what else. Do you want a wife and kids someday?"

Chris nods.

"Of course you do, and you want them to grow up in an environment that is safe and free, not under the control of

Jewish bankers or media, not in fear of some Negro robbing you or raping your wife or killing your child. That happens all the time, especially in America. It is happening as we speak. It is very important that the blacks that aren't wiped out be sent back to Africa, and it is very important that the white man's money be taken from the Jewish banks. They have the real power over us. Our war is an important one indeed, and if you can't handle it, you had better toughen up or get out of our way."

Chris says nothing. He would like to get up and walk away, but he knows Father Crowley won't allow him to simply leave. There would be some price to pay. A price to pay to a man who is capable of murder, murder without even blinking or the slightest pang of conscience.

Crowley takes Chris's silence as compliance, and continues his strategizing.

"I think we should start with the Aberdeen synagogue. Chris, didn't you say that there were no windows that you could see?"

Chris nods. "Yeah, I think so."

"Excellent. I think that might be the place to start, but I also think it is worth a trip to verify that fact. We will count the windows and the doors and plan accordingly. Let's go."

Crowley grabs his coat and Chris and Brad follow him to his car. The engine whines as he drives the car fast and hard and north.

Despite the furiousness of his driving, the trip is still nearly half an hour. Chris stares out the window, wondering what he has gotten himself into and wondering how he is going to get out. What would he be doing now, at this moment, if he had opted not to join the service, to stay in Michigan?

He would be homeless, he decides, his mother having moved, his father indifferent, and his brother constantly stoned or drunk.

The lights of Aberdeen illuminate their drive through the city center, and they easily find the synagogue. They park in the street right in front of the door, separated only by a narrow swath of sidewalk. The synagogue is housed in an old building on the edge of the center of Aberdeen, surrounded by shops and storefront offices. The building stands alone, barely, with a narrow passage leading to the alley from the sidewalk on either side of the building. There is one window in the front, right by the door, and only one door leading into the alley.

"Splendid," says Crowley, while looking up and down the street and the alley, scanning the rooftops, the doorways and other possible places to hide.

After only a few minutes, Crowley leads them back to the car and they head back to Lutherkirk.

He details his plan while driving south.

"This is so simple, it is brilliant." He grins from ear to ear. "On a day of my choosing, in the not too distant future, we will go to Aberdeen, during a service in the synagogue. Brad and Chris, you will take the front door, and I will take the back. Remember the wine bottles in Glasgow?"

Nods and uh-huhs from inside the car.

"Well, we will have an arsenal of those, at least two bagfuls, and we will simply light them and throw them inside. We will fill them with gasoline and oil. The gasoline will burn, and the oil will allow the fire to stick wherever our bottles are thrown. Chris, you will have to do the throwing, because Brad will be holding Thor's hammer, to deal with any sort of insurrection. We will also cover the doorways in gasoline, and will light those as we leave, so no one can get out. The building is old. The interior is made of wood and I am sure the pews are, too. If we do this right, the building will ignite rather quickly."

His plan is now clear in Chris's mind. He plans to burn people alive.

"What is Thor's hammer, Father?" Brad asks.

"Do you know who Thor is?"

Brad nods. Hesitant, he says, "Yes." He recalls a cartoon show from his youth and Crowley's occasional vague reference to the Norse gods.

"Thor is the son of Odin, a mighty god indeed. He rules the thunder, the lightning, and the rain. His hammer is a powerful weapon. He used to fight and slay giants in the ancient days, and he carries it now, in Valhalla, and returns to Earth occasionally to mete out justice as he sees fit.

"I have my own version of Thor's hammer that I've recently acquired. I have been waiting to show you, until the time was right. I ordered it through the mail, from the back of a mercenary magazine. It's a metal club with a five-pound metal ball with spikes on the end. I knew it was Thor's hammer the first time I saw it. It is, indeed, beautiful. As you are the largest and strongest among us, I thought it would be best for you to handle it. You will destroy anyone—man, woman or child—who tries to leave the synagogue or gets in our way."

"Not a problem, Father," says Brad, proud of himself, proud to be a mortal version of Thor, relishing the opportunity to slay the enemy.

Crowley deposits Brad and Chris right outside the gate of the base, and they walk back to their room. Brad is swinging an imaginary club through the air, making noises with his mouth, as if he is making contact with human flesh. His pantomime becomes quite animated. Chris walks alongside, silent, his eyes seeing only the ground.

"It is going to be awesome, Chris. People are going to hear of us around the world."

They enter their room and Chris immediately finds the bathroom.

He vomits, emptying his stomach and then some.

Chris spends the time off between the day and mid-watches with little or no sleep, while trying to avoid Brad as much as possible. He hides in the base library when it is open, mindlessly reading magazines. He even goes to the gym and tries to exercise, lifting weights among the larger and more athletic sailors but not remaining for too long, as he again feels awkward. He is unsure of how to exercise and self-conscious of his un-athletic form.

However, he can't avoid Brad in the evening, as he has to return to his room. To avoid conversation, he feigns sleep, the earpieces of his Walkman glued to his ears. Radio Luxembourg occupies these evenings, with European popular music that he finds puzzling but interesting and mildly distracting. Distraction is welcome, anything that takes his mind away from Crowley and fire and war.

He knows he can't go through with any plans that involve murder. At first, he was able to convince himself that the Jews and the blacks were all evil and inferior to his own race, and he felt superior because of that. Crowley managed to make him feel like he had some sort of special value, even though it was based solely on the color of his skin.

The priest's venom has changed all that, and he now knows what is truly evil. The barbaric images of people running to avoid flames and smoke, especially women and children, are too horrific for him to keep in his mind for very long.

Even more horrific is the imagined sight of Brad clubbing the frightened masses, clubbing them to a bloody and charred submission, with the beastly device coined by Crowley as Thor's hammer.

His mind while awake—with the irregular rhythms of Radio Luxembourg reverberating in his head—scrambles for a solution.

He could hide and avoid the priest, staying away from his house and from the chapel. He doubts the priest has been granted a security clearance, and doubts he has access to his worksite.

Hinckley—because of his roommate status—is a permanent fixture in Chris's life, as permanent as a layer of skin.

That leaves him with no other option but to confront the priest, to tell him he's out, out of the Trinity, and sorry, but he hopes there's no hard feelings.

Chris knows this approach is not possible. He bears too many of the priest's secrets, the graffiti and fire and murder that he has left in his wake. There is no way the priest will let Chris just walk away.

He, too, could die of an apparent suicide.

He thinks about running away from the base and trying to immerse himself into the Scottish countryside. Maybe he could find a job or something and become as anonymous as the countless sheep that dot the hills just underneath the nearly perpetual gray sky.

Not possible. He has no place to live, and he doesn't see Scottish society putting up with a vagrant American, wandering from village to village seeking food and shelter.

He thinks briefly about reaching out to his family, maybe his father, but this idea is also rejected. He doubts his father would even open a letter from him.

He has no address for his mother.

That leaves him with one option. The Navy has always stressed using the chain of command. One should always go to their direct supervisor with any questions or concerns, and if that supervisor feels it is necessary, they can forward the information further up the chain.

That leaves him Karen, and he knows this is the best option of all. She seems to emanate a certain sort of serene wisdom, and he knows though she may be shocked with what he reveals to her, she may offer a solution.

His first mid-watch comes. Bleary-eyed from a lack of sleep, shaking from an overindulgence of cola and stress, he enters the building with trepidation and hope. He is nervous about what he has to tell Karen. The details are unpleasant to think about, let alone to explain with words.

He is also hopeful. Something will happen because of this. His career in the Navy may be over, but that is better than the alternative: having a hand in mass murder.

He arrives for his watch and takes the pass-down from the outgoing seaman. There has been a bit of activity in the Mediterranean and a flurry in the Arctic Ocean as an American destroyer has been shadowing a Soviet sub. All part of the endless charade of cat-and-mouse that is part of this Cold War.

Normally, Chris would be excited by such details, the flurry of activity stirring his sense of duty and patriotism. But not on this night. On this night, he would prefer the oceans and seas surrounding Europe to be devoid of any military activity.

Karen takes her pass-down from the outgoing supervisor, another Petty Officer Second Class like herself. They chat idly for a while, longer than Chris would like. He wants to get his confession and his plea for help delivered as soon as possible, and he needs to wait until all ears have left the room, leaving just Karen and himself.

He enters his initials in the logbook, and the printer starts to buzz with the traffic of the Arctic Ocean and the North Atlantic. He ignores the printer as the scrolling paper piles up on the floor. Karen stares at him as her peer leaves the room. Chris has been distant lately, she realizes, but still dutiful.

"Are you going to get that?" she asks, pointing at the paper piled on the floor. "There's stuff going on. You need to pass it along."

"I need to tell you something," he says, tearing off the paper from the printer and scooping the pile off the floor, placing the heap of paper on top of the table that serves as a common desk.

"I'm guessing this is important, seeing how you're putting the welfare of the Atlantic Fleet at stake," she says, pointing at the pile of messages on top of the table.

"It is." He draws a deep breath. He tells her everything, slowly at first. The speed of his words increases. He tells her everything, from the beginning, the first meeting with Crowley at the chapel, concluding with a breathless account of Crowley's plan to ignite the Jews. He deliberately leaves no fact out; he even relays the embarrassing tale of the Aberdeen prostitutes.

Slowly, she digests the information, information that takes nearly half an hour to relate, and longer to understand.

And she does understand. She understands the loneliness that Chris feels. She understands the desperation that led him to the unholy alliance with the priest and Brad. It is no fun wandering through life without having someone to share it with, male or female.

Everyone needs friends. Everyone needs lovers... Even though friends and lovers come with a price.

Chris has had to pay a price that is steep, a price that is climbing still.

There are some things that she needs to explain to him. She is a woman of the world, so to speak, her life a myriad of experiences more varied and tragic than Chris has previously imagined. Her existence has been wrought with pitfalls, several minor and one very major, and these tragedies give her that mysterious air. These tragedies explain the melancholy that perpetually shrouds her countenance, leading to her enigmatic presence that has long confounded Chris.

This enigma, this melancholy, she feels compelled to explain.

"So, you think you hate blacks and Jews, do you?" she asks Chris upon the conclusion of his confession.

"Well, I don't know. I thought at first I did, because of what Father Crowley said, but deep down, if I take away what he's told me, then no, I have no reason to hate blacks or Jewish people or anyone else."

"That's right. You have absolutely no reason to hate anyone based on race or religion." She sighs, takes a deep breath, as she readies her body, her mind, to tell Chris the tragedy of her life. Not for a number of years has she revealed herself to anyone.

"You know how I said I was married once?"

Chris nods slowly. "Yes, you did mention that. I figured you got divorced."

She shakes her head. "No. I'm not divorced. We were very much in love. We met in college, and got married right after I got my teaching certificate. He was in law school, and I was the breadwinner, teaching while he went to school.

We also had twin babies, a boy and a girl. They would be eight now. Marc and Michele.

"We were married for just about three years when it happened. My husband and I, along with the twins, who were just over a year old, went out to dinner at a fairly nice restaurant in Silver Spring, near where we lived. We were celebrating. My husband had just finished law school, and our possibilities were endless. He had finished near the top of his class, and we knew it was just a matter of time before we left our apartment and would be able to afford a house and a new car.

"It was hard on us, me the only one working, paying for law school and babies. We did without a lot of things, but we didn't care. We were happy, very, very happy. We were happy being poor, and our potential for a wonderful life was boundless. So when he finished school, we went out to eat, something we never did. We lived on macaroni and cheese and hot dogs for weeks at a time, trying to feed the twins as best as we could.

"Dinner was wonderful. The kids sat in highchairs and ate, smiling all the while, and my husband and I had a couple of drinks. He had more than I did. We were so happy. We talked and laughed and I remember thinking that it was the most wonderful night of my life.

"Until we went home."

She now removes her glasses and wipes her eyes with the back of her hand. She pulls out a tissue, wipes her nose and blows and rubs it so hard that Chris notices the normally pale tip of her nose is now a temporary shade of scarlet.

"We both had a few drinks. We weren't accustomed to drinking. Not since our college days had we really drunk more than a glass of wine. I think maybe that night we split almost a whole bottle. Henry drank most of it.

"That's why I drove home, because he drank more. Every day, every moment since then, I wish we'd taken a cab.

"I felt a little tipsy when we left, you know, relaxed and sort of giddy. I wasn't drunk, but maybe a little too relaxed, too relaxed and happy, very, very happy."

She stands up and removes her utility jacket, something Chris has never seen her do, exposing her blue dungaree shirt, obviously one or two sizes too big. Chris guesses correctly that she has lost weight since she first purchased the shirt. He can barely make out her arms in the sleeves, and her neck appears lost in the vast collar.

"It was still daylight when we left the restaurant, but it was fading fast. The sun was setting and the clouds were almost bright red. It's funny, I never notice the sky, but I remember it that evening. It was beautiful in a surreal sort of way. The red clouds made the blue of the sky a pale shade of pink, as if God put a piece of cellophane over the sun.

"We had only a few miles to drive. Henry loaded the babies into the back of our old '71 Mercury, which he had in and out of the shop since we bought it a few years before. We couldn't afford a newer car, though I would have liked one. It was white and rusty and huge, and I felt so small behind the wheel, but I also felt safe, being inside such a big car.

"We laughed all the way home, and Henry talked about the Maryland bar exam, how hard it was going to be, and what sort of work he was going to do. He wanted to be a civil rights lawyer. That was his dream. He didn't want to be a lawyer to be rich. He wanted to provide well for his family, but he wasn't greedy. He wanted to make a difference in other people's lives. He made a difference in mine.

"I can remember the number of traffic lights between our house and the restaurant. Five. I remember hitting every single one red, having to stop but not minding at all, as we were in no hurry. Except for the last light. I thought it was green.

"But it was red."

Now there are tears streaming from her eyes, and she is breathing hard, almost in cadence with the scrolling printer, which continually feeds paper to the floor.

"There wasn't another car stopped there, so I guess, I don't know, I must have assumed the light was green. I could see our apartment building just a block away, on the left hand side, and I was already checking the oncoming traffic, to see how quickly I could turn into our parking lot. I went through the light and almost made it through the intersection, except a gravel truck demolished the car and the only three people in the world that I cared about, Henry and my two babies.

"The truck hit the car so hard that it spun like a crushed top in the middle of the intersection, and somehow I fell through the door, which popped open, and I landed on the asphalt. I passed out. I didn't wake up until later that night, in a hospital bed in the emergency room of the same hospital in Silver Spring where Marc and Michele were born.

"I knew, when I woke up, that the world was blacker than I last remembered, and I also knew, as I still know today, that it was all my fault. It is a heavy burden, though it gets lighter every day. The years pass and memories fade and I get to where in my mind I forget what Henry looked like, and how sweet my babies were, but I have pictures, trapped in an album under my bed, and I drag it out now and then and sit down and cry as I remember them. I just don't remember how they looked, but how they smelled, how the babies felt as I held them in my arms, how I felt when Henry held me in his arms.

"I suppose you're wondering why I'm telling you all this, how it's relevant to your situation. It is and it isn't. Henry was black. I guess our society would say my babies were black, even though they were half-white, and I never realized how ugly our American way of life is until Henry and I first started dating, and I brought him home to meet my parents.

"It was Thanksgiving. We were in our junior year at the University of Maryland. I grew up in Rockville, and Henry was from Washington, D.C., not even half an hour away. We were both going to meet our respective families then. Dinner at my house, pumpkin pie at his.

"I never thought Henry's color would be a concern with my family. I heard my father make snide comments about blacks before, you know, the same things your father probably said, how black neighborhoods aren't safe, how they commit crimes more than white people do, and how they shouldn't be trusted. I didn't think he meant anything by it, and it obviously didn't plant any kind of racist seed in me.

"So I thought when I brought Henry to my family's house, there would be no problem. I thought since he was with me and was important to me, he would be welcome, no matter what. That's how strong I thought my family's love was. I wasn't even nervous. I didn't think it would be an issue.

"Henry didn't even get his coat off. My father made a scene. He said no niggers were allowed in his house, and he'd be damned if his daughter was going to date one. I had never heard him use the word 'nigger' before. It shocked me, but it embarrassed me more than anything. As Henry walked out of the house, my father tried to pull me in, grabbing my coat as I stood in the doorway. I wanted nothing to do with him, and I still don't. That was the last time I spoke with my father. A year later, we were married, and then the babies and then the funeral, and I never saw hide nor hair of my father. My mother called when they died, but she wouldn't come over. She said my father was too upset, still, and she didn't want to upset him more. She took my father's side, and ignored the needs of her daughter. Having been a mother, it is unfathomable to me how a mother could ignore her children. I think it is instinctive to care for and protect your children first, and then worry about spouses and the rest of your family."

Chris can relate. He feels a chill as Karen speaks of her disappointment with her mother.

"I had tried to call my mother, right after that Thanksgiving so many years ago. She asked me if I was still seeing my Negro friend. I said, yes, of course. Well, you really shouldn't come around then, your father is very upset, she said.

"So I didn't come around. I invited them to the wedding, which of course was very simple, as I had grown up expecting my family to pay for it, and they didn't."

"How did Henry's family treat you?" Chris interrupts.

"They were nice to me. They weren't thrilled with the idea of their son marrying a white girl, but they loved their son more than they hated my race, and they were there for everything, reaffirming my conviction at the arrogance of my own race. For a while, I was ashamed to be white.

"Whenever we went anywhere together, it would be white people, especially white men, who would point at us and shake their heads, as if we were committing some sort of terrible sin. Their disapproval just strengthened my resolve.

"Henry's family disappeared from my life after the funeral. My family remained missing. I felt all alone surrounded by the people I had loved growing up; they lived just minutes away. That's why I joined the Navy, to get away from all that.

"I think Henry's family disappeared because they blamed me for the accident, as I blame myself. I tried reaching out to them, and they took my phone calls from the hospital, but they never came to see me, never reached out to me in the days and weeks afterward as I sat and cried and screamed in our apartment, surrounded by Henry's and the babies' things.

"I left the apartment the way it was. I up and left and joined the Navy, leaving everything behind. I went to boot camp like you, only the clothes on my back and maybe fifty dollars in my wallet.

"So, as you can imagine, I have no love for racists. Racism is ignorance. Racism is a reflection of the inadequacy one has in one's own identity. Racism keeps our society polarized, never moving forward. One race is always worried about what the other race is doing while other aspects of our culture and society are ignored. The schools deteriorate; I should know. Our country would be so much better off, economically and socially, if racism were a part of the past and not the present. Blacks in America have been denied so much for so long, and most of them have to go to poorer schools, which means no college, which means a low paying job, which in turn leads to their own children growing up in the same circumstances. It's a type of society unique to America. Race, for the most part, doesn't have stigmas attached to it in the rest of the world. It's the devil's work, I'm sure, and it all is born in ignorance and hate, and nothing good has ever come from it. Nothing. All because of racism there was a civil war that left nearly a million men dead in gruesome battle, causing wounds in our country that never really healed, and an assassination that left a most brilliant and peaceful man dead—Dr. King—who was starting to lead our country out if its hateful slumber. Then he got murdered in cold blood by a coward. And now, right in front of me, I have some idiot following an insane priest, killing Jewish people and god knows who else in a country that doesn't even belong to us."

Chris is irritated being called an idiot, but it's true. He feels more connected now to Karen than he ever has. He has found a common thread. They are both adrift in this world without the anchor of a family, without the anchor of a place that they can call home. More significant still, he knows her secret, and he realizes every hardship he has ever encountered in his brief life is quite trivial in comparison.

It's one thing to lose a parent to lust or selfishness (his mother), or slothful indifference (his father), but for a mother to lose a child is quite terrible. Even Chris can feel that.

"Now, as for your predicament," Karen continues after taking a deep breath, "we have no choice. We must let the master-at-arms know, probably Chief Lassiter, and god knows who else. You need to confront Father Crowley. Tell him you're done." Her sorrow has turned to anger, and Chris sees crimson splash over her ever-pale face, as if she has a sense of purpose that she hasn't realized before.

Chris explains his fear of confronting the priest. He fears for his own safety, fears a man who can murder without the slightest remorse.

"I realize that," she says, "but you need to sever ties any way you can. You probably are already in trouble, at least a little bit, and the sooner you distance yourself from this mess, the better off you are. I understand trying to fit in, and feeling like an outsider. I get all that, but the Navy might see it different. You have to toughen up and take responsibility for your actions."

Chris is comforted, though fearful. He doesn't feel as alone. Sharing his dilemma with someone else, someone he can trust, removes his burden.

His feelings of attraction for Karen have returned. Her display of emotions has touched him. He knows they are alike in many ways.

"Do you have a home of record?" he asks, after they have both sat in thought quietly for just a moment, privately pondering Chris's situation.

"What do you mean?"

"You know, for your service record. A home of record back in the States."

She understands the nature of his question. "My home of record is wherever I happen to be."

"Me too," he says, smiling only slightly.

They conclude their mid-watch in a flurry of busyness, dealing with the tremendous pile of messages that have gathered at their feet.

They both agree to deal with Chris's situation that morning, when the mid-watch is done and the day staff of the base wanders in.

Karen will wait for Chief Lassiter and the ensign, and tell them what she knows.

Chris will make his way to the chapel and wait for Father Crowley.

Chris goes to the galley at the end of his watch and tries to eat breakfast. His stomach is hungry, but his nerves are ablaze and the food is hard to put down. He sits alone and knows he will be returning to that old kind of life again, a friendless existence.

Karen called him a racist, a word he has associated with a certain ugliness ever since his childhood. He never thought of himself in that light before.

A racist.

It's a label that he knows doesn't suit him. There are other labels that suit him better, and he shifts these inside his mind as he sits alone at the end of a long table. Timid? Yes. A compliant lackey? Absolutely.

He is not one with a penchant for hate, just a desire for love and acceptance.

He is also disturbed by Karen's history, a history more tragic than his own, more tragic than the history he is currently making. If she can persevere after what she has gone through, then so can he.

As he leaves the galley, he spies Brad walking in through the front door, greedily grabbing his tray and cutlery. Chris has taken perhaps two bites of his scrambled eggs, ignoring the rest of his plate.

He goes to his room and waits for the red digits of his alarm clock to read 08:00. That's when Crowley should be at the chapel. He tries to compose a speech in his mind, responses to Crowley's possible questions and statements. His anxiety heightens and he runs to the bathroom.

He vomits, regurgitating the contents of his nearly empty stomach.

He walks to the chapel as soon as the clock arrives at eight. He thinks about not going at all, about ignoring the priest altogether, and to just let Karen get things moving.

As he walks, he feels like a prisoner on death row, like a dead man taking his last steps. He prays, even though he has never prayed before. He prays with a furrowed brow, concentrating on his thoughts, hoping his plea for help makes its way to heaven.

Not to Valhalla.

He walks into the chapel and finds that Crowley is not alone. Crowley and Chaplain Lambert are talking just outside their office doors. Lambert looks irritated as Chris walks in. Crowley smiles.

"Father, I need to talk to you privately," says Chris in a way that betrays his fear and exasperation.

"Certainly, certainly. Come into my office." Crowley is glad to get away from his supervisor, who had been chastising him for the less than satisfactory state of his khaki uniform. Crowley had spent the previous evening in the company of too much wine and this morning had to grab a uniform from the bottom of his closet.

"Well, well, it is a surprise to see you here at this time of day, on this day of the week. It is certainly welcome, like a breath of fresh air."

"I can't do it, Father." Chris is direct. "I can't do it. I'm sorry, but I can't come to our meetings anymore. I can't light a synagogue on fire. I'm sorry, but I can't do it."

Chris says all this without looking at the priest. He stares at the tops of his polished boots. He feet tap nervously.

If he were looking at the priest, he would see a trembling of the lips, a face rapidly going from pale to scarlet, a jaw clenching, and a grinding of the teeth.

Chris waits for a response but hears nothing but Crowley tapping his fingers on the desk. After a span of silence, Chris looks up at the priest.

Crowley's face softens and his color returns to normal just as Chris's eyes meet his.

He has developed a strategy, a way to deal with this insubordination. The Trinity must remain intact no matter what, and he will see that it does.

"There, there," he says, resting his hand on Chris's knee and leaving it there. Chris's gaze returns to his feet, which are still tapping, but not as quickly.

"We can scale things back a notch," continues the priest. "I certainly wouldn't want you to do anything that you are not comfortable with. Not everyone has the Viking spirit for war. Some of us are dreamers and thinkers. Perhaps that's what you are, and that's important, too. We can stop. It's all for one, or it's none at all, and that's okay, too."

Relieved, Chris sniffles and tells the priest how he appreciates going to his house, relaxing and drinking and how his friendship has been important in his life—and prior to the events at the synagogues—the best thing that ever happened to him.

"Well, how about we just do that, then?" replies the priest. "We'll keep things simple. I can deal with the enemy later; they're not going anywhere. You are off this Friday, aren't you?"

Chris nods in affirmation.

"Good. Why don't you come over, and we'll just drink and relax and we'll put all this behind us?"

Against his better judgment, Chris agrees to go to the priest's house Friday, early in the evening. The back of his mind knows this may change. There will be a reaction to Karen's report to Chief Lassiter, and he is still fearful of that result.

But somehow he feels comfortable again here in the company of the priest, as if he is in a place that is very safe. The priest's confident demeanor serves as a tonic for his shattered nerves.

Not as fearful, he shakes the priest's hand and returns to his room, where he sleeps soundly for the first time in several days.

When Chris leaves, the priest's face again turns red. He has issued a deadline to the Jews of Scotland, and it expires in exactly ten days. They will pay for ignoring that deadline. Chris or no Chris.

At lunchtime, Crowley goes to the base exchange and purchases a video camera on in-store credit, his rank giving him a generous credit limit.

He returns to his office and reads the instructions. He needs to be proficient in the use of the camera by Friday.

He closes the door to his office and calls the supply department. Cloaking his voice, he asks for Seaman Hinckley.

Karen waits for Chief Lassiter. She sits blankly at his desk and waits nearly an hour for him to arrive for work.

This night has been emotional. She has talked about things that she finds unpleasant to even think about, but somehow her soul feels rinsed; the weight of memory isn't quite as heavy as it was before.

Still, she is far from smiling.

The chief arrives and finds Karen at his desk. He is irritable, as his mind and body have yet to receive the necessary rush of caffeine.

"I need to talk."

"Okay, but can you wait just one minute?" He grabs a mug off of his desk, a stained white mug with an image of a gold anchor, the symbol of the rank of Chief Petty Officer, his name scripted underneath the anchor. He then finds the coffee mess in the next room, no larger than a closet, and returns, steaming mug in one hand, a donut in the other.

He sits down, and Karen tells him as thoroughly and briefly as she can the dilemma that Chris now faces.

She makes no mention of her own history, though it is there somewhere in the recesses of her service record.

Chief Lassiter listens with rapt attention. The tale holds his interest like a good movie or novel. And that's what he thinks it is, a fictional tale, though he doesn't relay that impression to Karen. Even though he was aware of Rodgers's suicide, the details are too wildly fantastic to possibly be true. A priest firebombing synagogues? A Navy chaplain trying to establish some white, Nordic cult? No way. He thinks that perhaps Seaman Fairbanks has read a few too many of the paperback novels available at the base bookstore. With a bit of duty-bound irritation, he tells Karen that he will pass the information on. He dismisses her, tells her to get a good day's sleep and be ready for the upcoming mid-watch.

She walks out, concerned about what tempest will now be set in motion.

Chief Lassiter tells the young division officer, the same militant ensign who first saw Chris on his arrival at RAF Lutherkirk. The chief relays Chris's account as though it is a work of fiction, and he tells it with a bit of mirth and laughter. The ensign, because of the chief's description, believes it to be fiction, too, and tells the chief to contact the base master-at-arms.

"There's no reason to take this further up the chain. Let the base police take care of it. We would be wasting everyone else's time and energy," the ensign tells the chief, proud of his own decisiveness, proud of his ability to seemingly think on his feet.

Chief Lassiter finishes a few more cups of coffee and drives down to the quarterdeck to find Chief Wilson, the base master-at-arms, head of the four-man police department. The base police are a distinctive group, allowed to carry handguns in a country whose own police are forbidden to carry such things. Their uniform is different, too; they wear camouflage gear, not unlike the Army or Marines, instead of the dungaree or dark blue or khaki uniform that the rest of the base is required to wear.

Chief Lassiter tells Chief Wilson the story, again with the same amount of mirth and laughter, as if the whole thing is amusing, better suited to be told over a couple of beers at the Chiefs and Officers Club.

Chief Wilson smiles and nods. He doesn't tell Chief Lassiter that the priest has been cast in a suspicious light before. What's the point? The priest had been investigated before and was cleared of any wrongdoing.

He takes a few notes, mainly for show, and tells Chief Lassiter that yes, this is probably too bizarre to be true, but he will look into it.

Wilson lets out a big sigh as Chief Lassiter leaves. He can taste his upcoming retirement and doesn't want to be bothered by anything cumbersome; he wants his remaining days in the Navy to be as placid as a frozen lake.

He does feel that the story is a bit far-flung, too far-flung to be true. He recalls being puzzled at the priest's involvement in the suicide of Lee Rodgers, and his forehead scrunches as he sits at his desk, recalling those days, those turbulent days interrupting the idyllic life of RAF Lutherkirk.

He dons his camouflage hat and hops into a blue Chevrolet, not unlike a police car found in the States, the car even possessing a left-sided steering wheel. He drives the quarter mile to the chapel and walks into the office of Chaplain Crowley.

The priest is sitting calmly at his desk, apparently doing nothing. Chief Wilson sees no papers on his desk or any other sign of activity.

Just Father Crowley sitting there in an unkempt khaki uniform underneath the navy blue cardigan that only officers are allowed to wear. The shoulders of the sweater are covered in dandruff and renegade hair. Chief Wilson surveys the uniform crossly, but he doesn't confront an officer and he doesn't confront a man of the cloth.

Crowley smiles upon seeing Chief Wilson. He instantly recognizes and recalls the face and the uniform.

On the outside, Crowley appears calm and carefree. On the inside, he is cringing, his heart beating so fast that he can feel its tremors in his throat. His temples start to pulse.

"Good morning, Chief, good morning. What brings you here to our Father's house?"

"Nothing, really. I just want to make sure that everything is okay with you. Some things have been mentioned about some extracurricular activities of yours, and, you know, it's all kind of related to the suicide of that pathetic young seaman a few months back. I was just wonderin' if anything has come up because of that."

"No, no," replies Crowley with an unbroken smile. He is sure that the obese Dundee inspector has contacted the base. He burns with anger at the thought.

"That's kind of what I thought. I'll leave you to your prayers." Chief Wilson assumes that he had interrupted Crowley praying, as there would be no other explanation for him sitting at his desk so calmly.

Crowley hasn't been praying. He has been inside his current favorite daydream, a daydream full of fire and smoke and the suffocated coughs of Jewish men, women and children. He sees himself standing outside the Aberdeen synagogue, long enough to watch the building collapse as it weakens in flames. He joins hands with Chris and Brad and they raise them in triumph.

"Anytime, anytime," replies Crowley, angry with the Tayside Police, not suspecting Chris of divulging any of their privileged information.

Chris awakens late in the afternoon. His sleep was deep and dreamless, and he is awake a full minute before he can remember the events of last night and of this morning.

He somehow expects the world to be different as he peers behind a drawn shade and sees only the damp and empty courtyard of the barracks.

Hinckley enters the room a bit earlier than normal and rather abruptly, almost slamming the door open as he comes in.

Chris is nervous. He doesn't know what the priest has told Brad. He is afraid Brad may antagonize him.

The priest did call Brad, only to tell him to be sure to come over this Friday evening, and that Chris needed a bit more convincing. That was all.

"I hear you talked to Father today," says Brad, flipping on the light switch.

"Yep."

"Well, he didn't tell me much about it. He says we'll all talk Friday. That's cool. I'm looking forward to relaxin' and kickin' back a few beers and not have to go anywhere. You got a cigarette?"

Chris fishes a fresh pack from a carton in his locker and gives the whole pack to Brad.

Brad opens the pack and lights a cigarette without thanking Chris.

Chris readies himself for work, showering quickly and getting dressed.

He hopes to find Brad gone when he exits the bathroom, but there he is, sitting on his bed, surrounded by a cloud of smoke.

"You wanna eat?" he asks Chris.

Chris shrugs his shoulders and grabs his coat.

They eat. Chris is sullen, and Brad talks incessantly.

"It will be something, you know, when we do it," says Brad. "We'll be famous. If you ain't white, you'll be afraid to come to Scotland, that's for shit-sure."

Chris spins his neck to make sure no one can hear Brad's boasting. As usual, no one in the half-full galley pays any attention to them. No one is interested in what he or Brad has to say. They are just part of the galley's landscape, no different than a table or a chair.

"I bet," Brad continues, "after we do what we're gonna do, people will hear of it around the world. They'll know about it everywhere. Nebraska, Detroit, Israel, heck, probably even Russia."

Chris realizes that Father Crowley has not told Brad everything, that he hasn't learned of his desire to abstain from the group's violent activity.

He doesn't fill him in. Brad thinks Chris is still a part of the fold.

Chris enters his building for the mid-watch, anxious to hear the result of Karen's conversation with Chief Lassiter.

Chris pictures a snowball rolling from the top of a mountain, turning into an avalanche.

He somehow expects the watch floor to be covered in snow, but it isn't. He takes his pass-down from the departing seaman. The night promises to be busy, which Chris is excited about. On this night, his mind is elsewhere. Although he was comforted by the priest's reassuring words this morning, he is still haunted by the specter of a Father Crowley angered by his reluctance to continue their racial and religious war. A man of a sort of god capable of murder with his bare hands.

He is dreading Friday. He hopes the evening will be innocent, the way he envisioned his relationship with the priest would transpire, merely a place to go off base, to drink and relax and enjoy semi-intelligent conversation without any sort of social pressure. No need to worry about being without a girlfriend in the company of a priest or to be accepted by the larger social circles. It was okay to be a misfit and still be a friend of the priest. Chris liked that.

Chris asks Karen how her talk with Chief Lassiter went as soon as the outgoing watch leaves the work space.

"Fine," she says numbly. She slept little during the day. Her adrenaline was raised by her confession to Chris, as if she had just completed a vigorous exercise, causing her to be too wound up to relax.

"Did he say anything?" Chris asks, concerned about his own culpability.

"No. I'm going to wait for him in the morning and see what happened. Otherwise, we'll have to wait and see."

Chris tells her about his conversation with Father Crowley. He tells her that it went well, that the priest didn't seem to mind his reluctance to carry on their relationship.

He omits one important detail. He is too embarrassed to tell her that he has agreed to spend Friday evening in the company of the priest.

The night goes on, and they forget about their situation in the midst of their work. The morning comes and Chris goes to the galley and then the barracks. Karen remains an extra hour or so, smoking cigarettes and drinking coffee while waiting for Chief Lassiter.

She confronts him as he walks in, again groggy from a lack of caffeine. She asks what is going to happen next, if the priest should be arrested, or even Chris.

"It's done," he says.

"What do you mean?"

"The priest and the situation have been investigated, and there is no reason to examine it further." Lassiter sips his coffee and avoids eye contact with Karen.

"What do you mean? The man is evil! Look at what he's done already!"

"Just because the young seaman told you something doesn't mean it's true. Did you ever consider that?"

Karen is silent. She gets it. The Navy will not persecute one of its own, especially an officer, unless there is something solid. If the priest is doing something wrong, well, they won't need to do anything until a corpse lands on their doorstep.

Until another corpse lands on their doorstep.

Dejected, Karen drives home. She wonders how she will contact Chris, to warn him of the impotence of the chain of command.

She also wonders—driving home with the window of her Austin Mini rolled down to combat the sweat she has developed—if there is anything she can do to confront the priest herself.

She has only seen the priest once before, coming out of the exchange. She knew he was a chaplain by the gold cross pinned on the collar of his khaki uniform. She rubbed up against him accidentally and said, "Pardon me, sir" with a smile.

He didn't return the smile, and she felt a certain sense of dread, a feeling like so many hot knives shredding her stomach, which reacted in twists and turns. Immediately thereafter, she forgot the very brief encounter, and didn't recall it until just now, driving home in the approaching sunlight, sunlight filtering through the branches of the grand trees along the narrow road leading from Lutherkirk to the A92.

It is Friday, the Friday of Chris's unfortunate decision to visit the priest at his cottage.

Chris sleeps until noon and then spends the day kicking around the base, trying to stay out of his room as much as possible. He is trying to avoid the many thoughts that enter his mind while confined to four walls, paperback novels, and the lonely headset of his radio.

He is also trying to avoid contact with his roommate. He is already dreading the evening ahead, an evening where he is bound to feel uncomfortable, having spurned the priest's request to participate in the firebombing of the Aberdeen synagogue.

The afternoon is also filled with regret. He regrets choosing the friends that he has. It would have been easier and wiser to remain anonymous and alone. He also regrets the crassness of his first feminine encounter—the insidious event at the George Hotel. He had enjoyed a sort of pristine picture of the end of his virginity, envisioning it as some sort of magical event. The night in Montrose shattered all his daydreams and expectations.

He still considers himself a virgin, and is now more resolved than ever to fall in love in the truest sense. There have been no prospects, and in this, too, he is disappointed. He expected the path to companionship to be open to him upon his arrival in Scotland. He expected a smorgasbord of suitable girls. The only candidate he has encountered so far is a widow more than ten years his senior. Still, she is a widow he cares about very much, and he also suspects that she cares about him.

He also regrets, deeply, being secretive about his appointment on this evening with Crowley. He feels as if he is betraying Karen—she has gone out of her way to help him—staying after the mid-watch to talk to the chief and seeming to understand how he got into this predicament, the desperation of his friendlessness, the naïveté of his blind devotion to a man so much older and wiser and kinder than any he has ever known.

Obvious to him, too, is the fact that Karen hasn't passed any sort of judgment on him, even though he knows his character deserves to be assassinated a thousand times or more. She seems to understand his humanness and he takes her lack of censure as a sort of backhanded forgiveness, forgiving him for taking the path that has led him to where he is on this day.

He knows that if she knew about his plans for the evening she would be angered and even more disappointed. However, he still feels a sort of allegiance to Crowley, and felt obliged to take his invitation. And hope lies in that obligation—the vague promise of Crowley being nothing more than an innocent mentor, a sort of lovable uncle who lets the nephews come over and drink beer and smoke without the parents knowing.

He will also come to regret not being in the barracks on this afternoon. If he were in his room, he would find Karen standing at his door, wanting to warn him about the inaction of the chain of command and of her decision to take another course of action.

She wants to talk to the Scottish police, and knows the small office in the village of Lutherkirk is the logical station to go to, as the base would obviously fall under its jurisdiction.

But she needs Chris to go with her, as he is the only link to the activity of Father Crowley and his Trinity.

She gets his room number from the Scottish gentleman on duty in the barracks office. He tries to summon Chris via an intercom system that is present in every room. There is no answer, and, boldly, Karen marches up the steps to find his room. She bangs on the door. There is no answer. Impatiently, Karen paces along the balcony for nearly fifteen minutes, smoking four cigarettes in a nearly continuous inhalation.

She leaves as her intuition tells her Chris won't be around for a while, and against her intuition, she decides not to go to the Tayside Police. It can wait till Monday, she decides, upon the conclusion of their day watch. She goes home to

Brechin and spends the day and evening in melancholy, staring at photographs from her past, thinking about the possibilities of her life, what those possibilities were, and what they are now. She knows now she will stay in the Navy as long as possible, until they tell her it's time to go. Then, maybe, she will find some small town somewhere in the center of the United States and live simply off of her retirement, spending her days reading books and still wondering about what her life's possibilities could have been. She sees herself very much alone, but she knows she would be happier in the company of someone else, someone who would want to live a simple life, someone who can understand the disappointment that life can bring, the disappointment that one's own loved ones can bring.

She thinks of Chris. His life has been similar, in a way. He too has felt unloved by the people he has spent all of his life loving.

As the late afternoon comes, Chris finds his way to the barracks, knowing he can avoid his roommate no more. Soon, it will be time to go to Father Crowley's. Chris buys a six-pack of beer from the small convenience store attached to the base exchange. It is a cheap American beer, loaded with preservatives for the purpose of export. It is barely palatable, but he forces it down, needing the alcohol to wash away the dread that goes hand in hand with his concerns about this evening.

By the time Brad returns to the room at the end of his workday, Chris has consumed three beers and is more than relaxed; he has already drowned his anxiety in a flood of alcohol. Brad sees the remaining beers attached to a plastic ring on top of the refrigerator and takes one without asking. Chris has another and leaves the sixth for Brad, who drinks his two beers in a rapid succession of long swallows. They make their way to the galley and eat a large amount of mashed potatoes and gravy and roast beef as Brad talks quietly about the deadline that is approaching at the end of next week. "I bet Father will have it all mapped out tonight, what our roles are gonna be," he says. Even though Chris has lost much of his inhibition, he decides not to tell Brad of his decision. He just nods and eats, scraping his nearly empty plate with a spoon.

Shortly after eating, they find themselves in a taxicab driving in the fading daylight through the village of Lutherkirk, heading to Father Crowley's.

Chris is feeling pleasant, enjoying the ride, but as he passes the castle in Lutherkirk, just a quarter mile or so from the priest's cottage, the euphoric feeling of alcohol begins to give way to anxiety. He is sweating underneath his collar as the cab deposits them at the end of the gravel driveway.

His anxiety is quickly washed away by the hospitality of Father Crowley. Chris expected to read a sort of hostility in the eyes of the priest. There is nothing but warmth as he welcomes Brad and Chris and quickly brings them each a beer. They sit down on the couch in the living room, and even though the mood is ostensibly light, Chris can feel as if things have changed, that this evening is the end of something.

"So, Mr. Hinckley," begins the priest, "I suppose Chris has told you of his change of heart. He no longer wants to be in the Trinity."

Hinckley glares at Chris in anger, and then turns his head towards the priest with a look that is searching for an explanation.

"It's all right, it's all right." The priest holds up his hand to shush Brad as he sees a protest forming on his lips. "If he doesn't feel comfortable and if he's not with us one hundred percent, then frankly, he's no good to us. We'll just have to wait. This is a war that has been going on for centuries. We can stand a setback for a few weeks or even months and maybe even years. Our day will come.

"Besides, Chris," he says without looking at either of them, swirling wine in his silver goblet, "I love you very much, like a father loves his son. I could see you were upset in my office the other day. If a father sees that his child is upset, then he, too, feels upset. I want you to be happy, more than anything, and if you can't stomach what needs to be done, then so be it. More beer?"

Chris and Brad both nod, and Crowley rises from his sagging chair. He stirs the coal in the fireplace and throws more on, brushing the black dust off his hands on his trouser legs. He asks Brad to come into the kitchen and help him with the beers, as he wants to grab some snacks.

Brad follows him into the kitchen obediently. They are gone for more than a moment, and Chris can hear frantic and low whispers coming from the open doorway between the kitchen and living room. Brad and Crowley return silently.

Brad returns to the couch and sits as far from Chris as possible. He continues to stare at him with loathing, as if Chris is touched with some sort of plague.

If Chris were sober, this sudden coldness on the part of Brad would have caused some alarm, but on this night, in his state of nearly complete drunkenness, he barely notices.

The priest returns to his chair at the head of the coffee table with a bottle of wine in his hand. He doesn't release the bottle, just constantly refills his goblet as he empties it rapidly.

"Chris, I want you to remember one thing," Crowley says as he settles into his seat. "I want you to remember one thing about this night, now, while you still can. I want you to remember that whatever happens will only happen because of the choices you've made. Does that make sense?" This the priest asks with an innocent smile, his eyes twinkling. And inside those eyes, Chris can see the reflection of the burning coal, the reflection causing the priest's normally pale blue eyes to appear to be a bright red, a red that grows with intensity as the night colors the sky.

"Okay," replies Chris calmly, returning the priest's smile. He feels quite content right now, warmth from the alcohol, warmth from the fireplace, and warmth from the priest. In his comfort, Chris's mind starts to wander. He wonders what Karen would think if she saw him here now. She would undoubtedly be angry. Chris wonders at what lengths he would go to to include Karen in this sick group of friends. This daydream quickly passes. Even drunk, he knows that it is an impossibility.

The priest uses his gift of inane conversation to keep the mood light, not expanding any more on the result of Chris's choices. He shuffles beer from the kitchen almost constantly, making sure Chris always has a full can in front of him. One other thing odd that Chris would normally notice but doesn't on this night: Crowley is constantly pulling on his penis through his pants. Chris does not notice the outline of an erection bulging behind Crowley's zipper.

Once again, Crowley summons Brad into the kitchen.

If Chris were more cognizant, he would also notice that Brad is drinking much less than he, and is sitting silently with arms crossed while he and the priest talk.

Brad and the priest return from the kitchen, the priest holding a beer for Chris, and Brad holding a video camera. Chris wonders why he has a camera, but doesn't ask aloud.

Crowley is feeding Chris Valium in his beer, not quite the same amount that he fed Lee, but combined with the eight or nine tall tins of beer that Chris has consumed, the effect of the drug is rapid and severe. Chris collapses on the couch. His eyes flutter but remain open. If he were more aware, he would feel the priest's hands grab his legs and swing them onto the floor. The priest forces Chris's face down on the couch, placing his knees on the floor. He would also feel the priest reach around his waist to unbutton his pants and slide them down around his ankles.

He does feel the priest sodomize him. But he is too powerless to move or protest, and through the haze, the entire evening is starting to make sense to him. It lasts only a few moments as the priest pulls out in a mix of blood and excrement and semen. Chris will feel the pain later, in the morning, when he wakes up feeling a severe hangover and a feeling in his body where the priest has been.

Brad videotapes the whole thing. He doesn't feel queasy or disgusted at all. It is a necessary act, to force Chris's compliance.

The priest is acting out a long fantasy, and there is a bit of a letdown when it is over. In his fantasy, Chris had been a more willing participant, not a near-zombie. It is a longtime craving that he has satisfied. He now knows that he will have to do it again—and often.

Clumsily, the priest pulls Chris's pants back up and swings his legs back onto the couch. Chris lays there motionless as his mind falls away and he lands in a dreamless sleep.

Chris wakes up to the sight of sunlight shining through the very dirty window above the priest's chair. It takes a moment for him to recall the evening, and when he does, he is washed in dread and shame. The half-memory of the assault makes him feel lower than he ever has before, even lower than the moment he realized his family had finally disintegrated. He sits up feebly on the couch, catching the sight of a patch of dried blood gathered on the floor.

His blood, he realizes, tenderly patting his behind, horrified.

He hears Brad sleeping on the floor, snoring loudly. He spies the camera on the mantel and makes the connection—Brad taped the whole sordid scene—and he knows from the dry taste in his mouth and the way he passed out last night that the priest drugged him somehow, with god-only-knows what.

He is startled by the sight of the priest walking out of the kitchen. He is naked except for his bathrobe, which he fails to close. He leans against the wall at the foot of the couch and smiles at Chris. Chris doesn't return the smile.

"You see, Chris, I told you a bit of a fib before. It is not okay. You can't leave the Trinity. We are bound by blood and a sacred oath to enforce a deadline, which is now only a week away. As intelligent and able bodied white men, we are also bound by a certain responsibility. It is up to us to liberate our race and our nations and send those of color packing and send the Zionists where they belong—straight to hell." He pats his penis. "I just reinforced that bond, that is all, and if you should still decide to leave us, well, then," he points to the camera, "your family back in Michigan will have to see what kind of man their son has become."

Chris can understand the nature of blackmail. He has witnessed blackmail at least a thousand times in movies and on television. But for someone to blackmail him, that is almost unfathomable, so unfathomable that the whole thing seems unreal. And to be blackmailed in such a fashion, such a grotesque fashion...

There is one fact that the priest doesn't know, and Chris does not enlighten him—Chris doesn't care what his family thinks of him—and though Crowley could probably glean the address of his original home of record from his service jacket, the video tape would arrive on a stranger's porch.

"Plus," Crowley says with a touch of a smile, running his hands through his tousled red and graying hair, "I rather enjoyed it. Didn't you?"

Chris thinks about flying off the couch with his arms flailing and pummeling the priest. This he decides against; he is still too feeble from the effects of Valium and his hangover, and the lower half of his body feels as if it's been branded by a hot and sharp iron.

Instead, tears well up in his eyes. He walks out the priest's front door as quickly as he can. He walks the long miles back to the base, not aware of the red outline of blood that is visible in the seat of his pants, causing him to be quite a sight as he walks through the village of Lutherkirk, High Street just showing the first signs of Saturday commerce.

He walks past the storefront office of Constable Robertson, who is working this morning in his civilian clothes. There are reports to write, as one of the pubs in the village enjoyed a raucous Friday evening, and he had to drive three individuals to Brechin for a night in jail.

He spies the disheveled Chris walking in front of his window and studies him over the top of his typewriter, above the rim of his steaming mug of tea.

Another sick American, he thinks while shaking his head.

What is normally a five-minute cab ride turns into nearly an hour-long walk. Chris wearily approaches the gate of the base, flashing his ID card as he is carefully scrutinized by the MoDP sentry on duty, who reluctantly lets him pass.

The barracks are quiet. Chris knows that he can't linger here. He doesn't want to confront Brad, at least not know, not until he has a plan of action. Courageous under fire, he will not let the priest go unpunished. He is going to strike back. He is full of vengeance, an emotion he has never felt before.

He showers and changes clothes quickly and grabs a few items and shoves them into his gym bag.

He calls for a cab from the payphone in the barracks lounge and again makes the trek to the main gate, where the same MoDP sentry studies him seriously as he exits the base. Chris stands along the side of the road, waiting for his taxi.

There is only one place he can go that will provide him a haven, and he isn't exactly sure where she lives, but he needs to find her.

"Brechin," he tells the cab driver as he seats himself tenderly in the back of the small Fiat.

The ride is brief, too brief for him to try to figure out how he is going to find Karen. The cab driver deposits him in the middle of town, and he enters a pub that is just opening. The dryness of his mouth has not disappeared, and he knows he can get something besides beer in a pub. He tries Irn-Bru, thinking that the iron may give him some sort of vitality. He guzzles the first can, makes a face, and orders another. He drinks the second more slowly as he gets his bearings. He spies a thin phonebook next to the register behind the bar and asks the proprietor if he can use it.

He finds her name quickly, Freeman, Karen, and he fishes 10p out of his pocket and finds the yellow payphone in the doorway of the pub. He dials the number with a bit of fear. Although she has been nothing but kind to him, she may not want to help him anymore because he spent the evening with the priest without telling her. The fear she may turn him away causes his hands to tremble just slightly.

She answers after several rings. He can tell from her throaty hello that the ringing of the telephone has ended her sleep. He identifies himself and asks if he can come over.

"Sure, but it's kind of early."

"He raped me." The sound of his own voice mentioning the unspeakable act brings forth a torrent of tears and emotion. He feels shame, sadness and a strong sense of rage.

"Come over."

She directs him to her flat. He is only two blocks away. He walks up the gentle slope of Brechin's High Street. He enters a narrow alley and walks up a flight of wooden stairs to Karen's flat above a chemist's shop.

She opens the door. She immediately puts her arms around him, and he is touched by the emotion of tenderness.

Again, more tears. She leads him to her sofa, and he tells her about it, how he was lured to the priest's house, how he was drugged, and how he woke up to the sight of blood.

She leaves him alone on the couch and enters her tiny kitchen, which isn't separated from her sitting room at all. She makes coffee. He studies her. He is attracted to the way she looks in the morning, and he feels a certain sense of intimacy in seeing her in such a private light. He admires her disheveled hair, her unmade face, and the casualness of her attire: exercise shorts and a long-sleeved t-shirt that she wears for sleeping.

She returns to the couch with two mugs of coffee and places them on the coffee table. She sits somewhat close to him, with her legs curled behind her. He places his face in his hands and rests his elbows upon his knees. He feels safe.

"We're going to have to go to the Scottish police," she says with a certain amount of gravity.

"And tell them, I know. I have to tell them everything." He shudders at the thought that his blood adorned the synagogue door in Aberdeen, that his footprints and fingerprints can be found in the cemetery in Glasgow, and that the priest had...

His immaturity causes him to ask Karen a question, out of context, and somewhat startling. "This doesn't mean I'm gay, does it?"

In spite of herself and the situation, she smiles. "No."

"Good," he says, and abruptly he confesses his lack of carnal experience. Though she is not surprised, the intensity of the confession makes her realize it is a burning issue in his life.

"There will be time for girls later. I suggest you eat something and then we go to the police."

Chris forsakes food and drinks coffee and smokes cigarettes while Karen showers. He walks around her one-room flat, a full-sized bed and dresser in one half of the room, a couch and two chairs and an old-fashioned black and white television in one half, and a sort of nook for a kitchen. There is little in the way of a feminine touch, a few nondescript paintings on the wall, and books—books are on every flat surface and along a row of shelves above the bed. He likes the effect the books have on the room, as if the occupant of the flat has spent a lot of time in solitary thought. He can relate.

They drive to Lutherkirk and find that the police station is closed. On the door is an emergency telephone number, the home number of Constable Robertson. Chris looks at Karen, wondering if his situation constitutes an emergency.

"We're calling," she says, and he likes her constant choice of the word "we". She is grouping herself with him as if they are a team, or even a couple. He finds another 10p in his pocket and makes his way to the payphone in front of a café two doors down. He calls the number. He almost freezes when a woman, the constable's wife, answers the phone.

He blurts out everything almost at once, and the wife is sure there is a lunatic, a Yankee lunatic, at the other end of the line. She gets her husband. Chris starts again, but to the constable, none of this sounds like lunacy. It sounds like the call he's been waiting for.

"I'll be right there." He hangs up while Chris is still speaking.

And he is right there. Chris and Karen stand in front of the door of the station and just as they light their cigarettes, the constable comes from around the corner, walking briskly. He may have been running before he came into Chris's and Karen's sight. He acknowledges them with a nod and unlocks the door with a key from a big ring of keys he keeps clipped to his waist. He is wearing his civilian clothes, the same clothes he was wearing when Chris happened by in the morning: blue cotton pants, a blue sweater over a plaid shirt, and black shoes in need of polishing.

There are brief introductions and a shaking of hands. Before he takes any sort of statement from Chris, he telephones Dundee and tracks down Inspector Holliday.

"How soon can you get here?" he asks. "Well, we may nail this priest just yet. I have a member of that wee little group called the Trinity sitting in front of me." He pauses. Chris and Karen can hear Holliday from the other end of the phone.

Holliday tells Robertson not to let Chris leave. He'll be there in half an hour.

The constable hangs up the phone and explains why he phoned Dundee, and why he is waiting for another officer.

"You mean you've known about this priest?" Karen asks in disbelief.

"Indeed, we have. We just haven't been able to nail him down. We've even been to his place on a few occasions. He's a crafty one, that priest is." He tells an angry Karen and a still bewildered Chris of his first visit to the priest and the sight of a swastika on top of his mantel.

"Did you contact the base and tell them about your suspicions?"

"Yes and no. The Americans have always been fond of whisking their own kind out of the country when something isn't going right. You know, they have to keep their squeaky-clean, apple-pie, Ronald Reagan image intact. We didn't want to tip their hand too much—and we didn't want to alarm the priest. We wanted him sort of relaxed, and, unfortunately, he's never been an official suspect in anything. The inspector and I have always had a hunch. I even spent time outside his house in surveillance, but he gave us nothing." He explains how letters were delivered to different synagogues in Aberdeen and Edinburgh while the priest remained at home.

"I delivered those," Chris says. "Hinckley and I did. Father Crowley sent us."

"Well, then," says the constable, dropping his pen in resignation on the top of his faded wooden desk, badly in need of refinishing, "I guess he buggered us." He shrugs. "My not-so-discreet cover was blown, anyway," he admits, exposing his provincial incompetence to a pair of strangers. "He picked me out straight away. We had to shift gears, the inspector and I."

Their gears ground, and they knew there would be a certain amount of vigilance required around the synagogues when the deadline promised in the notes expired. They would have to catch the priest and his troupe red-handed. Unless of course someone could deliver them a golden egg. Chris at first promises deliverance, but as Inspector Holliday comes puffing into Lutherkirk, it is apparent that Chris's words fall short of being golden.

"We need proof," says Holliday after pondering Chris's tale in wordless attention as Robertson shuffles through his little office dispensing tea.

"Proof?" asks Karen with a certain amount of tense incredulity. "What more can he say? He's laid it all out for you—blood and swastikas and Norse gods and everything. What else can you possibly need?"

"Ms. Freeman, though I don't doubt your young friend's story—in fact, it is too far-fetched to be anything but true—how does any of it link the priest to anything? Whose blood is on the doors of the synagogues? In whose hand were the letters written? He has given us nothing, unfortunately, except a most useful witness when this does go to trial."

"Can't you just arrest him or something?" Karen asks. "Tell him he's under suspicion, or arrest him for not stopping all the way at a stop sign. Can't you arrest him for anything, or do we have to wait for more corpses to arrive at synagogue steps?"

"We need proof, something solid." Holliday looks at Chris, waiting to hear words out of his mouth that can alleviate the futility of their current situation. "Having a swastika on his mantel is no crime, and he was cleared in that apparent suicide, and that's all we have."

They sit in silence until Holliday looks at Chris. "Do you think it would be possible to return to the priest's fold and feign an interest in taking part in the activities of the Trinity?"

Chris says nothing, and recalls only his last encounter with the priest, the thrust of evil inside him, the words of evil spoken just before Chris departed.

He shakes his head. "No."

Karen places her hand on his arm, and says to Holliday and Robertson, "Let me talk to him, but first, you would have to assure his safety."

"We can't do that, Ms. Freeman, as much as we'd like to. Ours is a sticky business and your young friend here has put himself in the stickiest of situations. We will do our best, but we can't guarantee anything. The only guarantee is that the priest will be arrested upon the receipt of something solid, something that can be proven in court."

Holliday lights a cigarette and offers one to each member of his present company. All accept, save the constable, whose face shows a sign of irritation as his little office quickly fills with the bluish smoke of exhaled tobacco.

"Inspector, give me your card. Chris and I will talk, and we'll see if we can figure something out. He has had a night from hell, and he's still just a teenager. It's a lot for him to think about right now, and I'm sure he's scared. I know I would be and so would you. Can we call you tomorrow?"

"You can call me anytime, and I'm sure the same is true for the constable." The inspector doesn't possess any cards, so he scribbles his phone number on a piece of paper from the tiny notepad he keeps inside his jacket.

Chris and Karen leave the office. An instant later, the blue Austin Allegro of Father Crowley drives slowly by, spying the familiar and formidable figure of Inspector Holliday climbing into his Cortina.

Karen takes Chris back to her flat in Brechin. She knows it is necessary for Chris to go back to the priest and try to come up with something, anything, that can link him to the crimes of the past and the threatened crimes of the future.

But she doesn't want to force him. She knows he is scared and has been through a lot. Most people in his situation would probably flee as far from the priest as possible.

Gently, she reminds him that he put himself into this situation, and for the sake of others, he should try to do what he can.

They arrive back at her flat, and she offers to make a late lunch. Chris still can't eat. He sits morosely on her couch, torn between what he knows he should do and what he wants to do. He wants to remain in Karen's flat forever and not have to face Brad or the priest ever again. He could ride with Karen to work and then exit the base immediately. He could spend the time off with her, traveling around the country visiting castles and towns.

But this isn't an option. He knows he couldn't live with himself if he doesn't do what the police and Karen have asked. He has to reach deep inside and wrestle a certain amount of courage that he has always lacked. Never in his life has he been made to face such fear, other than the fear of walking through hallways and sitting in cafeterias alone, a chronic fear that has plagued him since so very early in his adolescence.

He smokes a cigarette. He watches his hand and studies his fingers as he draws the cigarette to his lips and lets it hang above the ashtray on the coffee table. He wonders how he looks to Karen while smoking, and he wonders if it makes him seem older. He thinks back to the time when he was perhaps fourteen or fifteen, standing in front of his bathroom mirror, watching himself smoke. He smiles at the silliness of the memory and contemplates the change in his life since those days. Those were sad days. His mother had just started dating other men without hiding it. Lord knows what she had been doing in secret. He confronted her, and she told him to mind his own business and that the only reason why she and his father hadn't divorced was because of him. They might as well have, he thinks now, looking back. They weren't there for him very much. He brought home his report cards to no one, leaving them exposed on the kitchen table and they would remain there, undisturbed, until he threw them away.

He sighs, finishes his cigarette and immediately lights another. He ponders the consequences of his inaction. The priest will ultimately be caught; he will slip somehow, somewhere, with or without Chris. Chris's blood is left on the synagogue door in Aberdeen, already gathered in evidence bags in the Grampian Police HQ. The priest won't go down alone; Chris knows this to be true. The priest will go down kicking and crying and naming all of his associates, as he will need company to share in his misery.

He contemplates the worst-case scenarios of his return to the priest's fold. He knows he won't be sodomized again. He won't allow the priest to do that, and he won't eat or drink in the priest's presence ever again. He could die, somehow, during the attack on the synagogue or during the police break-up of such an act. He could be murdered by the priest, if the priest somehow gets wind of his contact with the police. Death is the worst thing that could possibly happen. The best result is that the priest's plans are thwarted and Chris, due to his cooperation, is absolved of all his earlier participation in the desecration of the synagogue and cemetery.

He thinks only briefly about Brad—his friend, but not really his friend. They were only friends while drinking. He knows Brad is a hateful young man. His heart is full of rage. He is without a conscience. He even hit a girl, Chris recalls. He has been with the priest since early on and has shown no sign of remorse over past murders or the possibility of future murders. He is a willing participant.

Chris finishes his cigarette. Karen is in the kitchen, cleaning up from the morning, the clutter of coffee cups and her own cereal bowl.

"I'll do it," he says suddenly. "I'll do what I have to do." He puts his head in his hands and he knows his words have just now sealed his fate. He could never go back on his word—not his word to Karen.

She nods slowly while walking to the couch. She sits next to Chris, very closely. The closeness is almost uncomfortable for Chris, but not unwelcome.

Karen is touched. She knows this requires a lot of courage on Chris's part, a sort of bravery that has never been required of him before at this tender age. She has been somehow attracted to Chris from early on. There is something about his gentle nature that is endearing, and she realizes now that he reminds her of her late husband. He too was gentle and unassuming, not brash and obnoxious like the boys she knew and dated in high school. He was sensitive; he showed his emotions to her often and readily. So has Chris.

"I just want you to know that you won't do this alone. I'll be with you and worrying about you while you're gone." She kisses him on the cheek and a thought crosses her mind, a thought that she would not have expected in a million years.

She has not been with a man since her husband and children passed away. She hasn't been interested, not even a little. She has been propositioned probably a thousand times. She is, after all, a not-so-unattractive woman in a mostly male Navy. Adak, Alaska was especially tiresome; the island was military-only. There was no place off base for sailors to go. She dared not show her face in the enlisted club at night. She stayed locked away in her room—her shelves lined with books borrowed from the base library or ordered through the mail.

She has known all along that her celibacy would end. She has, as of late, felt a sort of longing for companionship, and she realized after showing Chris some of Scotland that experiences are better and richer if they can be shared. His youth doesn't bother her; he hasn't been alive long enough for the world to harden him.

So she decides to make love to Chris.

Her reasoning is two-fold. The first reason is to satisfy her own needs; the length of mourning has been long enough where she doesn't feel a sense of guilt. The second reason is that Chris needs to cross the threshold into manhood. He needs to make love to a woman in a genuine way, in a way that will build his confidence. He needs a certain swagger in his step that one can only have when involved with a new love. He will need all the swagger and confidence he can muster when he goes back to the priest.

She kisses him once on the cheek, and she sees his face redden with a probable mix of embarrassment and desire. She kisses him again on the other cheek and then on the lips. She is surprised at her own aggressiveness. He kisses her back gently, and the softness of his kiss enthralls her even more.

She then seduces him completely, there on her couch, removing his clothes before removing her own. It has been a long time, but it is an act she hasn't forgotten. The sensation of desire fans across her body, a feeling that she realizes she has missed.

Chris, at first, is more than dumbfounded. This is a behavior that he doesn't expect from Karen, though it is a behavior that he has longed for and has imagined with her. His first inclination, out of shame and decency, is to resist her. He, of course, doesn't resist her; he surrenders completely and follows her lead with his own instinct.

They make love and the span of time is brief. The event is a less torturous one for him than the night in the George Hotel—he doesn't think about the procedural things quite so much. He is awkward at first, tumbling on top of her as she lays down on the couch, but he quickly learns the cadence of her body and he orgasms inside her, deep and passionately.

He is now quite sure that he is no longer a virgin.

They sit on the couch naked for a moment in the afterglow. They smoke cigarettes halfway and then get dressed, and decide to walk to a café for supper. The thought of dealing with the priest is nowhere near his mind as Chris walks along High Street with that certain amount of swagger. He is again in love, a lopsided smile set upon his face.

Chris eats heartily, as he is hungry from the act of love and the fast induced by the stress of the previous day.

"You know," she says, interrupting Chris's amorous reverie, "we need to call Inspector Holliday and let him know that you're going to help."

Chris's smile fades. Karen reaches for his hand. A trace of a smile returns in answer to her touch. Fear is no longer so visible on his face, as Karen's overture of affection is effective. He has a sense of confidence that he didn't possess just an hour before. The look on his face underlines that confidence.

Karen pays the bill and they return to her flat. They call the inspector. It is agreed that Chris will return to the priest as if nothing tragic happened, as if Crowley's predatory behavior wasn't so disturbing and that his blackmail was effective. Chris will be a good soldier right up until the attack on the synagogue in Aberdeen. Chris will be asked to alert Holliday of when the priest plans his assault, and Holliday in turn will alert the Grampian Police and Scotland Yard, who will wait as the priest arrives in Aberdeen. They will then pounce, arresting Father Crowley and Brad, as well as Chris, but only for show. He is to be granted a degree of immunity for his cooperation.

Chris agrees to the terms, and Holliday reminds him of the haste that is required.

"You need to head back to the base straightaway," the inspector tells Chris. "You can't deviate too much from your normal routine, and you can't alert them of your contact with Karen. Call us when you know something."

Chris nods as he hangs up the phone and tells Karen what the inspector said. She drives him back to the base. She kisses him goodbye, and he passionately returns her kiss. He morosely exits her car and walks through the front gate. He approaches his barracks and his room with dread. He hopes Brad isn't there, but he knows he is.

Chris enters his room. Brad is sprawled out on his rack, listening to Chris's Walkman radio.

"What's up, faggot?" he asks. "Where the hell you been?"

Chris says nothing as he thinks of a response. He sits heavily on his bed. "Nowhere. I was just walking around the countryside, trying to think."

"Oh." Brad hands the radio back to Chris. "Well... Father wants to know what you're going to do. He wants us to go out there tonight, if you're still in. If you're not in—"

"I'm in."

"Then let's get rollin'."

Crowley lets Chris and Brad into his cottage wordlessly. His mood is more solemn than it has been in the past. Before, he has assumed an air of friendliness, his face always adorned with a smile.

On this night, a Saturday after he has conducted a soulless Mass, he is all business. His deadline is less than a week away, and he has heard nary a mention in the news of any exodus of the Jews in Scotland. He knows their number is small, not even five thousand, but still, he had hoped the fear he has spread would make more of an impact. There was some talk dispensing fear on the radio at first, when the cab driver was murdered and when notes were deposited in Edinburgh and Aberdeen.

The lack of concern is insulting to him. He is irritated that he hasn't been taken more seriously. His ego is definitely bruised.

"Sit down," he commands as Chris and Brad walk in. He points to the chair for Brad, and sits himself down on the couch next to Chris, without even allowing an arm's width to separate them.

Brad makes a detour to the kitchen. He opens the refrigerator, as his body is aching for beer. The refrigerator is empty. Crowley barks, "You're not here for fun, you damn lush. Sit down. You will drink when I say you're damn good and ready to drink."

Morosely, Brad sits down. Crowley sits silently for a moment, satisfied that his Trinity is intact and loyal. He is smug in his role as the Trinity head, as if Chris and Brad are his subjects, mere extensions of his will.

"Now, gentlemen," Crowley continues. He is still wearing his khaki uniform that he wore under his robe for Mass. "I suggest we get to business first, and if time permits, maybe we will go over to Lutherkirk and grab a drink." Chris notes

Crowley's selfishness; he is armed with his goblet, and the smell of wine hangs over the couch, mingling with the smell of Crowley himself. Crowley hasn't showered in the past twenty-four hours. If Chris knew the reason for Crowley's lack of hygiene, he would be horrified. Crowley is keeping the smell and flesh of Chris on his genitalia as a sort of trophy. It is an attempt to prolong the memory of his intercourse with Chris. Several times throughout the day, he has pulled his pants down and smiled at the sight of Chris's dried blood and feces on his penis. It is the first fantasy he has ever fulfilled.

He plans to fulfill a second.

The plan to attack the Aberdeen synagogue is simple in its brutality. Father Crowley instructs Brad to stand at the door of the synagogue, armed with Thor's hammer. He is to keep the spike in constant motion, striking any man, woman or child that tries to exit the synagogue. Chris and the priest are going to dispense Molotov cocktails through the lone window after the door is ignited with gasoline.

Crowley shows Brad and Chris the assortment of pipe bombs and wine bottles and even a small propane torch he has purchased for the occasion. He salivates at the image of the synagogue in smoke and flames and wonders how he will feel when he hears the screams of the Jews as they meet their certain end.

His mood lightens. He tousles Brad's hair and puts his arm around Chris's shoulder. Gently, Chris pulls himself away.

"Chris, when is your next Saturday off?" He asks the question merely out of ceremony. He has long memorized Chris's schedule.

"I have a mid-watch next Saturday," Chris replies, knowing that the priest already knows the answer.

"Excellent, excellent," continues Crowley. "You will both stay here Friday night, and then on Saturday morning we will make our assault on Aberdeen. If that isn't effective enough, we will turn to Glasgow, Edinburgh, and finally Dundee. I am afraid I have become a blip on the radar of the Tayside Police, and I should really stay out of Dundee, until the end, anyway."

Father Crowley's last sentence causes Chris alarm, as if the priest knows Chris has betrayed him. Chris studies his face and sees no sign of resentment pointed in his direction.

They will conduct a rehearsal Wednesday evening, timing the drive to Aberdeen and how long it takes them to assume their positions.

When next Saturday comes, Father Crowley will take the license plate off his Allegro. They will wear black ski masks that Crowley acquired long ago for just such an occasion.

He wants their appearance to be as fearsome as possible.

"How about a drink, gentlemen? Let's have a drink to celebrate the last Saturday of freedom for the Jews in Scotland."

Father Crowley's earlier suggestion of driving to Lutherkirk for a drink is discarded. There is too great a chance they will run into fellow Americans so close to the base, and the existence of their Trinity must be kept a secret, especially now in these furious, last days. Crowley decides to drive to Finavon, a village slightly larger than Lutherkirk to the South and West, away from the coast. It is perhaps twenty minutes away, and the chance of coming across other Americans is nil.

Chris breaks his self-imposed vow of abstinence in the priest's presence. They spend nearly two hours in a dark little pub in the heart of Finavon. There is precious little else to do besides drink. He drinks slowly, making one of his pints last as long as three of Brad's. The evening is not entirely unpleasant; Chris enjoys traveling to a village that he's never seen and inhaling the atmosphere of the village from the bottom of a pint glass.

Chris and Brad remain mostly silent while Crowley talks vaguely about their impending greatness. They are to be the liberators of the white world, he says. Statues of them will adorn the great cities of Europe and North America by the time the war is complete.

"The blacks and Jews and Asians that are scattered away from their ancestral homes will be grateful to us, too, in the end," the priest predicts. "They will find more fulfillment in their natural realms."

He also talks about the need for reservations, not unlike those occupied by Native Americans in North America. Not all the blacks will be able to go to Africa, and not all the Jews will be able to return to Israel.

"There is a lot of empty land out west," Crowley says, thinking of Utah and Nevada. "There is acre upon acre upon acre of federally owned land that would be perfect. Reservations could be made and the whites that live out west would still be miles away from these encampments. We could even let the blacks and Jews govern their own affairs, but of course, they would be corralled. Like Soweto in South Africa—a brilliant move by the whites there, creating black homelands that are only partially self-governed, and still under white control. The same thing should happen in America, for those blacks and Jews and Asians that remain behind."

"What about spics, Father?" Brad asks, recalling the sight of migrant workers in the summertime fields of Nebraska.

"The same, the same. They can be sent back to Mexico or Central America or wherever they came from. It is easier to repatriate someone to a neighboring country than it is to send them across the oceans."

They drive back to Crowley's house. The priest and Brad are both quite drunk. Chris, who would normally be drunk in their presence, is nearly sober. The priest's driving terrifies him. He grabs the handle of the door tightly, his fingers and knuckles turning white as the priest fails to slow down for the many curves and rises in the road.

They return to Crowley's house. Looking at Chris, the priest invites them both to stay the night.

Chris declines. He says he doesn't feel good.

He starts walking towards the base, not bothering to see if Brad is coming with him.

Brad doesn't follow Chris to the barracks, and Chris is relieved; he needs a certain amount of privacy as he arrives at the base after walking in the dark.

He calls Karen from a payphone in the barracks lounge; the time is nearing 11 p.m. She listens to his account of the evening, and tells him to telephone Holliday straight away in the morning, before Brad returns.

"Can't I just come and stay with you?" Chris asks. "It would be easier for me to call Inspector Holliday from your place, without the chance of running into Brad."

"You know the answer to that one. Of course you can't. You will only be able to see me at work until this is done, but don't worry, I plan to be in Aberdeen when this whole thing goes down, and you can come home with me then. I'm going to be there, just to make sure that you're okay."

Chris feels a sensation of warmth in the base of his stomach, the same sensation he feels when he thinks about Karen, his mind constantly playing back the image of her underneath him while he made love to her—the smoldering look in her eyes, the sight of her unclothed body, the sound of pleasure from her lips. His mind has been too busy and too afraid to think about that moment for very long.

"Okay," Chris replies, smiling, feeling better about the whole situation. It has brought him Karen, and he can sort of consider her a girlfriend. The companion that he has wanted all along, coming from the unlikeliest of sources.

"And Chris?"

"Yes?"

"You should go to Mass tomorrow. You know, you have to play the part of a good soldier. You can show no wavering of loyalty or else your cover may be blown. But call the inspector first. Call me tomorrow if you can."

They say farewell. Chris hangs up and looks at the telephone with longing, wishing he were in the company of the voice that was on the other end.

Chris calls the inspector after a mostly sleepless night. The night has been spent with his headphones attached to his ears, the sounds of Radio Luxembourg intermingling with the fear of the priest and the lust and affection for Karen. His mind is a cacophony of images and emotions. He fell asleep finally as the sight of dawn just started to appear over the base.

Inspector Holliday is full of reassurances. There will be many policemen on the scene in Aberdeen when Saturday rolls around. Chris gives him a description of Brad and a description of the Allegro. The inspector thanks him and tells him not to worry. Chris is only slightly reassured.

Chris lingers in front of the television in the barracks lounge as he exits the phone booth. A situation comedy from the States is blaring, the sound of canned laughter echoing through the nearly empty lounge. The sound of laughter reminds Chris of a sad detail of his life—his life has been devoid of laughter.

He returns to his room to shower and dress for church. Brad is in the room and is sprawled across his bed fully clothed.

"What's up, faggot?" he asks as Chris exits the bathroom with only a barracks-supplied towel wrapped around his waist.

Chris ignores him and proceeds to get dressed. "You going to church?" Chris asks Brad.

"Naw. Father would like that, but I told him as we drove back to base that I need more shuteye. I can't sleep for shit in that damn house of his. It's too musty or dusty or somethin'. I always wake up with a headache."

"I think it's called a hangover," Chris replies with mild sarcasm.

"Fuck you. I can drink you under the table any day. Good drinkers like me don't get hangovers."

Chris leaves. He stops in the galley for breakfast. He eats alone, and it really doesn't bother him. He would now rather eat alone than with Brad. Besides, he has something more than anyone else in the galley. Chris studies the scattered faces in the dining hall, most in groups of two or more stuck inside inane conversations. He has something more than dining companions; he has love, and he knows that none of these people know what love is. He eats quickly and thoughtfully, his mind on Karen for a while instead of the priest. He longs to see her naked again, he longs to sit on her couch in comfortable silence. He sees himself there, in her small flat, reading a book beside her as she too reads, the sound of pages turning the only noise in the room.

He goes to church and is shocked at how empty the pews are. Only a few of the very devout seem to be attending, those who need to take communion to proceed with their lives. Crowley enters the chapel, and Chris can tell he is still under the influence of his constant flow of wine. His eyes and face are tinged with red and his hair is greasy and uncombed. He sees Chris sitting in the back and smiles and waves without regard to the handful of congregants.

The Mass is brief, and Chris spends it inside a daydream. He is looking forward to the day when all his trouble with Father Crowley is behind him and his free time can be spent exclusively with Karen.

The Mass concludes, and Chris tries to sneak out of the chapel without talking to Crowley. He is unsuccessful. Crowley stands by the doorway that separates the lobby from the chapel and puts his arm around Chris and leads him into his office.

"You know," he says to Chris with wine-laden breath, "you can spend the day with me—just you, not Brad. I want to go to Dundee and take care of some business, and I'd rather not go there myself. What do you say?"

Chris feels like a mouse that has been dropped into a cage with a boa constrictor. He feels that any time alone with the priest could be dangerous.

"No thanks, Father. I have to do laundry, and I need the rest. We have a big week ahead of us, and I want to be one hundred percent."

"Of course, of course."

"I'll see you Wednesday." Chris leaves the office without waiting for a response from the priest.

Working with Karen is now euphoric for Chris. It's like not even working at all. The long hours spent inside a windowless building are his sole refuge—the only place where he feels safe from the demons that occupy most of the other aspects of his life.

Karen is a bit cool to him while working. He tries to show her affection, but she halts him as he leans forward to peck her on the cheek as she enters their workspace.

"Not at work. We'll get in trouble. Fraternization is a big no-no. My record is blemish-free, and yours is going to look real interesting pretty soon. We don't need any extra stress in our lives. Just be patient. I'll be waiting for you in Aberdeen the minute it's all over."

And that's how the next two watches go, Chris staring at Karen longingly and giving little thought to the priest and the task required him of him in less than a week. Nothing seems worth worrying about while he is in the presence of Karen.

Until Wednesday evening. Chris is in between days and mids, and it is the day Crowley set aside for a trial run. Crowley stealthily drives off the base with Brad and Chris in tow, as there are no cabs queued outside the base on a Wednesday evening.

Chris can feel the stare of the MoDP officer as he waves the priest's car off the base. Chris is embarrassed to be seen in the company of the priest and Brad, even though he knows the officer knows nothing of the Trinity, and knows nothing of Chris's secret life.

"No time to eat, no time to eat," Crowley says as they spill out of his car in front of his cottage.

Carefully, he shows them his weapons of choice: empty bottles of South African wine soon to be filled with gasoline and oil, with gasoline soaked rags as wicks. And then, lovingly, he picks up the metal spiked ball at the end of a wooden handle that he has leaning against the wall by the fireplace. Chris was frightened by the sight of it the first time he saw it, and is even more terrified now. Crowley could bash his head just for spite in an instant. Chris hopes his secret with the Tayside Police is safe.

"This," he says, handing the weapon to Brad, "is Thor's Hammer."

Hinckley grabs the weapon with two hands, studying his fists as they clench the wood.

"Go on," Crowley urges with an enthusiasm similar to what a parent shows at Christmas as a child unwraps a special gift. "Let's take it outside and give it a few swings."

The trio walks into the scrubby woods behind Crowley's cottage. Thin, young hardwood trees jockey for position in this small forest. Brad swings the spiked ball in a circular motion over his head and forces a three-inch-wide sapling down in one swing. That's how powerful and heavy the weapon is.

"Excellent, excellent," says Crowley, who all but claps his hands. "You are indeed a true and natural Viking. No lessons necessary for you. You will be able to do the same with Jewish men, women, and children?"

"Sure, Father. Niggers and gooks, too."

"That's my boy. Let's get going."

They return Thor's hammer to the living room and hop in Crowley's Austin, which is rapidly approaching dilapidation. Crowley makes Chris the timekeeper and Chris sets his watch, utilizing the stop clock function of the digital watch he bought at the exchange in Pensacola.

"Of course, this won't be one hundred percent accurate," says the priest, speaking of their rehearsal. "We won't be igniting anything tonight. I just want to get our parking situation crystallized, as well as our stations in front of and behind the synagogue."

They drive to Aberdeen in relative silence, parking a street away from the synagogue and approaching it from the back, via a wide and clean alley. Chris and the priest position themselves, Chris standing in front of the window and Crowley in front of the door. Brad stands on the city sidewalk, allowing himself a wide-angle view of the front of the synagogue, enabling him to see any and all would-be escapees.

"We will probably only spend about four minutes here, gentlemen, and by then I suspect we should hear sirens. When we do, I want you to drop everything, and the three of us will run in three different directions. I will proceed across the alley, and the two of you with your younger legs will have to run a bit farther. Chris, you run one block north, one block west, and then backtrack to the car. If no one is watching, I want you to walk instead of run. Remove your mask as quickly as possible, discarding it anywhere. Brad, the same goes for you, except you will travel south instead of north, and you both should find me driving up and down the same street where we parked. I expect to pick up both of you as casually as someone waiting for a taxicab. I wish to see no signs of commotion. If you think you are going to be seen, then don't get into my car. I want you to hide, until night falls, if necessary, at least until several hours after the sirens have subsided. I will make sure you each have cab fare to get back home. And, most importantly," he adds, shaking a plastic container of pills, "should you be arrested, you can't be taken alive. You will swallow seven of these and wait for the Valkyries to arrive."

They drive back to Lutherkirk. They agree to meet at Crowley's cottage on Friday at 5 p.m.

"We will have an immaculate feast," promises Crowley, "and plenty to drink. We have to be well fed to undertake such a task, and we have to be relaxed and well rested. We will drink plenty, but we will drink early. In bed by ten and off to Aberdeen by eight Saturday morning."

The priest drops Brad and Chris off at the gate of the base. They walk to their room as Brad talks in an agitated excitement about the blow they are going to deal to the Jews around the world. Brad immediately climbs into his rack when they reach their room, and Chris retrieves his sea bag from his locker. His sea bag serves as a sort of dirty clothes hamper. He walks to the laundry room attached to the barracks lounge and does his washing.

He also calls Holliday and tells him of their rehearsal and their estimated time of arrival in Aberdeen.

"Thank you, Mr. Fairbanks," replies Inspector Holliday. "We will see you Saturday, then?"

Chris mumbles in affirmation and returns to his laundry, mindlessly watching the washer until it stops spinning.

Wednesday and Thursday night, Chris can't sleep and he can barely eat. His thoughts are a mixture of lust and fear and longing. Images of Karen and the priest alternate space in his consciousness, and he pictures a variety of scenarios for Saturday.

His favorite daydream has the police swarming all over them immediately Saturday morning, almost as soon as the feet of the Trinity hit the Aberdeen sidewalks.

He will then ride back to Brechin with Karen, and the rest of his days in the Navy and life will flow with tranquility.

But he also has horrifying daydreams. The priest finds out, somehow, beforehand that Chris has betrayed him. He sodomizes him again by force and then kills him, either in Aberdeen or while he sleeps Friday night in his cottage. And in his least favorite daydream, he survives until the police come, but Karen is not there, and their relationship is over. This horrifies him more than death. He has no other reason for living, other than Karen.

Friday. He is exhausted and listless as the time comes for him and Brad to go to Father Crowley's house.

He takes all the letters he has written and never mailed and places them in a large manila envelope. A sort of will, he thinks, the only thing he wishes to leave behind if the worst does happen on Saturday morning. He marks the envelope to the attention of Petty Officer Second Class Karen Freeman, and leaves them on top of the desk in his room, easily found in case he never returns.

April 24, 1986

Dear Wife,

Do you have regrets? I've never really regretted anything
before, but I've made some bad decisions that have put me
in a bad situation. These decisions are so bad, and the consequences so steep, that I may never meet you (but I think I
may already have). I could end up in jail or out of the Navy
for some of the things that I've done. It has to do with that
priest that I mentioned earlier. Even though I've done some
bad things, I want you to know that in my heart I never felt
any anger or hatred at anyone. I just wanted to be a part of
something.

I have desecrated synagogues, showing a huge lack of respect for places of worship that mean so much to many people. I did it just to fit in, just to have a couple of friends.
Friends like that aren't worth keeping, I know now. I'm not
any happier with them than I was without them. I was better
off being alone.

Hopefully, I come out of this okay. Saturday, tomorrow,
is going to be a huge day and an important one. I will become a better person because of this, and I will always try to
be kind, no matter what. Love and kindness are the most
important things, and tolerance too, I think. We're not all
the same, but we have to be together, somehow, in this very
goofy world.

More later, no matter what.

Love,
Chris

Father Crowley had come home for lunch to start cooking a turkey, just like Thanksgiving. It is ready when Brad and Chris arrive at his cottage as passengers in his car. There is no time to waste waiting for a taxi; they have to eat and drink quickly and retire early. Crowley insists that their minds and bodies be well rested for tomorrow morning.

"And we must drink in moderation, gentlemen," he says in contrast to his earlier promise of plenty to drink. "We must have full command of our faculties. We can't disappoint—they are watching in Valhalla, and I know they are relishing this moment. It will be a defining moment in the white man's struggle. Of this, you can be sure."

Chris thinks briefly about the reception waiting for them tomorrow morning in Aberdeen. He had spoken with Inspector Holliday briefly in the afternoon, calling him from a payphone outside the base commissary.

"Not to worry, lad," Holliday told him with assurance. "The finest of the island will be there, even some from Scotland Yard."

"When are we going to tell the Navy?" Chris asked.

"When it's done. We will make them promise to leave you alone, or else we parade the priest in front of the television cameras."

Chris knows that scene will be ugly, explaining it all to the chain of command as Chaplain Crowley and Brad are locked away in some Scottish prison. Chris imagines a stone fortress surrounded by fog tucked away in a remote part of the Scottish Highlands.

Crowley and Brad need to be locked away for a very long time, if not forever, he thinks.

They sit down and eat the driest of turkey, and Crowley forgets about his vow of moderation. He pours them all tall glasses of wine. He constantly empties his own goblet in one or two swallows, refilling it again and again.

Chris sips his wine timidly, remembering what happened the last time he became too intoxicated in the priest's presence. Brad drinks with abandon, finishing one glass of wine before foraging the priest's refrigerator for tins of beer.

Fortunately, the priest doesn't seem to be feeling too amorous on this night.

"The Jew, the Jew," he says after their meal is done and he commands Brad to clear the table, "is not expecting this, not expecting us. Sure, sure, they know about fringe groups in the States and in Europe, you know, the skinheads and the like who chant on and on but do nothing. Look at us—we look like everyone else, normal, average citizens, but we've been enlightened by the will of Odin. The fog of mental control by the Zionists has been removed from our eyes. We have seen the lies of the Holocaust exposed. We have seen through the Jewish manipulation of Hollywood and the Jewish control of our central banks. Enough is enough. We, the sons of Odin and keepers of the white flame, can no longer stand idly by as our race is inbred and our children become morally corrupted by the lies of schools and churches and the media. The time is high."

He drinks from his goblet, wipes his mouth with his sleeve and stands at the head of the table, looking very thoughtful.

"Now, as you know from history, the Jew has always been able to turn tragedy into triumph. In fact, they thrive on tragedy. The murder of one Jew two thousand years ago gave rise to the religion that has deceived the white man for ages—Christianity. And the supposed murder of six million Jews during World War II gave them what they have always wanted—the nation of Israel." He drinks again. "That, my friends," he says, favoring Brad and Chris with separate gazes, "was the beginning of the end. Israel gave them credibility, gave them the opportunity to war with the Arabs, and war with the Arabs was merely a practice round for the battles with the rest of the world that are yet to come. But they didn't count on the tenacity of the Arabs; they thought the Middle East would have been under their control by 1975. And, it goes to show," he says, laughing, "though they are a lesser race, those Arabs sure can fight. They are more devoted to their beliefs than the Jews. The Jews have more devotion to things that are material rather than spiritual. The Jews want the world. They want to control all of the money, and the only way to control all the money is to control the banks of all the countries. They already do in America and most of Europe. We are going to stop them. They won't be able to turn the wounds we inflict on them into their benefit. We are not an identifiable enemy. We are not as big as the Romans or as powerful as the Nazis. No, we are small and lethal and completely shrouded in secrecy."

Chris shivers at the last sentence as he thinks about his fate if Crowley finds out about his betrayal before the police get a hold of him.

The priest concludes his sermonizing and they retire to the living room, where Crowley feeds the fire with more coal. They talk about nothing in particular, just the vague notion of a white utopia when their work has been completed.

"After Scotland is liberated, and if we are still here, we will work on England. London is chock-full of Zionists. If somehow we are gone, transferred out of here before our work is complete, then the three of us will find each other in America and start our work there," Crowley says, showing signs of inebriation.

Brad and the priest drink constantly, well into the dark, laughing and talking loudly. Chris feigns laughter as well, still sipping his beer cautiously, resisting the temptation to abandon his fear and enjoy the feeling of being drunk.

"Well, well, gentlemen," Crowley says as the hour approaches eleven. "We have stayed up way too late, and we have drunk way too much. Is our gear ready?" he asks of Brad.

"Yes, Father, you made sure of that after Wednesday. The bottles are full of gas and oil and stuffed with rags. You put them in three duffel bags out back, and Thor's hammer is right here." Brad points to the spike leaning against the fireplace.

"Excellent." The priest rises from his armchair and stretches his arms with a yawn. "There will be a slight change of plans, gentlemen. Dundee, too, houses a synagogue. We never went there because the Tayside Police became suspicious of me. We never delivered a note to their synagogue because of that. However, we won't be expected in Dundee, and there may be a certain amount of vigilance in Aberdeen. I drove to Dundee on my own and checked the synagogue out. It is small, and it seems to be attached to the University of Dundee. Logistically, it will be similar, except there are two windows in front. We will be able to approach it just as stealthily and scatter in the same fashion when we hear the sirens."

Chris panics, knowing that the priest is expected in Aberdeen, fearing that somehow he knows what is waiting in the shadows on Saturday morning.

"But Father," Chris protests after gathering his thoughts, "Brad and I only know the Aberdeen synagogue. We already practiced that one. We've never even seen the Dundee synagogue." He is quite frightened. He pictures the scores of police waiting in Aberdeen tomorrow morning—waiting and waiting and waiting while a disaster is inflicted upon Dundee, while Crowley escapes.

"It doesn't matter. We need the element of surprise on our side. No one will expect Dundee. It is perfect." With that, Crowley walks upstairs to retire for the night, not wishing to discuss the choice of Saturday's destination any further. Brad collapses in a pile of blankets on the floor, and Chris places his rigid and now sweaty body on the couch with eyes wide open and his heart racing.

He must do something, but he's not sure what. He thinks of so many things, mainly of an attack on the synagogue in Dundee that goes unchecked. He pictures smoke pouring out of the synagogue. He can hear the screams of those trapped inside. He can picture Brad wielding Thor's hammer, crudely bludgeoning those who manage to leave the building.

He thinks about trying to leave the priest's house, running away once and for all, but that would alarm Crowley. He wouldn't try to attack a synagogue, again giving the police nothing to pin upon him. And he would know he had been betrayed. He would wait and plan an attack later, after the passage of a certain amount of time. Chris's safety would be in perpetual doubt.

And he also thinks about sneaking out, calling Holliday or Constable Robertson or Karen, whoever he can reach first, and warning them about the change of venue. He would then sneak back in the house and remain there until the morning.

This plan he ponders the longest, as it is the more feasible of his choices. It does pose a certain amount of risk. Brad or the priest may awaken as he sneaks in or out of the house, and he would have to explain his absence at such a late and inconvenient hour.

He rises from the couch and tiptoes towards the door. He plans to walk the short distance into Lutherkirk, find a payphone, and call the police. Brad stirs as Chris walks across the dusty floor, and, in fright, Chris flies back to the couch.

He remains awake, gripped by panic and fear and indecision. His eyes stay wide open, darting back and forth, studying the moonlight pouring through the window. The hands on his watch read two in the morning when he is struck with an epiphany, a frightening conclusion that he cannot ignore. It is the surest way to end the priest's reign of hate. It is the surest way to ensure Chris's security.

He rises from the couch, automatically, as if he is guided by some cosmic remote control. He goes outside, not caring that his footfalls or the opening or closing of the door will stir Brad or Father Crowley from their drunken sleep. He retrieves several of the wine bottles that the priest has carefully filled with gasoline and oil. He pours them over all the furniture in the house, over the carpet, across the blanket that covers Brad. He grabs Thor's hammer and purposefully walks up the narrow stairs to the priest's bedroom. He has never traveled up these stairs before, and he leans against the wall as he guides himself through the dark.

The priest is easy enough to find. There are only two rooms upstairs, and the priest's bedroom door is open. Chris enters, spying the priest lying naked on top of his bed, the moonlight making his pale and flabby skin appear nearly luminous.

He is sleeping on his back, his hands folded peacefully across his chest. Chris studies him for a moment, almost reverently. The priest has the smallest of smiles and his chest rises and falls slowly, as if he hasn't a care in the world.

He must feel at peace, Chris thinks, a feeling he has chased unknowingly for years, until the priest so clearly illustrated the common man's meandering through life.

He is at peace, Chris thinks as he closes his eyes and raises Thor's hammer above his head. The metal ball glistens briefly as it catches the moonlight and falls swiftly and silently, save the noise of the ball cutting through the still air of the room. The spikes crush the skull of the priest in one swing. Chris witnesses this through half-open eyes. He swings again, and this time the ball gets stuck in the mattress. Chris struggles to free it as he hears the sound of gurgling blood coming from the priest's neck and mouth. The sound makes Chris think of a shallow and slow moving stream, with water passing over rocks smooth and round.

Chris returns downstairs. He places Thor's hammer on the floor next to Brad, tenderly placing Brad's hand on top of the handle. He goes back outside and retrieves another duffel bag full of wrapped wine bottles filled with gasoline. He takes them upstairs, pouring gasoline on the stairs and on the floor of the priest's bedroom. He then goes to the front door, soaks the threshold and the wood of the door itself in gasoline. Finally, he is satisfied the house is sufficiently drenched. The smell of gasoline is overpowering, so powerful that Chris can hear Brad stir.

He stands outside and retrieves his lighter and pack of cigarettes from his left sock. He lights a cigarette and inhales it once before throwing it back in the house. It lands in the middle of the living room floor, its embers quickly igniting the gasoline soaked carpet. Chris closes the door as the blanket covering Brad becomes enflamed. He walks down the driveway and stands along the side of the road and watches as the inside of the cottage burns. He almost expects Brad to come crashing through the now burning front door, but he doesn't. Chris can hear a stifled scream for a moment and then only the sound of the fire as it passes up the stairs.

He lights another cigarette and feels, finally, at peace.

www.ingramcontent.com/pod-product-compliance
Lightning Source LLC
Chambersburg PA
CBHW022142010726
47493CB00002B/300